Sallust, John Clarke, John Adams

C. Crispi Salustii Bellum Catilinarium et Jugurthinum

cum versione libera

Sallust, John Clarke, John Adams

C. Crispi Salustii Bellum Catilinarium et Jugurthinum
cum versione libera

ISBN/EAN: 9783337380571

Printed in Europe, USA, Canada, Australia, Japan

Cover: Foto ©Andreas Hilbeck / pixelio.de

More available books at **www.hansebooks.com**

THE

PREFACE.

THE *Character* of SALLUST *as an Historian
is so well known, and so justly established in
the Learned World, that I judge it needless
to enlarge upon the Subject ; and I decline it
the rather, because I am sensible Encomiums of that Kind
from a Translator or Commentator are generally, and but
too justly, suspected by the most sensible Readers to pre-
ceed only from a Design to set off, or recommend more
effectually, his own Performance : Though how little I
am disposed to that selfish Piece of Pedantry the Preface
to my* FLORUS *may convince the Reader ; and, to give
him yet further Proof of it, I shall here take notice of
the only material Fault I know of in* SALLUST.

ONE *of the Qualifications indispensably required in
an Historian is Impartiality. I grant our Author has
given a remarkable Instance of this in undertaking to
write the History of* Catiline's *Conspiracy, wherein he
could not avoid speaking much of his Enemy* Cicero *in a
Manner that could not but be for his Honour, which he
has not only done decently, but with Commendation
of his Vigilance and Concern for ·the Publick, under
the Titles of* Clariffumus Conful, *and* Optimus Conful. *The former, indeed, he puts into the mouth of* Ju-

A 2   lius

lius Cæfar; *but he might, notwithftanding, have eafily avoided that elevated epithet, fince he has only given us the Senfe, and not the Words, of* Cæfar, *whofe Stile is very different from that of his Speech in* Salluſt. *This, I fay, is a commendable Inſtance of his Impartiality, if he was not at the writing reconciled to* Cicero, *as fome have imagined. But then, I think, he has failed as much in his Parallel between* Cato *and* Cæfar. *It is an Outrage upon common Senfe to run a Parallel betwixt two Men of fuch oppofite Characters fo as to leave it at laſt a difputable Point which was the greater and better of the two; infomuch that any one who was to know nothing of* Cæfar *but by our Author's Account of him would certainly take him for a very worthy, glorious Man, whereas his true Character is the reverfe. He was indeed a Perfon of vaſt Abilities; but then he had nothing in him that bore any Refemblance of a Virtue but what was directly intended to promote the worſt and moſt wicked defign that can enter into the Heart of Man to conceive, the Deſtruction of the Liberties of his Country. The Generofity, Eafinefs, and Clemency, our Author celebrates him for, were in him Arts or Tricks, practifed purely with a View to acquire, and fecure to himfelf, the Poffeffion of an arbitrary Power over his Fellow-Citizens; otherwife, he had fo little of thofe good Qualities feparated from fuch a View, that this generous, eafy Gentleman would have made no Scruple to have fwept the Globe of the Earth of one Half of its Inhabitants by Fire and Sword, or any other Methods of Deſtruction, in order to rule the Remainder at Pleafure. And, to ufe the Words of* Cato *in his Speech to the Senate, upon Occafion of* Catiline's *Confpiracy,* Shall any one talk to me in this cafe of Mildnefs and Mercy? *Shall that Man be accounted or ſtiled mild and merciful whofe infatiable Thirſt after Power made him wade through Seas of Blood to come*

at

at it. He was not a whit better Man than Catiline, *but had a great deal more Cunning, and much greater Abilities, whereby he at length executed with Succefs what the other attempted only to his own Deftruction. He was fhrewdly fufpected to be privy to* Catiline's *Defign, and engaged in it ; and the great Concern he fhewed to fave the reft of the Confpirators, makes it not unlikely. However, his having been concerned in a Plot of the like nature before, and indeed his whole Conduct from his early Youth to his Death, plainly demonftrate that his Concern for them proceeded not from any Tendernefs of Nature, or Regard to the Laws of his Country, as he pretended in his Speech to the Senate, but from a Defign to ufe them for the like Purpofe whenfoever a favourable Opportunity might prefent. It was abfurd, as* Cato *juftly obferved in his Anfwer to him, at fuch a Juncture, when the City was in immediate Danger of being involved in Blood and Fire, and the whole Commonwealth ready to be fwallowed up in one common Ruin, to ftand dallying and dodging, as if all was fafe and fecure, and proceed according to the Prefcription of Laws, which never were, nor ever could be, defigned for Cafes of fuch a Nature as that was. When Villainy is carried to fo dangerous a Height, by Power and Numbers together, as not to admit of the Obfervation of Laws defigned only for common and ordinary Cafes, without the Hazard of a general Ruin, or utter Diffolution of the Government, the Rulers of a Commonwealth in fuch a Cafe, are difcharged from all fuch Laws, and left to act by that of Nature or Reafon, which allows of all the Methods of Violence and Force that appear neceffary for the Prefervation of the State from the Deftruction that threatens it.* Cæfar, *in fhort, fpoke upon that Occafion like an artful, ill-defigning Man ;* Cato, *like what he was, a brave and a worthy Patriot : And to compare two fuch Men together, whofe*
Characters

Chara&ers were as oppofite to one another as black and white, in the Manner our Author has done, was vile Daubing, fetting a Glofs upon the mofi extreme Wickednefs, to give it the Air and Lufire of Virtue and commendable Accomplifhments.

BUT this, indeed, is the only Flaw in our Author of any Importance, or worth while to trouble the Reader about, that I know of. As to the Matter of his Hifiory, it is remarkable and engaging enough. Catiline's *Confpiracy was fuch a villainous, defperate Defign, as is fcarce to be parallelled in the Hifiory of Mankind, unlefs by the murtherous Proje&s contrived by the Roman Catholics in Favour of their Religion, as they call it, efpecially that famous Plot here in England againfi King* JAMES *the Firfi and his Parliament.*

THE War againfi King Jugurtha *too, for the Time of its Continuance, is as full of important and remarkable Incidents as any other in the whole Roman Hifiory befides. We fee there to what a Height Bribery and Corruption were at that Time got in Rome; to fuch a Height indeed, that the* Romans *wanted but one Thing to complete their Shame and Ruin at once, that is, to have had the Bill which was preferred to the People againfi the Penfioners to the King reje&ed. And this was what many of the Senate (in all likelihood a very great Majority) endeavoured by clandefiine Means and fly Pra&ices to bring about; but the People, corrupt as they were, yet were not wicked and fhamelefs enough to come into fo vile a Proje&, which, had it fucceeded, mufi in all Probability have made* Jugurtha *Mafier of* Rome. *To conclude, we may learn, from this and the fubfequent Part of the* Roman *Story 'till* Julius Cæfar *executed his long-proje&ed Defign upon his Country, this Leffon, that where* Bribery and Corruption prevail amongft the Governors

vernors of a free State, unlefs fome powerful Re-, medy can be fpeedily applied, there the Deftruction. of Liberty muft unavoidably and prefently enfue.

AS for the two Orations, as they are called, of Salluft. *to* Cæfar, *about fettling the Government, I have not thought fit to tranflate them, as well becaufe of the vile Flattery they are dafhed with, as. alfo becaufe, having. been lefs read and regarded than the Hiftory, they have not been conveyed. down to us fo correct, infomuch that. the Senfe feems to be quite loft in fome Places by the extreme Corruption of the Text, and in others the prefent. Reading is at beft difputable.*

AS Tranflations *of the* Claffick Authors, *both Literal. and Free, are exceedingly ufeful in .learning the* Latin *Tongue, I have thought fit to fubjoin to this Preface my. Differtation upon that Subject, but confiderably enlarged.. I am afraid, indeed, the moft judicious of my Readers may. think I have given myfelf a needlefs Trouble in dwelling. fo long upon fo plain a Subject; but I muft befeech fuch to. confider the great Importance of it, and withall the ftrong Prejudice many, even School-Mafters, are poffeffed with againft the Ufe of Tranflations, and perhaps they may find Reafon to be of a different Opinion. A Perfon that was a* Stranger *to the Abfurdities of the Church of* Rome *would certainly think it a very needlefs Thing for any one to go about to prove in a long Difcourfe that a Bit of Bread cannot be a human Body ; and yet to that Neceffity have the Reformed been. driven, infomuch that many Men of the greateft Learning and Abilities among them have writ largely to expofe the Madnefs of that Affertion of the* Ro-maniſts, *and were never blamed for it : And therefore, tho' the Abfurdity I write againft be indeed almoft as grofs as it is to maintain Bread to be Flefh, or a Penny Loaf to*
be

be a Man, yet since a great many think quite the contrary, or at least pretend so, and upon that pretence reject the Use of Translations, and plead against them, I hope the Reader who considers this will not think what I have urged against the common Method of proceeding in our Grammar-Schools in Favour of Translations at all too much or more than needed. For where Prejudice hinders People from seeing what is right, in Matters of great Concern to the Publick, and so disposes them to decline and decry the Practice of it, there it will not only be excusable, but highly useful and necessary, to multiply Words, in order to set the Truth of the Case in as strong and glaring a Light as possible, 'till Prejudice vanishes before it. Now, that the Opposition made by many to the Use of Translations is very absurd, and can therefore be founded upon nothing but Prejudice, or something worse, I have, I presume, in the Dissertation so abundantly demonstrated, that, if it has no good Effect upon the Advocates for the common Method, it may at least prevent indifferent and unprejudiced Persons from being misled by them, and so operate in time to a thorough Reformation of so palpable a Fault.

T H E Method of Education commonly followed in our Schools has long been the Subject of a general Complaint among the Learned. I very early became sensible of the Justness of that Complaint, and thought I saw clearly how it was faulty and deficient in several Respects ; and, as no Attempts were made by any one to reform it, I thereupon took up a Resolution to try what I could do towards it myself, which Resolution issued in the Publication of an Essay upon the Subject of Education, *and several other Books, to support and render practicable the Method laid down in the* Essay. *But, not finding myself at Liberty enough to*
pursue

purſue the Deſign ſo cloſely as I wiſhed, by reaſon of the cumberſome Employment I had upon my hands ; and being upon another Account quite weary of the Buſineſs, I quitted it, in order to employ my Studies and Pen more effectually in carrying on a Deſign I had ſo much at Heart, with this Aſſurance, that, if my Sentiments upon Education were right, I could not be employed in any way more uſeful to the Publick. And that my Sentiments were juſt, or at leaſt that I was not greatly out, or widely miſtaken, in the Method I propoſed, I thought I had ſome Reaſon to hope, from the great Approbation it met with from the moſt able Judges up and down the Kingdom ; of which I had good Aſſurance by Letters from ſeveral of them, as well as other Information. If, therefore, it ſhould pleaſe God to continue to me that fine State of Health I have hitherto enjoyed, and Gentlemen will be pleaſed to encourage me in my Pro-ject, I ſhall ſpare no Pains to furniſh our Schools with what further Helps are wanted in them. And I hope ſuch Gentlemen as have done, or ſhall do me the Honour to declare in my Favour, will further honour me, by ſupporting my Endeavours for the Service of the Publick with the Fa-vour of their Recommendation, in order to baniſh out of our Schools that Abſurdity in Practice which has hitherto generally prevailed therein. If they pleaſe but to intereſt themſelves in the Buſineſs, all Obſtructions to the Work ariſing from Ignorance or Prejudice, or what Motives ſoever, will quickly vaniſh ; and we may ſoon ſee ſuch a Revolution in our Schools as will tend greatly to the Advancement of Learning and Virtue among us.

A

DISSERTATION

Upon the USEFULNESS of

TRANSLATIONS *of* Claſſick Authors,

Both L I T E R A L and F R E E,

For the Eaſy Expeditious Attainment of the

L A T I N T O N G U E:

BEING

An EXTRACT from the ESSAY UPON EDUCATION, and other Books, publiſhed by Mr. CLARKE, late School-maſter of *Hull,* but very much enlarged with further Thoughts upon the Subject.

Humbly offered to the Conſideration of the Learned, in order to a Reformation of the vulgar Method of Proceeding in Grammar Schools, as to that important Article of Education, the Teaching of the LATIN TONGUE.

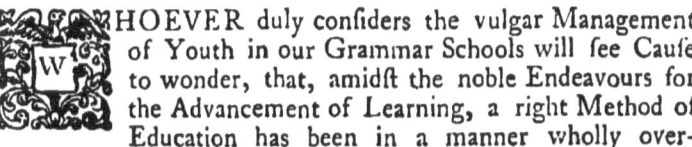HOEVER duly conſiders the vulgar Management of Youth in our Grammar Schools will ſee Cauſe to wonder, that, amidſt the noble Endeavours for the Advancement of Learning, a right Method of Education has been in a manner wholly over-looked. Whilſt the Great Men in the Commonwealth of Letters have been buſily and ſucceſsfully employed in im-proving and carrying on the ſeveral Arts and Sciences, they

B 2　　　　　　　　　have

have neglected what was equally neceffary, the Care of
Youth : For had but this been as duly attended to as the Importance of the Matter required, their Labours would have been
of vaftly more Ufe to the World. Grammars, and Notes
upon Authors, we have indeed in Abundance, and more by far
than are good for any Thing; yet thefe, where they are ufeful,
are only fo to fuch as have made a confiderable Progrefs in
the *Latin* Tongue. But Beginners have been left wholly
without any proper Helps, 'till of late fome few have been
provided for them by one engaged in the laborious and troublefome Employment of teaching School, who confequently
had both lefs Time and lefs Eafe of Mind for that Work
than many others better qualified to promote a rational Method
of Education amongft us, had they been pleafed to turn their
Thoughts upon the Subject, and pufh the Matter, by fupplying our Schools with proper Books for the Purpofe. But
the Learned, it feems, have thought Things of this Kind
below their Notice. There was more Credit and Fame to be
got by writing for Men than Children; and therefore the
latter have been ftrangely neglected.

As the Courfe of Life I was feveral Years engaged in
obliged me to turn my Thoughts that Way, I have long fince
publifhed my Sentiments upon the Subject, in a Treatife under
the Title of *An Effay upon the Education of Youth in Grammar
Schools.* What I have there faid, and elfewhere, upon the
Ufefulnefs of Tranflations for the eafy and expeditious Attainment of the *Latin* Tongue, I have thought proper, in this
Preface, to draw together under one View, in order to turn
more effectually the Attention of the Publick upon a Matter
of fuch great and general Concern.

TRANSLATIONS are of two Kinds, or there are two
Ways of tranflating Authors for the Ufe of Schools; the
one *Literal* or *Verbal,* in which the *Latin* is rendered into
Englifh Word for Word, or the Senfe and Meaning of every
Word in the Original is given in the Tranflation; the other
Free and *Proper,* wherein Regard is only had to the Senfe,
which the Tranflator endeavours to exprefs in the moft juft
and handfome Manner, without pretending to give the precife Meaning of every individual Word, as in the Literal or
Verbal Way. Now both thefe Sorts of Tranflations are fo
highly and apparently ufeful for the ready Attainment of the
Latin Tongue, that it is really amazing the World fhould
not long fince have been fenfible of it : And it is yet more
amazing, that after fo much has been faid upon the Subject,

and

and Tranflations too of feveral Authors provided for the Ufe
of Schools, to which no Exception has been taken as ill done,
that ever I could hear; yet a great many of our Mafters
fhould fhew fo ftrong an Averfion to what is fo manifeftly
calculated for their Eafe, as well as for the greater Improvement of Youth under their Care. In order to open the Eyes
of fuch, if poffible, in a Matter, in which both their Intereft
and Credit is fo highly concerned, I have thought fit to prefent
them with this Differtation. I fhall, therefore, fpeak diftinctly
to the Ufefulnefs of TRANSLATIONS, both *Literal* and *Free*.
And firft of the *Literal*.

WHEN Boys fet forward in the reading of *Latin* Authors,
there are but three feveral Ways for them to proceed in:
1, By the Help of a Mafter to conftrue their Leffons to them:
2, By the Help of a Dictionary: Or, 3, By that of Literal
Tranflations.

I. As to the firft, our Schools are very few of them provided with any more than two Mafters; in which Cafe it is
impoffible for a Man that has three or four Claffes to take
Care of, to give that Attendance to them all, in the Way of
conftruing their Leffons to them, as to keep them employed
a third Part of the Time they have to fpend in the School.
For it is not fufficient for a Mafter to conftrue to Boys a
Leffon once over from Beginning to End in a Hurry, (as is
ufual, I believe) and fo clear his Hands of them, in Expectation
that fhould ferve the Turn, by keeping them properly employed,
and he be no more troubled with them for his Affiftance upon
that Leffon. Alas! this will fignify juft nothing at all. If
he would affift them to any Purpofe, he muft go over each
Period of a Leffon diftinctly and flowly by itfelf, more than
once; and then try the Boys in it one after another, helping
them out, where he finds them faulter, or at a ftand; and
not advancing further, 'till the floweft of them are pretty
perfect in what they are upon. But then, whilft he is thus
engaged with one Clafs, the reft, for want of Help, will
have little or nothing to do, but gape and ftare about them,
if they be not worfe employ'd. Befides, this is fuch a Piece
of Drudgery, as few Mafters, I believe, will care to undergo.
For where the Ufe of Tranflations is rejected, and the
Mafter's Lungs are to fupply the Want of them, he, in regard to his own Eafe, and to fave his Breath, is apt to make
very fhort Work of it, by fetting the Boys very fhort
Leffons, not a third, or not a fourth Part of what they
B 3   might

might eafily get, and to greater Perfection, by the Help of a Literal Tranflation, without giving him any Trouble at all. Two Thirds, then, of their Time, at leaft, muft be fpent in Sauntering, or Trifling ; and therefore this Way of Proceeding will not anfwer the Defign propofed, or produce the defired Effect, the fpeedy Progrefs of Youth in their Bufinefs.

I MAY add too, that, perhaps, not very many Mafters are qualified to furnifh their Scholars, in conftruing their Leffons to them, with Words fo fit and proper for their Purpofe, as Literal Tranflations will, done by a Perfon qualified with a competent Skill in the Language for the Work. If any one wants to be convinced of this, let him make a Trial upon fome of the Claffick Authors already publifhed with Literal Tranflations, *Juftin* or *Florus* for Inftance, by tranflating three or four Chapters together, and comparing what he does with what is already done, and I doubt not, but he will receive ample Satisfaction of the Truth of what I have faid. For though he may find his Performance to have the Advantage upon the Comparifon, yet he will certainly find it coft him fome Thought and Trouble here and there, to work it up to that Perfection. For the *Latin* Idiom differs fo widely from the *Englifh*, that it is no fuch eafy Bufinefs, as fome may perhaps imagine, to tranflate the Clafficks Literally, and at the fame Time with tolerable Juftnefs and Propriety of Language, fo as the *Englifh* may bear a Reading, without appearing abfolutely barbarous and ridiculous. It was this Difficulty of the Work, I guefs, which deterred thofe whofe proper Bufinefs it was, from attempting it, and fo has been the principal, if not the fole Occafion, that our Schools have not been long fince provided with that admirable and obvious Help of Literal Tranflations, fo obvioufly fuch, that many could not but be fenfible of it, who yet being deterred by the Difficulty of the Undertaking, and the Fear of Cenfure, would not engage in the Tafk of fupplying our Schools with any thing in that Way. Now if this be the Cafe, if it be no fuch eafy Matter to tranflate the Claffick Authors Literally, with any tolerable Juftnefs or Propriety of Language, muft it not be a vaft Advantage to many School-Mafters, to be delivered from the Vexation of hunting for proper Words, and oftentimes to no Purpofe, by being provided with good Tranflations, juft and exact in their Kind ? In fhort, I fhall be bold to fay, that not only Boys, but Mafters themfelves may,

many

many of them, receive great Improvement in their Bufinefs, from Literal Tranflations of Claffick Authors.

II. As to the Ufe of a Dictionary. That Way is yet more improper than the former. Young Boys are but very aukward at finding Words in a Dictionary, which Work will confequently make a fad Confumption of their Time, a fingle Word requiring as much as will fuffice them for the getting two or three Lines perfectly to conftrue by the Help of a Literal Tranflation. And then what a tedious while muft they be in getting fo many Lines to conftrue by the Ufe of a Dictionary, where they may have Occafion, as muft often happen, to look out half a Dozen Words or more for that Purpofe? Does not the Abfurdity of fuch a Method of Proceeding ftare the Reader in the Face? And how can Gentlemen be eafy in having their Sons carried on in a Way fo manifeftly trifling? Which will appear yet more fo, when it is confidered, that young Boys can indeed make but little Ufe of a Dictionary, for want of Senfe to diftinguifh, amongft the various Significations many Words have, fuch as are proper for their Purpofe; not to fay too, that the beft Dictionaries will in this Cafe frequently fail them. But fuppofe all this was otherwife, yet by what Kind of Conjuration muft young Lads, betwixt Ten and Fourteen, unravel that perplexed Order of Words in the *Latin* Tongue? This they can never do, give them what Inftructions you will for it, 'till they come to have a pretty general Knowledge of Words; fo as that, upon reading a Sentence once or twice flowly and attentively over, they either difcover the Senfe, or come pretty near it. That alone, and not any Directions you can give Boys fo young, will enable them to unravel the intricate Order Words ufually have in the *Latin* Tongue. Now Literal Tranflations direct them immediately to the Order in which Words are to be taken, and at the fame Time immediately fupply them with the Meaning of fuch Words as they want to know the Meaning of. All that has been faid upon this Head appears to me fo very evident and inconteftable, that, for my Part, I fee not how it can be difputed by any one.

III. THERE is, then, no other proper Help left for young Lads in the Reading of Authors, for the firft three or four Years at leaft of their being at School, but that of *Literal Tranflations.* If Boys, who cannot conjure to come at the Meaning of Words, muft be helped to the Meaning of them fome Way or other, is not the moft eafy and expeditious Way

the

the teft? And fuppofing a Mafter could affift them to keep them conftantly employed, (which every one muft fee to be utterly impoffible) or fuppofing they might make a hard Shift to do their Bufinefs in a poor blundering Manner by a Dictionary, (which is the utmoft any one of the leaft Knowledge in thefe Matters can fuppofe) yet what Occafion can there be for either, when it is to the laft Degree vifible, their Bufinefs may be more eafily and effectually done by the Help of Literal Tranflations? Is it not vaftly more eligible for a Boy, when he is at a Stand for want of the proper Order or Meaning of Words, to be fet a going immediately by one fingle Caft of his Eye, than to be obliged to fpend Time in tumbling and toffing the Leaves of a Dictionary backward and forward, or trotting perpetually up and down the School to the Mafter, or his Schoolfellows for their Help? Is it not as abfurd to deny this, as it would be to affirm that the beft Way for a Workman to go on eafily and expeditioufly with a Piece of Work is not to have his Tools and Implements in the Shop or Workhoufe about him, all ready at hand, but to have them all to feek, fome in the Kitchen, others in the Garret, others in the Yard, or the furtheft Part of the Town; to be all carefully hid again every Night, that he may be fure to have them all to feek again the next Day when he wants them? Juft like this is the common Way of Proceeding in our Schools, where the Ufe of Literal Tranflations is rejected. Help of the beft Kind is provided for Boys, by Virtue whereof they may proceed eafily, chearfully, and expeditioufly, in their Bufinefs; and yet a great many Mafters will not let them make ufe of it, but inftead thereof will oblige the poor Children to wafte two Thirds at leaft of their Time in Sauntering and Play, or thumbing the Leaves of a Dictionary to Pieces, for the Benefit of the Bookfellers, who alone reap any Benefit from this Piece of Wifdom, whilft the poor Boys only lofe their Time, and the Parents their Mouey by it.

But perhaps it may be alledged, (for fome I have known weak enough to make the Allegation) ' That the getting their Leffons by a Dictionary fixes the Meaning of Words better in ' the Memory of Boys than the Ufe of Tranflations.' To which I anfwer, fuppofing it practicable for young Boys to get their Leffons by the Help of a Dictionary, which I have fhewn it is not, yet does the toffing over the Leaves of a Dictionary to find a Word contribute to fix the Meaning of it, when found, in the Memory? If fo, the longer Boys are in finding a Word, that is, the longer they are 'e're they come at the

Senfe

Senfe of a Word, the better they will remember it. As much as to fay, that the lefs Bufinefs they do, the greater Progrefs they will make ; which I fear is too ridiculous to pafs with any body. The turning over the Leaves of a Dictionary, 'tis evident, can fignify no more to the Purpofe, than the toffing of a Ball, or the knocking down of Nine-Pins. What is it then that is of Ufe for fixing the Meaning of a Word in the Memory ? 'Tis plainly nothing but feeing it in the Dictionary, and repeating it over and over again. And is there any thing of Charm in the Name of a Dictionary, that the feeing the Meaning of a Word in a Tranflation running in a Column along with the Original, join'd with the like Repetition of it, fhould not produce the fame Effect, and conduce as much to fix it in the Memory ? The Reading a Word three or four Times over in a Dictionary, you fay, will make a ftrong Impreffion upon the Mind. Will not Reading the fame Word as often over in any other Book, under any other Denomination, produce the like Impreffion ? If not, it muft be becaufe the Leaf of a Dictionary, as fuch, has fome ftrange bewitching Virtue in it, a Power of operating upon the Mind, and affecting it, which the Leaf of no other Book can poffibly have.——*Rifum teneatis ?*

I HAVE likewife heard it alledged, ' That the Ufe of Tran' flations will make Boys idle ;' an Allegation more ridiculous, if poffible, than the former. As Boys' Bufinefs is by the Ufe of Tranflations rendered vaftly more eafy to them, if their Tafk or Leffon is increafed in Proportion, as it ought to be, how is there any Encouragement given, or Allowance made, for Idlenefs ? Tranflations are defigned to affift Boys in getting their Leffons only, not in faying them to the Mafter. In this latter Cafe the Tranflations are to be under clofe Cover, that, by the Manner of the Boys acquitting themfelves, the Mafter may have Proof of their Diligence, or the contrary. And if the fame Methods are taken to encourage Induftry, and difcourage Idlenefs, where Boys are helped by a Tranflation, as where they have the Help of a Mafter, or are left to the Ufe of a Dictionary, why fhould they not have the fame Effect ? If Sugar-Plums, Fruit, Play-things, or Half-pence, will make Boys attend diligently to the Inftructions of a Mafter, or thumb their Dictionary heartily, will they not operate as ftrongly to make Boys diligent in the Ufe of a Tranflation ? Or, if Correction be neceffary, why fhould it not work up a Lad to Induftry, as well where .he has the Affiftance of a Tranflation, as where he has not ? Will a Tranflation make

him

him thicker fkinned, or lefs fenfible of Pain ? *O rem ridiculam*, *Cato, & jocofam !* It is therefore a very fenfelefs thing to pretend, that Tranflations will make Boys idle. One Way to encourage them to Induftry is, to make their Bufinefs eafy and pleafant to them ; which Tranflations certainly do : And therefore are a vifible Means, not to make them idle, but induftrious. Whereas in the vulgar Method of our Schools, Boys find it impracticable to do their Bufinefs to Content, and fo are oftentimes rendered defperately idle, as being convinced by frequent and woful Experience, that no Pains, no Induftry they can ufe, will avail to fecure them effectually from the Lafh.

THESE Objections againft the Ufe of Tranflations have not, however, hindered but that Tranflations have been thought fo neceffary for the eafy and fpeedy Attainment of the Greek Tongue, that, for above thefe hundred and fifty Years laft paft, no Authors in that Language have been publifhed without them. This might, one would think, have naturally led the World to the Purfuit of the fame Method, at leaft with the eafier Authors of the Latin Tongue, for the Ufe of Schools. For muft it not needs appear to any confiderate Man a little unaccountable, that Tranflations fhould be thought ufeful and neceffary for Men or elder Boys, in order to their more eafy and fpeedy Progrefs in the Greek Tongue, but neither neceffary nor ufeful for younger Boys in the Attainment of the Latin ? Is it agreeable to Reafon or common Senfe, to fuppofe a Boy of fixteen or feventeen Years of Age ftands in need of a Tranflation, to affift him in reading of Greek, but that a Boy of ten or twelve may do his Bufinefs in the Latin Tongue eafily and expeditioufly enough without any fuch Help ? Has a Child of that Age more Senfe for the confulting and ufing a Latin Dictionary, than he has for making Ufe of a Greek Lexicon when he is arrived almoft at the Years of Manhood ? And what forry Work would Boys make of it, if, upon entering the Greek Teftament, they fhould be denied the Ufe of a Latin Teftament, to help them in getting their Leffons, and be obliged to pick the Meaning of their Words out of a Lexicon ? Every body can fee the Abfurdity of fuch a Manner of proceeding in this Inftance, and would be forward enough to cry out againft any Mafter that fhould be guilty of it. And yet the like Abfurdity committed in the Teaching of the Latin Tongue goes glibly down, and paffes for the moft proper Way of Proceeding. Now what is it that difpofes Men to make fo wide a Difference, where there is none at all in the Nature of Things ? Nothing but Cuftom, the great Rule that moft Men ufually go by in the

moft

moft important Affairs of Life without confulting their Reafon at all. Very few have the noble Freedom of Mind to
examine Things ftrictly and impartially, in order to make the
Refult of fuch Examination the Rule of their Conduct. The
Generality chufe to fave themfelves that Trouble, by going
with the Herd, *qua itur, non qua eundum eft*, as a great Man
among the Antients words himfelf upon Occafion of making
the fame Remark, if my Memory fails me not.

As for the Hebrew Tongue, to facilitate the Learning of that,
Arias Montanus long fince publifhed the Hebrew Bible with an
interlineary Verfion, for which, I doubt not, fuch as apply
themfelves to the Study of the Hebrew Language, are thankful
to his Memory, at leaft they have a good deal of Reafon, I am
fure, having received myfelf a great deal of Benefit from the
Ufe of it in learning that Language. And Mr. *Locke* was fo fenfible of the vaft Help to be had frcm Literal Tranflations, that
he did not think it below him to publifh *Æfop*'s Fables in the
fame Form as *Montanus* did the Hebrew Bible, with an interlineary Verfion. I grant indeed that Way of publifhing Authors with the Tranflation fo intermixed with the Original, is
not proper for Schools. But however, what thofe two Gentlemen did in that Way, fhews fufficiently their Opinion of the
Ufefulnefs of Literal Tranflations. And the latter, Mr. *Locke*,
thought fo well of them, that he declares in his *Book of Education*, Mothers may by the Help of them teach their Sons the
Latin Tongue themfelves, if they pleafe. *Whatever Stir*, fays
he, *there is made about getting of Latin, his* (a young Gentleman's) *Mother may teach it him herfelf, if fhe will but
fpend two or three Hours in a Day with him, and make him
read the Evangelifts in Latin to her. For fhe need but buy a
Latin Teftament, and having got fomebody to mark the laft
Syllable but one, in Words of above two Syllables (which is
enough to regulate her Pronunciation) read daily in the Gof-
pels, and then let her avoid underftanding them in Latin, if
fhe can. And when fhe underftands the Evangelifts in Latin, let
her in the fame Manner read Æfop's Fables, and fo proceed on
to* Eutropius, Juftin, *and other fuch Books. I do not mention
this as an Imagination of what I fancy may do, but as of a Thing
I have known done, and the Latin Tongue with Eafe got this
Way.*

To conclude, the Ufe of *Literal Tranflations* has no Difficulty in it, employs nothing but Memory. The Boys have
proper Words all ready at hand, without the tedious and oftentimes fruitlefs Labour of hunting and poring in a Dictionary, or
that

that of troubling their Mafter or School-fellows for them; and
fo go fmoothly forward, without any Rubs in their Way, or
Lofs of Time, and with a great deal of Satisfaction to find
their Bufinefs to very eafy. And I fhall venture to fay, what I
believe few Men of Senfe, that will but duly confider what has
been faid above, will gainfay, That a Boy by the Help of Literal Tranflations would make a better Progrefs in the Language
in one Year, than without them he could do in three or four.

Nor are Literal Tranflations of Latin Authors ufeful only
for the lower Forms of a School, but likewife for the higher,
or fuch as can read them pretty well, without any fuch Help,
as well to bring them to a more complete Acquaintance with
them, in the moft expeditious Manner, as likewife to a Readinefs in the writing and fpeaking of proper Latin, by reading the
Tranflation into the original Latin of the Author. Conftant
Converfation in Latin, with fuch as talk it well, would indeed
be of great Ufe for that Purpofe. But then very little can be
done in that Way at School. For to confine Boys to the
talking of Latin amongft themfelves, before they have attained
any tolerable Skill in the Language, is abfurd, and a Means to
prevent their ever fpeaking or writing it well. If Boys are to
be fo confined, they ought to be conftantly attended by a good
Mafter, to help them out upon all Occafions, by furnifhing
them with proper Language: But this is manifeftly impracticable, where there are but two Mafters in a School, or, as is
oftentimes the Cafe, but one. A ready and proper Ufe of the
Latin Tongue is a Matter of very great Difficulty, and never
to be attained by Boys talking barbaroufly amongft themfelves;
if it is at all attainable at School. For my Part, I never yet
knew fo much as one Inftance of its being attained there, in any
School that has come within the Reach of my Obfervation, or
indeed any thing like it. Nay I have talked with very inge-
nious Men, of uncommon Learning, and befides Perfons of
confiderable Experience in that Way, who looked upon the
bringing Boys at School to any thing of a true and genuine Latin Stile wholly impracticable. Now, tho' I will not affirm
this, yet I muft be allowed to fay, it is a Matter of very great
Difficulty, infomuch that I greatly queftion, whether any Method that can be taken with them will be found generally fuccefsful, in any reafonable Time, befides this I here recommend.
All the Grammar, indeed, neceffary for the Purpofe may eafily
be taught them: But when that is done, the Main of the Difficulty is ftill behind, as every one muft be fenfible that knows
much of the Latin Tongue. A ready Ufe of proper Terms,
and

and of proper Phrafes, or Forms of Expreffion, upon all Occafions, feems hardly attainable in any reafonable Time, or the
longeft Term of the Continuance of Boys at Grammar-
Schools, but in the Method I propofe. This, I fay, will be
the moft ready, expeditious Method that can be taken, at
School however, to furnifh the Mind with a Plenty of Words,
and a Variety of Phrafes and Expreffions for the fame Senfe,
and that without any Danger of Error, which the Ufe of Dictionaries and Phrafe-Books would be attended with. For none
indeed can receive any great Benefit from them for that Purpofe, but fuch as are good Judges in the Latin Tongue, and
well acquainted with the Idiom thereof already.

LITERAL TRANSLATIONS Boys are to begin with; and
after they have gone through four or five Authors, in the Method of reading fuch Tranflations into the very original Latin
of the Authors, they are to be advanced to *Free* and *Elegant*
Tranflations. Two or three of the fineft Claffick Hiftorians,
with *Terence*, and fome of the Epiftles, and other Pieces of
Tully, publifhed with fuch Tranflations, would, in Conjunction with the Claffick Hiftorians I have already publifhed with
Literal Tranflations, be fufficient for the Purpofe of attaining
a ready Ufe of a good Latin Style, perhaps equal to Converfation itfelf, if not preferable to it, at leaft in one Refpect
more advantageous, by furnifhing the *Tyro* with better Latin
for his Englifh, as oft as he wants it, than any, even the
greateft Mafters of the Latin Tongue, could help him to, in
the Way of Converfation. For the great Advantage of conftant Converfation for the Attainment of any Language, lies
in the perpetual Exercife of the Invention, in what a Man
fays himfelf, and the like perpetual Affiftance given to his Invention, in the conftant Suggeftion of proper Language by
thofe he converfes with. Now both thefe Advantages are to be
had from the Method of Proceeding here advifed, and the
latter of them to a greater Degree of Perfection, than can be
had in the Way of Converfation. For in converfing to attain
the Ufe of a Language, the Learner employs his Invention to
exprefs his Thoughts properly ; he hunts and cafts about continually for Words and Phrafes that may fuit his Defign. If he
delivers himfelf improperly, or fticks and ftammers for want of
Language, thofe he converfes with correct his Improprieties,
and help him to what is proper, which he carefully attends to,
and repeats it, may be, two or three Times to himfelf, to make
it ftick by him, againft another Occafion. Juft fo too in
attempting to read a Tranflation into Latin, the Learner
ftretches

ftretches his Invention, and ftudies for·proper Words and Phrafeology, *viz.* that of the Original, which he has perufed carefully over, comparing it Period ·by Period, with the Tranflation, to prepare him for the Work he is upon. If he cannot fatisfy himfelf therein, or is at a Stop, one fingle Caft of his Eye upon the Latin Column informs him in what he wants, which he reads with clofe Attention over and·over, in order to remember it againft a repeated Perufal of the Paragraph or Chapter. Thus the Invention is as much exercifed and affifted in this Way of ufing Tranflations, as in Converfation; in which Exercife and Affiftance given to the Invention lies the whole Advantage of Converfation for the attaining of a Language. Nay, the Invention is more fubftantially affifted in the former Cafe. For the Claffick Authors were Men of the moft eminent Parts, who writ in their native Language, writ at Leifure and upon Deliberation, reviewed and corrected their Works over and over, thereby reducing them to fuch an Accuracy and Exactnefs, as no modern Talker of Latin muft pretend to in an Extempore Effufion, or the Swiftnefs and Hurry of Converfation. So that I think, I need not fcruple to pronounce, that the Way of ufing Tranflations for the attaining to fpeak Latin, which I here advife, is even preferable to the beft Converfation that is to be had in that Language.

BUT *Literal Tranflations* of Latin Authors are not only very ufeful for Boys at School, but Men too, efpecially fuch as having got a pretty good Infight into the Latin Tongue at School, but through Difufe forgot it in a great Meafure, are defirous to recover it : Which may de done with a great deal of Eafe, by the Help of fuch Books as I have publifh'd, viz. *Cordery, Erafmus, Eutropius, Florus, C. Nepos, Suetonius, Juftin, Introduction to the Making of Latin, A new Grammar of the Latin Tongue.* One Hour or two employed in reading Claffick Authors with fuch Tranflations as the above, every Day, for a Year together, will bring Gentlemen that are ignorant of the Latin Tongue, to read Profe with Eafe and Pleafure; after which the Poets will not be difficult for them to underftand, by the Help of fuch Notes as they are publifhed with, efpecially now the Way is paved for them, by a Literal Tranflation of *Ovid's Metamorphofes.* So that I am not wholly without Hopes, I may, by the Books I have pub-lifhed, to facilitate the Learning of the Latin Tongue, h.. : done a piece of acceptable Service to fuch Gentlemen, as are defirous of regaining or improving the Skill they had acquired

at

at Schoel. Few grown People will ever have the Patience to
hammer out fuch a Language as the Latin, by the Help of a
Dictionary. That would require more Time than any one in
a thoufand can or will fpare. But in this Way of Proceeding,
the regaining, or improving in the Latin Tongue, will but be
a new Kind of Diverfion, which the World has hitherto been
unacquainted with. The Time Gentlemen need to employ
that Way, is lefs than thofe who are the moft taken up with
Bufinefs, ufually fpend upon their Pleafures.

I PROCEED now to treat of *Free* and *Proper Tranflations*,
wherein a large Liberty is taken of departing from the Letter of
the Latin, in order to make the moft handfome proper Englifh.
Now the great Ufefulnefs of Claffick Authors, publifhed with
fuch Tranflations, is fo very apparent, that I wonder no body
has attempted any thing of this Kind before me. Englifh
Tranflations indeed of many of them have been publifhed by
themfelves, as being defigned, I fuppofe, purely for the Ufe
of fuch as are ignorant of the Latin Tongue, by prefenting
them, for their Information or Amufement, with that in Englifh, which they could not come at in the Original, without
any further View or Intention at all. But then fuch Tranflations may be of the greateft Ufe for other important Purpofes,
upon account of which it is highly convenient to have them
publifhed along with the Originals. As,

I. CLASSICK Authors, fo publifhed, will be vaftly ferviceable
for the eafy and fpeedy Improvement of fuch as, having no
great Acquaintance with the Latin Tongue, are defirous of
attaining a competent Skill therein, fo as to read Authors of all
Sorts eafily and familiarly. I do not fay that Tranflations,
wherein a good deal of Freedom is taken of departing from the
Letter or Words of the Original, are at all for the Purpofe of
fuch as have but little or no Knowledge of the Latin Tongue,
to begin with in order to their learning of that Language. No.
Such ought, in the firft Place, to make Ufe of Literal Tranflations, 'till they have got a pretty general Acquaintance with
Words; after which they may proceed to fuch as are Free and
Proper, by the Help whereof they will read an Author fubftantially over in a fourth Part of the Time they could do without,
to fpeak within Compafs.

II. THE publifhing of Claffick Authors, with proper and
handfome Tranflations, will be very convenient for thofe that
are defirous to attain a Faculty of writing and fpeak ig Latin
with Propriety and Readinefs. The Way will be t ead the
Original and Tranflation together, 'till they can read render
the

the latter into the Words of the original Latin precifely and exactly. The being thus accuftomed to fee the Idiom of the two Languages go conftantly together, joined with continual Efforts for rendering the one by the other, will make the Idiom of the Latin Language almoft as familiar to the Mind as that of the Englifh. And I.fhall be bold to fay, that this is far beyond every thing elfe that can be done, at School however, for the eafy and ready Attainment of a good Latin Stile. But upon this Point I have enlarged fufficiently above.

III. Another Ufe that may be made of Claffick Authors, fo publifhed, is for the eafy quick Attainment of a good Englifh Stile. And the Way thereto is here again for a Perfon to compare the Original and Tranflation together 'till he is able to render the Latin Text very readily into the precife Words of the Tranflation. What woful Stuff do Boys at School, for want of this Help, ufually render the Claffick Authors into, in the conftruing of their Leffons! By which we may eafily account for what fome have obferved, (Mr *Locke* and the *Spectator*, if my Memory fails me not) that Men educated to Letters, who have threfhed hard at Latin for nine or ten Years together, are oftentimes very deficient in their own Language: And no Wonder. For how fhould thofe who have, for fo many Years together at School, been fo much inured to vile barbarous Language, be able to deliver themfelves in much better, with any great Eafe or Readinefs. It is Ufe makes Perfectnefs in every thing Mankind have occafion to learn in order to practife. And therefore it is not to be expected that our Youth, after they have run through the Courfe of a Grammar School, fhould have any Talent at the writing or fpeaking handfome Englifh, with any Eafe or Fluency, if they have never been ufed to any thing of that Kind there, but, inftead thereof, have had the Relifh of their Minds vitiated by a perpetual Run of improper barbarous Language, or meer Gibberifh. But, in the Way of proceeding here advifed to, the Cafe is the reverfe. The Invention's being fo conftantly exercifed in Search of proper handfome Language, and withal as conftantly affifted in the moft fubftantial Matter, and prefently fet a going again, in cafe of any Stop or Difficulty, muft needs render fuch Language very familiar to the Mind, and make it occur, upon all Occafions of writing or fpeaking, with great Eafe and Readinefs. In fhort, I fay this Way of ufing Free and Proper Tranflations of Claffick Authors is fo apparently of the greateft and moft excellent Ufe for the Purpofe of writing and fpeaking good Englifh with Eafe and Fluency, that, in

my

my Opinion, the Matter can admit of no Difpute amongft Perfons of any Senfe or Confideration at all.

THE feveral Ufes before-mentioned to be made of Claffick Authors, publifhed together with handfome elegant Tranfla-tions, fhew of what prodigious Advantage it would be to our Grammar-Schools, to have fome of the choiceft among them fo publifhed. Half a Dozen fuch thrown into our Schools, and ufed there as they fhould be, would certainly work a won-derful Effect, fuch as would foon be very vifible all the Nation over, by much greater and quicker Improvement of Youth in both the Languages of Latin and Englifh together. Now the Way of exercifing Boys in Clafficks fo publifhed would be to make them get three or four Leffons in the Original, to read exactly into the Tranflation, and, when that is done, to make them go the fame Leffons over again, and get the Tranflation to read as exactly back again into the original Latin. This (I fay it again, and defire the Reader will take Notice of it) will, in my Opinion, be the moft effectual expeditious Method to bring Youth to an eafy elegant Ufe of both Languages, that can poffibly be taken with them.

FROM the Whole of what has been faid upon this Subject of Tranflations, I fhall venture to draw this Conclufion, that a Man of but a very moderate Skill in the Latin Tongue may acquit himfelf, in the Teaching of it, by the Help of Tranfla-tions, with much greater Succefs, than the moft able Critick in the Language can do without. I have had as much Experience in the Bufinefs of Education as moft Men that have engaged in it. I have taught in the common Method, and in my own, fo far as it was practicable, (for we are yet far from having all the Clafficks publifhed with Tranflations that are neceffary for the Affiftance of our Youth at School, to fay nothing of other Helps that are wanting) and I add too, that I have thought as much upon the Subject of Education, as perhaps any Man whatever : and I do pretend to fay, that, in the common Me-thod of Education, where the Ufe of Literal Tranflations is difallowed, Youth muft thereby alone fuffer a Lofs of at leaft two Years' Time, upon a moderate Computation. So that take two Boys of equal Age and Capacity, and let one ftart two Years before the other, in the reading of Authors, accord-ing to the vulgar Way of proceeding, and I will be anfwerable for it, that the latter fhall, by the Help of Tranflations, in a Year, or two at the moft, clearly out-do the former, that had fo much the ftart of him. Now if this be fo, as I am pretty fure of it, here is two Years' Time quite loft ; to which if we

C   add

add two Years more Boys lose by trifling in *Lilly*'s Grammar,
which I am sure is but a reasonable Supposition, here is a Loss
of no less than four Years of the propereft Time in human Life
for the learning of Languages, to be charged to the Account of
the usual Management of Youth in Grammar-Schools, with ·
respect to those two articles alone, the rejecting of proper
Helps for reading the easier Authors, and the Use of an ill-con-
trived Grammar in Latin.

Now if this Time was to be saved by receiving into our
Schools a competent Number of the Classicks with Literal
Translations, and the Use of a compendious methodical
Grammar in English; and the other Faults in the vulgar Way
of teaching, which I have taken Notice of in my *Essay upon
Education*, were reformed, and other Helps provided for
Schools, which I have there directed to, what a prodigious Advantage would it be to the Youth of the Nation? How finely
might such as are naturally qualified to make Scholars (for all are
not so) go furnished to an University, by the Age of eighteen
or nineteen Years? which is as soon, I think, as Youth ought
to be sent thither, let their Parts be what they will. They
would not only acquire a much greater Acquaintance with the
Languages and Antiquities of ancient *Greece* and *Rome*, than
they now usually do in the best Schools, but go off prettily ac-
complished in their own Language, with a competent Skill in
History and Geography, both Ancient and Modern, the Use
of the Globes, Chronology, &c. What a noble Foundation
would thus be laid for Academical Studies? And if this be so,
the Matter may well deserve the most serious Consideration of
all sober worthy Gentlemen, concerned for the Good of their
own Children, and that of their native Country together.

I HAVE now done with this important Article of Education,
and, I hope, done enough to satisfy any reasonable unprejudiced Reader, of the Necessity for a further Reformation of the
vulgar Method of Proceeding in our Schools, as to this Particular. I flatter myself, that what has been said, carries so much
Light and Evidence along with it, that very little, if any thing
at all, can be said against it, with any Appearance of Reason.
And if so, it were much to be wished, our School-Masters,
who still stand out against a Thing so plainly for their own Ease
and Interest, as well as the Good of the Publick, would take
the Matter under their most serious Consideration. But whilst
Prejudice, or a supine Neglect of Information in some, and a
haughty Disdain in others to receive any Instructions, or accept
of any Helps, from one they conceive perhaps to be much below

low them, keep fo many of our Mafters up to old Forms, the Youth of the Kingdom fuffer miferably by it in their Education. And therefore it were further to be wifhed, that Gentlemen who are convinced of the Reafonablenefs of what I have been pleading for, would be pleafed to add the Weight of their Authority to my poor Endeavours, and difcountenance, by their Refentment, the Practice of fuch Abfurdity upon their Sons, as ftill generally prevails in the Education of Youth in Grammar-Schools. All I fhall add is, that fuch Gentlemen as like the Sentiments delivered in this Differtation, may, I humbly prefume to hope, find many more equally agreeable to them, upon all the Branches of Education, in my *Effay* upon the Subject, as likewife upon all the Branches of Literature, in a Book I publifhed fome Time ago, under the Title of, *An Effay upon Study, wherein Directions are given for the due Conduct thereof, and the Collection of a Library proper for the Purpofe, confifting of the choiceft Books in all the feveral Parts of Learning.*

JOHN CLARKE.

The

The following BOOKS, *all by Mr.* CLARKE, *are fold by* HAWES, CLARKE, *and* COLLINS, *in* Pater-Nofter-Row, LONDON.

I. AN Effay upon Study; wherein Directions are given for the due Conduct thereof, and the Collection of a Library proper for the Purpofe, confifting of the choiceft Books in all the feveral Parts of Learning. The 2d Edition. Price 3s.

II. An Effay upon the Education of Youth in Grammar Schools, wherein the vulgar Method of Teaching is examined, and a new one propofed for the more eafy and fpeedy training up of Youth in the Knowledge of the Learned Languages, with Hiftory, Geography, Chronology, &c. The 3d Edition, as large again as the firft. · Price 2s.

The Seven following BOOKS *are Literally Tranflated.*

III. Eutropii Hiftoriæ Romanæ Breviarium. The 9th Edition. Price 2s. 6d.

IV. C. Nepotis Vitæ excellentium Imperatorum. The 6th Edition. Price 3s. 6d.

V. L. Annæi Flori Epitome Rerum Romanarum. The 5th Edition. Price 2s. 6d.

VI. Juftini Hiftoriæ Philippicæ.. The 5th Edition. Price 4s.

VII. P. Ovidii Metamorphofeon. The 4th Edition. Price 5s.

VIII. Corderii Colloquiorum Centuria felecta. The 10th Edition. Price 1s.

IX. Erafmi Colloquia felecta. The 16th Edition. Price 1. 6d.

The following is with a Free Tranflation.

X. Suetonii XII Cæfares. The 3d Edition. Price 5s.

XI. A New Grammar of the *Latin* Tongue. The 4th Edition. Price 1s. 6d.

XII. An Introduction to the Making of *Latin*. The 16th Edition. Price 2s.

XIII. A Supplement to the Introduction to the Making of *Latin*. Price 1s.

C. CRISPI

C. CRISPI SALLUSTII

VITA.

ONORUM virorum timiditati, inconftantiæ,
aut imprudentiæ vix ignofcere · poffumus, fi
quid aliquando moribus fuis indignum, & ante-
actæ vitæ minus confentaneum protulerint. Sed multo
magis iram noftram movent improborum honefti fer-
mones; quibus, ut nequitiam fuam occultent, certiuf-
que noceant, uti folent : nihil enim fceleratius, quam
armis virtutis uti, ut vitium tuearis. Non puto autem
quemquam pravæ hujus fimulationis labe magis infectum vixiffe, quam celeberrimum hiftoricum C. CRIS-
PUM SALLUSTIUM, ut liquebit ex ejus vita; quam ex
veteribus colligere ftatui, ut quicumque eam legent,
hoc exemplo intelligant, non effe propterea exiftiman-
dum bonum quemquam fuiffe, quod virtutem calamo
defenderit, nifi conftet mores cum fermonibus confen-
fiffe. Nemo certe elegantius & acrius in fuæ ætatis
vitia, quam Salluftius, invectus eft; nec quifquam .
vitæ minus feveræ fuit.

C 3   Natus

xxx   *C. CRISPI SALLUSTII*

Natus erat *(a)* Amiterni, in Sabinis, apud quos
extant etiamnum antiquæ feveritatis reliquiæ, anno
ab urbe condita *(b)* DCLXIX. L. Cornelio Cinna III.
& Cn. Papirio Carbone coff. Hi Sullæ infenfi bellum
civile concitarunt, quod non defiit, nifi poftquam
Sulla, triennio poft, rerum potitus eft. His annis,
omnis generis flagitia in Italia commiffa, plebeiæque
& nobiles familiæ graviffimas calamitates paffæ funt:
unde intelligere licet miferrimo ac flagitiofiffimo ævo
natum effe Salluftium, & quo multo plura, quæ vi-
taret, quam quæ fequeretur, videbat. Parentes tamen ejus inculpatæ vitæ fuiffe credibile fit, quod
prifcus declamator, qui nomine Ciceronis in Salluftium
invectus eft, omniaque conquifivit, quæ in eum dici
poffent, nihil in fama, rumoribufque fubfequentis
ætatis invenerit, quod iis exprobraret. Patrem certe
Salluftii fe *præterire* ait ; *qui fi,* inquit, *numquam in
vita fua peccaffet, tamen majorem injuriam reipublicæ
facere non potuiffet, quam quod eum talem filium ge-
nuerat.* Subjicit, fe *non exfequi fi qua in pueritia
peccaffet Salluftius, ne parentem ejus accufare videretur,
qui eo tempore fummam ejus poteftatem habuit.* Quæ
verba fatis oftendunt, probra nulla in hiftorici noftri
parentes tunc temporis jacta ; neque enim iis vehemens
declamator peperciffet, ut Salluftii nequitiam credi-
biliorem redderet.

Plebeiam ejus familiam, non patriciam, ut nonnulli
volunt, fuiffe liquet, ex eo quod tribunus plebis fuerit;
ac fane ubique in nobiles invehitur, ac præfertim in
hiftoria belli Jugurthini, & pofteriore epiftola ad C.
Cæfarem *De Republica Ordinanda.*

(a) Vide Eufebium in chron. ad ann. MDCCCCXXXI.
(b) A. C. LXXXV.

A

A teneris annis excultam eloquentiam, & oper.im
diligentem literis a Salluftio datam, fatis oftendunt
ejus fcripta ; neque enim ita fcribunt, qui ferius fefe
ad literarum ftudia contulerunt. Ideo fidem ei minime
detraxerim dicenti, epift. 11. ad Cæfarem, *poftquam fibi
ætas ingeniumque adolevijfet, fe haud ferme armis atque
equis corpus exercuijfe, fed animum in literis agitajfe ;
&, quod natura firmius erat, ingenium in laboribus habuiffe.* Sed & hoc diferte teftatur *(a) Suetonius* ; præceptorem enim ejus fuiffe docet Atteium Prætextatum,
nobilem grammaticum Latinum, qui fe *Philologum*
vocavit, & qui Salluftium familiariffime coluit. Vix
tamen videtur, more aliorum, caufas actitaffe, ut gratiam ac famam fibi actionibus forenfibus compararet.
Nulla certe memoria ejus rei apud veteres ; nec Cicero, qui tot æqualium fuorum, qui operam fuam ven-
ditarunt in foro, meminit, C. Crifpi Salluftii mentio-
nem ullam ufquam fecit. Si quis filentii caufam fuiffe
inimicitiam, quæ inter eos fuit, fufpicetur : doceat,
cur Cicero ejus faltem obiter non meminerit, ut vitupe-
raret. Ac fane genus eloquentiæ Salluftianæ minus
aptum foro fuit, aptiffimum hiftoriæ, quæ ab otiofis
legitur. Quare *(b)* Quintilianus, vitari oportere judicat in caufis agendis illam Salluftianam (quamquam in
ipfo virtutis locum obtinet) brevitatem, & abruptum
fermonis genus, quod otiofum fortaffe lectorem minus
fallit, audientem tranfvolat.

Declamator, *(c)* quem dixi, turpiffimam adolefcentiam Salluftio exprobrat, nefandarumque voluptatum
amorem objicit ; quæ criminationes, ut falfæ effe
poffunt, non omnino incredibiles ob fequuta flagitia
videntur. *Domum paternam,* fi accufatori credimus,

_____

(a) In lib. de illuftribus grammaticis, c. 10.   *(b)* Lib. iv.
cap. 2.   *(c)* cap. 5.

vivo patre, turpiffime venalem habuit, ac vendidit; morique coegit ex mœrore patrem, quo nondum mortuo, jam pro herede omnia gerebat. Nec ætatis tirocinio lapfus, poftea fe correxit, fed abiit in fodalitium facrilegi nefcio cujus Nigidiani : bis accufatus eft apud judices, bis abfolutus ; verum ita ut non innocens eſſe, fed judices perjuraſſe viderentur.

Cum ad capeſſendos reipublicæ honores contenderet, *(a)* quæfturam eft confequutus, quam fi petiit legitimo anno, hoc eft, vigefimo quinto, quæftor fuit A. U. C. *(b)* DCXCIV. Quinto Cæcilio Metello Celere & L. Afranio coſſ. Aliofne honores ambiverit, an difficultatibus deterritus ad privatam vitam, iis miſſis, conceſſerit, non fatis liquet. Ab hoc certe tempore nullos honores, ad tribunatum ufque plebis, geſſit. In ipfo adolefcentiæ ardore, videtur ea admifiſſe, quæ æternam nomini ejus infamiam inuſſerunt. M. Varro, *(c)* fcriptor graviſſimus, in libro quem infcripferat Pius, aut de Pace, C. Salluftium in adulterio deprehenfum cum Faufta, Sullæ filia, a Milone ejus viro loris bene cæfum, &, cum pecuniam dediſſet, dimiſſum fuiſſe prodidit.

Attamen A. U. C. DCCII. *(d)* tribunatum plebis adeptus eft, tempore quo ufque adeo turbata erat refpublica, ut eo deventum fit, ut Cn. Pompejus Magnus conful fine collega crearetur. Cum autem paullo ante T. Annius Milo P. Clodium occidiſſet, Pompejufque legem de vi tuliſſet, qua inftituebatur quæftio de ea cæde ; ulcifcendi occafionem naćtus Salluftius, fibi non defuit. Cum duobus aliis tribunis plebis inimiciſſimas conciones, ut fcribit Afconius Pedianus in Ciceronis Milonianam, de Milone habuit, invidiofas etiam de Ci-

(a) Ibidem. *(b)* A. C. LX. *(c)* Apud Aul. Gellium, lib. XVII.. c. 18. Vide et veterem Scholiaften Horatii ad Sat. lib. 1. *(d)* A. C. N. LII.

cerone, quod Milonem fummo ftudio defenderet ; erat-
que maxima pars multitudinis infenfa non folum Miloni,
fed ipfi etiam, propter invifum patrocinium, Ciceroni.
Poftea tamen cum de accufandi ftudio multum remi-
fiffet Salluftius, in fufpicione fuit in gratiam rediiffe
cum Milone & Cicerone.

Crediderim, hifce temporibus, fcriptam fuiffe hiftoriam Catilinariæ conjurationis ; cum Salluftius, exaĉto
tribunatus tempore, privatus ageret, nec Ciceroni
effet infenfus ; rem enim ita narrat, ut, ea leĉta hiftoria,
nemo non aĉta Ciceronis fit probaturus. Forte & bellum Jugurthinum, & civilia, quæ id infequuta funt,
aliaque cum iis connexa, eodem illo tempore confcripfit, aut aliquanto pofterius. Certe non funt ea fcripta
hominis adolefcentis, teftaturque ipfe, initio conjurationis Catilinariæ, fe tum demum hiftoriam aggreffum
fcribere, *(a) ubi animus ex multis miferiis atque periculis
requievit, & fibi reliquam ætatem a republica procul habendam decrevit* ; quod vix ante tribunatum, quem
anno ætatis xLi. geffit, fieri potuit. Tum vero ftatuit *res geftas populi Romani carptim,* (fic ipfe loquitur)
ut quæque memoria digna viderentur, perfcribere ; *eo magis, quod ei a fpe, metu, partibus reipublicæ, animus liber
erat.* Hæc funt verba hominis honores nullos amplius
fperantis, aut certe ambitionem egregie diffimulantis.
At nec ante diffimularat honorum cupiditatem, nec
poftea, rerum potiente Cæfare, eorum contemptum
præ fe tulit.

Itaque ante omnia Catilinariam conjurationem, quæ
contigerat anno ejus vitæ xxx. ac proinde cujus teftis
fuerat, fcribere undecim circiter poft annis aggreffus eft,
fi calculos recte ponimus. Tum Jugurthinum bellum,
quod, diu antequam nafceretur, & civile, quod eo pu-
ero geftum eft, confcripfit. Periit poftremum opus,

(a) Cap. 3.

fi

fi fragmenta quædam excipias, quæ tamen fat ampla ad nos' pervenerunt, ut ex iis intelligere poffimus, non minus accurate ac cetera perfcriptum fuiffe. Sed *(a)* mihi videor ex loco Aufonii poffe colligere tempora, quorum hiftoriam fcripferat Salluftius, in iis libris qui perierunt. Aufonius in idyllio xxxII. ad nepotem, docet puerum, quos libros legere eum oporteat, & quos ipfe in gratiam ejus in manum iterum fumere fit paratus. Itaque memorato Terentio, fic loquitur de Salluftii libris:

Jam facinus, Catilina, tuum, Lepidique tumultum ;
Ab Lepido & Catulo jam res & tempora Romæ
Orfus, bis fenos feriem connecto per annos.
Jam lego civili miftum Mavorte duellum,
Movit quod focio Sertorius exful Ibero.

Hæc funt omnia opera Salluftii, excepto bello Jugurthino, quod cur omiferit Aufonius, non intelligo. Forte aliquot verfus vetuftate interciderunt. I. Occurrit bellum Catilinarium, de quo nihil neceffe eft dicere. II. Hiftoria tumultus excitati a Marco Æmilio Lepido, anno urbis conditæ DCLXXXVII. poftquam anno fuperiori conful fuiffet : is tumultus a Pompejo & Catulo oppreffus eft, eodem anno. III. Inde Salluftius fcripferat hiftoriam rerum in republica Romana per duodecim annos geftarum, ante Lepidi tumultum ; quorum duodecim annorum initium fecerim circiter ab anno U. C. DCLXIII. quo bellum Marficum inchoatum ; ab eo enim tempore, ufque ad extremam dictaturam Sullæ, duodecim circiter anni fluxerunt. Multa autem inveniuntur fragmenta Salluftii, ex quibus liquet eum res a Sulla geftas fcripfiffe ; quæ ea temporis intercapedine continentur. IV. Bellum fcripferat Sertorianum, quod cœperat fub finem vitæ Sullæ, proximeque duodecim annos memoratos confequebatur ; Metellus enim in Hifpaniam contra Sertorium miffus eft anno

---

(a) Suetonius de Ill. Gramm. cap. x.

U. C.

U. C. DCLXXIV. qui duodecim illorum annorum ul-
timus fuit. Si ea hiftoria ad receptas ufque Hifpanias
pertexta eft, quod credibile videtur, pertinuit ad annum DCLXXXI. nam eo demum anno, occifis Sertorio
& Perperna, pacatæ funt Hifpaniæ.

Hinc videmus quamvis Salluftius carptim fcripfiffet
hiftoriam Romanam, nec continua temporum ferie lu-
cubrationes fuas edidiffet, ex tribus poftremo memora-
tis operibus potuiffe contexi circiter octodecim annorum hiftoriam; quæ utinam fane extaret! Fragmenta
enim ejus fitim noftram excitant, non reftinguunt.
Hi autem libri, quamvis ab auctore eo ordine, quem
memorat Aufonius, editi, videntur poftea a grammaticis in ordinem quemdam redacti, ut ex tribus operibus
una conflaretur hiftoria, librique ejus perpetuo ordine a
primo ad ultimum decurrerent, commodiufque ad tef-
timonium citarentur. Afinius Pollio, in libro quo Salluftii fcripta reprehenderat, ut nimia prifcorum verborum adfectatione oblita, tradebat, *In eam rem adjutori-
um ei feciffe maxime quendam Atteium Prætextatum, nobilem grammaticum Latinum, declamantium deinde adju-
torem atque præceptorem.* Ab hoc aiebat, *Salluftium,
hiftoriam fcribere aggreffum, breviario rerum omnium Romanarum, ex quibus quas vellet eligeret, inftructum fuiffe,
antiquaque ei verba & figuras folitum eum effe colligere.*
Videtur grammaticus non ignobilis ea in re ingenio ac
voluntati Salluftii gratificatus effe, potius quam fuum
ipfius judicium fequutus; nam in præceptis rhetoricis
ad Afinionem Pollionem, ei *nihil aliud fuadebat,* ut prodidit Suetonius, *quam ut noto, civilique & proprio fermone uteretur, vitaretque maxime obfcuritatem & audaciam
in tranflationibus.* Credibile eft, Salluftium ea re gravi-
tatem ftyli captaffe, & prifcorum illorum Romanorum
fermonem imitatum, quorum moribus erat diffimilli-
mus, ut flagitiofæ vitæ maculas elueret, perfuaderetque
iis, quibus fatis notus non erat, falfa effe omnia, quæ
de illo minus honefta jactabantur.

Verum

Verum hæ artes belle homini non cefferunt, nam anno *(a)* U. C. DCCIV. coff. L. Æmilio Paulo & C.
Claudio Marcello, Appius Claudius Pulcher Cenfor,
non repugnante collega L. Calpurnio Pifone, omnes
libertinos, ut docet Dio, lib. XL. multos etiam nobilium, atque inter eos Crifpum Salluftium, qui hiftoriam
confcripfit, fenatu ejecit.   Quod factum, fi veteribus
(b) grammaticis credimus, propter adulteria : dicitur
enim ab iis *Salluftius tanto ardore infaniviffe in libertinas,*
quanto mœchus in matronas, quod cum illi in fenatu a
cenforibus objectum effet, refpondit fe non matronarum, fed
libertinarum fectatorem effe. *Quare ex fenatu,* inquiunt,
ejectus eft. Hoc quoque ei exprobrat perfonatus ille *(c)*
Cicero, qui declamatione in ejus mores invectus eft.
Idem nos docet, poftquam cenfores fenatum more
majorum legiffent, nufquam confpectum effe Salluftium
Romæ, fufpicaturque tum fe *conjeciffe in ea caftra, quo*
omnis fentina reipublicæ confluxerat ; hoc eft, in Galliam
ad Cæfarem fe contuliffe.   Non minoribus *(d)* convi-
ciis eum exagitavit Lenæus, Pompeji Magni libertus,
ex amore erga patroni memoriam, quem Salluftius
fcripferat *oris probi, animo inverecundo fuiffe.*   Ideo Lenæus poftea hiftoricum noftrum *acerbiffima fatyra,* ut
docet Suetonius, *laceravit,* laftaurum & lurconem &
nebulonem popinonemque *appellans,* & vita fcriptifque
monftrofum, *præterea* prifcorum, Catonifque verborum
ineruditiffimum furem.   Qua ex occafione, fic de Pompejo fcripfiffet Salluftius, poft interitum ejus hiftoriæ,
conjicere non poffumus ; at conftat Cæfarianis partibus
e fenatu expulfum faviffe.

Certe pofteaquam refpublica armis oppreffa eft, anno fequente, *(e)* U. C. DCCV. C. Claudio Marcello &

(a) A. Chr. N. L.   *(b)* Schol. in Sat. II. lib. 1.   Horatii.
(c) Cap. 5 & 6.   *(d)* Suetonius de illuftr. Gramm. cap. 15.
(e) Cicero in Salluft. cap. 6.

L. Cornelio Lentulo coff. a Cæfare *(a)* eft in fenatum
reductus ; quæftura iterum accepta, ut honeftius in
ampliffimum ordinem reciperetur. Eum autem *ho-*
norem, fi adverfæ famæ credimus, *ita geffit, ut nihil*
in eo non venale habuerit, cujus aliquis emptor fuit. Nihil
non æquum ac verum duxit, quod ipfi facere collibuiffet.
Propter iteratam quæfturam, prifcus declamàtor, cujus verba protulimus, *bis fenatorem, bis quæftorem fac-*
tum; ait. At Dio, lib. xLII. vult, ut recuperaret
dignitatem fenatoriam, prætorem creatum. Malim,
quæftura in eum collata, factum hoc effe ; eo enim
magiftratu capto, Romana juventus ingrediebatur fenatum.

Hoc tempore, viris doctis videtur fcripfiffe ad Cæfarem duas illas literas, quæ perperam orationes infcri-
buntur, *De republica ordinanda.* Sed pofteriores quidem,
hoc tempore, fcripfiffe potuit ; at priores non nifi
propemodum confecto bello fcripfit. Malim ergo hafce
differre in annum DCCVII, aut certe ad finem anni an-
tecedentis, cum victus effet Cn. Pompejus.

Igitur fub finem *(b)* anni DCCVI. cum in Afia effet
Cæfar, ab iis *(c)* qui Roma ad eum venerant cognovit,
literifque urbanis animadvertit, multa Romæ male &
inutiliter adminiftrari, neque ullam partem reipublicæ
fatis commode geri ; quod & contentionibus tribunitiis
perniciofæ feditiones orirentur, & ambitione atque in-
dulgentia tribunorum militum, & qui legionibus præerant, multa contra morem confuetudinemque militarem fierent, quæ diffolvendæ difciplinæ, feveritatif-
que effent. Hanc crediderim occafionem fuiffe fcri-

(a) A. C. N. xLIx. Id. c. 7. *(b)* A. C. N. xLVII. *(c)* Hirtius de Bel. Alexand. cap. 65.

bendi

bendi iterum ad Cæfarem de ordinanda republica : qua de re, cogitare ferio non potuit, nifi poft victum Pompeium. Antea quidem Salluftius, Cæfare nondum in Macedoniam profecto, vigenteque bello, multa monuerat, ea de re, in epiftola quæ II. oratio perperam dicitur, ubi de 'M. Bibulo & L. Domitio quafi viventibus loquitur, cum Bibulus mortuus fit ante pugnam Pharfalicam, & Domitius ex ea fugiens interfectus. Sed in altera epiftola, in qua de bello quafi confecto loquitur, rem eamdem iterum aggreditur. Itaque, quæ prior eft, eam oportet effe pofteriorem, quod ipfum ejus, quæ pofterior eft, procemium fatis oftendit.

Antequam autem Cæfar contra Scipionem, Pompeji focerum, in Africam iret, anno U. C. DCCVII. quo Cæfar iterum dictator fuit, M. Antonius magifter equitum, prætor factus eft Salluftius ; qui 'honor videtur non tam monitorum de republica ordinanda, quam turpium adulationum iis admiftarum præmium fuiffe. At Salluftio propemodum fatalis fuit ; *(a)* 'cum enim effet in Campania, apud Cæfarianos milites, mox in Africam tranfmittendos, motaque ab iis effet feditio, quam fruftra compefcere tentavit, ab iis ferme eft interfectus. Quin etiam cum Romam ad Cæfarem contenderet, ut hac de re certiorem faceret, infequuti eum complures militum, obvios quofque occiderunt ; ipfum, fi adipifci poffent, e medio fublaturi.

Cæfar vero, placatis militibus, fub. brumam in Africam, cum parte exercitus, trajecit, fecumque Salluftium duxit, quem, paucis diebus poftquam adpuliffet, cum penuria annonæ premeretur, *(b)* ad Cercinam in-

---

(a) Ex Dione, lib. XLIII. *(b)* Hirtius de Bello Afric. cap. 8.

fulam,

fulam, quam adverfarii tenebant, cum parte navium,
ire juffit, quod ibi magnum numerum frumenti effe
audiebat. Ejus adventu *(a)* C. Decimius Quæftorius,
qui ibi cum grandi familiæ fuæ præfidio præerat com-
meatui, parvulum navigium nactus confcendit, ac fe
fugæ commendavit. Salluftius interim a Cercinatibus
receptus, magno numero frumenti invento, naves one-
rarias, quarum ibi fatis magna copia fuit, complevit,
atque in caftra ad Cæfarem mifit. Quid aliud in eo
bello gefferit Salluftius, nemo prodidit, fed fidelem ac
ftrenuam operam Cæfari navaffe, ex præmio intelligere
eft. Anno *(b)* enim U. C. DCCVII. confecto Africano
bello, *(c)* Cæfar eum in Numidia recepta, verbo quidem adminiftrandæ provinciæ caufa, reipfa autem ex-
pilandæ, pro prætore reliquit. Itaque dona multa
Salluftius accepit, multa rapuit, Romamque deinde re-
verfus, cum a Numidis accufaretur, maximam infamiam retulit ; quod cum libros fcripfiffet, in quibus
copiofa & acerba oratione invectus erat in eos qui ex
provinciis queftum feciffent, rebus ipfis quod fcripferat non exprefiffet. Ne *(d)* tamen caufam diceret,
(e) feftertio duodecies cum Cæfare pactus eft, fi credimus perfonato Ciceroni. Graviffimus certe hiftoricus
Dio prodidit eum, licet a Cæfare dimiffum, fuis ipfius
fcriptis perennem infamiam fibi creaffe, quod vita ab
iis prorfus diffentiret.

Ea præda, *(f)* qui modo ne paternam quidem domum redimere poterat, repente tanquam fomnio beatus,
hortos pretiofiffimos, qui *(g)* Salluftiani, ab ejus nomine, dicti funt, villam Tiburtinam, & alias pof-
feffiones fibi comparavit.

(a) Ibid. cap. 34.   *(b)* A. C. N. XLVI,   *(c)* Dion. lib.
XLIII.   *(d)* Cicer. in Salluft. cap, 8.   *(e)* Nonagies mille ff.
eoque amplius.   *(f)* Cicero in Salluft. cap. 8.   *(g)* De iis vide
Fam. Nardinum vet. Romæ, lib. IV. cap. 7.

Qua ratione vitam poſtea traduxit Salluſtius, veteribus tacentibus, nobis non liquet. Credibile eſt ornandæ domui, exſtruendis villis, deliciiſque undiquaque parandis occupatum fuiſſe ; ita ut ſaluberrimis præceptis, quæ in hiſtoriis tradiderat, exemplo ſuo, vim pondufque detrahere pergeret. De ejus oratione in Ciceronem, & Ciceronis in Salluſtium, nihil addam ; quia, licet antiquæ ſint, nec infra ævum Tiberianum, animi cauſa, a rhetore quopiam confictas nemo amplius dubitat.

Septuageſimo ætatis anno, fato functus eſt, quadriennio (*a*) ante bellum Actiacum, hoc eſt, anno (*b*) U. C. DCCXIX. S. Pompejo & S. Cornificio coſſ. Vir ſane fuit memorabilis, ſi hiſtorias ejus ſpectes ; quæ, ſi nimium antiquioris ſtyli ſtudium excipias, nullis aliis poſtponendæ ſunt, principemque locum inter Romanos hiſtoricos, etiam judicio veterum, ei pepererunt. Nec brevitatem ac efficaciam ſingularem dictionis duntaxat laudant, ſed etiam veritatis ſtudium ; quod ita intelligendum, ut de aliis loquenti fides habeatur, de ſe ipſi nihil credatur niſi quod re ipſa comprobatum eſt. Facile credo, cum ſe reipublicæ longum vale dixiſſe putaret, (*c*) *conſilium ei non fuiſſe*, ut ipſe dicit, *ſocordia atque deſidia bonum otium conterere, neque vero, agrum colendo ac venando, ſervilibus officiis intentum, ætatem egiſſe*, ſed honeſtioribus ſtudiis & ſcriptionibus, operam dediſſe. At nec oblitum deliciarum ac voluptatum opinor ; quibus & puer & adoleſcens & ſenex, quaſi ſirenibus quibuſdam, adhæſit : nec, ut puto, dum hiſtorias florente ætate, ſcriptitaret, nuncium remiſit.

(*a*) Vide Euſeb. in Chron.   (*b*) A. C. N. xxxv.
(*c*) Conjur. Catil. cap. 4.

Idem

Idem fecit, quod *(a)* plerique philofophorum, *difer-orum in convicium fuum, quos fi audias in avaritiam, in ibidinem, in ambitionem perorantes, indicium profeſſos pu-es, adeo redundant ad ipfos maledicta in publicum miſſa !* nterea ejus hiftoria, ut ceteris omnibus, utamur opor-et, quippe quæ non minus gravia ac utilia præcepta, xemplaque continet, quam fi fcriptor fanctitate mo-um prifcos omnes fuperaſſet.

(a) Seneca apud Lactant. lib. III. cap. 15.

D   *C. CRISPI*

C. CRISPI SALLUSTII

BELLUM CATILINARIUM:

SIVE DE

CONJURATIONE CATILINÆ.

OMNIS homines qui fefe ftudent præftare cæteris animalibus, fumma ope niti decet, ne vitam filentio tranfeant, veluti pecora, quæ natura prona atque ventri obedientia finxit. Sed noftra omnis vis in animo & corpore fita eft. Animi imperio, corporis fervitio magis utimur. Alterum nobis cum dis, alterum cum belluis commune eft. Quo mihi rectius videtur, ingenii, quam virium opibus gloriam quærere ; &, quoniam vita ipfa, qua fruimur, brevis eft, memoriam noftri

ALL men, who are defirous to excel other animals, fhould endeavour by all means not to pafs their days in filence, like cattle, which nature has formed in an inclining pofture, and a ftate of fubjection to their bellies. But our faculties are of two different kinds, of the body and the foul. 'Tis the bufinefs of the foul to command, and that of the body to obey. The one we have in common with the Gods, and the other with brutes. And therefore to me it appears more advifeable to purfue glory by the abilities of the mind, than thofe of the body ; and fince the life we enjoy, is but fhort, to make our memories as lafting as poffible in the world. The fplendour, riches

quam

quam maxume longam efficere. Nam divitiarum & formæ gloria fluxa atque fragilis eft ; virtus clára æternaque habetur. Sed diu magnum inter mortales certamen fuit ; vine corporis, an virtute animi, res militaris magis procederet. Nam & prius quam incipias, confulto ; &, ubi confuleris, mature facto opus eft : ita utrumque per fe indigens, alterum alterius auxilio veget.

II. Igitur initio reges (nam in terris nomen imperii id primum fuit) diverfi, pars ingenium, alii corpus exercebant. Etiam tum vita hominum fine cupiditate agitabatur ; fua cuique fatis placebant. Poftea vero quam in Afia Cyrus, in Græcia Lacedæmonii & Athenienfes cœpere urbes atque nationes fubigere ; lubidinem dominandi caufam belli habere ; maxumam gloriam in maxumo imperio putare : tum demum periculo atque negotiis compertum eft, in bello plurimum ingenium pofle. Quod fi regum atque imperatorum animi virtus in pace ita, ut in bello, valeret : æquabilius atque conftantius fefe res humanæ haberent : neque

and beauty yield, is fading and frail ; but virtue is thought to give an everlafting luftre. Yet it has been a long time a matter of no fmall debate among men, whether fuccefs in war has more depended upon ftrength of body, or the abilities of the mind. For enterprizes of that kind ought not to be undertaken but upon previous deliberation, and when refolved upon, ought vigoroufly to be put in execution. Thus whilft neither of thefe things is of itjetf fufficient, they fucceed by the mutual aid of each other.

II. Wherefore in the early ages of the world, Kings (for monarchy feems to have been the firft kind of government amongft men) fome of them laboured the improvement of their minds, and others of their bodies. At that time indeed mankind were ftrangers to covetoufnefs, every one being content with his own. But after Cyrus in Afia, and in Greece the Athenians and Lacedemonians, begun to conquer cities and whole nations, and to look upon the luft of dominion as a fufficient ground of war, and to reckon the greateft glory to confift in the large extent of their conquefts ; then it was found by experience, that an able head was the moft ferviceable in war. And if the great abilities of Kings and Commanders produced but as good effects in peace as in war, the affairs of mankind would be in a much more calm and fettled ftate. Nor fhould we fee fuch hurly-burly, fuch diftraction and confufion fpread over the face of the earth.

aliud

aliud alio ferri, neque mutari ac mifceri omnia cerneres. Nam imperium facile iis artibus retinetur, quibus initio partum eft. Verum, ubi pro labore defidia, pro continentia & æquitate lubido atque fuperbia invafere, fortuna fimul cum moribus immutatur. Ita imperium femper ad optumum quemque ab minus bono transfertur. Quæ homines arant, navigant, ædificant, virtuti omnia parent. Sed multi mortales, dediti ventri atque fomno, indocti, incultique, vitam ficuti peregrinantes tranfiere : quibus profecto, contra naturam, corpus voluptati, anima oneri fuit. Eorum ego vitam mortemque juxta æftumo ; quoniam de utraque filetur. Verum enimvero is demum mihi vivere, & frui anima videtur, qui, aliquo negotio intentus, præclari facinoris, aut artis bonæ famam quærit. Sed in magna copia rerum, aliud alii natura iter oftendit.

III. Pulchrum eft bene facere reipublicæ: etiam bene dicere haud abfurdum eft. Vel pace vel bello clarum fieri licet. Et qui fecere, & qui facta aliorum fcripfere, multi laudantur. Ac mihi quidem, tametfi haudqua-

For dominion is eafily fecured by the fame arts by which it was firft acquired. But when idlenefs has fucceeded in the place of induftry, and inftead of moderation and equity, luft and pride prevail, then the fortune of a people changes with their manners. And thus power is ever fhifting about from the worfe to the better part of men ; and the advantages of plowing, failing, and building, become the perquifites of virtue. But a great many men who minded nothing but eating and fleeping, illiterate and unpolifhed, have fpent their days like ftrangers in the world, whofe happinefs, contrary to nature, lay in pampering their bodies, whilft their fouls were a burthen to them. The life and death of fuch as thefe I reckon much the fame, fince no notice is taken of either. But he indeed appears to me to be truly alive, and to enjoy life, who is engaged in fome ufeful employment, and endeavours to acquire fame by noble actions, or the practice of fome commendable art. But in the midft of plenty for that purpofe, nature has pointed out to different men different ways.

III. It is a glorious thing to be ferviceable to the ftate ; and eloquence is no defpicable talent. A man may make himfelf famous in peace or in war. Many, as well thofe that have performed great actions, as thofe that have given us the hiftory thereof, are highly applauded. And though I cannot

D 3   quam

quam par gloria fequatur
fcriptorem & auctorem
rerum, tamen in primis
arduum videtur res geftas
fcribere : primum, quod
facta dictis exæquanda
funt ; dein, quia plerique,
quæ delicta reprehende-
ris, malevolentia & invi-
dia dicta putant. Ubi de
magna virtute atque glo-
ria bonorum memores,
quæ fibi quifque facilia
factu putat, æquo animo
accipit : fupra, veluti ficta pro falfis ducit. Sed
ego adolefcentulus initio,
ficuti plerique, ftudio ad
rempublicam latus fum :
ibique mihi multa advorfa
fuere. Nam pro pudore,
pro abftinentia, pro vir-
tute, audacia, largitio,
avaritia vigebant. Quæ
tametfi animus afperna-
batur, infolens malarum
artium ; tamen inter tan-
ta vitia imbecilla ætas
ambitione corrupta te-
nebatur. Ac me, cum
ab reliquis malis mori-
bus diffentirem, nihilo-
minus honoris cupido
eadem, quæ cæteros, fa-
ma atque invidia vexa-
bat.

IV. Igitur, ubi animus
ex multis miferiis atque
periculis requievit, & mihi
reliquam ætatem a repub-
lica procul habendam de-
crevi ; non fuit confilium

indeed say, that the historian and the hero are entitled to the same share of glory ; yet it appears to me a matter of no small difficulty to write history well. First, because in the relation of noble actions the style must be suited to the grandeur of the subject ; and in the next place, because most readers are apt to look upon the censure of any miscarriages as proceeding from ill-nature and envy. And in accounts of the gallant behaviour and glorious atchievments of worthy men, such things as any one looks upon to have no great difficulty in them, he can read with patience, as credible ; but all beyond he treats as mere fiction, and utterly false. When I was a young man, I was, like most other gentlemen, very inclinable to engage in the service of the state, but every where found great difficulties in the way of such my design ; for instead of modesty, justice, and virtue, impudence, bribery, and avarice carried all before them. Which though I had an abhorrence of, as having never been accustomed to such vile practices, yet those being now become the fashion of the times, my unexperienced youth exposed me to be caught by the baits of ambition. And though I did not fall entirely in with a vicious age in other respects, yet I had the same spirit of ambition and envy in me as others had.

IV. Being at last happily delivered from a world of vexation and danger, and resolved no more to meddle in state-affairs, I was not, however, minded to spend my days in idleness and sloth, or to
focor-

ocordia atque defidia bo-
ium otium conterere :
ieque vero, agrum colen-
lo, aut venando, fervili-
ius officiis intentum, æ-
atem agere ! fed a quo
ncœpto ftudioque me
imbitio mala detinuerat,
eodem regreffus ftatui res
geftas populi Romani
trictim, uti quæque me-
noria digna videbantur,
perfcribere : eo magis,
quod mihi a fpe, metu,
partibus reipublicæ, ani-
mus liber erat. Igitur
le Catilinæ conjuratione,
quam veriffime potero,
paucis abfolvam. Nam
d facinus in primis ego
memorabile exiftumo,
fceleris atque periculi no-
vitate. De cujus hominis
moribus pauca prius ex-
plananda funt, quam ini-
tium narrandi faciam.

V. Lucius Catilina,
nobili genere natus, fuit
magna vi & animi & cor-
poris, fed ingenio malo
pravoque. Huic ab ado-
lefcentia bella inteftina,
cædes, rapinæ, difcordia
civilis, grata fuere ; ibique
juventutem fuam exercu-
it. Corpus patiens inediæ,
algoris, vigiliæ fupra
quam cuiquam credible
eft. Animus audax, fub-
dolus, varius, cujuflibet
rei fimulator ac diffimula-
tor, alieni appetens, fui
profufus, ardens in cupi-
ditatibus : fatis loquentiæ,

employ my life in agriculture,
hunting, or the like fervile offices;
but immediately refumed the purfuit of my former defign, from
which wicked ambition had diverted me, and determined to fet
about writing the hiftory of the
Roman people, fuch parts of it, I
mean, as appeared to me moft worthy of the notice of pofterity ; and
the rather, becaufe my mind was
not at all influenced by hope, fear,
or party-prejudice. Accordingly,
I fhall in the firft place give a
brief account of Catiline's confpiracy, and that with all poffible
regard to truth. For I look upon
that defign to have been one of the
moft memorable that ever were,
for the ftrange wickednefs and
danger of it. Which I fhall begin with a fhort character of the
man.

V. Lucius Catiline was defcended of a noble family, and
endowed with an extraordinary
vigour both of body and mind, but
of a wicked perverfe difpofition.
Who had from his youth nothing
fo much at heart as civil war,
rapine, and embroiling of the
ftate ; in which he fpent the prime
of his years. His body was incre-
dibly qualified for the enduring of
hunger, want of fleep, and cold.
His mind was daring, crafty,
fickle, capable of the moft profound diffimulation, and of acting any part whatever ; greedy of
what was not his own, and lavifh of what was ; extremely eager

D 4   fapi-

sapientiæ parum. Vastus animus immoderata, incredibilia, nimis alta semper cupiebat. Hunc, post dominationem L. Sullæ, lubido maxuma invaserat reipublicæ capiundæ : neque id quibus modis adsequeretur, dum sibi regnum pararet, quidquam pensi habebat. Agitabatur magis magisque indies animus ferox inopia rei familiaris, & conscientia scelerum : quæ utraque his artibus auxerat, quas supra memoravi. Incitabant præterea corrupti civitatis mores : quos pessuma ac diversa inter se mala, luxuria atque avaritia, vexabant. Res ipsa hortari videtur, quoniam de moribus civitatis tempus admonuit, supra repetere, ac paucis instituta majorum domi militiæque, quomodo rempublicam habuerint, quantamque reliquerint ; &, ut paulatim immutata, ex pulcherrima & optuma pessuma ac flagitiosissuma facta sit, disserere.

VI. Urbem Romam, sicuti ego accepi, condidere atque habuere initio Trojani ; qui, Ænea duce, profugi, sedibus incertis vagabantur ; cumque his Aborigines, genus hominum agreste, sine legibus, sine imperio, liberum, atque solutum. Hi,

in the gratification of his desires ; eloquence enough he had, but little wisdom. His wild soul was ever engaged in the most extravagant projects, things unattainable, and above his sphere. After the tyranny of Sulla, he became passionately fond of seizing the government ; and, provided he could but bring his purpose about, he cared not at all by what means he did it. His savage soul was more and more agitated with his poverty, and a sense of guilt, both which he had increased by the vile practices above mentioned. He was moreover encouraged in his enterprize by the wickedness of the times, the city being sadly overrun with two of the worst, but very different sorts of vices, luxury and avarice. And since I am got upon this subject, it may not perhaps be an improper occasion of running back into the early ages of the Roman people, to give an account of the conduct of our ancestors, how they managed their affairs both in peace and war, and to what a height they brought the Roman state, how by degrees it has been changed, and of the most glorious and best is become the worst and most flagitious.

VI. The city Rome, as far as I can find, was built and first inhabited by the Trojans, who being obliged to fly from their native country strolled about from place to place, under the leading of Æneas. But with them were joined the Aborigines, a wild sort of people, under no restraint from law or government at all. How-
post-

poftquam in una mœnia convenere, difpari genere, diffimili lingua, alius alio more viventes, incredibile memoratu eft, quam facile coaluerint. Sed poftquam res eorum civibus, moribus, agris aucta, fatis profpera, fatifque pollens videbatur; ficuti pleraque mortalium habentur, invidia ex opulentia orta eft. Igitur reges populique finitimi bello tentare. Pauci ex amicis auxilio effe. Nam cæteri, metu perculfi, a periculis aberant. At Romani, domi militiæque intenti, feftinare, parare, alius alium hortari, hoftibus obviam ire, libertatem, patriam, parentefque armis tegere. Poft, ubi pericula virtute propulerant, fociis atque amicis auxilia portabant; magifque dandis, quam accipiundis, beneficiis amicitias parabant. Imperium legitimum, nomen imperii regium habebant. Delecti, quibus corpus annis infirmum, ingenium fapientia validum erat, reipublicæ confultabant. Hi, vel ætate vel curæ fimilitudine, *Patres* appellabantur. Poft, ubi regium imperium, quod initio confervandæ libertatis atque augendæ reipublicæ fuerat, in fuperbiam dominationemque

ever, upon their uniting and cohabiting in the fame city, notwithftanding the wide difference betwixt them, with refpect to their language, and manner of life, yet it is incredible to fay, how eafily they became one people. But after this new ftate received fuch an improvement in number of people, manners, and territory, as to appear in a profperous and vigorous condition, their happy circumftances, as is ufual in fuch cafes, drew down the envy of their neighbours upon them. Accordingly the neighbouring princes and ftates prefently engaged in war againft them; wherein fome few of their friends ftood by them, whilft the reft, for fear of the worft, kept themfelves out of danger. The Romans, however, were not wanting in their endeavours, both at home and abroad, for a vigorous defence; but animated by mutual encouragements, boldly faced their enemy for the fecurity of their liberty, country, and parents. And after they had by their bravery repelled the dangers that threatened them, gave in their turn affiftance to their allies and friends; and added to the number of them, more by the conferring of favours, than the receiving of them. Their government was a legal one, under the name of a monarchy. Perfons weak of body by reafon of their age, but eminent for their wifdom and abilities of mind, were appointed as a council of ftate, to provide for the publick fecurity; who from their age, or their obligation to a paternal concern for the good of the common-

. con-

convertit, immutato mo- re, annua imperia, binos imperatores fibi fecere. Eo modo minume poffe putabant per licentiam infolefcere animum humanum.

wealth, were called Fathers. *But when kingly government, which at firft proved a means of preferving their liberty, and advancing the publick intereft, degenerated into haughtinefs and tyranny, it was laid afide, and in room thereof,*

two magiftrates were yearly appointed to govern the ftate. For this they thought the moft likely means to prevent a licentious infolence in their governors.

VII. Sed ea tempefta- te cœpere fe quifque ma- gis magifque extollere, ingeniumque in promptu habere. Nam regibus boni, quam mali, fufpec- tiores funt; femperque his aliena virtus formidolofa eft. Sed civitas, incredi- bile memoratu eft, adepta libertate, quantum brevi creverit : tanta cupido gloriæ incefferat. Jam- primum juventus, fimul ac belli patiens erat, in caftris per laborem ufu militiam difcebat; magif- que in decoris armis & militaribus equis, quam in fcortis atque conviviis, lubidinem habebat. Igi- tur talibus viris non la- bos infolitus, non locus ullus afper aut arduus e- rat, non armatus hof- tis formidolofus : virtus omnia domuerat. Sed gloriæ maxumum certa- men inter ipfos erat. Quifque hoftem ferire, murum afcendere, con- fpici, dum tale facinus faceret, properabat. Eas divitias, eam bonam fa-

VII. *Now every one began to exert himfelf, and employ all his faculties, for the publick fervice. For under kings, perfons of worth and merit are more apt to be look- ed upon with a jealous eye, than thofe of a contrary charaćter. For princes are ever appprehenfive of great abilities in their fubjećts. But after the Roman ftate had thus recovered its liberty, it is in- credible to fay, what a mighty im- provement it prefently received ; fuch an appetite for glory had now prevailed amongft that people. Now the youth, as foon as capable of bearing arms, were trained up in the fatigues of a camp, to the bufinefs of war. Handfome arms, and fine war-horfes, were much more their concern, than the praćtice of lewdnefs and luxury. To fuch men as thefe hardfhip was no novelty, no place too rugged or difficult, no enemy was terrible, their refolution bore down all be- fore it. But at the fame time there was the higheft emulation amongft them in point of glory ; every one being zealous to diftin- guifh himfelf in fight, or the fca- ling of walls, in the view of his fellow-foldiers. This was their riches, their glory, and what* mam,

ıam, magnamque nobi-
ilitatem putabant. Lau-
is avidi, pecuniæ libera-
:s erant. Gloriam in-
entem, divitias honeftas
olebant. Memorare pof-
:m, quibus in locis max-
mas hoſtium copias po-
ulus Romanus parva ma-
u fuderit, quas urbes na-
ıra munitas pugnando ce-
:rit ; ni ea res longius
ɔs ab incœpto traheret.
VIII. Sed profecto for-
ına in omni re domina-
ır. Ea res cunctas, ex
ıbidine magis, quam ex
:ro, celebrat obſcurat-
ıe. Athenienfium res
:ſtæ, ficut ego exiſtu-
.ɔ, fatis amplæ magni-
:æque fuere : verum
iquanto minores tamen,
ıam fama feruntur. Sed
ıia provenere ibi magna
riptorum ingenia, per
:rrarum orbem Atheni-
ıſium facta pro maxu-
ıis celebrantur. Ita eo-
ım, qui ea fecere, vir-
ıs tánta habetur, quan-
ım verbis ea potuere ex-
ɔllere præclara ingenia.
ıt populo Romano num-
ıuam ea copia fuit : quia
rudentiffimus quifque ne-
otiofus maxume erat.
ıgcnium nemo fine cor-
ore exercebat. Optu-
ıus quifque facere, quam
icere ; fua ab aliis bene
ıɕta laudari, quam ipfe
liorum narrare, malcbat.

alone ennobled them, in their opinion. They were greedy of honour, but laviſh of their money.
Glory they could never have too
much of, but for riches a handſome
competency ſufficed them. And
here I could entertain the reader
with numerous inſtances of mighty
armies defeated by inconſiderable
numbers, and cities wonderfully
fortified by nature taken by them.
But that would detain me too long
from my purpoſe.

VIII. But fortune has indeed
a mighty ſway in all things ; raĩſes
or depreſſes them at pleaſure, rather than according to truth. The
actions of the Athenians were, in
my opinion, great and glorious
enough, but not altogether ſo conſiderable as fame repreſents them.
But becauſe that city produced
great plenty of fine authors, the
exploits of that people are throughout the world celebrated for the
greateſt that ever were performed by men. Accordingly the courage and conduct of the actors
have been as much magnified as
it was in the power of the fineſt
wits to do it. But this was an
advantage the Roman people never
had, becauſe the wifeſt men were
always the moſt engaged in the ſervice of the ſtate ; for none purſued
the improvement of the mind only,
without regard to that of the body.
The beſt men chofe rather the part
of acting than ſpeaking ; and to
have their own atchievements celebrated by others, rather than write
thoſe of others themſelves.

IX. Igi-

IX. Igitur domi militiæque boni mores colebantur. Concordia maxuma, minuma avaritia erat. Jus bonumque apud eos non legibus magis, quam natura, valebat. Jurgia, difcordias, fimultates cum hoftibus exercebant. Cives cum civibus de virtute certabant. In fuppliciis deorum magnifici, domi parci, in amicos fideles erant. Duabus his artibus, audacia bello, ubi pax evenerat, æquitate, feque remque publicam curabant. Quarum rerum ego maxuma documenta hæc habeo; quod in bello fæpius vindicatum eft in eos, qui contra imperium in hoftem pugnaverant, quique tardius revocati prælio excefferant, quam qui figna relinquere, aut pulfi, loco cedere aufi erant. In pace vero, beneficiis magis, quam metu, imperium agitabant; & accepta injuria, ignofcere quam perfequi, malebant.

X. Sed, ubi labore atque juftitia refpublica crevit; reges magni bello domiti; nationes feræ, & populi ingentes vi fubacti; Carthago, æmula imperii Romani, ab ftirpe interiit; cunĉta maria terræque patebant; fortuna fævire ac mifcere omnia cœpit. Qui laborcs,

XI. *Good manners therefore were practifed both at home and abroad, in the wars. Their unanimity was great, but defires very moderate. Juftice and equity prevailed amongft them, not more by the force of laws, than natural inclination. All the differences and quarrels they had were with the enemies of the ftate. But one with another they had no other conteft, than who fhould behave beft. In the worfhip of the gods they were magnificent, but thrifty at home, and faithful to their friends. And by the practice of bravery in war, and equity in peace, did they manage themfelves and the publick affairs. Of which thefe things are fufficient proofs, that fuch as fought the enemy contrary to orders, or kept the field after founding a retreat, were ofter punifhed, than fuch as deferted, or in time of action quitted their pofts. But in peace the adminiftration was managed more in the way of kindnefs than terror : and in cafe of an injury received, they chofe rather to forgive, than revenge it.*

X. *But when, by the practice of induftry and juftice, the Roman ftate was come to a confiderable height, great princes conquered, wild nations and mighty ftates brought under fubjection by dint of arms, and Carthage, that was rival with Rome for the empire of the world, utterly deftroyed ; ana all parts of it, whether by fea or by land, at the devotion of the peri-*

a, dubias atque af-
es facile tolerave-
is otium, divitiæ,
æ aliis, oneri mife-
fuere. Igitur pri-
:uniæ, dein impe-
lo crevit. Ea quafi
:s omnium malo-
ere. Namque a-
fidem, probitatem,
que artis bonas
it ; pro his fuper-
crudelitatem, deos
re, omnia venalia
edocuit. Ambitio
mortalis falfos fi-
:git ; aliud claufum
ore, aliud promp-
i lingua habere ;
as inimicitiafque
: re, fed ex com-
æftumare ; ma-
vultum, quam in-
i, bonum habere.
primo paullatim
e, interdum vindi-
Poft, ubi contagio,
peflilentia, invafit ;
immutata, impe-
ex juftiffimo atque
), crudele intole-
ique factum.
Sed primo magis
), quam avaritia,
i hominum exerce-
quod tamen vitium
s virtuti erat. Nam
n, honorem, im-
i, bonus, ignavus,
fibi exoptant. Sed
ra via nititur : huic
ionæ artes defunt,
atque fallaciis con-
, Avaritia pecuniæ

*Romans ; fortune began to shew
her malice, and confound all. For
they who had endured fatigues,
dangers, and the most severe
trials, with ease, found peace and
plenty, desirable things with the
rest of men, to be their bane.
First the love of money, and then
of power, grew upon them, and
proved the occasion of all manner
of mischief. For avarice was the
destruction of faith, honesty, and
other good qualities ; and in the
room thereof brought in fashion,
pride, cruelty, profaneness, and a
mercenary spirit. Ambition obliged
many to breach of faith, and to
have one thing in their hearts,
and another upon their tongues ;
to contract or break friendship, not
as honour, but their interest required ; and to seem good, rather
than be really so. These vices
grew up but slowly for some time,
and were now and then punished.
But the infection at last carrying
all before it like the plague, the
state was hugely altered, and the
government, from being the most
just, and the best that ever was,
became cruel and intolerable.*

XI. *But at first ambition more
than avarice influenced the minds
of the Romans : which vice, however, had some resemblance of a
virtue. For the brave, and the
base-spirited, are equally fond of
glory, honour, and power. But
the former pursues them in the
right way ; whereas the latter, as
destitute of all good qualities, endeavours to come at them in the
way of trick and deceit. Avarice*

ftudium

ſtudium habet ; quam nemo ſapiens concupivit. Ea, quaſi venenis malis imbuta, corpus animumque virilem effeminat : ſemper infinita, inſatiabilis eſt ; neque copia, neque inopia, minuitur. Sed poſtquam L. Sulla, armis recepta republica, bonis initiis malos eventus habuit ; rapere omnes, trahere. Domum alius, alius agros cupere ; neque modum neque modeſtiam victores habere ; fœda crudeliaque in civis facinora facere. Huc accedebat, quod L. Sulla exercitum, quem in Aſia ductaverat, quo ſibi fidum faceret, contra morem majorum, luxurioſe nimiſque liberaliter habuerat. Loca amœna, voluptaria facile in otio ferocis militum animos molliverant. Ibi primum inſuevit exercitus populi Romani amare, potare ; ſigna, tabulas pictas, vaſa cœlata mirari ; ea privatim ac publice rapere ; delubra ſpoliare ; ſacra profanaque omnia polluere. Igitur hi militeſ, poſtquam victoriam adepti ſunt, nihil reliqui victis fecere. Quippe fecundæ res ſapientium animos fatigant : nedum illi, corruptis mo-

is nothing but an extravagant deſire of money, which no wiſe man was ever fond of. And this paſſion, as if it was enforced by the power of enchantment, enervates both the bodies and ſoulſ of men, is ever boundleſs and inſatiable, not to be reduced by either plenty or want. But after Lucius Sylla ſeized upon the government by force of arms, and though he began well, yet run into great outrages, rapine and violence prevailed univerſally. The conquerors, one ſet his heart upon a fine houſe, another upon lands; and in the proſecution of their ſeveral deſires, had not the leaſt tincture of moderation or modeſty at all, but practiſed all the moſt abominable exceſſes of cruelty upon their fellow-citizens. Beſides this, L. Sylla, in order to engage the army he had commanded in Aſia to ſtand by him, did, contrary to the uſage of our anceſtors, ſlacken the reins of diſcipline in the way of indulgence and profuſion, to a great exceſs. And the pleaſant voluptuous country of Aſia had, after the war was ended there, ſtrangely ſoftened the rugged minds of the ſoldiery. There firſt of all did the Roman troops contract a paſſion for whoring and drinking, ſtatues, pictures, and fine-wrought plate, which they publickly and privately made plunder of, robbing the temples of the gods, and ſparing no places whatever, whether ſacred or profane. For thoſe ſoldiers, after their conqueſt in thoſe parts, left the conquered nothing at all. Succeſs indeed makes a ſtrong impreſſion upon

ribus,

ribus, victoriæ temperarent. an army fo corrupted by ufe of their conqueft.

the minds of wife men, and therefore it is not to be wondered at, if ill difcipline, fhould make fo bad a

XII. Poftquam divitiæ honori effe cœperunt, & eas gloria, imperium, potentia fequebatur : hebefcere virtus, paupertas probro haberi, innocentia pro malevolentia duci cœpit. Igitur ex divitiis juventutem luxuria atque avaritia cum fuperbia invafere. Rapere, confumere ; fua parvi pendere, aliena cupere ; pudorem, pudicitiam, divina atque humana promifcua, nihil penfi neque moderati habere. Operæ pretium eft, cum domos atque villas cognoveris in urbium modum exædificatas, viferç templa deorum, quæ noftri majores, religiofiffumi mortales, fecere. Verum illi delubra deorum pietate, domos fuas gloria decorabant ; neque victis quidquam præter injuriæ licentiam, eripiebant. At hi contra, ignaviffumi homines, per fummum fcelus omnia ea fociis adimere, quæ fortiffumi viri victores hoftibus reliquerant : proinde quafi injuriam facere, id demum effet imperio uti.

XII. *When riches now began to be in fuch vaft efteem, and to be attended with glory, command, and power ; virtue began to languifh, poverty to be accounted matter of reproach, and innocence to pafs for ill-nature. Hereupon our youth became infected with luxury, avarice, and pride, all together. They now ravaged and wafted all before them, and never fatisfied with what was their own, were ever longing for what was not ; trampled upon modefty, friendfhip, chaftity, and every thing elfe, divine or human, without diftinction ; and throwing off all reftraint, had not the leaft care or concern for any thing that was good. It is worth while to take a view of the fine houfes in town and country, and then to vifit the temples of the gods, built by our forefathers, the moft religious of mankind. But they graced the temples of the gods with their piety, and their houfes with glory ; and took nothing from thofe they conquered, but the licence of doing mifchief. But thofe I fpoke of above, the moft worthlefs of men, have in the moft wicked manner ravifhed from our allies all the brave old conquerors would have left to their vanquifhed enemies ; as if the ufe of power confifted in the doing of mifchief.*

XIII. Nam quid ea memorem, quæ, nifi his

XIII. *For why fhould I fpend time in the relation of things,*
qui

qui videre, nemini credibilia funt; a privatis compluribus fubverfos montis, maria conftrata efle? Quibus mihi ludibrio videntur fuiffe divitiæ; quippe, quas honefte habere licebat, per turpitudinem abuti properabant. Sed lubido ftupri, ganeæ, cæterique cultus non minor incefferat. Viri pati muliebria : mulieres pudicitiam in propatulo habere : vefcendi caufa terra marique omnia exquirere : dormire prius, quam fomni cupido effet : non famèm aut fitim, neque frigus neque laffitudinem opperiri, fed ea omnia luxu antecapere. Hæc juventutem, ubi familiares opes defecerant, ad facinora incendebant. Animus imbutus malis artibus, haud facile lubidinibus carebat : eo profufius omnibus modis quæftui atque fumptui deditus erat.

XIV. In tanta tamque corrupta civitate, Catilina, id quod factu facillumum erat, omnium flagitioforum atque facinoroforum circum fe, tamquam ftipatorum, catervas habebat. Nam, quicunque impudicus, adulter, ganeo, alea, manu, ventre, pene bona patria laceraverat, quique alienum æs grande conflave-

which can appear credible to no one that has not feen them; as the levelling of mountains, building fine palaces in the fea itfelf, by many private perfons? who feemed to play with their riches, in the way of bantering, as it were, and abufing them in the moft fcandalous manner, when they might have enjoyed them with honour. Nor were they lefs extravagant in their amours, and all the articles of furniture and equipage : the men and women were guilty of the moft barefaced proftitution. Sea and land were ranfacked to furnifh out their tables with dainties. And the natural return of fleep, hunger, and thirft, were anticipated by a luxurious indulgence. The practice of thefe vices firft reduced the youth of Rome to want, and then pufhed them upon all manner of villainy. The mind being once inured to thofe vile practices, knew not how to forego the gratification of its lufts, and fo was the more violently bent upon all the ways of both getting and fpending.

XIV. In fo great and fo wicked a city, Cataline, as was no hard matter to be fure, had troops of flagitious, profligate fellows, like fo many life-guard men, always about him. For all your catamites, cuckold-makers, rakes, that had fpent their eftates in all the ways of luxury and lewdnefs, all fuch as had run over head and ears in debt, to fcreen themfelves from the punifhments due to their crimes : parricides befides from all quar-rat,

ut fa-
ræte-
: par-
nvic-
factis
; ad
atque
ngui-
oftre-
flagi-
nfcius
ii Ca-
nilia-
od fi
acuus
cide-
atque
fimi-
ieba-
ado-
itates
ani-
iuxi,
capi-
i cu-
etate
præ-
ie e-
emo
mo-
dum
fque
uiffe
exi-

ters, *facrilegious rafcals, fuch as had been already legally convicted of horrid villainies, or feared fo to be ; and further, all fuch as maintained themfelves by perjury or murder ; finally, all whom wickednefs, want, or a guilty confcience made uneafy ; thefe were Catiline's neareft and moft intimate friends. And if any innocent perfon happened to be engaged in any friendfhip with him, by daily converfation and wheedling, he was foon made like the reft of the crew. But thofe he chiefly affected to draw into his party were young gentlemen. Their minds being, by reafon of their age, foft and pliable, were eafily cajoled. For, according to their feveral inclinations, fome he furnifhed with whores, for others he would buy dogs and horfes. Finally, he ftuck at no coft, or breach of modefty, whatever to get them into his power, and fecure them to his intereft. I am fenfible, fome people were of opinion, that the youth that frequented Catiline's houfe were engaged in unnatural lewdnefs ; but this fancy proceeded, I fuppofe, not fo much from any certain evidence of the thing, as other reafons.*

em, quæ domum Catilinæ frequenta-
udicitiam habuiffe. Sed ex aliis rebus
iiquam id compertum foret, hæc fama

a-
ulta
erat,
cum
alia
jus

XV. *Catiline himfelf, when a young fellow, had been engaged in feveral villainous intrigues with a young lady of high quality, one of the Veftal nuns, and many other the like abominable pranks. At*

E   fafque,

fafque. Poftremo, captus amore Aureliæ Oreftillæ, cujus præter formam nihil unquam bonus laudavit, quod ea nubere illi dubitabat, timens privignum adultum ætate ; pro certo creditur, necato filio, vacuam domum fceleftis nuptiis feciffe. Quæ quidem res mihi in primis videtur cauffa fuiffe facinoris maturandi. Namque animus impurus, dis hominibufque infeftus, neque vigiliis neque quietibus fedari poterat : ita confcientia mentem excitam vexabat. Igitur color ei exfanguis, fœdi oculi ; citus modo, modo tardus inceffus ; prorfus in facie vultuque vecordia inerat.

XVI. Sed juventutem, quam, ut fupra diximus, illexerat, multis modis mala facinora edocebat, ex illis teftis fignatorefque falfos commodare ; fidem, fortunas, pericula vilia habere. Poft, ubi eorum famam atque pudorem attriverat, majora alia imperabat. Si cauffa peccandi in prefens minus fuppetebat ; nihilominus infontes, ficuti fontes, circumvenire, jugulare. Scilicet, ne per otium torpefcerent manus, aut animus, gratuito potius malus atque crudelis erat. His amicis

last he fell in love with Aurelia Oreftilla, in whom no good man ever commended any thing but her beauty ; and becaufe fhe made a fcruple of marrying him, by reafon his fon was at man's eftate, it is believed for a certainty, he murdered him, to make way for fo wicked a match. Which, indeed, I believe, might be the reafon of his pufhing his enterprize with fo much violence as he did. For his polluted foul, fired with rage gainft both gods and men, could find no reft either waking or fleeping ; fo much was he haunted with the terrors of an evil confcience. Accordingly his complexion was very pale, his eyes ghaftly, his gait fometimes quick, fometimes flow : in fhort, his whol appearance was perfectly that of a madman.

XVI. Now the young men h wheedled in to join him, as hat been above faid, he trained up villainy by various ways ; fro among ft them he ufed to furnij falfe witneffes, and others to fig forged deeds, teaching them that means to fet light by thei honour, eftates, and danger. An after he had utterly fuppreffed them all regard to credit or fham he put them upon greater project And if no prefent opportunity pr fented for the exercife of the talent, yet he kept them doing, employing them to circumvent a murder fuch as had given him offence, as if they had ; that to keep their hands and minds ufe, he was wicked and cru

fociifq

)ciifque confifus Catilina, mul quod æs alienum er omnis terras ingens rat, & quod plerique ullani milites, largius io ufi, rapinarum et vic-oriæ veteris memores, ivile bellum exoptabant, pprimundæ reipublicæ onfilium cepit. In Ita-a nullus exercitus : Cn. 'ompeius in extremis erris bellum gerebat ; ip-confulatum petundi 1agna fpes ; fenatus ni-il fane intentus.; tutæ ranquillæque res omnes. ed ea prorfus opportuna 'atilinæ.

without any provocation fo to be. Catiline confiding in thefe friends and accomplices, and becaufe the number of perfons involved in debt was every where very great, and becaufe too moft of Sylla's old fol-diers, having made an end of what they had gotten, and re-membering full well the plunder they had made upon Sylla's fuccefs, wifhed for a civil war ; Catiline. I fay, putting thefe feveral things together, entered into a defign of ufurping the government. There was no army in Italy ; Cn. Pom-pey was carrying on a war in the remoteft parts of the earth : he himfelf had great hopes of obtain-ing the confulfhip ; the fenate ap-peared very fecure ; and all was fafe and quiet ; which fe-veral things feemed to prefent Catiline with a favourable op-portunity of carrying his point.

XVII. Igitur circiter alendas Jan. L. Cæfa-e & C. Figulo confuli-us, primo fingulos ap-ellare : hortari alios, ali-s tentare ; opes fuas, mparatam rempublicam, nagna præmia conjurati-nis docere. Ubi fatis ex-lorata funt, quæ voluit ; n unum omnis convocat, uibus maxuma necefli-udo & plurimum auda-iæ inerat. Eo conve-ere fenatorii ordinis P. entulus Sura, P. An-onius, L. Caffius Lon-inus, C. Cethegus, P. Ser. Sullæ Servii filii . Varguntejus, Qu. An-ius, M. Porcius Læcca, . Buftia, Q. Curius :

XVII. Wherefore about the firft of January, in the year of the confulfhip of L. Cæfar and C. Figulus, he applies himfelf to his affociates feparately firft ; fome he encouraged, others he tried ; he acquaints them with his ftrength, how little the government was provided to oppofe him, and what vaft advantages they might promife themfelves from the fuccefs of the confpiracy. After he had fuf-ficiently fifted them with relation to his defign, he draws together fuch of them as were under the greateft difficulties, and appeared the moft daring. Upon that occa-fion affembled of the fenatorian rank, Publius Lentuins Sura, Pub-lius Antonius, Lucius Caffius Lon-ginus, Caius Cethegus, Publius and Servius the fons of Sylla Ser-

E 2   præ-

præterea, ex equeſtri ordine, M. Fulvius Nobilior, L. Statilius, P. Gabinius Capito, C. Cornelius : ad hoc, multi ex coloniis & municipiis domi nobiles: ·Erant præterea complures paullo occultius conſilii hujùſce participes nobiles ; quos magis dominationis ſpes hortaɓatur, quam inopia aut alia neceſſitudo. Cæterum juventus pleraque, ſed maxume nobilium; Catilinæ incœptis favebat. Quibus in otio vel magnifice vel molliter vivere copia erat, incerta pro certis, bellum, quam pacem, malebant. Fuere item ea tempeſtate, qui crederent M. Licinium Craſſum non ignarum ejus conſilii fuiſſe : quia Cnejus Pompejus, invifus ipſi, magnum exercitum ductabat, cujuſvis· opes voluiſſe contra·illius potentiam creſcere : ſimul confiſum, ſi conjuratio valuiſſet, facile apud· illos principem ſe fore. Sed antea item·conjuravere pauci, in quibus Catilina. De quo, quam veriſſume potero, dicam.

XVIII. L. Tullio, M. Lepido ﹐ coſſ. P. Autronius & P. Sulla, deſignati conſules, legibus ambitus interrogati, pœnas dederant. Poſt paullo Catili-

vius, Lucius Varguntejus, Quintus Annius, Marcus Porcius Lacca, Lucius Beſtia, Quintus Curius ; and beſides theſe, of equeſtrian rank, Marcus Fulvius Nobilior, Lucius Statilius, Publius Gabinius Capito, Caius Cornelius ;. and over and above this company,· many from the colonies and borough-towns nobly deſcended there. There were likewiſe a good many noblemen, who under·hand countenanced the deſign, whom the hopes of power, more than want, or any other neceſſity, engaged therein. But moſt of the youth, eſpecially amongſt the nobility, favoured Catiline's undertaking ; who might have lived in great· quiet, ſplendidly, and pleaſantly : but they choſe rather uncertainties for things certain, and war rather than peace. There were ſome too at that time, who did really believe, that Mark Craſſus was not unacquainted with the deſign ; becauſe Cn. Pompey, whom he mortally hated, commanded a great army, to reduce whoſe power he was ready to raiſe any one whatever ; but hoped too, if the conſpiracy ſucceeded, to have the chief ſway. But before this time, ſome few gentlemen had entered into a conſpiracy againſt the ſtate, of which Catiline was one, concerning which I ſhall here give as true an account as I can.

XVIII. In the conſulſhip of Lucius Tullus and Mark Lepidus, Publius Autronius and· Publius Sulla conſuls elect, had· been proſecuted for bribery, and puniſhed. Some little time after, Catiline
na,

ietun-
iibitus
tum ;
s dies
Erat
Pifo,
fum-
, fac-
ertur-
m in-
mores
hoc
onius,
embr.
icato,
o ka-
Cot-
iatum
i, faf-
onem
inen-
mit-
, rur-
bruar.
anftu-
non
d ple-
per-
antur.
matu-
gnum
, poft
mam,
patra-
ndum
onve-
filium

being likewife profécuted for extortion, was not allowed to ftand candidate for the confulfhip, becaufe he could not enter his name for that purpofe, within the time limited by law. There was at that time Cn. Pifo, a noble youth, of great boldnefs, poverty, and a factious fpirit.: whom vice and want together excited to difturb the government. With him Catiline and Autronius entering into a cabal, about the nones of December, came to a refolution of affaffinating, the firft of January following, the confuls Luke Cotta and Luke Torquatus; whereupon they were to feize the confulfhip, and fend Pifo with an army to be governor of the two Spains. But the plot being difcovered they deferred the intended murder to the nones of February. And now they propofed not only to take off the confuls, but moft of the fenators too. And had not Catiline been too hafty in giving the fignal for that purpofe before the fenate-houfe, that day would have been executed the horrideft villainy that had ever been perpetrated from the building of Rome to that time. But as there was no great appearance of the confpirators, that prevented the execution of their defign.

ifo in
aniam
: mif-
raffo ;
i Cn.
iverat.

XIX. *Afterwards Pifo was fent Quæftor, but with the authority of Prætor, into Spain, by the intereft of Craffus, becaufe he knew him to be a bitter enemy of Cn. Pompey, the fenate not*

E 3   Neque

Neque tamen fenatus provinciam invitus dederat. Quippe fœdum hominem a republica procul abeffe volebat : fimul, quia boni complures præfidium in eo putabant, & jam tum potentia Cn. Pompeji formidolofa erat. Sed is Pifo, in provinciam, ab equitibus Hifpanis, quos in exercitu ductabat, iter faciens, occifus eft. Sunt qui ita dicant, imperia ejus injufta, fuperba, crudelia barbaros nequiviffe pati. Alii autem, equites illos, Cn. Pompeji veteres fidofque clientes, voluntate ejus Pifonem aggreffos : numquam Hifpanos præterea tale facinus feciffe ; fed imperia fæva multa antea perpeffos. Nos eam rem in medio relinquimus. De fuperiori conjuratione fatis dictum.

XX. Catilina, ubi eos, quos paullo ante memoravi, conveniffe videt, tametfi cum fingulis multa fæpe egerat, tamen in rem fore credens univerfos appellare & cohortari, in abditam partem ædium feceffit, atque ihi, omnibus arbitris procul amotis, orationem hujufcemodi habuit. *Ni virtus fidefque veftra fatis fpectata mihi foret, nequicquam opportuna res cecidiffet ; fpes magna, domi-*

being averfe to the thing, in order to get rid of fo troublefome a fellow, as alfo becaufe a great many honeft men thought good ufe might be made of him, in oppofition to the power of Pompey, which was now become formidable. But Pifo was in his march for Spain, affaffinated by fome Spanifh horfe he had in his army. The reafon whereof, fome fay, was his unjuft, haughty, cruel behaviour in his command, which the barbarians were not able to endure. But others will have it, that thofe horfe were fome old trufty clients of Cn. Pompey's, and took off Pifo by his encouragement. For the Spaniards had never been guilty of any thing like that before, but had borne the cruelty of feveral other governors with patience. We fhall leave the matter undetermined. And fo much for that confpiracy.

XX. *When Catiline faw his company above mentioned affembled, though he had before had much conference with them fingly and feparately, yet judging it proper to fpeak to them all together, and encourage them to the work, he retired with them into a private part of his houfe, where he addreffed them in the following harangue.* If your virtue and honour were not fufficiently known to me, a moft lucky opportunity for our intended project would have prefented itfelf in vain ; vaft hopes and dominion would have

n manibus fruf-
iffe : neque per
m aut vana inge-
ncerta pro certis
n. Sed, quia mul-
magnis tempeftati-
cognovi fortis fi-
mihi, eo animus
ft maximum atque
·imum facinus in-
fimul, quia vobis
quæ mihi, bona
? effe intellexi.
idem velle atque
lle, ea demum fir-
citia eft. Sed, ego
ente agitavi, om-
n antea divifi au-
Cæterum mihi in-
agis animus accen-
cum confidero, quæ
i vitæ futura fit,
ofmetipfos vindica-
libertatem. Nam
m refpublica in
um potentiam, jus
ditionem conceffit ;
illis reges, tetrar-
ectigales effe ; po-
nationes ftipendia
? ; cæteri omnes,
, boni, nobiles at-
nobiles, vulgus fui-
fine gratia, fine
itate, his obnoxii,
, fi refpublica va-
formidini effemus.
omnis gratia, po-
honos, divitiæ
illos funt, aut ubi
olunt : nobis reli-
it pericula, repul-
judicia, egeftatem.
quoufque tandem

drooped into our hands to no purpofe. Nor would I for certainties
purfue uncertainties, by the help of
forry fellows not to be depended
upon. But as I have, upon many important occafions, found you gallant and faithful to me, I have
thereby been encouraged to engage
in the greateft and moft glorious
undertaking that ever was, and the
rather, becaufe I am fenfible our
interefts are the very fame. For *Catilines Idea of Friendship!*
union of intereft is the only laft-
ing bond of friendfhip. But you
have already each of you heard
apart what it is I propofe to go
upon. And I am daily more heartily difpofed thereto, when I confider what fort of life we muft lead,
if we do not endeavour the recovery of our liberty. For fince all
power and authority has been en-
groffed by a few great men, kings
and tetrarchs have been tributary
to them ; to them only have the
feveral nations and provinces of
the empire paid taxes. The reft
of us, however brave and honeft,
whether noble or ignoble, have
been treated as mob only, without intereft or authority, in a flavifh fubjection to thofe to whom
we fhould be a terror, if the government was upon a right foot.
Now all intereft, power, honour,
and riches, are with them, or
where they pleafe. They have
left us nothing but dangers, dif-
honour, impeachments, and want.
And how long, my moft gallant
friends, will you take all this at
their hands ? Is it not better to
die bravely, than to lofe a miferable difhonourable life in a dif-

patiemini, fortiffumi vi-
ri ? Nonne emori per vir-
tutem præstat, quam vitam
miferam atque inhoneftam, ubi alienæ fuperbiæ ludibrio fueris,
per dedecus amittere ?

XXI. Verum enimvero,
prob deum atque homi-
num fidem ! victoria in
manu nobis eft : viget
ætas, animus valet. Con-
tra illis, annis atque divitiis, omnia confenue-
runt. Tantummodo in-
cæpto opus eft : cætera
res expediet. Etenim quis
mortalium, cui virile in-
genium eft, tolerare po-
teft, illis divitias fuperare,
quas profundant in ex-
truendo mari & montibus
coæquandis ; nobis rem
familiarem etiam ad ne-
ceffaria deeffe ? illos bi-
nas, aut amplius, domos
continuare ; nobis larem
familiarem nufquam ul-
lum effe ? Cum tabulas,
figna, toreumata emunt,
nova diruunt, alia ædi-
ficant : poftremo omnibus
modis pecuniam trahunt,
vexant: tamen fumma lu-
bidine divitias fuas vin-
cere nequeunt. At nobis
eft domi inopia, foris æs
alienum; mala res, fpes
multo afperior. Denique,
quid reliqui habemus,
præter miferam ani-
mam? Quin igitur ex-
pergifcimini ! En illa,
illa, quam fæpe optaftis,
libertas ; præterea divi-
tiæ, decus, gloria in ocu-

graceful manner, after you have
been expofed to the infults of their
haughty difdain.

XXI. But, O gods ! victory
is in our hands ; we are in the
prime of our ftrength, our minds
in full vigour ; they upon the
decline both from age and luxury.
We need but begin, the project
will execute itfelf. For what
mortal, that has the fpirit of a
man in him, can endure with patience, that they fhould fo wal-
low in riches as to wafte them in
ftraitening the very feas by their
large and ftately buildings, and in
the levelling of mountains, whilft
we are in want of neceffaries ?
that they fhould have two houfes,
or more, and we none at all ?
They, though they are ever pur-
chafing fine pictures, ftatues, and
veffels of fine workmanfhip, are
ever pulling down even new
houfes, and building them up
again : in fhort, though they con-
trive all the ways and means imaginable to wafte and confume
their money, yet with all their
extravagance they can fee no end
of their riches ; whilft we have
nothing but want at home, and
debt abroad, our condition bad,
and our expectations worfe. Finally, what have we left, but a
wretched life ? Rouze then, gentlemen ! See now the liberty you
have fo often wifhed for ; riches
moreover, honour, and glory, are
all in view. Fortune offers all
thefe rewards to the conquerors.
Let the cafe itfelf, the juncture,

lis

funt. Fortuna ea victoribus præmia Res, tempus, pe- egeflas, belli fpolia :a magis, quam o- ica, vos hortentur.. ?eratore .vel milite îini. Neque ani- 'ue corpus a vobis Hæc ipfa, ut fpero, n una conful agam : 'e me animus fallit, êrvire magis, quam e, parati eflis.
I. Poftquam ac- :a homines, quibus unde omnia erant, que res, neque 'na ulla '; tamet- quieta movere, merces videbatur ;)oftulare plerique,)oneret, *quæ con- li foret, quæ armis petarent ;* quid *ipis aut fpei habe- 'um* Catilina polli- *bulas novas, pro- iem locupletium, itus, facerdotia, alia omnia, quæ itque lubido victo- t. Præterea, effe ania citeriore Pi- in Mauritania cum* P. *Sitium Nu- , confilii fui par- Petere confulatum inium, quem fibi fore fperaret, i & familiarem ibus neceffitudini- :unventum. Cum 'ulem fe initium*

your danger, want, and the noble fpoils of a war, work upon you more than my fpeech. You fhall have me either for your leader or your fellow-foldier. Neither my body nor mind fhall ever forfake you. The things I am now fpeak- ing to you about I hope to act in poffeffion of the confular dignity conjointly with you, unlefs my guefs fail me, and you prefer flavery before power and domi- nion.

XXII. *The company, upon hear- ing this fpeech, though they were all wretched to the laft degree, and without the leaft hope of any a- mendment of their condition ; and though they were inclinable too to think they might poffibly find their own account in a publick confu- fion ; yet moft of them defired to* know, upon what terms they were to engage in this war, or what advantage they were to reap by it ; what ftrength they had, or what hopes of fuccefs. *Then Catiline promifed them* a cancelling of all paft debts, a profcription of the rich, places in the magiftracy, or the priefthood, free plunder, and all things elfe that war, and the licence of conqueft, are apt to produce. *Befides, he told them,* there was Pifo in hither Spain, and Publius Sitius Nucerinus in Mauritania, with an army, who were both embarked with him in the defign. That C. Antonius was candidate for the confulfhip, whom he hoped to have for his colleague, a man that was his in- timate friend, and engaged in all
agendi

agendi fa\u0303urum. Ad hoc, maledictis increpabat omnis bonos ; fuorum unumquemque nominans, *laudare, admonere alium egeftatis, alium cupiditatis fuæ, complures periculi aut ignominiæ, multos victoriæ Sullanæ, quibus ea prædæ fuerat.* Poftquam omnium animos alacris videt ; cohortatus ut petitionem fuam curæ haberent, conventum dimifit.

poffible ties and obligations to him; that he would enter upon the affair in conjunction with him. *To this he added a great deal of bitter reflection upon all the honeft party, and then naming his own fingly each,* one he highly commended, another he put in mind of his poverty, another of fomething he longed for, moft of them of their danger or fhame, and many of their fuccefs under Sylla, whereby they had been enriched. *And perceiving them all to be much elevated, he advifed them to take care of his intereft in the enfuing election, and then broke up the affembly.*

XXIII. Fuere ea tempeftate, qui dicerent, Catilinam, oratione habita, cum ad jusjurandum populares fceleris fui adigeret, humani corporis fanguinem vino permixtum in pateris cicumtuliffe ; inde, cum poft exfecrationem omnes deguftaviffent, ficuti in folemnibus facris fieri confuevit, aperuiffe confilium fuum : atque eo dictitare feciffe, quo inter fe magis fidi forent, alius alii tanti facinoris confcii. Nonnulli ficta & hæc & multa prætcrea exiftumabant ab iis, qui Ciceronis invidiam, quæ poftea orta eft, leniri credebant atrocitate fceleris eorum, qui pœnas dederant. Nobis ea res pro magnitudine parum comperta eft.

XXIII. *There were at that time fome who faid that Catiline, after the making of this fpeech of his, adminiftered an oath to his fellow-confpirators, and obliged them to drink a mixture of wine and man's blood, handed about in bowls; which when they had done, in imitation of the cuftom of drinking wine round in folemn facrifices, he more fully difclofed to them his intentions, and told them, he had made ufe of that ceremony, to engage them the more effectually to a faithful unanimous execution of fo noble a defign. But fome believed all this, and much more of the like kind, was mere fiction, proceeding from fuch as thought the odium, which Cicero afterwards fell under, might be abated by the horrid wickednefs of thofe that were punifhed by him. For my part, I muft own I have not met with any fufficient evidence for fo heinous a charge.*

XXIV. Sed

XXIV. Sed in ea conjuratione fuit Q. Curius, natus haud obfcuro loco, flagitiis atque facinoribus coopertus ; quem cenfores fenatu probri gratia moverant. Huic homini non minor vanitas inerat, quam audacia. Neque reticere quæ audierat, neque fuamet ipfe fcelera occultare; prorfus neque dicere, neque facere, quidquam penfi habebat. Erat ei cum Fulvia, muliere nobili, ftupri vetus confuetudo. Cui cum minus gratus effet, quod inopia minus largiri poterat, repente glorians, *maria montifque polliceri ; minari interdum ferro, ni fibi obnoxia foret.* Poftremo, ferocius agitare, quam folitus erat. At Fulvia, infolentiæ Curii caufa cognita, tale periculum reipublicæ haud occultum habuit ; fed, fublato auctore, de Catilinæ conjuratione, quæ quo modo audierat, compluribus narravit. Ea res in primis ftudia hominum accendit ad confulatum mandandum M. Tullio Ciceroni. Namque antea pleraque nobilitas invidia æftuabat, & quafi pollui confulatum credebat, fi eum, quamvis egregius, homo novus adeptus foret. Sed ubi periculum advenit, invidia atque fuperbia poftfuere.

XXIV. *Now in this confpiracy was engaged Q. Curius, defcended of no mean family, but a vile profligate wretch, whom the cenfors, for his fcandalous life, had ftruck out of the lift of the fenators. This man had an equal fhare of vanity and impudence ; was neither able to contain a fecret, nor even to conceal his own wicked pranks ; in fhort, he neither regarded what he faid, or what he did. He had an old intrigue with one Fulvia, a lady of noble birth ; but declining in favour with her, by reafon of his poverty, which difabled him from making the prefents fhe expected from him, he began all on a fudden to bounce, and promife her golden mountains, and fometimes threatened to ftab her, if fhe would not comply with his inclinations ; and, in fhort, behaved in a much more fawcy, haughty manner than he had ever been ufed to do before. Fulvia, when fhe came to underftand the occafion of all this infolence, made no fecret of the danger the ftate was in, but told to feveral all fhe had heard relating to Catiline's confpiracy, yet without naming her author. This difcovery made the people in general zealous for chufing M. Tully Cicero conful. For before this, almoft all the nobility ufed to fret with envy, and look upon the confular dignity as defiled, when any perfon of low birth, how excellently qualified foever he was, happened to procure the fame But now, upon the appearance of this danger, envy and pride vanifhed at once.*

XXV. Igi-

XXV. Igitur, comitiis habitis, confules declarantur M. Tullius & C. Antonius. Quod factum primo populares conjurationis concufferat. Neque tamen Catilinæ furor minuebatur; fed indies plura agitare; arma per Italiam locis opportunis parare; pecuniam, fua aut amicorum fide fumptam mutuam, Fæfulas ad Manlium quemdam portare; qui poftea princeps fuit belli faciundi. Ea tempeftate plurimos cujufque generis homines adfciviffe fibi dicitur; mulieres etiam aliquot, quæ primo ingentis fumptus ftupro corporis toleraverant; poft, ubi ætas tantummodo quæftui, neque luxuriæ modum fecerat, æs alienum grande conflaverant. Per eas fe Catilina credebat poffe fervitia urbana folicitare, urbem incendere, viros earum vel adjungere fibi vel interficere.

XXVI. Sed in his erat Sempronia, quæ multa fæpe virilis audaciæ facinora commiferat. Hæc mulier genere atque forma, præterea viro atque liberis fatis fortunata fuit: Literis Græcis & Latinis docta; pfallere, faltare elegantius, quam neceffe eft probæ; multa alia, quæ inftrumenta luxuriæ funt.

XXV. *Accordingly, at the enfuing election, M. Tully and C. Antonius were declared confuls, which at firft gave a great fhock to the confpirators. However, the madnefs of Cataline did not abate upon it at all.* He was every day more and more taken up with frefh projects; he lodged arms in the moft convenient places for his defign, up and down Italy; took up money upon his own credit, or that of his friends, and fent it to Fæfulæ to Manlius, who was afterwards the firft that appeared in arms for the caufe. He is faid at the fame time to have drawn in great numbers of all ranks, and fome women, who in the prime of their years had fupported their extravagance by proftitution; but when age put an end to that trade, though not to their luxury, had run themfelves into a great deal of debt. Catiline expected by their means to engage the city flaves, for him, to fire the town, and either draw over their hufbands to join him, or murder them.*

XXVI. *Amongft thefe was Sempronia, who had in her time, with a boldnefs very uncommon with the fex, played a great many mad pranks. This woman was happy in her extraction and perfon, as likewife a hufband and children; a great miftrefs of the Greek and Latin tongue; would play upon an inftrument, and dance more finely than any honeft woman needs to do; and in feveral*
Sed

Sed ei cariora femper omnia, quam decus atque pudicitia fuit. Pecuniæ an famæ minus parceret, haud facile difcerneres. Lubidine fic accenfa, ut fæpius peteret viros, quam peteretur. Sed ea fæpe antehac fidem prodiderat, creditum abjuraverat, cædis confcia fuerat, luxuria atque inopia præceps abierat. Verum, ingenium ejus haud abfurdum. Poffe verfus facere, jocum movere ; fermone uti, vel modefto, vel molli, vel procaci. Prorfus multæ facetiæ, multufque lepos inerat.

other articles of luxury fhe was very nice and dexterous. But for decency and modefty, thofe were the leaft of her care. It was hard to fay, whether fhe was more lavifh of her money, or her reputation. She was a woman of that furious luft, that fhe more frequently made advances to the men than they to her. She had frequently, contrary to her promife given, revealed fecrets, abjured what had been left in truft with her, had been guilty of murder, and, at the inftigation of luxury and poverty together, had run headlong into all manner of wickednefs. But fhe was a woman of parts, could write verfes, was very facetious, and equally fitted for modeft or wanton converfation. In fhort, fhe was an exceeding pleafant witty woman.

XXVII. His rebus comparatis, Catilina nihilominus in proxumum annum confulatum petebat ; fperans, fi defignatus foret, facile fe ex voluntate Antonio ufurum. Neque interea quietus erat, fed omnibus modis infidias parabat Ciceroni. Neque illi tamen ad cavendum dolus aut aftutiæ deerant. Namque a principio confulatus fui, multa per Fulviam pollicendo effecerat, ut Q. Curius, de quo paullo ante memoravi, confilia Catilinæ fibi proderet. Ad hoc, collegam fuum Antonium pactione provinciæ perpulerat, ne contra rempublicam fentiret :

XXVII. But notwithftanding thefe preparations for the execution of his project, Catiline declared himfelf a candidate for the confulfhip againft the next year ; in hopes, if he fhould be chofen, of making Anthony his tool. In the mean time he was not idle, but ufed his utmoft endeavours to take off Cicero, who wanted not cunning and dexterity on his part to countermine all his contrivances. For, as foon as he entered upon the office of conful, by large promifes to Fulvia, he prevailed with Quintus Curius, whom I have mentioned a little above, to difcover to him all the defigns of Catiline. And further, by the affurance of a province, he engaged Anthony not to act againft the government ; and had privately guards of friends and clients about him.

circùm

circum fe præfidia amico-
rum atque clientium oc-
culte habebat. Poftquam
dies comitiorum venit, &
Catilinæ neque petitio,
neque infidiæ, quas con-
fuli fecerat, profpere cef-
fere ; conftituit bellum
facere, & extrema omnia
experiri ; quoniam, quæ
occulte tentaverat, afpera
fœdaque evenerant.

XXVIII. Igitur C.
Manlium Fæfulas, atque
in eam partem Etruriæ,
Septimium quemdam Ca-
mertem in agrum Pice-
num, C. Julium in A-
puliam dimifit ; præterea
alium alio, quem ubique
opportunum fibi fore cre-
debat. Interea Romæ
multa fimul moliri : con-
fuli infidias tendere. Parare incendia. Opportuna
loca armatis hominibus
obfidere. Ipfe cum telo
effe, item alios jubere,
hortari, uti femper intenti
paratique effent. Dies
noctifque feftinare. Vi-
gilare, neque infomniis
neque labore fatigari.
Poftremo, ubi multa agi-
tanti nihil procedit, rurfus
intempefta nocte conjura-
tionis principes convocat
per M. Porcium Læccam,
ibique multa de ignavia
eorum queftus, docet *fe
præmififfe Manlium ad
eam multitudinem, quam
ad capiunda arma para-
verat ; item alios in alia
loca*

When the day of election came,
and Catiline found that neither
his fuit for the confulfhip, nor
his plot for affaffinating the conful in the field of Mars, fucceeded, he refolved upon open war,
and to try the utmoft extremity ;
fince all his underhand contrivances
had miferably mifcarried.

XXVIII. Accordingly he difpatched away C. Manlius to Fæfulæ, to take care of his concerns
there, and in the neighbouring
parts to Etruria ; one Septimius
Camers into the territory of Picene ; and C. Julius into Apulia.
Others likewife he fent off, one
one way, and another another,
where he thought they might be
moft fubfervient to his defign. In
the mean time he was carrying on
feveral projects, one to murder
the conful ; another to fire the city ;
another to fecure proper places with
an armed force. He had always
a fword about him, and ordered
the reft to be provided after the
fame manner ; and defired them to
be always ready and prepared for
action. He was day and night
in a hurry, got little fleep, and yet
was not fatigued with the want
of it, or all the pains he under-
went. Finally, when all his endeavours proved abortive, he again
fummons the principal of the confpirators, by M. Porcius Læcca,
to repair to his houfe in the dead
time of the night ; and there
complaining heavily of their want
of fpirit and activity, he informs
loca

loca opportuna, qui in- them, that he had fent Manlius
itium belli facerent ; fe- before him to the people he had
que ad exercitum pro- prepared to take up arms, and had
ficifci cupere, fi prius likewife difpatched away others
Ciceronem opprefiffet : eum into proper places to begin the
fuis confiliis multum offi- war : and that he himfelf was de-
cere. firous to go to the army, but
wanted to take off Cicero firft ; for that he very much obftructed his defigns.

XXIX. Igitur, per-   XXIX. *All the reft being difpi-*
teritis ac dubitantibus *rited, and not at all forward to*
cæteris, C. Cornelius e- *engage in fuch an affair, C. Cor-*
ques Rom. operam fuam *nelius, a Roman knight, offered his*
pollicitus, & cum eo L. *fervice, and together with him*
Varguntejus fenator, con- *Lucius Varguntejus, a fenator.*
ftituere ea nocte paullo *They propofed to go that very night*
poft, cum armatis homi- *with armed men to Cicero's houfe,*
nibus, ficuti falutum, in- *and enter it, under pretence of*
troire ad Ciceronem, & *paying their refpects ; and then to*
de improvifo domi fuæ *fall unexpectedly upon him, and*
imparatum confodere. *ftab him, unprovided for a defence.*
Curius, ubi intelligit *Curius, upon finding how great a*
quantum periculum con- *danger the conful was in, imme-*
fuli impendeat, propere *diately difpatches away Fulvia to*
per Fulviam Ciceroni do- *him, to give him notice of the de-*
lum, qui parabatur, enun- *fign. Whereupon the affaffins were*
ciat. Ita illi janua prohi- *denied admittance, and that plot*
biti, tantum facinus fruftra *was blafted. In the mean time,*
fufceperant. Interea Man- *Manlius in Etruria follicits the*
lius in Etruria plebem fo- *common people to rife, who were*
licitare, egeftate fimul ac *ripe for a rebellion, inftigated by*
dolore injuriæ novarum *their poverty, and refentment of the*
rerum cupidam ; quod *injuftice that had been done them,*
Sullæ dominatione agros *having been ftripped of their lands*
bonaque omnia amiferat ; *and goods under the tyranny of Sylla.*
præterea latrones cujufque *He likewife encouraged robbers of*
generis, quorum ea in re- *all kinds to come in to him, of*
gione magna copia erat, *which there was great plenty in*
nonnullos ex Sullanis co- *that country. Some likewife he*
lonis quibus lubido atque *picked up from amongft the old*
luxuria ex magnis rapinis *foldiers of Sylla, whom he had*
nihil reliqui fecerant. *fettled in the poffeffion of lands in*
that country, to whom lewdnefs and luxury had left nothing
of all the great fpoil they had made under him.

XXX. Ea

XXX. Ea cum Ciceroni nunciarentur, ancipiti malo permotus, quod neque urbem ab infidiis privato confilio longius tueri poterat, neque exercitus Manlii quantus, aut quo confilio foret, fatis compertum habebat; rem ad fenatum refert, jam antea vulgi rumoribus exagitatam. Itaque, quod plerumque in atroci negotio folet, fenatus decrevit, *darent operam confules, nequid refpublica detrimenti caperet.* Ea poteftas per fenatum, more Romano, magiftratui maxuma permittitur, exercitum parare, bellum gerere, coercere omnibus modis focios atque civis; domi militiæque imperium atque judicium fummum habere. Aliter, fine populi juffu, nulli earum rerum confuli jus eft.

XXXI. Poft paucos dies L. Senius fenator in fenatu literas recitavit, quas Fæfulis allatas fibi dicebat a Q. Fabio; in quibus fcriptum erat, C. Manlium arma cepiffe, cum magna multitudine, ante diem vi. kal. Nov. Simul, id quod in tali re folet, alii portenta atque prodigia nunciabant: alii, conventus fieri, arma portari, Capuæ atque in Apulia fervile bellum moveri.

XXX. *Upon advice of this, Cicero being moved with a fenfe of the double danger that threatened the commonwealth, becaufe it was neither poffible for him, by his own fingle endeavours, any longer to fecure effectually the city againft the plot; nor had he any certain account of the number of Manlius's army, or how he defigned to proceed; he lays the matter before the fenate, which was already become the common talk of the town. Upon this, according to ancient cuftom in a time of great danger, the fenate paffed a vote,* That the confuls fhould take care, and provide for the fecurity of the ftate. *Now by fuch a vote as this, the confuls became invefted with a very extraordinary authority of raifing troops, levying war, and exercifing a fort of defpotick power, as well over the Romans, as their allies, both at home and abroad. Otherwife, without the people's order, a conful has no authority for any of thefe things.*

XXXI. *A few days after this, Lucius Senius, a fenator, read a letter in the houfe, which he faid was brought him from Fæfulæ by Quintus Fabius, giving an account, that C. Manlius had taken up arms, with a vaft number of people, upon the fixth of the calends of November. At the fame time, as it ufually happens in fuch cafes, fome brought news of ftrange omens and prodigies, others of unufual affemblies, and the hurrying of arms from place to place; and that the flaves were up at Capua,*

Igitur

gitur fenati decreto Q. Marcius Rex Fæfulas, Q. Metellus Creticus in A- uliam, circumque ea lo- a miffi. Hi utrique ad rbem imperatores erant; npediti, ne triumpha- ent, calumnia pauco- um, quibus omnia ho- efta atque inhonefta ven- ere mos erat. Sed præ- ores Q. Pompejus Ru- ıs Capuam, Q. Metel- ıs Celer in agrum Pice- um; hifque permiffum, ti pro tempore atque pe- iculo exercitum compa- arent. Ad hoc, fi quis idicaffet de conjuratione, uæ contra rempublicam ıƈta erat, præmium, rvo libertatem & fef- rtia centum; libero npunitatem ejus rei & ftertia cc. Itemque de- ·evere, uti familiæ gla- iatoriæ Capuam & in etera municipia diftri- terentur, pro cujufque ıbus; Romæ per totam ·bem vigiliæ haberentur, fque minores magiftratus ·æffent.

XXXII. Quibus re- us permota civitas, at- ue immutata facies ur- is erat: ex fumma læ- tia atque lafcivia, quæ iuturna quies pepererat, pente omnis triftitia in- afit. Feftinare, trepi- are, neque loco neque

and in Apulia. Wherefore, by or- der of the fenate, Q. Marcius Rex was difpatched away to Fæfulæ, Q. Metellus Creticus into Apulia, and the places thereabout. Thefe two gentlemen were at that time in the command of armies, attend- ing nigh the city, in expectation of the honour of a triumph; but were baulked by the fpiteful endeavours of fome, whofe cuftom was to do any thing, right or wrong, for money, and nothing without. The præ- tors too, Q. Pompeius Rufus was fent to Capua, and Q. Metellus Celer into the territory of Picene, with commiffions to levy troops as the exigency of the times and the danger might require. Befides, the fenate voted a reward of his free- dom, and a hundred thoufand fef- terces, to any flave, and a pardon, with two hundred thoufand fefter- ces, to any freed-man, that would make any difcovery relating to the confpiracy then on foot againft the government. They likewife ordered, that gladiators fhould be difperfed in Capua, and other bo- rough-towns, in numbers propor- tioned to the abilities of each town for the fupport of them, and that conftant guards fhould be kept up and down Rome, commanded by the inferior magiftrates.

XXXII. By all thefe things the city was put into a mighty con- fternation, and the appearance thereof very much changed; and from a ftate of jollity and wan- tonnefs, which a long quiet had produced, a difmal concern fpread through the whole town. There was nothing but hurry and fright

F   homini

homini cuiquam fatis credere ; neque bellum gerere, neque pacem habere. Suo quifque metu pericula metiri. Ad hoc, mulieres, quibus pro reipublicæ magnitudine belli timor infolitus incefferat, afflictare fefe : manus fupplices ad cœlum 'tendere ; mifereri parvos liberos ; rogitare ;. omnia pavere ; fuperbia atque deliciis omiffis, fibi patriæque diffidere. At Catilinæ crudelis animus eadem illa movebat, tametfi præfidia parabantur, & ipfe lege Plautia interrogatus erat ab L. Paulo. Poftremo, diffimulandi cauffa, & quafi fui expurgandi, ficuti jurgio laceffitus foret, in fenatum venit. Tum M. Tullius conful, five præfentiam ejus timens, five ira commotus, orationem habuit luculentam atque utilem reipublicæ, quam poftea fcriptam edidit. Sed ubi ille adfedit, Catilina, ut erat paratus ad diffimulanda omnia, demiffo vultu, voce fupplici, *poftulare a patribus, ne quid de fe temere crederent : ea familia ortum, ita ab adolefcentia vitam inftituiffe, ut omnia bona in fpe haberet. Ne exiftumarent, fibi patricio homini, cujus ipfius atque majorum pluri-*

every where. No one thought any place, or any company fufficiently fecure. They had neither war nor peace, and every one meafured the danger by his own fears. Now the women, full of their apprehenfions of war, which, by reafon of the grandeur of the Roman ftate they had not been before ufed to bemoaned their cafe moft difmally lifted up their hands in prayer t heaven, bewailed their little chil dren, were full of enquiry afte news, afraid of every thing, an dropping their pride, nicenefs, an finery, all at once, gave up them felves and their country for gon But the cruel foul of Catiline fi purfued the fame wild project, notwithftanding all the precautio that were taken againft him, a though he himfelf was impeach upon the Plautian law by Luci. Paulus. At-laft he made his a, pearance in the fenate-houfe, order to cloak his villainy, a under pretence of clearing himfel as if he had been wrongfully a famed. Then M. Tully the co ful, whether apprehenfive of confequences from his appearar there, or fired with refentme made a very fine fpeech, very fu. able to the occafion ; which he a terwards put in writing, and pu lifhed. But after he fat down, C tiline, as he was finifhed maf in the art of diffimulation, w a dejected look, and humble to began to beg of the houfe, r rafhly to believe what was faid him ; that his family was fuc and he had from his youth led life in fuch a manner, that he h

ma beneficia in plebem R. essent, perdita republica opus esse; cum eam servaret M. Tullius, inquilinus civis urbis Romæ. Ad hoc, maledicta alia cum adderat, obstrepere omnes, hostem atque parricidam vocare. Tum ille furibundus: Quoniam quidem circumventus, inquit, ab inimicis præceps agor, incendium meum ruina extinguam.

reason to expect every thing he could wish for. *He requested of them,* they would not believe, that he a nobleman, who had himself, as well as his ancestors, done many services for the people of Rome, should have any occasion to seek the destruction of the common-wealth, whilst M. Tully, who was but a tenant in town, stood up for its preservation. *As he proceeded in his reflections upon the consul, there was a general outcry raised against him by the house,* as an enemy to his country, and a parricide. *Upon which he,* in a mighty rage, *said,* Since I find myself circumvented, and pushed upon extremities by my enemies, I will put out the fire of your houses with the utter demolition of them.

XXXIII. *Dein se ex curia domum proripuit. Ibi multa secum ipse volvens, quod neque insidiæ consuli procedebant, & ab incendio intelligebat urbem vigiliis munitam, optumum factu credens exercitum augere, ac prius, quam legiones scriberentur, multa anteapere quæ bello usui forent, nocte intempesta cum paucis in Manliana castra profectus est. Sed Cethego atque Lentulo, cæterisque, quorum cognoverat promptam audaciam, mandat, quibus rebus possent, opes factionis confirment, insidias consuli maturent; cædem, incendia, aliaque belli facinora parent: sese propediem cum magno exercitu ad urbem accessurum.*

XXXIII. *With that he got hastily out of the house, and went home; where considering with himself, that his designs upon the consul came to nothing, and that the city was secured against his intention of burning it, by watch and ward constantly kept; he thought his best course would be to increase his army, and to make his advantage by seizing of proper places for his purpose, before the legions designed to oppose him were raised. Accordingly, about midnight he went off, with a few attendants, for Manlius's camp. But recommended to Cethegus and Lentulus, and others, whose zeal and boldness he was assured of, by all possible means to strengthen their party, to get rid of Cicero as soon as possicle, and prepare for a massacre, firing of the town, and other acts of war: that he would immediately come to the city with a great army.*

F 2   XXXIV. Dum

XXXIV. Dum hæc Romæ geruntur, C. Manlius ex suo numero legatos ad Q. Marcium Regem mittit, cum mandatis hujuscemodi : *Deos hominesque teſtamur, imperator, nos arma neque contra patriam cepiſſe, neque quo periculum aliis faceremus, ſed uti corpora noſtra ab injuria tuta forent ; qui miſeri, egentes, violentia atque crudelitate fœneratorum, plerique patria, ſed omnes fama atque fortunis expertes ſumus. Neque cuiquam noſtrum licuit, more majorum, lege uti ; neque amiſſo patrimonio, corpus liberum habere ; tanta ſævitia fœneratorum atque prætoris fuit. Sæpe majores noſtri, miſeriti plebis R. decretis ſuis inopiæ ejus opitulati ſunt. Ac noviſſume, memoria noſtra, propter magnitudinem æris alieni, volentibus omnibus bonis, argentum ære ſolutum eſt. Sæpe ipſa plebes, aut dominandi ſtudio permota, aut ſuperbia magiſtratuum armata, a patribus ſeceſſit. At nos non imperium, neque divitias petimus ; quarum rerum cauſſa, bella atque certamina inter mortalis ſunt ; ſed libertatem, quam nemo bonus, niſi cum anima ſimul, amittit. Te atque ſenatum*

XXXIV. *Whilſt theſe things are doing at Rome, C. Manlius ſent ſome of his lieutenant-generals to Q. Marcius Rex, with a meſſage to this effect :* We call gods and men to witneſs, noble general, that we have not taken up arms either againſt our country, or to bring others in danger, but only to defend our own perſons from ill uſage, who being reduced to a ſtate of miſery and want, by the violence and cruelty of our creditors, are moſt of us baniſhed our country, but all of us ſtript entirely of our credit and fortunes. Nor could any of us have the uſual benefit of the law for our protection, or enjoy the liberty of our perſons, after the loſs of our eſtates ; ſuch was the cruelty of our creditors and the prætor together. Our fore elders frequently took pity of the commons of Rome, and by their decrees relieved their want. And lately in our own times, by reaſon of the great debt that multitudes were involved in, by the vote of every honeſt man, braſs was made to paſs in payment for ſilver, weight for weight. The commons have frequently in their ſtruggles for a ſhare of power and authority in the government, or upon provocation from the pride of the magiſtrates, come to an open breach with the ſenate. But we neither deſire power nor riches ; for the ſake of which all the wars and contentions that happen amongſt mankind, are raiſed. 'Tis liberty only that we requeſt, which no brave man is willing to loſe but with his life. We there-

ob-

obteſtamur, conſulatis mi- fore beg of you and the ſenate, to
ſeris civibus ; legis præſi- take the care of us your fellow-
dium, quod iniquitas præ- citizens under conſideratiön, and
toris eripuit, reſtituatis : reſtore us the protection of the
neve nobis eam nceceſſitu- law, which the iniquity of the Præ-
dinem imponatis, ut quæ- tor has taken from us ; and that
ramus, quonam modo, you would not lay us under a ne-
maxume ulti ſanguinem ceſſity of conſidering how we may
noſtrum pereamus. ſell our lives at the deareſt rate.

XXXV. Ad hæc Q. **XXXV.** *To this Q. Marcius*
Marcius reſpondit : *Si* made anſwer, If they had any
quid ab ſenatu petere vel- thing to requeſt of the ſenate, they
lent, ab armis diſcedant, ought to lay down their arms, and
Romam ſupplices proficiſ- apply with all due ſubmiſſion to
cantur. Ea miſericordia Rome. That the ſenate and peo-
atque manſuetudine ſena- ple of Rome had alway ſhewn
tum populumque Roma- themſelves of ſo mild and merci-
num ſemper fuiſſe, ut ne- ful a diſpoſition, that no one ever
mo unquam ab eo fruſtra applied to them for their aſſiſtance
auxilium petiverit. At in vain. *But Catiline in his jour-*
Catilina ex itinere pleriſ- *ney ſent letters to moſt of the conſu-*
que conſularibus, præte- *lar gentlemen in Rome, eſpecially*
rea optumo cuique literas *thoſe of the beſt character among ſt*
mittit : *Se, falſis crimini-* *them, ſignifying,* That whereas he
bus circumventum, quo- had been on all hands perſecuted
niam factioni inimicorum with charges of a heinous nature,
reſiſtere nequiverit, for- utterly falſe, and found it impoſ-
tunæ cedere, Maſſiliam in ſible to ſtand againſt the faction of
exſilium proficiſci : non his enemies, he ſubmitted to his
quo ſibi tanti ſceleris fate, and was going to Marſeilles,
conſcius eſſet, ſed uti reſ- to ſpend his days in baniſhment
publica quieta foret, neve there ; not that he was conſcious
ex ſua contentione ſeditio to himſelf of the villainy he was
oriretur. Ab his longe charged with, but in regard ſolely
diverſas literas Q. Ca- to the quiet of his country, and
tulus in ſenatu recitavit ; to prevent the diſturbance his con-
quas ſibi nomine Catilinæ teſting with his enemies might oc-
redditas dicebat. Earum caſion. *But Q. Catulus read in*
exemplum infra ſcriptum *the ſenate-houſe, a letter quite dif-*
eſt. *ferent from all theſe, which he ſaid*
was delivered him as from Catiline;
a copy of which follows.

XXXVI. L. Catilina XXXVI. L. Catiline to Q. Ca-
Q. Catulo, S. Egregia tua tulus, greeting. Your extraordi-
F 3 *fides,*

fides, re cognita, grata mihi, magnis in meis periculis, fiduciam commendationi meæ tribuit. Quamobrem defensionem in consilio novo non statui parare : satisfactionem ex nulla conscientia de culpa proponere decrevi : quæ medius fidius licet vera mecum cognoscas. Injuriis contumeliisque concitatus, quod, fructu laboris industriæque meæ privatus, statum dignitatis non obtinebam, publicam miseforum caussam pro mea consuetudine suscepi. Non quin æs alienum meis nominibus ex possessionibus solvere possem ; cum & alienis nominibus liberalitas Aureliæ Orestillæ suis filiæque copiis persolveret. Sed, quod non dignos homines honore honestatos videbam, meque falso suspicione alienatum esse sentiebam ; hoc nomine satis honestas pro meo casu spes reliquæ dignitatis conservandæ sum secutus. Plura cum scribere vellem, nunciatum est mihi vim parari. Nunc Orestillam tibi commendo, tuæque fidei trado. Eam ab injuria defendas, per liberos tuos rogatus. Haveto.

nary honour, known to me by experience, and for which I am obliged to you, gives me the assurance of recommending my case to you in my present distress. And in dependance upon your undertaking it, I would not stand upon my defence in the uncommon measures taken against me, but for the present contented myself with the satisfaction arising from a consciousness of my innocence, which I do aver upon my honour to be real. Provoked by injuries and indignities, in being robbed of the fruits of my labour and industry, and not suffered to keep the honourable station that belonged to me, I publickly undertook the cause of poor oppressed people, agreeably to my former way of life. Not but that I could have satisfied my own creditors out of my own estate, whilst the generosity of Orestilla would have done the same for others my friends out of her own and her daughter's estate. But finding worthless men advanced to places of trust and power in the government, and myself set aside upon a groundless suspicion, I have, I think, considering my circumstances, pursued means honourable enough for the preservation of the remainder of dignity left me. I should have said more to you, but word is just brought me that we are going to be attacked. I recommend to your protection Orestilla. Suffer her not to be ill used, I beg of you, as you wish well to your own children. Farewel.

XXXVII. Sed

XXXVII. Sed ipfe, ucos dies commoratus ud C. Flaminium in ro Reatino, dum vici-:atem antea folicitatam nis exornat, cum faf-)us atque aliis imperii fignibus in caftra ad anlium contendit. Hæc i Romæ comperta funt, natus *Catilinam & Man-m hoftis* judicat; *cæte-:multitudini diem ftatuit, te quam liceret fine frau-ab armis difcedere, præ-· rerum capitalium con-mnatis.* Præterea de-rnit, *uti confules delec-m habeant; C. Antonius m exercitu Catilinam per-qui maturet; Cicero urbi æfidio fit.* Ea tem-ftate mihi imperium ipuli R. multo maxu-e miferabile vifum eft; ti cum ad occafum ab ·tu folis omnia domita mis parerent, domi :ium atque divitiæ, quæ ·ima mortales putant, fluerent; fuere tamen ves qui feque remque iblicam obftinatis animis :rditum irent. Nam-1e, duobus fenati decre-s, ex tanta multitudine, :que præmio inductus)njurationem patefece-it, neque ex caftris Ca-linæ quifquam omnium ifcefferat. Tanta vis iorbi, atque uti tabes, ple-ofque civium animos in-aferat.

XXXVII. *He ftaid a few days with C. Flaminius in the territory of Reate, 'till he could provide the neighbourhood, which had been engaged in the caufe before, with arms, and then marched with the fafces, and other enfigns of command, to Manlius's camp. When the news of this was carried to Rome, the fenate voted Catiline and Manlius enemies, and fixed a day for the troops under their command, within which, if they laid down their arms, they were affured of a pardon, except fuch as had been condemned for capital crimes. They likewife ordered the confuls to levy an army, which C: Antonius was to lead with all expedition againft Catiline, whilft Cicero was to provide for the fecurity of the city. The Roman ftate at that time feemed to me to be in a moft piteous condition; when, though all nations from the rifing of the fun to the fetting of the fame were reduced to their obedience, and there was at home a profound peace, and a prodigious affluence of riches, which men are apt to prefer before every thing elfe; yet was there a fort of people, and Romans too, who were obftinately bent upon their own ruin, with that of the commonwealth. For, notwithftanding the two. votes above mentioned, there was not one of fo great a number concerned in the plot that was prevailed upon by the reward offered to make the leaft difcovery, nor one deferted Catiline's camp. So ftrangely were their minds infected with a difpofition to rebellion and mifchief.*

F 4   XXXVIII. Ne-

XXXVIII. Neque folum illis aliena mens erat, qui confcii conjurationis fuerant ; fed omnino cuncta plebes, novarum rerum ftudio, Catilinæ incœpta probabat. Id adeo more fuo videbatur facere. Nam femper in civitate, quibus opes nullæ funt, bonis invident, malos extollunt ; vetera odere, nova exoptant ; odio fuarum rerum mutari omnia ftudent ; turba atque feditionibus fine cura aluntur, quoniam egeftas facile habetur fine damno. Sed urbana plebes ea vero præceps ierat multis de cauffis. Primum omnium, qui ubique probro atque petulantia maxume præftabant ; item alii, per dedecora, patrimoniis amiffis ; poftremo omnes, quos flagitium aut facinus domo expulerat ; hi Romam, ficuti in fentinam, confluxerant. Dein multi, memores Sullanæ victoriæ, quod ex gregariis militibus alios fenatores videbant; alios ita divites, ut regio victu atque cultu ætatem agerent ; fibi quifque, fi in armis foret, ex victoria talia fperabat. Præterea juventus, quæ in agris manuum mercede inopiam toleraverat, privatis atque publicis largitionibus excita, urba-

XXXVIII. *Nor was this the cafe only of thofe that were concerned in the confpiracy; but the whole body of the common people were defirous of a revolution in the government, and approved of Catiline's defign. And herein they feemed to act only according to their ufual temper and difpofition. For, in all governments, the poorer fort are apt to envy the good, and extol the bad ; hate a conftitution they have been ufed to, and wifh for a new one ; and from a diffatisfaction with their own circumftances, endeavour to have all things turned upfide-down ; becaufe in a time of publick diforder and confufion they find an eafy fubfiftence, as having, by reafon of their poverty, nothing to lofe. But the commonalty of Rome, efpecially at this time, were from feveral caufes grown extremely corrupt. In the firft place, the moft profligate wretches every where, and fuch as had wafted their eftates by fcandalous extravagance ; finally, all whofe villainies had forced them from their native country, flocked to Rome, as a common fewer for the reception of all manner of filth. And then again, many reflecting upon Sylla's fuccefs, and how they had feen many raifed from the degree of common foldiers to the dignity of fenators, and many fo enriched as to live like kings all their lives after, every man, in cafe of a war, hoped for the like, from the fuccefs of his party. Befides, the young fellows that lived in the country by their labour, tempted to town by the num*

num otium ingrato labori prætulerat. Eos atque alios omnis malum publicúm alebat. Quo minus mirandum eft, homines egentis, malis moribus, maxuma fpe, reipublicæ juxta ac fibi confuluiffe. Præterea quorum, victoria Sullæ, parentes profcripti, bona erepta, jus libertatis imminutum erat, haud fane alio animo belli eventum expectabant. Ad hoc, quicunque aliarum atque fenati partium erant, conturbari rempublicam, quam minus valere ipfi, malebant. Id adeo malum multos poft annos in civitatem reverterat.

XXXIX. Nam poftquam Cn. Pompejo & M. Craffo coff. tribunitia poteftas reftituta eft, homines adolefcentes, fummam poteftatem nacti, quibus ætas animufque ferox erat, cœpere, fenatum criminando, plebem exagitare; dein largiundo atque pollicitando, magis incendere; ita ipfi clari potentefque fieri. Contra eos fumma ope nitebatur pleraque nobilitas fenati fub fpecie, pro fua magnitudine. Namque, uti paucis verum abfolvam, per illa

private and publick largeffes there ſtirring, preferred an idle life there to hard working in the country. Theſe, and the reſt I mentioned, were ſubſiſted by the troubles of the commonwealth ; and therefore it is not to be wondered, that a pack of ſcrubby raſcally fellows, with ſuch a view before them, ſhould juſt be as much concerned for the good of the publick, as they had been for their own before. Beſides too, all thoſe whoſe parents had been proſcribed under the tyranny of Sylla, who had had their eſtates confiſcated, or been disfranchiſed, had much the like expectations from a war, as the others had. And moreover, they who were of the party oppoſite to the ſenate, choſe rather to have the ſtate involved in confuſion, than not carry their point : a humour which had for many years laid dormant, but was now ſtarted up in the city again.

XXXIX. For after the revival of the tribunitian authority, in the conſulſhip of Cn. Pompey and M. Craſſus, raw young gentlemen of great ſpirits, getting into poſſeſſion of that high dignity, began by railing at the ſenate, to incenſe the commonalty againſt them ; and then by throwing away their money upon them, and making mighty promiſes of what great things they would do for them, they inflamed them ſtill the more, and were themſelves in high vogue, and carried all before them. Theſe were oppoſed by the greateſt part of the nobility, under pretence of promoting the power of the ſenate, but in reality for their own. For, to

tem-

tempora quicumque rempublicam agitavere, honeſtis nominibus, alii, ſicuti jura populi defenderent, pars, quo ſenati auctoritas maxuma foret, bonum publicum ſimulantes, pro ſua quiſque potentia certabant; neque illis modeſtia, neque modus contentionis erat: utrique victoriam crudeliter exercebant.

XL. Sed, poſtquam Cn. Pompejus ad bellum maritimum atque Mithridaticum miſſus eſt, plebis opes imminutæ, paucorum potentia crevit. Hi magiſtratus, provincias, aliaque omnia tenere: ipſi innoxii, florentes, ſine metu ætatem agere, cæteroſque judiciis terrere, quo plebem in magiſtratu placidius tractarent. Sed ubi primum dubiis rebus novandis ſpes oblata eſt, vetus certamen animos eorum arrexit. Quod ſi primo prælio Catilina ſuperior, aut æqua manu diſceſſiſſet: profecto magna clades atque calamitas rempublicam oppreſſiſſet: neque illis, qui victoriam adepti forent, diutius ea uti licuiſſet; quin defeſſis & exſanguibus, qui plus poſſet, imperium atque libertatem extorqueret.

ſay the truth at once, all the diſturbers of the publick at that time, under plauſible pretences, ſome of aſſerting the rights and privileges of the people, others of advancing the authority of the ſenate, pretending all to have nothing ſo much at heart as the publick good, did in reality ſtickle every one only for their own power; and that without any regard to modeſty or moderation at all. And both ſides, as they happened to prevail, made a cruel uſe of their victory.

XL. But when Cn. Pompey was ſent to the war againſt the pirates and Mithridates, the power of the commons began to decline, and that of a few to riſe upon it. Theſe engroſſed the publick offices of ſtate, the provinces and all things elſe; liv'd in great eaſe, grandeur, and ſecurity, and kept the reſt in conſtant apprehenſions of proſecutions and impeachments, in order to render the commons more tame and ſubmiſſive. But as ſoon as any hopes of a revolution preſented, the commons took heart, and begun to play the old game over again. And if Catiline in the firſt battle had come off conqueror, or but with equal advantage, the publick would have been engaged in the moſt terrible circumſtances of ruin and deſolation; nor would thoſe who got the victory, have long enjoyed it; but the moſt potent amongſt them, would have forced from the reſt, weary and lifeleſs with the diſpute, all power, and their liberty withal. However there were ſeveral not concern'd in the conſpicacy, who

Fuere

tamen extra con-
iem complures ;
Catilinam initio
i funt. In his erat
ius,fenatoris filius;
etractum ex itine-
necari juffit. Iif-
:mporibus Romæ
is, ficuti Catilina
:rat, quofcunque
; aut fortuna no-
us idoneos crede-
it per fe aut per
olicitabat ; neque
cives, fed cujuf-
li genus hominum,
nodo ufui bello

at *firſt went over to Catiline, a-*
mongſt them A. Fulvius, a fenator's
fon ; who was fetch'd back again,
before he could reach the camp,
and put to death, by the order of
his father. At the fame time Len-
tulus at Rome, agreeably to the in-
ſtructions of Catiline, endeavoured
by himſelf or others to engage in
the cauſe all ſuch as he looked upon
to be diſpoſed by their vices or ill
circumſtances for a rebellion, and
not citizens only, but any kind of
men whatever, if they could but be
of any ſervice in the war.

. Igitur P. Um-
cuidam negotium
i legatos Allobro-
quirat ; eofque, fi
impellat ad focie-
belli ; exiftumans
privatimque ære
oppreffos, præte-
iod natura gens
bellicofa effet, fa-
tale confilium ad-
offe. Umbrenus,
Gallia negotiatus
erifque principibus
m notus erat, at-
noverat. Itaque
ora, ubi primum
in foro confpexit,
ftatus pauca de
ivitatis, & quafi
ejus cafum, requi-
rpit, *quem exitum*
malis fperarent.
am illos vidit *queri*
aritia magiſtratu-
accuſare fenatum,

XLI. *Accordingly he employs*
one P. Umbrenus to feek out the
ambaſſadors of the Allobroges, and
perſuade them, if poſſible, to join
in the war ; ſuppoſing that as the
ſtate of the Allobroges, as well as
great numbers of private perſons
amongſt them, were ſadly encum-
bered with debts, and as the whole
nation of the Gauls was naturally
warlike, they might eaſily be drawn
into ſuch a deſign. Umbrenus ha-
ving followed the employment of a
merchant in Gaul, was acquainted
with moſt of the leading men there.
Wherefore, without more ado, as
foon as he fet fight on the ambaſſa-
dors on the forum, he briefly en-
quired how matters went at home
with them. *And as if he was*
concerned for their condition, he
began to aſk them, whether they
had any hopes to fee an end of their
misfortunes ? *Upon their complain-*
ing of the greedinefs of the magiftracy of Rome, and railing at the
quod

quod in eo auxilii nihil *effet ; miferiis fuis reme-dium mortem expectare ; at ego,* inquit, *vobis, fi modo viri effe vultis, ra-tionem oftendam, qua tan-ta mala ifta effugiatis.* Hæc ubi dixit ; Allobro-ges, in fpem maxumam adducti, Umbrenum ora-re, *uti fui mijereretur. Nihil tam afperum, neque tam difficile effe, quod non cupidiffime facluri effent, dum ea res civitatem ære alieno liberaret.* Ille eos in domum Decimi Bruti perducit ; quod foro pro-pinqua erat, neque aliena confilii, propter Sempro-niam. Nam tum Brutus ab Roma aberat. Præ-terea Gabinium accerfit, quo major auctoritas fer-moni ineffet. Eo præfente conjurationem aperit, no-minat focios, præterea multos cujufque generis innoxios ; quo legatis a-nimus amplior effet : De-in eos pollicitos operam fuam, domum dimittit.

XLII. Sed Allobroges diu in incerto habuere, quidnam confilii cape-rent. In altera parte erat æs alienum, ftudium belli, magna merces in fpe vic-toriæ. At in altera ma-jores opes, tuta confilia, pro incerta fpe certa præ-mia. Hæc illis volventi-bus, tandem vicit fortu-na reipublicæ. Itaque Q.

fenate for giving them no relief; and faying that they expected death muft be the only cure for their mifery : but, *fays he,* if you will act like men, I'll fhew you a way how to get rid of all your misfortunes. *The Allobroges hear-ing this from him, and thereupon conceiving mighty hopes, begged of Umbrenus* to take pity of them. There was, *they faid,* nothing fo harfh or fo difficult, they would not gladly do, to eafe their ftate of fuch a vaft load of debt. *He car-ries them to the houfe of D. Bru-tus, becaufe it was nigh the forum, and the family no ill-wifhers to the defign, through Sempronia. For Brutus was at that time abfent from Rome. Umbrenus fends too for Gabinius, to give the greater weight to what he fhould fay. Af-ter he came, he difcovered the plot to them, names thofe that were con-cerned in it, and a great many more of all ranks that were not, to be-get in the ambaffadors a better lik-ing of the bufinefs. Upon promifing their affiftance, Umbrenus difmiffed them.*

XLII. But the Allobroges were a long time in doubt what courfe to take. On one fide were their debts, an inclination to war, and great advantage to be hoped for from a victory. But on the other, greater benefit to themfelves, fafe meafures, certain rewards inftead of uncertain hopes. After they had mufed fome time upon the matter, at laft the fortune of Rome pre-vailed. Accordingly they difcover
Fabio

Fabio Sangæ, cujus pa-rocinio civitas plurimum utebatur, rem omnem, uti cognoverant, aperi-unt. Cicero, per San-gam confilio cognito, le-gatis præcipit, ut ftudium conjurationis vehementer imulent; cæteros adeant, ene polliceantur ; dent-que operam, ut eos quam naxume manifeftos ha-eant.

XLIII. Iifdem fere emporibus, in Gallia ci-eriore atque ulteriore, tem in agro Piceno, Bru-io, Apulia motus erat. Namque illi, quos ante Catilina dimiferat, incon-ulte, ac veluti per de-nentiam, cuncta fimul gere. Nocturnis confi-iis, armorum atque telo-um portationibus, fe-tinando, agitando omnia, lus timoris, quam peri-uli, effecerant. Ex eo umero complures Q. Metellus Celer prætor, :x S C. caufla cognita, in 'incula conjecerat; item n citeriore Gallia C. Mu-æna, qui ei provinciæ egatus præerat.

XLIV. At Romæ Lentulus cum cæteris, qui principes conjuratio-nis erant, paratis, uti vi-lebatur, magnis copiis, conftituerat, uti, cum Catilina in agrum Fæfu-anum cum exercitu ve-niffet, L. Beftia tribunus

the whole affair, as they had heard it, to Quintus Fabius Sanga, whofe patronage the ftate of the Allobro-ges much ufed. Cicero underftand-ing the matter from Sanga, orders the ambaffadors to pretend a huge liking and zeal for the confpiracy, to get into the company of the reft of thofe concerned in it, promife their utmoft affiftance, and endea-vour to have as plain and ample proof againft them as poffible.

XLIII. About the fame time, there was great buftle in hither and further Gaul, os alfo in the country of Picene, the Brutii, and Apulia. For thofe whom Ca-tiline had difpatched thither, in-confiderately and madly acted all things at once; and by their right affemblies, the carriage of arms up and down, and huge hurry, and hafty action, caufed more of fright than danger. A great ma-ny of them the prætor Q. Metel-lus Celer, as impowered by the au-thority of the fenate, tried, and clapt in chains ; as likewife did C. Muræna in hither Gaul, who prefided as deputy-governor over that province.

XLIV. But at Rome, Len-tulus, with the other ringleaders of the confpiracy, having provided, as they thought, a fufficient force, refolved, that, as foon as Catiline was come with his army into the country of Fæfulæ, L. Beftia Tri-bune of the commons, fhould call the people together, and complain

plebis

plebis, concione habita, quereretur de actionibus Ciceronis, bellique graviffumi invidiam optumo confuli imponeret ; eo figno, proxuma nocte cætera multitudo conjurationis fuum quifque negotium exfequeretur. Sed ea divifa hoc modo dicebantur. Statilius & Gabinius uti cum magna manu duodecim fimul opportuna loca urbis incenderent, quo tumultu facilior aditus ad confulem cæterofque, quibus infidiæ parabantur, fieret. Cethegus Ciceronis januam obfideret, eumque vi aggrederetur, alius autem alium. Sed filii familiarum, quorum ex nobilitate maxuma pars erat, parentes interficerent ; fimul, cæde & incendio perculfis omnibus, ad Catilinam erumperent. Inter hæc parata atque decreta, Cethegus femper querebatur de ignavia fociorum : Illos, dubitando & dies prolatando magnas opportunitates corrumpere; facto, non confulto, in tali periculo, opus effe : Seque, fi pauci adjuvarent, languentibus aliis, impetum in curiam facturum. Natura ferox, vehemens, manu promptus erat : Maxumum bonum in celeritate putabat.

of Cicero's proceedings, and lay the odium of fo dangerous a war upon the beft of confuls : and that, upon this fignal, the night following, the reft of the confpiracy fhould every one mind the proper bufinefs affigned them ; which was as follows. Statilius and Gabinius, attended with a confiderable body of men, were to fire the city, in twelve places the moft convenient for their purpofe, that in the confufion occafioned thereby, they might the more eafily come at the confuls, and others they defigned to affaffinate. Cethegus was to fecure the entrance into Cicero's houfe, and fall upon him, whilft others were elfewhere employed in the like wicked defigns Then young gentlemen, the greateft part of which were of nobl families, were to kill their fathers and during the diftraction of th town, from the maffacre and th fire together, they were all to fal ly out, and march off to Catiline In the midft of thefe preparation and refolves, Cethegus was conti nually complaining of the backwardnefs of the reft, That they b their hefitation and delay ruined very hopeful caufe ; that in an er terprize of fo much danger, ther was, he faid, more occafion fo action than debate ; and that fo his part, he was ready, if a fe only would but ftand by him, le the reft fleep if they would, t attack the fenate. Cethegus w naturally of a daring violent fpiri and thought the fuccefs of the caufe depended upon pufhing with vigour.

XLV

XLV. Sed Allobroges, ex præcepto Ciceronis, per Gabinium cæteros conveniunt : ab Lentulo, Cethego, Statilio, item Caffio poftulant jusjurandum, quod fignatum ad civis perferant : aliter haud facile eos ad tantum negotium impelli poffe. Cæteri nihil fufpicantes dant. Caffius femet eo brevi venturum pollicetur, ac paullo ante legatos ex urbe proficifcitur. Lentulus cum his T. Volturcium quendam Crotonienfem mittit, uti Allobroges, prius quam domum pergerent, cum Catilina, data atque accepta fide, focietatem confirmarent. Ipfe Volturcio literas ad Catilinam dat ; quarum exemplum infra fcriptum eft.

Quis fim, ex eo, quem ad te mifi, cognofces. Fac cogites, in quanta calamitate fis, & meminecris, te virum effe. Confideres, quod tuæ rationes poftulent. Auxilium petas ab omnibus, etiam ab infimis. Ad hoc, mandata verbis dat ; cum ab fenatu hoftis judicatus fit, quo confilio fervitia repudiet. In urbe parata effe, quæ jufferit. Ne cunctetur ipfe propius accedere.

XLV. *But the Allobroges, according to Cicero's inftructions, procured by Gabinius's means, a meeting with the reft of the confpirators, at which they infifted upon an oath from Lentulus, Cethegus, Statilius and Caffius, under their hands and feals, to carry to their mafters at home, pretending it would be otherwife impoffible to engage them in an affair of fo great importance; which the reft, having no fufpicion of their defign in it, readily granted. But Caffius affured them he would be in their country very fpeedily, and accordingly left the town a little before the ambaffadors. Lentulus fent along with them one T. Volturcius of Croton, that they might further ratify what had been agreed on, with Catiline himfelf, before they went home; and gave Volturcius a letter for Catiline, a copy of which follows.*

You will underftand who I am that write to you, by the bearer. Confider the calamitous circumftances you are in, and remember you are a man ; and confider further too what your caufe requires. Seek affiftance from people of all conditions, even the meaneft. He moreover inftructed Volturcius to afk him, fince he was declared an enemy by the fenate, what he meant by refufing to accept of the affiftance of flaves. That all things in town were ready according to his order ; and therefore that he fhould not delay to advance forthwith.

XLVI.

XLVI. His rebus ita actis, conftituta nocte qua proficifcerentur, Cicero, per legatos cuncta edoctus, L. Valerio Flacco & C. Pomtino prætoribus imperat, uti in ponte Mulvio per infidias Allobrogum comitatus deprehendant. Rem omnem aperit, cujus gratia mittebantur. Cætera, uti facto opus fit, ita agant. Homines militares, fine tumultu præfidiis collocatis, ficuti præceptum erat, occulte pontem obfidunt. Poftquam ad id loci legati cum Volturcio venerunt, fimul utrimque clamor exortus eft. Galli cito cognito confilio, fine mora prætoribus fe tradunt. Volturcius'primo, cohortatus cæteros, gladio fe a multitudine defendit; dein, ubi a legatis defertus eft, multa prius de falute fua Pomtinum obteftatus, quod ei notus erat; poftremo timidus ac vitæ diffidens, velut hoftibus, fefe prætoribus dedit.

XLVII. Quibus rebus confectis, omnia propere per nuncios confuli declarantur. At illum ingens cura atque lætitia fimul occupavere. Lætabatur intelligens, conjuratione patefacta, civitatem periculis ereptam effe : porro autem anxius erat, in

XLVI. Upon this, the night being fix'd for the departure of the ambaffadors, Cicero being informed by them of all that had paffed, orders the prætors, L. Valerius Flaccus, and C. Pomtinus, to go and lie in wait for the ambaffadors at the Mulvian bridge, acquainting them at the fame time with the whole affair, and leaving the management to their difcretion. Thefe gentlemen having been in the military fervice, according to their orders, without any bustle, plant themfelves with an armed force nigh the bridge, and lie fnug there 'till the arrival of Volturcius with the ambaffadors ; upon which a fhout was fet up on both fides. The Gauls quickly underftanding the matter, immediately furrender themfelves up to the prætors. Volturcius at firft calling upon his men to ftand by him, drew his fword in his defence; but being deferted by the ambaffadors, he begged hard of Pomtinus, with whom he had had an acquaintance, to fpare his life, and then in great fright and defpair, furrendered himfelf to the prætors, as if they had been enemies.

XLVII. An account of this affair was immediately carried to the conful, who was thereupon full of concern and joy all at once. He was glad to think, that by fo full a difcovery of the plot, the city now was delivered from the danger it had been in; and then again, as the perfons concerned in the villany, were of the higheft

max-

maxumo fcelere tantis civibus deprehenfis, quid facto opus effet ; pœnam llorum fibi oneri, impunitatem perdundæ reipublicæ fore credebat. Igitur, confirmato animo, vocari ad fefe jubet Lentulum, Cethegum, Statilium, Gabinium, itemque Cœparium Terracinenfem, qui in Apuliam ad concitanda fervitia proficifci parabat. Cæteri fine mora veniunt. Cœparius, paullo ante domo egreffus, cognito indicio, ex urbe profugerat. Conful Lentulum, quod prætor erat, ipfe manu tenens, in fenatum perducit ; reliquos cum cuftodibus in ædem Concordiæ venire jubet. Eo fenatum advocat, magnaque frequentia ejus ordinis, Volturcium dum legatis introducit ; Flaccum prætorem fcrinium cum literis quas a legatis acceperat, eodem adferre jubet.

XLVIII. Volturcius interrogatus de itinere, de literis, poftremo quid, aut qua de cauffa, confilii habuiffet ; primo fingere alia omnia, diffimulare de conjuratione ; poft, ubi fide publica dicere juffus eft, omnia, uti gefta erant, aperit, docetq; fe paucis ante diebus a Gabinio & Cœpario focium afcitum : nihil amplius fcire, quam

rank and quality, he was in fome doubt with himfelf how to proceed againft them. The punifhment of them might fall heavy upon himfelf he thought, and to let them pafs unpunifhed would be ruinous to the publick. Wherefore taking courage, he orders Lentulus, Cethegus, Statilius, and Gabinius, to be fummoned before him, as alfo Cœparius of Terracina, who was upon the point of going into Apulia, to raife the flaves there. The reft of them came immediately. Cœparius being gone from home a little before the fummons came, and having fome notice of the bufinefs, had flipt out of town. The conful taking Lentulus by the hand, becaufe he was a prætor, conducts him into the fenate-houfe ; and orders the reft under a guard to repair to the temple of Concord. Thither he fummons the fenate, and there being a full houfe upon the occaffon, he introduces Volturcius with the embaffadors, and orders the prætor Flaccus to bring in a box with the letters, which he had from the embaffadors.

XLVIII. Volturcius being queftioned about his journey, and the letters, and what his defign was, or upon what account he had undertaken the journey, at firft made ufe of fome idle pretences, without faying a word of the confpiracy. But being affured upon the publick faith of his pardon, if he would declare the truth, he made a full difcovery of all ; and told them that a few days before he had been drawn in by Gabinius and Cœpa-

G

legatos ;

legatos ; tantummodo au-
dire folitum ex Gabinio,
P. Autronium, Ser. Sul-
lam, L. Varguntejum,
multos præterea in ea
conjuratione effe. Eadem
Galli fatentur. At Len-
tulum diffimulantem co-
arguunt, præter literas,
fermonibus, quos ille ha-
bere folitus erat, ex libris
Sibyllinis, regnum Romæ
tribus Corneliis portendi.
Cinnam atque Sullam an-
tea, fe tertium effe, cui
fatum foret urbis potiri ;
præterea ab incenfo Ca-
pitolio illum effe vigefi-
mum annum, quem fæpe
ex prodigiis harufpices re-
fpondiffent bello civili cru-
entum fore. Igitur per-
lectis literis, cum prius
omnes figna fua cogno-
viffent, fenatus decernit,
uti, abdicato magiftratu,
Lentulus itemque cæteri
in liberis cuftodiis habeantur. Itaque Lentulus
P. Lentulo Spintheri, qui
tum ædilis erat, Cethegus
Q. Cornificio, Statilius
C. Cæfari, Gabinius M.
Craffo, Cœparius (nam
is paullo ante ex fuga re-
tractus erat) Cn. Teren-
tio fenatori, traduntur.

rius to join in the confpiracy; that
he knew no more than the embaffadors ; he only ufed to hear of
Gabinius, that P. Autronius, Ser.
Sulla, and L. Varguntejus, with
many others, were concerued in
the plot. *The Gauls confirmed
what he faid ; and charged Lentulus, who pretended to know nothing
of the matter, not only with his
letters, but with fome things he
was ufed to fay in converfation, as*
that there was a prophecy in the
books of the Sibyls, that three of
of the Cornelian family fhould be
mafters of Rome, two of which,
Cinna and Sulla, had already been
fo ; fo that he was the third, for
which that honour was referved
by the fates ; befides, that was the
twentieth year from the burning
of the Capitol, which the harufpices, from divers prodigies, had
often foretold would be remarkable for a bloody civil war. *Upon
this the letters were read, aftev
each of the writers had owned hi.
Seal ; and the fenate voted, thal*
Lentulus fhould abdicate his office, and that both he and the reft
fhould be fecured in the cuftody o'
gentlemen. *Accordingly Lentulus is delevered up to Publius Lentulus Spinther, who was at tha.
time ædile, Cethegus to Quincu.
Cornificius, Statilius to Caiu.
Cæfar, Gabinius to Mark Craffus
Cœparius (for he had been fetchei
back to town a little before) to Cn
Terintius a fenator.*

XLIX. Interea plebes,
conjuratione patefacta,
quæ primo, cupida rerum
novarum, nimis bello fa-

XLIX. *In the mean time th|
common people, who, upon the firf|
difcovery of the plot, from the lov:
of novelty, had too much favourei|
vebat*

vebat, mutata mente, Catilinæ confilia exfecrari; Ciceronem ad cœlum tollere; velut ex fervitute erepta, gaudium atque lætitiam agitabat. Namque alia belli facinora prædæ magis, quam detrimento, fore: incendium vero crudele, immoderatum, ac fibi maxume calamitofum putabat; quippe cui omnes copiæ in ufu quotidiano & cultu corporis erant. Poft eum diem quidam L. Tarquinius ad fenatum adductus erat, quem, ad Catilinam proficifcentem, ex itinere retractum ajebant. Is cum fe liceret de conjuratione ndicaturum, fi fides publica data effet; juffus a confule, quæ fciret, edicre, eadem fere, quæ Volturcius, de paratis incendiis, de cæde bonorum, de itinere hoftium, fenaum edocet. Præterea, 'e miffum a M. Craffo, jui Catilinæ nunciaret; ie eum Lentulus & Cehegus, aliique ex conjuatione deprehenfi terreent; eoque magis propearet ad urbem accedere, iuo & cæterorum animos eficeret, & illi facilius periculo eriperentur. Sed, ubi Tarquinius Crafium nominavit, hominem nobilem, maxumis divitiis, fumma potentia;

the war, now changing their minds, began to curfe the defigns of Catiline, and to extol Cicero to the heavens; and, as being now fecured againft the flavery they were threatened with, were full of joy and jollity. For the other acts of war they thought might turn more to their advantage than detriment; but the firing of the town they looked upon as a cruel wild project, and what would have been pernicious to them efpecially, whofe fubftance confifted entirely in cloaths and a few houfhold goods. After this, one Lucius Tarquinius was brought before the fenate, who was faid to be going over to Catiline, and had been therefore brought back to town. He offered to make a full difcovery of the plot, if he might have the publick faith for his pardon; and being thereupon ordered by the conful to declare what he knew, he gave much the fame information Volturcius had done, as to firing of the town, the defigned maffacre, and the march of the enemy. He added, that he had been difpatched by M. Craffus to tell Catiline not to be frighted at the feizing of Lentulus, Cethegus, and others of the confpirators, but make the more hafte to town, for the encouragement of the reft, and for the releafe of thofe that were prifoners. But when Tarquin named Craffus, a perfon of the higheft quality, a vaft eftate, and mighty power; fome looking upon what was faid as incredible, and others, though they believed it true, yet becaufe fo powerful a man was rather to be wheedled

G 2　　　　　　alii

alii rem incredibilem rati; pars, tametsi verum exiſtumabat, tamen quia in tali tempore tanta vis hominis magis leniunda, quam exagitanda, videbatur, plerique, Craſſo ex negotiis privatis obnoxii, conclamant, *indicem falſum eſſe*; deque ea re poſtulant uti referatur. Itaque, Cicerone conſulente, frequens ſenatus decernit. *Tarquinii indicium falſum videri, eumque in vinculis retinendum ; neque amplius poteſtatem faciundam, niſi de eo indicaret, cujus conſilio tantam rem eſſet mentitus.* Erant eo tempore, qui exiſtumarent indicium illud a P. Autronio machinatum ; quo facilius, appellato Craſſo, per ſocietatem periculi reliquos illius potentia tegeret. Alii Tarquinium a Cicerone immiſſum ajebant ; ne Craſſus, more ſuo, ſuſcepto malorum patrocinio, rempublicam conturbaret. Ipſum Craſſum ego poſtea prædicantem audivi, tantam illam contumeliam ſibi ab Cicerone impoſitam. Sed iiſdem temporibus Q. Catulus & C. Piſo neque gratia, neque precibus, neque precio Ciceronem impellere quivere ; uti per Allobroges aut alium indicem C. Cæſar falſo no-

than provoked at ſuch a juncture, being meſt of them too under particular obligations to Craſſus, they all cried out the informer was a raſcal, *and deſired the houſe might immediately go upon that affair. Which Cicero complying with, and moving the houſe accordingly, they voted by a great majority,* That Tarquin's information appeared to them to be falſe, and that he be kept in cuſtody, and not be enlarged, 'till he diſcovered the perſon at whoſe inſtigation he had forged that lie. *There were ſome at that time, who did believe that the thing was a project of Publius Autronius, in order to ſcreen the conſpirators, by naming Craſſus as one. Some ſaid Tarquin was put upon it by Cicero, leſt Craſſus ſhould, according to his way, take upon him the protection of the villains, and thereby confound the proceedings of the government againſt them. And I myſelf afterwards heard Craſſu. ſay, that that baſe trick had been put upon him by Cicero. But a the ſame time Q. Catulus and C Piſo could by no intereſt, importunity, or money, prevail upon Ci cero to have Cæſar falſely named as a conſpirator, by the Allobroges or any one elſe. Both thoſe gen tlemen were bitter enemies to him Piſo having been proſecuted by hi in an action of damages, for th unjuſt puniſhment of a certain per ſon of Gallia beyond the Po. Ca tulus bore him a grudge, ever a fter the time of his ſtanding for th place of high-prieſt, when he, th a man in years, that had borne th greateſt offices in the ſtate, can minaretu*

minaretur. Nam uterque cum illo gravis inimicitias exercebant ; Pifo, oppugnatus in judicio repetundarum, propter cujufdam Tranfpadani fupplicium injuftum ; Catulus, ex petitione ponteficatus odio incenfus ; quod extrema ætate, maxumis honoribus ufus, ab adolefcentulo Cæfare victus difcefferat. Res autem opportuna videbatur ; quod is privatim egregia liberalitate, publice maxumis muneribus grandem pecuniam debebat. Sed ubi confulem ad tantum facinus impellere nequeunt, ipfi fingillatim circumeundo, atque ementiendo quæ fe ex Volturcio aut Allobrogibus audiffe dicerent, magnam illi invidiam conflaverant ; ufque adeo, uti nonnulli equites Rom. qui præfidii cauffa cum telis erant circum ædem Concordiæ, feu periculi magnitudine, feu animi nobilitate impulfi, quo ftudium fuum in rempublicam clarius effet, egredienti ex fenatu Cæfari gladio minitarentur. Dum hæc in fenatu aguntur, & dum legatis Allobrogum & T. Volturcio, comprobato eorum indicio, præmia decernuntur, liberti & pauci ex clientibus Lentuli, diverfis itineribus,

off baffled by Cæfar, who was at that time but a very young man. The charge feemed likely to pafs, becaufe he by his private generofity, and publick diverfions, for the entertainment of the people, was got into a world of debt. But being not able to engage the conful in fuch a piece of roguery, they by going about, and falfely reporting what they pretended to have heard from Volturcius and the Allobroges, brought him under a very great odium, infomuch that fome gentlemen of the equeftrian order, who were pofted in arms about the temple of Concord, as a guard to the houfe, whether pufhed on by a fenfe of danger, or fome nobler motive, to fhew their zeal for the publick, threatened Cæfar at his coming out of the houfe with their drawn fwords. Whilft thefe things are done in the fenate, and rewards are voted for the Allobroges and T. Volturcius, whofe information was approved of ; fome freed-men and clients of Lentulus difperfed themfelves in town, and endeavoured to engage the workmen and flaves they met with in the ftreets, to refcue him. And fome would gladly have prevailed with the leaders of the mob to head them, who were ufed for hire to give difturbance now and then to the government. But Cethegus by meffengers begged of his flaves and freed-men choice blades, and fuch as had been trained up in the practice of bold wicked pranks, to form themfelves into a body, and break in to him with arms. The conful being informed

G 3

opi-

opifices atque fervitia in vicis ad eum eripiendum follicitabant. Partim exquirebant duces multitudinum, qui precio rempublicam vexare foliti erant. Cethegus autem per nuncios familiam, atque libertos fuos, lectos & exercitatos in audaciam, orabat ; uti, grege facto, cum telis ad fefe irrumperent. Conful, ubi ea parari cognovit, difpofitis præfidiis, uti res atq; tempus monebat, convocato fenatu refert, *quid de his fieri placeat, qui in cuftodiam traditi erant.* Sed eos paulo ante frequens fenatus judicaverat contra rempublicam feciffe. Tum D. Junius Silanus, primus fententiam rogatus, quod eo tempore conful defignatus erat, de his, qui in cuftodiis tenebantur, & præterea de L. Caffio, P. Furio, P. Umbreno, Q. Annio, fi deprehenfi forent, fupplicium fumendum decreverat. Ifque poftea, permotus oratione C. Cæfaris, pedibus in fententiam Ti. Neronis iturum fe dixerat, quod de ea re, præfidiis additis, referundum cenfuerat. Sed Cæfar, ubi ad eum ventum eft, rogatus fententiam a confule, hujufcemodi verba locutus eft.

of thefe attempts, placed guards as the occafion required, and then calling the fenate together, defired to know their pleafure with relation to the prifoners, what they would have done with them. A full houfe had already voted them guilty of a traiterous defign againft the government. Then D. Junius Silanus being firft afked what he thought of the matter, for he was at that time conful elect, declared for capital punifhment to be inflicted upon thofe in cuftody, as alfo L. Caffius, P. Furius, P. Umbrenus, and Q. Annius, if they fhould be taken. But being afterwards much affected with a fpeech of C. Cæfar to the houfe, he declared for the opinion of Tiberius Nero, who was for having the further debate of that matter deferred, 'till the houfe was provided with a better guard. Now Cæfar, when the conful was come to him, and defired his fentiments, fpoke to the effect following.

asar.

L. Omnis homines, patres confcripti, qui de rebus dubiis confultant, ab odio, amicitia, ira, atque miferi- cordia vacuos effe decet. Haud facile animus verum providet, ubi illa officiunt ; neque quifquam omnium lubidini fimul & ufui paruit. Ubi inten-

L. Illuftrious fathers, all men in their debates upon matters of difficulty, ought to be free from the paffions of hatred, love, anger, and pity. The mind of man does not eafily fee the truth where thofe obftructions are in the way ; nor has ever any man been able to confult his intereft and his paffion together. Where the underftand-
deri

deris ingenium, valet. Si lubido poſſidet, ea dominatur ; animus nihil valet. Magna mihi copia eſt memorandi, P. C, qui reges aut qui populi, ira aut miſericordia impulſi, male conſuluerint. Sed ea malo dicere, quæ majores noſtri, contra lubidinem animi ſui, reɛte atque ordine fecere. Bello Macedonico, quod cum rege Perſe geſſimus, Rhodiorum civitas, magna atque magnifica, quæ populi Rom. opibus creverat, infida atque advorſa nobis fuit. Sed poſtquam bello confeɛto, de Rhodiis conſultum eſt, majores noſtri, ne quis divitiarum magis, quam injuriæ cauſſa, bellum inceptum diceret, impunitos cos dimiſere. Item bellis Punicis omnibus, cum ſæpe Carthaginienſes & in pace & per inducias multa nefanda facinora feciſſent, nunquam ipſi per occaſionem talia fecere ; magis, quod ſe dignum foret, quam quod in illos jure fieri poſſet, quærebant. Hoc item vobis providendum eſt, P. C. ne plus valeat apud vos P. Lentuli & cæterorum ſcelus, quam veſtra dignitas ; neu magis iræ veſtræ, quam famæ, conſulatis. Nam ſi digna pœna pro faɛtis eorum reperitur, novum

ing is in any caſe duly applied, it does its work effectually. But if paſſion of any kind poſſeſſes the mind, that rules, a man's ſenſe or parts ſignify nothing. I could bring many inſtances of kings and ſtates, that have by anger or pity been led into pernicious miſtakes. But I chuſe rather to take notice to you of the behaviour of our anceſtors, wherein they ſhewed a noble ſelf-denial. In the Macedonian war, which we had with king Perſes, the Rhodians, a great and flouriſhing people, who had been raiſed by the ſupport of the Romans, proved baſe and treacherous to us. Yet when, upon the concluſion of the war, the caſe of the Rhodians came under conſideration, our anceſtors, to leave no pretence for ſaying that the war had been undertaken out of a covetous humour, more than upon account of injury received, pardoned them. In all the Carthaginian wars too, tho' that people in time of peace, or ceſſation of arms, had been guilty of many wicked things againſt us, yet our anceſtors never upon any occaſion returned them the like uſage, regarding more what was worthy of themſelves, than what might have been fairly practiſed againſt them. And in like manner ought you, gentlemen, to take care, that the wickedneſs of Lentulus and the reſt of the conſpirators, have not more influence upon you than your own honour, and not gratify your reſentment at the expence of your reputation. For if a puniſhment equal to their crime be

conſi-

*onfilium apprebo. Sin magnitudo fceleris omnium ingenia exfuperat ; iis utendum cenfeo, quæ legibus comparata funt. Plerique eorum, qui ante me fententias dixerunt, compofite atque magnifice cafum reipublicæ miferati funt ; quæ belli fævitia effet, quæ viêtis acciderent, enumeravere ; rapi virgines, pueros ; divelli liberos a parentum complexu ; matres familiarum pati, quæ viêtoribus collibuiffent ; fana atque domos exfpoliari ; cædem, incendia fieri ; poftremo armis, cadaveribus, cruore atque luêtu omnia compleri. Sed, per deos immortalis, quo illa oratio pertinuit ? An, uti vis infeftos conjurationi facerent ? Scilicet, quem res tanta atque tam atrox non permovit, .eum oratio accendct. Non ita eft. Neque cuiquam mortalium injuriæ fuæ parvæ videntur. Multi eas gravius æquo habuere. Sed alia aliis licentia eft, P. C. Qui demiffi in obfcuro vitam agunt, fi quid iracundia deliquere, pauci fciunt ; fama atque fortuna eorum pares funt. Qui magno imperio præditi, in excelfo ætatem agunt, eorum faêta cunêti mortales novere. Ita in maxuma fortuna minuma li-

poffible to bé found, I approve of the ftrange advice given. But if the greatnefs of their villainy be fuch, as to puzzle the beft invention to find out a punifhment equal to it, I think we ought to content ourfelves with fuch as are provided by law. Moft of the gentlemen that fpoke before me have very elegantly and nobly lamented the misfortune of the commonwealth; have enumerated all the cruel confequences of a war, and the miferable circumftances the vanquifhed party muft needs be in ; fuch as the ravifhing of virgins, the unnatural abufe of boys, the tearing away of children from the embraces of their parents, the expofing of matrons to the luft of the conquerors, thé plundering of temples and houfes, flaughter, the firing of towns; and finally, the filling of all places with arms, dead bodies, blood, and lamentation. But, for heaven's fake, what does all that way of talking tend to ? to incenfe you againft the confpiracy? Words, I warrant, will inflame thofe whom fo monftrous and villainous a crime cannot move. No, no. No man is apt to under-rate the injuries done to himfelf. Many aggravate them beyond all reafon. But all men have not the fame liberty allowed them. If perfons in low life, through paffion, are guilty of any mifdonduêt, few know of it ; the fame and fortunes of fuch men are generally equal. But thofe in great power and authority, ftand high, and their aêtions are known to all men. Thus in the greateft

centie

centia eſt. Neque ſtudere, neque odiſſe, ſed minume iraſci decet. Quæ apud alios iracundia dicitur, ea in imperio ſuperbia atque crudelitas appellatur. Equidem ego ſic exiſtumo, P. C. omnis cruciatus minores, quam facinora illorum, eſſe. Sed plerique mortales poſtrema meminere; & in hominibus impiis, ſceleris eorum obliti, de pœna diſſerunt, ſi ea paulo ſeverior fuerit. D. Silanum, virum fortem atque ſtrenuum, certo ſcio, quæ dixerit, ſtudio reipublicæ dixiſſe, neque illum in tanta re gratiam aut inimicitias exercere. Eos mores eamque modeſtiam viri cognovi. Verum ſententia ejus mihi non crudelis, (quid enim in talis homines crudele fieri poteſt?) ſed aliena a republica noſtra videtur. Nam profecto aut metus aut injuria te ſubegit, Silane, conſulem deſignatum, genus pœnæ novum decernere. De timore ſupervacaneum eſt diſſerere; cum, præſertim diligentia clariſſumi viri conſulis, tanta præſidia ſint in armis. De pœna poſſumus equidem dicere id, quod res habet; in luctu atque miſeriis mortem ærumnarum requiem, non cruciatum eſſe; eam cunc-

fortune is there the leaſt licence allowable. In that there muſt be no party-prejudice, or hatred, and paſſion leaſt of all. What is called anger upon other occaſions, in perſons inveſted with great power, goes by the name of pride and cruelty. Truly, gentlemen, I am of opinion, that no puniſhment can be thought of bad enough for their crimes. But moſt men remember the upſhot of things, and in the caſe of villains, forgetting their wickedneſs, talk only of their puniſhment, if that be a little too ſevere. I am well aſſured that the worthy brave gentleman D. Silanus ſaid what he did out of zeal to the publick ſervice, without the leaſt regard to favour, or ill-will to any one: ſuch is his virtue and modeſty to my knowledge. But his advice appears to me, not cruel indeed, (for what can be cruel againſt ſuch wretches?) but not agreeable to the proceedings of our government. For certainly, Silanus, either your fear, or the injury deſigned the publick, moved you to adviſe a puniſhment unknown to our laws. As to your fear, I need ſay nothing, eſpecially ſince, by the diligence of our glorious conſul, ſo ſufficient a force has been provided for our ſecurity. And as to the puniſhment, we may ſay indeed, what is the truth in reality, that in a ſtate of mourning and miſery, death is a deliverance, not a puniſhment. That puts an end to all the miſeries of mankind, beyond which there is no room for either ſorrow or joy, But by heaven, tell me why did

ta

ta mortalium mala diffol-
vere ; ultra neque curæ
neque gaudio locum effe.
Sed, per deos immortalis,
quamobrem in fententiam
non addidifti, uti prius
verberibus in eos animad-
verteretur ? An, quia lex
Porcia vetat ? At aliæ
leges item condemnatis civibus non animam eripi,
fed exilium permitti ju-
bent. An quia gravius eft
verberari, quam necari ?
Quid autem acerbum, aut
nimis grave eft in homines
tanti facinoris convictos ?
Sin, quia levius eft ; qui
convenit in minore nego-
tio legem obfervare, cum
eam in majore neglexe-
ris ? At enim quis repre-
hendet, quod in parrici-
das reipublicæ decretum
erit ? Tempus, dies, for-
tuna, cujus lubido gentibus
moderatur. Illis merito ac-
cidet, quicquid evenerit.
Cæterum vos, P. C. quid
in alios ftatuatis, confiderate. Omnia mala exem-
pla ex bonis initiis orta funt.
Sed, ubi imperium ad ig-
naros aut minus bonos per-
venit ; novum illud exemplum ab dignis & idoneis ad indignos &
non idoneos transfertur.

LI. Lacedæmonii, de-
victis Athenienfibus, triginta viros impofuere, qui
rempublicam tractarent.
Ili primo cœpere peffu-
mum quemque & omnibus
invifum indemnatum ne-
care. Eo populus lætari,

you not advife too to have them
feverely lafhed, before they were
put to death ? Was it becaufe the
Porcian law exprefly forbids it ?
But there are other laws too, that
equally forbid the putting a condemned Roman to death, and
allow him the favour of banifhment. Or was it becaufe whipping is a feverer punifhment than
death ? But what can be too
cruel or fevere againft men convicted of fo horrid a villainy ? But
if it was becaufe whipping is really
a leffer punifhment, is it fit to regard the law in a matter of fmal-
ler moment, whilft you flight it
in a greater ? But who will blame,
you'll fay, what fhall be refolved
upon againft men bent upon the
deftruction of the commonwealth?
Time and fortune, who rule the
world at pleafure. They certainly
deferve the worft that can befall
them. But do you, worthy fathers, confider well what you refolve upon againft them. All ill
examples had their rife from harm-
lefs beginning. But when power
comes into the hands of ignorant
or wicked men, the precedent fet
is transferred from deferving and
proper objects to fuch as are not
fo.

LI. After the Lacedemonians
had conquered the Athenians,they
lodged the government in the
hands of thirty perfons ; who at
firft began to put to death, without tryal, the wickedeft amongft
them, and fuch as were univerfally odious. This the people re-

*& merito dicere fieri. Poft, ubi paullatim licentia crevit, juxta bonos & malos lubidinofe interficere, cæteros metu terrerè. Ita civitas, fervitute oppreffa, ftultæ lætitiæ gravis pænas dedit. Noftra memoria victor Sulla, cum Damafippum & alios hujufmodi, qui malo reipublicæ creverant, jugulari juffit, quis non factum ejus laudabat? Homines fceleftos & factiofos, qui feditionibus rempublicam exagitaverant, merito necatos ajebant. Sed ea res magnæ initium cladis fuit. Namque, uti quifque domum aut villam, poftremo aut vas aut veftimentum alicujus concupiverat, dabat operam, uti is in profcriptorum numero effet. Ita illi, quibus Damafippi mors lætitiæ fuerat, paulo poft ipfi trahebantur. Neque prius finis iugulandi fuit, quam Sulla omnis fuos divitiis explevit. Atque ego hoc non in M. Tullio, neque his temporibus vereor. Sed in magna civitate multa & varia ingenia *funt. Poteft alio tempore, alio confule, cui item exercitus in manu fit, falfum aliquid pro vero credi. Ubi hoc exemplo, per fenati decretum, conful gladium eduxerit, quis illi finem ftatuet, aut quis moderabitur?*

joiced at, and faid was right proceeding. But prefently, as this humour grew upon them, they proceeded to put good and bad promifcuoufly to death at their pleafure, and filled the reft with apprehenfions of the like ufage. Thus the poor city being miferably enflaved fuffered fufficiently for their filly rejoicing. In our times too, when Sulla, after his fuccefs in the war, ordered Damafippus, and fome others like him, who had raifed themfelves by the misfortunes of their country, to be put to death, who did not commend him for it? Every body faid, that thofe wicked factious rafcals, who had plagued the publick by their feditious practices, were defervedly put to death. But that was the firft part only acted in one of the moft bloody fcenes that ever was. For, as any of the party chanced to take a fancy for any gentleman's houfe in town or country, nay but any piece of plate, or fine coat, he took care to get him put upon the lift of the profcribed. Thus they who rejoiced at the death of Damafippus were themfelves foon after hurried away to execution. Nor was there any end of this butchery, 'till Sulla had glutted all his followers with riches. I apprehend indeed nothing like this in Mark Tully, or thefe times. But in a mighty ftate there are many various humours. At another time, another conful, who fhall have an army at his command, may be under a miftake; and then, when upon this precedent the conful fhall by a vote of the fenate draw the fword, who fhall ftop, or over-rule it? LII.

LII. Majores nostri, Patres conscripti, neque consilii neque audaciæ unquam eguere. Neque superbia obstabat, quo minus instituta aliena, si modo proba erant, imitarentur. Arma atque tela militaria ab Samnitibus, insignia magistratuum ab Tuscis pleraque sumpserunt. Postremo, quod ubique apud socios aut hostis idoneum videbatur, cum summo studio domi exsequebantur. Imitari, quam invidere bonis, malebant. Sed eodem illo tempore Græciæ morem imitati, verberibus animadvertebant in civis, de condemnatis summum supplicium sumebant. Postquam respublica adolevit, & multitudine civium factiones valuere, circumvenire innocentes, alia hujuscemodi fieri cœpere ; tum lex Porcia, aliæque leges paratæ sunt ; quibus legibus exilium damnatis permissum est. Hanc ego caussam, P. C. quo minus consilium novum capiamum, in primis magnam puto. Profecto virtus atque sapientia major in illis fuit, qui ex parvis opibus tantum imperium fecere, quam in nobis, qui bene parta vix retinemus. Placet igitur, eos dimitti, & augeri exercitum Catilinæ? Minume.

LII. Our fore-elders, worthy fathers, never wanted either conduct or courage; nor did a spirit of pride hinder them from imitating the laudable customs of other nations. They borrowed from the Samnites arms and weapons of war, most of the ornaments of our magistrates from the Tuscans. In fine, they studiously put in practice at home whatsoever appeared, either amongst friends or foes, worthy of their reception. They chose rather to imitate than envy the good. Now at that time, according to the usage of Greece, they used to punish by scourging, and put citizens to death. But when the Roman state was grown up to its full magnitude, and in a numerous people factions prevailed, innocent men began to be trepanned, and other the like wickedness to be practised; then the Porcian law, and other laws were provided, by which all such as should be condemned for capital crimes were allowed the favour of banishmint. And therefore I think this a very substantial reason against the new proceedings advised to. Certainly their conduct and wisdom, who from a small rise produced so vast an empire, was far aboue ours, who have much ado to keep what was so well provided to our hands. Well, you'll say, would I have them discharged, to augment Catiline's army? By no means. But my sentence is this, Let their estates be confiscated, themselves kept in close custody, in the most substantial boroughs. Let no one

Se

Sed ita cenſeo, publicandas eorum pecunias ; ipſos in vinculis habendos per mu-nicipia, quæ maxume opi-bus valent ; neu quis de his poſtea ad ſenatum referat, neve cum populo agat. Qui aliter fecerit, ſenatum exiſtumare, eum contra rempublicam & ſalutem omnium faɛturum.

ever move the ſenate, or make the leaſt application to the people in their favour. And let it be de-clared as the opinion of this houſe, that whoever does is a traitor to his country, and an enemy to the commonwealth.

LIII. *Poſtquam Cæ-far dicendi finem fecit ; cæteri verbo, alius alii varie aſſentiebantur. At M. Porcius Cato, rogatus ſententiam, hujuſcemodi orationem habuit.*

LIII. *After Cæſar had made an end of his ſpeech, the reſt ſig-nified their aſſent, ſome to one and ſome to another. But M. Porcius Cato, being aſked what he thought of the matter, made a ſpeech to the following effeɛt.*

LIV. *Longe mihi alia mens eſt, patres conſcrip-ti, cum res atque pericula noſtra conſidero, & cum ſententias nonnullorum me-cum ipſe reputo. Illi mihi diſſeruiſſe videntur de pœna eorum, qui pa-triæ, parentibus, aris atque focis ſuis bellum paravere. Res autem monet, cavere ab illis magis, quam, quid in il-los ſtatuamus, conſulta-re. Nam cætera malefi-cia tum perſequare, ubi faɛta ſunt ; hɛc, niſi pro-videris, ne accidat, ubi evenit, fruſtra judicia implores. Capta urbe, nihil fit reliqui viɛtis. Sed per deos immortalis, vos ego appello, qui ſemper do-mos, villas, ſigna, tabu-las veſtras pluris, quam rempublicam, feciſtis. Si iſta, cujuſcumque modi ſint, quæ amplexamini,*

LIV. I am, gentlemen, of a quite different opinion from you in this caſe, when I conſider it, and the danger we are in, as alſo the advice that has been offered by ſome. The buſineſs they ſeem alone to have had in view is the puniſhment of thoſe who have formed a deſign to make war up-on their country, parents, and re-ligion. Now the nature of the thing obliges us to conſider rather, how we may guard effeɛtually againſt them, than how we are to puniſh them. For other crimes you may puniſh after they are committed ; but unleſs you pre-vent the commiſſion of this, it will be in vain to fly to the law for vengeance. When the city ſhall be taken, the conquered will have nothing left. But, by the immortal gods, I ſpeak to you, who have always had more regard to your fine houſes, ſtatues, and pictures, than the welfare of your country. If you have a mind to keep the things, be they what they

reti-

Cato.

retinere, si voluptatibus vestris otium præbere vultis; expergiscemini aliquando, & capessite rempublicam. Non agitur de vectigalibus, non de sociorum injuriis. Libertas & anima nostra in dubio est. Sæpenumero, P. C. multa verba in hoc ordine feci. Sæpe de luxuria atque avaritia nostrorum civium questus sum. Multosque mortalis ea caussa adversos habeo. Qui mihi atque animo meo nullius unquam delicti gratiam fecissem, haud facile alterius lubidini malefacta condonabam. Sed, ea tametsi vos parvi pendebatis, tamen respublica firma erat. Opulentia negligentiam toleravit. Nunc vero non id agitur, bonisque an malis moribus vivamus; neque quantum aut quam magnificum imperium populi Romani sit; sed hæc, cujuscumque modi videntur, nostra, an nobiscum una hostium futura sint.

LV. Hic mihi quisquam mansuetudinem & misericordiam nominat? Jampridem equidem nos vera rerum vocabula amisimus. Quia bona aliena largiri, liberalitas; malarum rerum audacia, fortitudo vocatur; eo respublica in extremo sita est. Sint sane, quoniam

will, you are so fond of and to find time for the pursuit of your pleasures; rouze at last, and stand up for the defence of your country. We are not now treating of the revenue of the state, or the ill usage of our allies. Our liberty, our lives are at stake. I have, gentlemen, spoke often and much in this house. I have often complained of the extravagance and avarice that prevail amongst us; and have, by so doing, made myself many enemies. Now I, who would never indulge myself in the least fault, could not easily pardon the crimes of others. But though you minded little what I said, yet our country was secure. Our great opulence would admit of some negligence in the management of our affairs. But a reformation of manners, or the aggrandizing the state, is not the business we have now under consideration; but whether what we enjoy, be it what it will, should be our own, or, together with ourselves, be delivered up a prey to the enemy.

LV. And shall any one talk to me in this case of mildness and mercy? We have long since indeed lost the right names of things from amongst us. The giving of what belongs to other people is called generosity, and the courage to venture upon wickedness is named fortitude; by which means it is, that the state has been brought upon the very brink of
ita

ita se mores habent, libe-
rales ex sociorum fortu-
nis. Sint misericordes in
furibus ærarii. Ne illis
sanguinem nostrum largi-
antur ; &, dum paucis
sceleratis parcunt, bonos
omnis perditum eant. Be-
ne & composite C. Cæsar
paullo ante in hoc ordine
de vita & morte disseru-
it, credo falso existumans
ea, quæ de inferis memo-
rantur ; diverso itinere
malos a bonis loca tætra,
inculta, fœda atque for-
midolosa habere. Itaque
censuit, pecunias eorum
publicandas, ipsos per municipia in custodiis habendos ; videlicet, ne, si Romæ sint, aut a popularibus
conjurationis, aut a multitudine conducta, per vim
eripiantur. Quasi vero
mali atque scelesti tan-
tummodo in urbe & non
per totam Italiam sint ;
aut non ibi plus possit
audacia, ubi ad defenden-
dum opes minores sunt.
Quare vanum equidem
hoc consilium est, si periculum ex illis metuit: Sin
in tanto omnium metu
solus non timet ; eo magis
refert, me mihi atque vobis
timere.

LVI. Quare cum de
P. Lentulo cæterisque
statuetis, pro certo habetote, vos simul de exer-
citu Catilinæ, & de om-
nibus conjuratis decerne-

destruction. Let them, since it
is now become the fashion of the
times, be generous out of the fortunes of our allies. Let them shew
compassion to the robbers of the
publick ; but let them not pretend
to make a present of our blood to
them, and by sparing a few villains bring destruction upon all
good people. C. Cæsar spoke
just now very handsomely and
prettily of life and death, as judging, I presume, the vulgar notions
of hell, where the bad are divided
from the good, and confined in
nasty, uncomfortable, filthy, dismal places, to be false ; and therefore advised to confiscate their
estates, and keep their persons under confinement in the boroughs ;
from an apprehension, I suppose,
if they should be kept at Rome,
of their being rescued, either by
their fellows, or a hired mob. As
if we had rascals and villains only
in town, and not all Italy over ;
or as if bold attempts would not
be more likely to succeed, where
there was the least ability to oppose them. This therefore is very
idle advice, if he fears any danger from them ; but if he alone
is not afraid, whilst every body
else is, I am the more obliged to
be afraid both for myself and
you.

LVI. Wherefore, in judging
the case of Lentulus, you may
depend upon it, you determine
that of Catiline's army, and the
rest of the conspirators, at the
same time. The more vigour you
re.

re. Quanto vos attenti-
us ea agetis, tanto illis
animus infirmior erit. Si
paullulum modo vos lan-
guere viderint, jam om-
nes feroces aderunt. No-
lite exiftumare, majores
noftros armis rempubli-
cam ex parva magnam
fecijfe. Si ita res ejfet;
multo pulcherrumam eam
nos haberemus. Quippe
fociorum atque civium,
praterea armorum atque
equorum major copia no-
bis, quam illis, eft. Sed
alia fuere, qua illos mag-
nos fecere; qua nobis
nulla funt. Domi in-
duftria, foris juftum .im-
perium; animus in confu-
lendo liber, neque delicto
neque lubidini obnoxius.
Pro his nos habemus luxu-
riam atque avaritiam;
publice egeftatem; pri-
vatim opulentiam. Lau-
damus divitias, fequimur
inertiam. Inter bonos &
malos difcrimen nullum.
Omnia virtutis pramia
ambitio poffidet. Neque
mirum; ubi vos fepara-
tim fibi quifque confilium
capitis, ubi domi volup-
tatibus, hic pecunia aut
gratia fervitis; eo fit,
ut impetus fiat in va-
cuam rempublicam. Sed
ego hac omitto. Conju-
ravere cives nobiliffumi
patriam incendere; Gal-
lorum gentem, infeftiffu-
mam nomimi Romano, ad

act with, the more difcouraged
they will be. But if they fee you
faint-hearted, they will all forthwith advance boldly upon us.
Do not think that our forefathers
brought the Roman ftate from a
low rife to its prefent height by
their arms. If they had, we fhould
then be in a much more happy fecure condition than they. For we
have more allies and people, as well
as more arms and horfes than they.
But there were other things which
made them great, which we have
nothing of. I mean induftry at
home, and juft management a-
broad; minds free from the influence of vice and humour in publick councils: in the room of
which, we have got luxury and
avarice, publick poverty and private wealth. We admire riches,
and are in love with idlenefs. We
make no diftinction between the
worthy and the worthlefs. Ambition is poffeffed of all the rewards of virtue. Nor is it to be
wondered at, whilft you each of
you purfue feparate meafures only
for your own intereft; whilft you
mind nothing but your pleafures
at home, and in this place wealth
and honour. 'Tis this behaviour
of yours that has encouraged the
villains to fall upon the abandoned
ftate. But I let thefe things alone.
Perfons of the higheft quality have
engaged in a confpiracy to fire the
city, and are endeavouring to
bring the Gauls, thofe mortal
enemies of Rome, to join them
in a war againft us. The commander of the enemy is at our
gates with an army; and do you
bellun

bellum arceſſunt. Dux hoſtium cum exercitu ſupra caput eſt. Vos cunĉtamini etiam nunc, & dubitatis, quid, intra mœnia deprehenſis hoſtibus, faciatis ?· Miſereamini, cenſeo. Dliquere homines adoleſcentuli per ambitionem. Atque etiam armatos dimittatis. Næ iſta vobis manſuetudo & miſericordia, ſi illi arma ceperint, in miſeriam vertet. Scilicet res ipſa aſpera eſt, ſed vos non timetis eam. Imo vero maxume ; ſed, inertia & mollitia animi, alius alium expeĉtantes, cunĉtamini ; videlicet diis immortalibus confiſi, qui hanc rempublicam in maxumis ſæpe periculis ſervavere. Non votis, neque ſuppliciis muliebribus auxilia deorum parantur. Vigilando, agendo, bene · conſulendo proſpere omnia cedunt. Ubi ſocordiæ tete atque ignaviæ tradideris, nequicquam deos implores. Irati infeſtique ſunt. Apud majores noſtros A. Manlius Torquatus bello Gallico filium ſuum, quod is contra imperium in hoſtem pugnaverat, necari juſſit. Atque ille egregius adoleſcens immoderatæ fortitudinis morte pœnas dedit. Vos de crudeliſſumis parricidis quid ſtatuatis, cunĉtamini ? Videlicet

pretend to demur upon the matter, or make any doubt what you ought to do with thoſe of the enemy you have catched within your walls ? You ſhould take pity of them, I ſuppcſe. They are only young fellows led away by the love of power, and therefore ought to be diſcharged. Truly that mildneſs and mercy, if they get but arms into their hands, will prove your deſtruĉtion. The caſe indeed is very diſmal ; but you are notwithſtanding, it ſeems, fearleſs about it. Far from it ; but, for want of ſpirit and vigour, you hang back, waiting one another's motions ; confiding, I ſuppoſe, in the providence of the immortal gods, who have frequently ſaved this ſtate of ours in the greateſt of dangers. But the aſſiſtance of the gods is not procured by vows and womaniſh prayers. All deſigns ſucceed by vigilance, induſtry, and wiſe counſels. If you give yourſelves up to idleneſs and ſloth, 'tis in vain to invoke the aſſiſtance of the gods. They are angry and enraged at you. In the days of old, Aulus Manlius Torquatus, in the Gallick war, ordered his ſon to be put to death for fighting contrary to his order. Thus was that excellent youth puniſhed for his ill governed courage. You are in doubt what to do with parricides ; moved, I ſuppoſe, by the great innocence of their lives before they engaged in this projeĉt. Yes, ſhew a regard to the quality of Lentulus, if ever he ſhewed the leaſt to his own chaſtity, or credit, to either gods or men.

H *vita*

vita cætera eorum huic
fceleri obftat. Verum par-
cite dignitati Lentuli; fi
ipfe pudicitiæ, fi famæ
fuæ, fi diis aut hominibus
unquam ullis pepercit.
Ignofcite Cethegi adolef-
centiæ, nifi iterum jam
patriæ bellum fecit. Nam
quid de ego Gabinio, Sta-
tilio, Cæpario loquar ?
Quibus fi quidquam penfi
umquam fuiffet, non ea
confilia de republica ha-
buiffent. Poftremo, pa-
tres confcripti, fi meher-
cle peccato locus effet, fa-
cile paterer vos ipfa re
corrigi ; quoniam verba
contemnitis. Sed undique
circumventi fumus. Cati-
lina cum exercitu in fau-
cibus urget. Alii intra
mœnia atque in finu urbis
funt hoftes. Neque para-
ri neque confuli quidquam
occulte poteft ; quo ma-
gis properandum eft.
Quare ita ego cenfeo :
cum nefario confilio fce-
leratorum civium refpub-
lica in maxuma pericula
venerit, hique indicio T.
Volturcii & legatorum
Allobrogum convicti, con-
feffique fint, cædem, in-
cendia, aliaq; fœda atq;
crudelia facinora in civis
patriamque paraviffe ; de
confeffis, ficuti de mani-
feftis rerum capitalium,
more majorum fuppliçium
fumendum.

Pardon the youth of Cethegus, if
this be not the fecond time he has
made war upon his country. For
what need I fay any thing of Gabinius, Statilius, and Cœparius?
who, if they had had but the
leaft confideration at all, would
never have engaged in fuch defigns
againft the publick. Finally, fathers, if there was in this cafe
room for mifconduct, I could eafily fuffer you to be fet right by
the event, fince you regard not
words. But we are pufhed home on
all fides. Catiline, with an army
is juft upon us. Others of the
enemy are within our walls, and
in the midft of the city itfelf.
No preparations or confultations
of ours can be concealed from
them, and therefore we muft ufe
expedition. Wherefore my fentence is this : Since the ftate has
been brought into the utmoft
danger by the villainous contrivance of fome wicked members
of it, and thefe have been fufficiently proved guilty of the fame,
by the evidence of T. Volturcius,
and the deputies of the Allobroges, and have confeffed their being concerned in a defign to affaffinate divers gentlemen, and
fire the city, and to commit various other difmal and cruel crimes
againft their fellow-citizens and
country, my fentence, I fay, is,
that they be punifhed according to
antient ufage, as being, by their
own confeffion, manifeftly guilty
of crimes worthy of death.

LVII.

LVII. Poftquam Cato adfedit ; confulares omnes, itemque fenati magna pars, fententiam ejus laudant, virtutem animi ad cœlum ferunt. Alii alios increpantes timidos vocant. Cato clarus atque magnus habetur. Senati decretum fit, ficut ille cenfuerat. Sed mihi, multa legenti, multa audienti, quæ populus Romanus domi militiæque, mari atque terra præclara facinora fecit, forte lubuit attendere, quæ res maxume tanta negotia fuftinuiffet. Sciebam fæpenumero parva manu cum magnis legionibus hoftium contendiffe. Cognoveram parvis copiis beila gefta cum opulentis regibus ; ad hoc, fæpe fortunæ violentiam tolerafle ; facundia Græcos, gloria belli Gallos ante Romanos fuiffe. Ac mihi multa agitanti conftabat, paucorum civium egregiam virtutem cuncta patravifle ; eoque factum, uti divitias paupertas, multitudinem paucitas fuperaret. Sed poftquam luxu atque defidia civitas corrupta eft ; rurfus refpublica magnitudine fua imperatorum atque magiftratuum vitia fuftentabat ; ac, veluti effœta parente, multis tempeftati-

LVII. *After Cato fat down, all the confular gentlemen, with the greateft part of the reft, applaud his fentence, and extol his refolution to the heavens, upbraiding and calling one another cowards, but magnifying and celebrating Cato for a hero. Accordingly a vote paffed conformable to his advice. Now, as I have read and heard much of the noble atchievements of the Roman people, both in peace and war, by fea and by land, I had a mind to make a ftrict enquiry into the true fpring of all their mighty fuccefs. I was fenfible, they had oftentimes with a handful of men engaged vaft armies of their enemies. I was not ignorant, they had carried on wars againft mighty princes with fmall forces ; and befides, had oftentimes felt the fevereft ftrokes of ill fortune ; that the Greeks were fuperior to them in eloquence, and the Gauls for reputation in war. Upon due confideration I found, that the prodigious bravery and conduct of a few fine men did all, and was the true caufe that poverty prevailed againft riches, and fmall numbers againft great. But after the city became debauched with luxury and idlenefs, ftill the commonwealth, by reafon of its grandeur, was able to bear up under all the vices of its commanders and magiftrates ; but yet Rome, like a woman effete with the production of a numerous brood, did not for a long time produce fo much as one man of any extraordinary character. But within the compafs of my own times, we have*

H 2

bus

bus haud fane quifquam Romæ virtute magnus fuit. Sed, memoria mea, ingenti virtute, diverfis moribus fuere viri duo, M. Cato, & C. Cæfar; quos, quoniam res obtulerat, filentio præterire non fuit confilium ; quin utriufque naturam & mores, quantum ingenio poffem, aperirem. Igitur his genus, ætas, eloquentia prope æqualia fuere. Magnitudo animi par, item gloria ; fed alia alii. Cæfar beneficiis ac munificentia magnus habebatur ; integritate vitæ Cato. Ille manfuetudine & mifericordia clarus factus ; huic feveritas dignitatem addiderat. Cæfar dando, fublevando, ignofcendo ; Cato, nihil largiundo, gloriam adeptus eft. In altero miferis perfugium ; in altero malis pernicies. Illius facilitas, hujus conftantia, laudabatur. Poftremo Cæfar in animum induxerat laborare, vigilare ; negotiis amicorum intentus, fua negligere ; nihil denegare, quod dono dignum effet ; fibi magnum imperium, exercitum, bellum novum exoptabat, ubi virtus enitefcere poffet. At Catoni ftudium modefliæ, decoris ; fed maxume feveritatis erat. Non divitiis cum divite,

had two perfons of huge abilities, but quite different difpofitions, M. Cato and C. Cæfar, whom I was not willing to pafs flightly by, fince fo fair an opportunity prefented of enlarging upon their charaders, They were pretty much upon a par, with refpeð to their extradion, age, and eloquence. They had both the fame greatnefs of foul, with an equal fhare of glory, but of a different kind. Cæfar was celebrated for a boundlefs and noble generofity ; Cato for the integrity of his life. The former became famous by his mildnefs and mercy ; his feverity gave a mighty reputation to the latter. Cæfar acquired glory by the praðice of generofity, compaffion, and clemency ; Cato by refufing to wafte his fubftance in bribing the people. In one there was a fure refuge for the miferable ; in the other certain deftruðion for the wicked. The eafinefs of the former was admired ; the fteady refolution of the latter. Finally, Cæfar was laborious, vigilant, intent upon all occafions of ferving his friends, to the negleð of his own concerns ; denied no body any thing that was worth their acceptance, and fought nothing for himfelf but the command of an army, with a new war, in order to difplay his vaft abilities to the world. Cato was a lover of moderation, decency, and, above all, ftrið difcipline. He did not vie with the rich in riches, nor in faðion with the faðious, but in bravery with the brave, in modefty with the modeft, and in juftice with the

neque

neque factione cum factioso; sed cum strenuo virtute, cum modesto pudore, cum innocente abstinentia certabat. Esse, quo minus gloriam petebat, eo magis illum adsequebatur.

innocent. He chose rather to be good, than appear so; and therefore the less he sought after glory, the more it followed him. quam videri, bonus malebat. Ita-

LVIII. Postquam uti dixi, senatus in Catonis sententiam discessit; consul optumum factu ratus, noctem, quæ instabat, antecapere, ne quid eo spatio novaretur, triumviros, quæ supplicium postulabat, parare jubet. Ipse, præsidiis dispositis, Lentulum in carcerem deducit. Idem fit cæteris per prætores. Est in carcere locus quod Tullianum appellatur, ubi paullulum ascenderis ad lævam, circiter XII. pedes humi depressus. Eum muniunt undique parietes, atque insuper camera lapideis fornicibus vincta; sed inculto, tenebris, odore fœdo, atque terribilis ejus facies. In eum locum postquam demissus est Lentulus; vindices rerum capitalium, quibus præceptum erat, laqueo gulam fregere. Ita ille patricius, ex gente clarissuma Corneliorum, qui consulare imperium Romæ habuerat, dignum moribus factisque suis exitum vitæ invenit. De Cethego, Statilio, Gabinio, Cœpario, eodem modo supplicium sumptum est.

LVIII. *After the senate, as I have said, gave into Cato's opinion, the consul thinking it the best way to have the sentence executed that very night, which was just at hand; for fear of any rising in the city, in case of delay, orders the triumviri to have all things ready for the same. He himself conducts Lentulus to prison, where he placed strong guards; whilst the prætors do the same by the rest of the conspirators. There is a place in the jail called Tullianum, upon a small rise to the left hand, as one enters, which is sunk twelve foot within the earth, secured on all sides by strong walls, and a good arch of stone above, but a nasty, dark, stinking, dismal place. As soon as Lentulus was let down into the same, the executioners appointed for the purpose strangled him. Thus did that gentleman of a patrician family, the great family of the Cornelii, who had been consul of Rome, come to an end suited to his manners and behaviour. Cethegus, Statilius, Gabinius, and Cœparius, were all punished in the same manner.*

LIX. Dum ea Romæ geruntur, Catilina ex omni copia, quam ipse

LIX. *Whilst these things are doing at Rome, Catiline formed two legions out of the troops h adduxe-*

adduxerat et Manlius habuerat, duas legiones inftituit, cohortes pro numero militum complet. Dein uti quifque voluntarius aut ex fociis in caftra venerat, æqualiter diftribuerat; ac brevi fpatio legiones numero hominum expleverat; cum initio non amplius duobus millibus habuiffet. Sed ex omni copia circiter pars quarta erat militaribus armis inftructa. Cæteri, ut quemque cafus armaverat, fparos aut lanceas, alii præacutas fudes portabant. Sed poftquam Antonius cum exercitu adventabat, Catilina per montis iter facere ; modo ad urbem, modo in Galliam verfus caftra movere ; hoftibus occafionem pugnandi non dare. Sperabat propediem magnas copias fe habiturum, fi Romæ focii incepta patraviffent. Interea fervitia repudiabat, cujus initio ad eum magnæ copiæ concurrebant, opibus conjurationis fretus; fimul alienum fuis rationibus exiftumans, videri caufam civium cum fervis fugitivis communicaffe. Sed poftquam in caftra nuncius pervenit, Romæ conjurationem patefactam, de Lentulo, & Cethego, cæterifque, quos fupra memoravi, fuppli-

had brought with him, and thofe of Manlius together, and makes up his battalions according to the number of his men ; and then as any voluntiers, or thofe that had before engaged in the plot, came in, he difpofed of them equally among his troops ; and in a fhort time made his legions full as to number, though he had not at firft above two thoufand men. Of thefe, about a fourth part were completely armed; the reft, as it happened, had fpears or lances, and fome only fharp ftakes. But after the approach of Anthony with his army, Catiline took to the mountains, and one while made a movement towards Rome, and then again towards Gaul ; but would give the enemy no opportunity of battle. He hoped he fhould fpeedily have a vaft army, if his fellows did but fucceed in the execution of their defigns in town. In the mean time, he refufed the flaves that came in to him at firft in great numbers, depending upon the ftrength of the confpiracy ; and at the fame time not thinking it confiftent with his pretenfions, to appear to jumble freemen and flaves together in the fame intereft. But after news arrived in the camp, that a full difcovery had been made of the confpiracy at Rome ; that Lentulus, Cethegus, and the reft mentioned above, had been all put to death, moft of Catiline's men, whom the hopes of plunder, or the love of change, had tempted to the war, flipt away. The reft Catiline led by great marches through craggy mountains, into

cium

cium fumptum, plerique, quos ad bellum fpes rapinarum, aut novarum rerum ftudium illexerat, dilabuntur. Reliquos Catilina per montis afperos magnis itineribus in agrum Piftorienfem abducit; eo confilio, uti per tramites occulte profugeret in Galliam Tranfalpinam. At Q. Metellus Celer cum tribus legionibus in agro Piceno præfidebat; ex difficultate rerum eadem illa exiftumans, quæ fupra diximus, Catilinam agitare. Igitur, ubi iter ejus ex perfugis cognovit, caftra propere movit, ac fub ipfis· radicibus montium confedit, qua illi defcenfus erat in Galliam properanti. Neque tamen Antonius longe aberat ; utpote qui magno exercitu locis æquioribus expeditos in fugam fequeretur. Sed Catilina, poft quam vidit montibus atque copiis hoftium fefe claufum, in urbe res adverfas, neque fugæ neque præfidii ullam fpem, optumum factu ratus in tali re fortunam belli tentare, ftatuit cum Antonio quam primum confligere. Itaque, concione advocata, hujufcemodi orationem habuit.

LX. *Compertum ego habeo, milites, verba viris virtutem non addere ; neque ex ignavo ftrenuum, neque fortem ex timido exercitum oratione imperatoris fieri. Quanta cujufque animo audacia natura aut moribus ineft,*

the neighbourhood of Piftorium, in order to make his way privately through fome narrow defiles into Tranfalpine Gaul. But Q. Metellus Celer was pofted with three legions in the territory of Picene, who gueffed by the ftreights Catiline was in, he had fuch a defign, as has been mentioned, in view. Wherefore, being informed by fome deferters from him, of the rout he had taken, he immediately march'd away, and encamp'd at the bottom of the mountains, where he was to pafs into Gaul. Nor was Anthony far off, who purfued the enemy flying with little or no baggage, with a good army, along the low country. But Catiline finding himfelf inclofed by the mountains, and the enemy's troops together, that all went wrong in the city, and that there were no hopes either of flight or defence within walls, thinking it the beft way in fuch a cafe, to try the fortune of a battle, he refolv'd to engage Anthony as foon as poffible. Wherefore, calling his army together, he made them a fpeech to the following purpofe.

LX. I am very fenfible, gentlemen, that words cannot infpire courage, and that an army of lubbers will never become vigorous and active, or of cowards brave, by any thing a general can fay to them. Juft as much courage as nature or ufe has given a man, will he fhew in time of bat-

H 4 *tanta*

*tanta in bello patere folet.
Quem neque gloria neque
pericula excitant, nequicquam hortere. Timor ani-
mi auribus officit. Sed ego
vos, quo pauca monerem,
advocavi; fimul uti cauf-
fam confilii mei aperirem.
Scitis equidem, milites,
focordia atque ignavia
Lentuli, quantam ipfi no-
bifque cladem adtulerit;
quoque modo, dum ex ur-
be præfidia opperior, in
Galliam proficifci nequi-
verim. Nunc vero, quo
in loco res nostræ stant,
juxta mecum omnes intelli-
gitis.*

LXI. *Exercitus hofti-
um duo, unus ab urbe,
alter a Gallia obftant.
Diutius in his locis effe, fi
maxume animus ferat,
frumenti atque aliarum
rerum egeftas prohibet.
Quocumque ire placet,
ferro iter aperiundum eft.
Quapropter vos moneo,
uti forti atque parato animo fitis; &, cum præli-
um inibitis, memineri-
tis, vos divitias, decus,
gloriam, præterea liber-
tatem, atque patriam, in
dextris veftris portare.
Si vincimus, omnia nobis
tuta erunt; commeatus
abunde, municipia atque
coloniæ patebunt. Sin me-
tu cefferimus, eadem illa
advorfa fient; neque lo-
cus neque amicus quifquam
teget, quem arma non*

tle. 'Tis in vain to encourage
one, whom neither glory nor danger can work upon; his fear pre-
vents all attention to what you
fay. I have therefore called you
together, only to give you a little
advice, and acquaint you with the
reafons of my proceedings. You
know full well, gentlemen, what
mifchief the dulnefs and inactivity of Lentulus has brought upon
himfelf and us all; and how,
whilft I wait here for reinforce-
ments from town, I have been
prevented from getting into Gaul.
Now you are all as fenfible as I
myfelf, of the ftate of our affairs.

LXI. We have two armies upon us, one from Rome, and another from Gaul. The want of
corn, and other neceffaries, will
not allow of our continuance here,
tho' we never fo much defired it.
And whitherfoever we think of
marching, we muft make our way
with the fword. Wherefore be
bold and refolute, and when you
engage, confider that you carry
riches, honour, glory, liberty,
and your country, in your right
hands. If we conquer, all will
be fafe; we fhall have plenty of
provifions, and the boroughs and
colonies all at our devotion. But
if we flinch thro' fear, our cafe
will be the reverfe. No place or
friend will be able to fecure him,
whom arms could not. Befides,
gentlemen, there is not the fame
neceffity incumbent upon us and
them We fight for our country,
liberty, and lives; they to ad-
texe-

exerint. Præterea, mi-
ites, non eadem nobis &
llis necessitudo impendet.
Vos pro patria, pro liber-
ate, pro vita certamus.
Illis supervacaneum est
ro potentia paucorum
ugnare ; quo audacius
geredimini, memores pri-
inæ virtutis. Licuit
otis cum summa turpi-
udine in exsilio ætatem
gere. Potuistis nonnul-
Romæ, amissis bonis,
lienas opes expectare.
Quia illa fœda atque in-
leranda viris videban-
ir, hæc sequi decrevi-
is. Si hæc relinquere
ultis, audacia opus est.
Jemo, nisi victor, pace
illum mutavit. Nam
i fuga salutem sperare,
im arma, quis corpus te-
itur, ab hostibus aver-
ris, ea vero dementia
?. Semper in prælio iis
iaxumum est periculum,
ui maxume timent. Au-
acia pro muro habetur.
ium vos considero, mili-
is, & cum facta vestra
stumo, magna me spes
ictoriæ tenet. Animus,
etas, virtus vestra me
ortantur ; præterea ne-
cessitudo, quæ etiam timi-
os fortis facit. Nam,
ultitudo hostium ne cir-
umvenire queat, prohib-
ent angustiæ loci. Quod

vance the power of a few, which
they have no need to do ; which
should encourage you to fall on
bravely, mindful of your former
courage. We might have lived in
banishment, but with the utmost
disgrace. Some of you too might
have lived at Rome in a starving
condition, and a state of dependance. But because those things
appeared dishonourable and intolerable to brave men, you resolved
upon the part you now act. And
if you desire to get out of your
present ill circumstances, courage
is the only way to it. None but
conquerors ever change war for
peace. For to expect security in
flight, when the arms that should
secure a man are turned from the
enemy, is madness. The most
timorous are always in the most
danger in time of battle. Valour
is a wall of defence. When I
consider you, and your gallant
behaviour, gentlemen, I am in
great hopes of victory. Your
spirit, youth, and courage, give
me heart ; as also the necessity
you are under, which makes cowards brave. For the narrowness
of the place we are to engage in,
secures us against being surround-
ed by the enemy's numbers But
if fortune envy your bravery, be
sure you fall not unrevenged Suffer not yourselves to be taken and
slaughtered like cattle ; but fight
like men rather, and leave the
enemy a bloody, and a sorrowful
victory.

i virtuti vestræ fortuna inviderit, cavete, ne inulti animam
mittatis ; neve capti potius, sicuti pecora, trucidemini, quam
irorum more pugnantes, cruentem atque luctuosam victoriam
hostibus relinquatis. LXII.

LXII. Hæc ubi dixit, paullulum commoratus ſigna canere jubet ; atque inſtruĉtos ordines in locum æquum deducit. Dein, remotis omnium equis, quo militibus, exæquato periculo, animus amplior eſſet, ipſe pedes exercitum pro loco atque copiis inſtruit. Nam, uti planities erat inter finiſtros montis, & ad dextera rupes aſpera, oĉto cohortis in fronte conſtituit ; reliqua ſigna in ſubſidiis arĉtius collocat. Ab his centuriones omnis, & evocatos, præterea ex gregariis militibus optumum quemque armatum in primam aciem ſubducit. C. Manlium in dextra, Fæſulanum quendam in ſiniſtra parte curare jubet. Ipſe cum libertis & colonis propter aquilam adſiſtit, quam bello Cimbrico C. Marius in exercitu habuiſſe dicebatur. At ex altera parte C. Antonius, pedibus æger, quod prælio adeſſe nequibat, M. Petrejo legato exercitum permittit. Ille cohortis veteranas, quas tumulti cauſſa conſcripſerat, in fronte ; poſt eas cæterum exercitum in ſubſidiis locat. Ipſe, equo circumiens, unumquemque nominans, appellat, hortatur, rogat, *uti meminerint ſe*

LXII. *Soon after the delivery of this ſpeech, he commanded the ſignal to be given for battle, and draws down his troops in proper order upon a ground commodiou. for him; and then having ordered all the horſes away, to put the more reſolution into his men by making the danger of all alike, he being himſelf on foot, marſhals his arm. as the nature of the place and the number of his men required For as the plain had on the left mountain, and on the right a craggy rock, he drew up eight battali ons in front, and the reſt he place cloſe in the rear, to relieve them upon occaſions. But he calle from amongſt them all the choice centurions and other old ſoldier. even common ſoldiers too, an poſted them in the foremoſt ran. He appoints C. Manlius to command on the right, and an of ficer of Fæſulæ on the left. F with his freed-men, and ſome Sulla's old ſoldiers that had ſettl in thoſe parts, took up his ſtand. the eagle, which, it was ſaid, (Marius had in his army in t. Cimbrick war. On the other ſia C. Antonius being rendered, by fit of the gout, incapable of takii the command himſelf upon this o caſion, commiſſioned his lieutenan general M. Petreius to ſupply l place. Accordingly he poſts the c battalions, which he had draw together upon the account of th rebellion, in the front, and behi them the reſt of the army, to rei force them if need required. I riding about, and calling upon men, here and there by name, ai*
cont

ntra latrones inermis, 'o patria, pro liberis, 'o aris atque focis fuis rtare. Homo militaris, ıod amplius annos tri- inta tribunus aut præ- :ctus, aut legatus, aut ·ætor, cum magna glo- a in exercitu fuerat, ple- ıfque ipfos, factaque eo- ım fortia noverat, ea ımmemorando militum ıimos accendebat.

mates, encourages, and begs of them, to confider that they were now to fight againft a parcel of unarmed robbers, for their coun- try, their children, and their all. *And as he had led the life of a fol- dier, having been employed in the military fervice with great repu- tation, for above thirty years toge- ther, as tribune, commander of horfe, lieutenant-general, or præ- tor, he was acquainted with moft of the foldiers, and the brave ac- tions they had performed, by taking notice of which, he very much raifed their courage.*

LXIII. Sed ubi, om- bus rebus exploratis, :trejus tuba fignum dat, ıhortis paullatim ince- :re jubet. Idem fecit ıftium exercitus. Poft- ıam eo ventum eft, un- : a ferentariis prælium ımmitti poffet ; maxu- o clamore infeftis fignis ıncurrunt ; pila omit- nt ; gladiis res geritur. eterani priftinæ virtu- memores, cominus riter inftare ; illi haud nidi refiftunt. Maxuma certatur. Interea Ca- ina cum expeditis in ima acie verfari ; la- ırantibus fuccurrere ; tegros pro fauciis accer- re ; omnia providere ; ultum ipfe pugnare, :pe hoftem ferire. Stre- ıi militis & boni impe- toris officia fimul cxfe- ıebatur. Petrejus, ubi det Catilinam, contra

LXIII. *After a thorough in- fpection into the difpofition of his troops, Petreius orders the fignal to be founded, and the battalions to advance flowly, whilft the ene- my's army does the fame. After they came near enough for the light-armed foldiers to begin the fight, both fides fall to work with a very great fhout, fword in hand, without making ufe of their fhort lances. The veterans mindful of their former bravery, engage the enemy in clofe fight with great fury ; whilft they make as gallant a refiftance, fo that a very defpe- rate battle enfued. In which Ca- tiline, with a detached party, moved about in the firft line, re- lieving the diftreffed, bringing up frefh men to fupply the place of the wounded, and providing for all exigencies ; fighting himfelf too in perfon very often, and performing at once all the duties of a ftout foldier, and a good commander. Petreius finding Catiline, contra- ry to his expectations, ftand to it*

ac ratus erat, magna vi tendere, cohortem prætoriam in medios hostis inducit ; eosque perturbatos, atque alios alibi resistentis interficit. Deinde utrimque ex lateribus cæteros aggreditur. Manlius & Fæsulanus in primis pugnantes cadunt. Postquam fusas copias, seque cum paucis relictum videt Catilina, memor generis atque pristinæ dignitatis suæ, in confertissumos hostis incurrit, ibique pugnans confoditur.

LXIV. Sed, confecto prælio, tum vero cerneres, quanta audacia, quantaque animi vis fuisset in exercitu Catilinæ. Nam fere, quem quisque vivus pugnando locum ceperat, eum, amissa anima, corpore tegebat. Pauci autem, quos medios cohors prætoria disjecerat, paullo diversus, sed omnes tamen adversus vulneribus, conciderant. Catilina vero longe a suis inter hostium cadavera repertus est, paullulum etiam spirans, ferociamque animi, quam habuerat vivus, in vultu retinens. Postremo, ex omni copia, neque in prælio, neque in fuga, quisquam civis ingenuus captus est. Ita cuncti suæ hostiumque vitæ juxta pepecerant. Neque tamen exercitus populi Ro-

with great obstinacy, the general's own sele upon their main body, broke them ; and tho' again, and faced abou here and there, yet h slaughter of them. A he attacks the rest upo Manlius and the Fæ amongst the first that line seeing his forces himself left with a that stood by him, re his family, and forn rushed in amongst th the enemy, and was fighting to the last.

LXIV. After the ended, you might hav tokens of the despe and spirit in the army They were generally upon the very spot they in at the beginning o Some few only of th which had been broken ral's guard, fell s and there at a little all with wounds befor tiline himself was fou distance from the rest, heaps of the slaugh not quite dead, and his looks his wont Finally, out of all not so much as one m quality of a slave, wa in the battle, or in that they seemed to their own lives, as li the enemy. Nor ha of the republick much joice in their victory very bloody one. Fo

ani lætam aut incruen-
m victoriam adeptus
at. Nam ftrenuiffumus
iifque aut occiderat in
ælio, aut graviter vul-
eratus difcefferat. Multi
item, qui e caftris vi-
ndi, aut fpoliandi gra-
a procefferant, volventes
oftilia cadavera amicum
ii, pars hofpitem aut
ognatum reperiebant. Fuere item, qui inimicos fuos cog-
ofcerent. Ita varie per omnem exercitum lætitia, mœror,
ictus atque gaudia agitabantur.

among them were all, either flain, or defperately wounded. Many that came out of the camp to view the field of battle, or plunder the flain, in tumbling over the dead bodies, fome found a friend, others a relation; and fome too light upon their enemies. So that there was throughout the whole army a ftrange mixture of mirth and forrow mourning and joy.

C. CRISPI

C. CRISPI SALLUSTII

JUGURTHA:

SIVE

BELLUM JUGURTHINUM.

FALSO queritur de natura sua genus humanum, quod imbecille atque ævi brevis, forte potius, quam virtute, regatur. Nam contra reputando, neque majus aliud, neque præstabilius invenias, magisque naturæ induftriam, hominum, quam vim aut tempus, deeſſe. Sed dux atque imperator vitæ mortalium animus eſt ; qui, ubi ad gloriam virtutis via graſſatur, abunde pollens, potenſque, & clarus eſt neque fortuna eget ; quippe quæ probitatem, induftriam, aliaſque artis bonas neque dare, neque eripere cuiquam poteſt. Sin captus pravis cupidinibus, ad inertiam & voluptates corporis peſſum datus eſt, pernicioſa lubidine paulliſper u-

Mankind complain of their nature without cauſe, as infirm and ſhort-lived, and more under the direction of chance than virtue. But upon conſidering the human frame in a different view, you will find nothing in the world more great and excellent ; and that men want induſtry more than abilities or time. Now the ſoul is the leader and commander in the life of man, which, whilſt it purſues glory in the way of virtue, is abundantly vigorous, able, and glorious, and ſtands in no need of fortune's help ; as who can neither give nor take away from any one probity, induſtry, or other good qualities. But if the mind, captivated by wicked luſts, ſinks into idleneſs and pleaſure, after it has for a while indulged its humour, to the ruin of its own vigour, and that of the body, beſides loſs of time, the weakneſs of human nature is blamed for it ; as people of ill conduct

ſus

rdiam
enium
infir-
Suam
&ores
erunt.
s bo-
cura
) alie-
utura,
:ulofa,
geren-
gerent
nitudinis procederent, ubi pro mortalibus
t.

us ho-
n ex
t ; ita
e cm-
alia,
m fe-
eclara
æ, ad
& alia
brevi
ngenii
ficuti
funt.
is &
i, uti
:, om-
nt, &
iimus,
s, rec-
s, agit
a ne-
Quo
m ad-
dediti
:r lux-
i æta-
m, in-
nelius,
ud in

are apt to transfer all blame from themselves upon the circumstances of affairs they are engaged in. Now if men were but as much concerned for things truly good, as they are for what are otherwise, and can avail them nothing, nay are really very dangerous, they would not be so much governed by chance, as over-rule it ; and arrive at that grandeur, as instead of being mortal, to live for ever in the records of fame.

II. For as man is made of two parts, body and soul; so all our concerns and pursuits have a near affinity with the nature of the one, or the other. Thus beauty, riches, and strength, with other things of the like kind, are soon gone ; but the noble productions of the mind are, like the mind itself, immortal. Finally, the goods of the body and fortune, as they have a beginning, so have they likewise an end ; and all things that rise, set ; and such as grow, grow old too. But the soul suffers no decay, is eternal, the guide of man, acts and possesses all things ; but is itself out of the power of every thing else. How wonderful is their weakness then, who give themselves up to sensual enjoyments, and spend their lives in luxury and idleness ; but suffer their minds, the best and the greatest thing in human nature, to lie fallow, without any cultivation or care at all of it ! especially, when there are so many, and such various ways of employ-
na-

natura mortalium eft, in-
cultu atque focordia tor-
pefcere finunt ; cum præfertim tam multæ variæque fint artes
animi, quibus fumma claritudo paratur.

III. Verum ex his ma-
giftratus & imperia, po-
ftremo omnis cura rerum
publicarum, minume mi-
hi hac tempeftate cupi-
unda videntur. Quoniam
neque virtuti honos da-
tur ; neque illi, quibus
per fraudem jus fuit, tuti,
aut eo magis honefti funt.
Nam, vi quidem regere
patriam aut parentes,
quamquam & poffis, &
delicta corrigas, tamen
importunum eft, cum
præfertim omnes rerum
mutationes cædem, fu-
gam, alia hoftilia porten-
dant. Fruftra autem niti,
neque aliud, fe fatigan-
do, nifi odium quærere,
extremæ dementiæ eft ;
nifi forte quem inhonefta
& perniciofa lubido tenet,
potentiæ paucorum decus
atque libertatem fuam
gratificari.

IV. Cæterum ex iis
negotiis, quæ ingenio ex-
ercentur, in primis mag-
no ufui eft memoria re-
rum geftarum. Cujus de
virtute quia multi dixere,
prætereundum puto ; fi-
mul, ne per infolentiam
quis exiftumet memet
ftudium meum laudando
extollere. Atque ego cre-
do fore, qui, quia decrevi

ing the mind, whereby a man may
render his name immortal.

III. But of thefe feveral ways,
offices civil and military, in fhort,
all publick places of truft and
power whatever, feem at this
time not at all defireable ; when
virtue has no regard paid it ; and
thofe who by bafe arts obtain them,
are not therefore more fecure or
honourable at all. For to govern
your country or parents in the way
of violence, tho' you have it in
your power, and may perhaps rec-
tify fome things that are amifs in
them, is however very vexatious ;
efpecially fince all revolutions are
fure to be attended with the mur-
ther and banifhment of great
numbers, and other calamities of
war. Now for a man to take a
world of pains to no purpofe, and
to get nothing by all his fatigue,
but to be hated by the world i.
meer madnefs, and what non
would furely be guilty of, but thof
of a humour bafe and perniciou.
enough, to facrifice their honour
and liberty both to the power of a
few.

IV. But of all the ways of em
ploying a man's parts, that of writ
ing hiftory feems to be of fingula
ufe. But this is fo beaten a fub
ject that I fhould fay nothing of it
and the rather leaft any one fhoul
think I magnified my own employ
ment, out of vanity only. An
as I have determined to decline a
preferment in the ftate, I doub
there will be fome ready to giv
the name of idlenefs to the ufefu
procu

procul a republica æta-
tem agere, tanto tamque
utili labori meo nomen
inertiæ imponant : certe,
quibus maxuma induftria
videtur, falutare plebem
& conviviis gratiam quæ-
rere. Qui fi reputaverint,
& quibus ego temporibus
magiftratum adeptus fim ;
& quales viri idem adfe-
qui nequiverint ; & po-
ftea, quæ genera homi-
num in fenatum perve-
nerint ; profecto exiftu-
mabunt, me magis meri-
to, quam ignavia, judici-
um animi mei mutaviffe ;
majufque commodum ex
otio meo, quam ex alio-
rum negotiis, reipublicæ
venturum. Nam fæpe
audivi, Q. Maxumum,
P. Scipionem, præterea
civitatis noftræ præclaros
viros folitos ita dicere,
*Cum majorum imagines
intuerentur, vehementif-
fume fibi animum ad vir-
tutem accendi.* Scilicet,
non ceram illam, neque
figuram, tantam vim in
fefe habere ; fed memoria
rerum geftarum eam
flammam egregiis viris in
pectore crefcere ; neque
prius fedari, quam virtus
eorum famam atque glo-
riam adæquaverit. At
contra, quis eft omnium,
his moribus, quin divitiis
& fumptibus, non probi-
tate, neque induftria, cum
majoribus fuis contendat ?

*way of life I have chofen ; fuch I
mean, who think the greateft induftry is fhewn in complimenting
and treating the mob. Who, if
they would but confider in what
times I was preferred in the government, and what confiderable
men mifcarried in their endeavours
to that purpofe, and what fort of
men have fince got into the fenate,
will certainly think that I altered my mind upon very good reafon, and not from a love of idlenefs ; and that the publick will receive greater advantages from my
declining of bufinefs, than from
others engaging therein. For I
have often heard, that Q. Maxi-
mus, Publius Scipio, and other
perfons of great figure in the government, ufed to fay, that, when
they looked upon the images of
their anceftors, their minds were
fired to the laft degree with an
emulation of their noble behaviour. Now, to be fure, the wax,
or its figure, had no fuch efficacy
in it ; but it was the reflection
upon their great actions, which
raifed that flame in the breafts of
thofe excellent men, and gave them
no quiet, 'till they arrived at the
fame height of reputation and glory
with their anceftors. But what
perfon have we, as the times now
go, that is not much more concerned to outftrip his forefathers
in riches and prodigality than
probity and induftry. Nay, gentlemen of low rank, who before
ufed by their good qualities to raife
themfelves above the nobles, now
endeavour to get into places of
power and truft, by underhand*

I   Etiam

Etiam homines novi, qui antea per virtutem soliti erant nobilitatem antevenire, furtim & per latrocinia potius, quam bonis artibus, ad imperia & honores nituntur. Proinde quasi praetura & consulatus, atque alia omnia hujuscemodi per se ipsa clara & magnifica sint, ac non perinde habeantur, ut eorum, qui ea sustinent, virtus est. Verum ego liberius altiusque processi, dum me civitatis morum piget taedetque. Nunc ad inceptum redeo.

V. Bellum scripturus sum, quod populus Romanus cum Jugurtha rege Numidarum gessit; primum, quia magnum & atrox, variaque victoria fuit; dein, quia tum primum superbiae nobilitatis obviam itum est; quae contentio divina & humana cuncta permiscuit; eoque vecordiae processit, uti studiis civilibus bellum atque vastitas Italiae finem facerent. Sed prius, quam hujuscemodi rei initium expedio, pauca supra repetam; quo, ad cognoscendum, omnia illustria magis, magisque in aperto sint. Bello Punico secundo, quo dux Carthaginiensium, Hannibal, post magnitudinem nominis Romani, Italiae opes maxume attriverat, Masinissa rex Numidarum, in amicitiam receptus a P. Scipione, cui

tricks and rogueries, more than laudable accomplishments. As if the praetorship, consulship, and other the like offices, were in themselves glorious and honourable, and not rendered such only by the good behaviour of those that enjoy them. But I have run out too freely, and too far upon this subject, out of pure indignation against the corruption of the times. Now I return to my purpose.

V. Which is to write the history of the war the Roman people had with Jugurtha, king of the Numidians; first, because it was a great and a terrible one, full of various turns of fortune; and secondly too, because then was the first stand made against the insolence of the nobility; which dispute confounded all things, both divine and human; and was carried to that height of madness that nothing but a war, and the desolation of Italy, could put an end to it. But before I enter upon this subject I must run back a little, in order to set the whole in a proper light. In the second Punick war, wherein Hannibal, general of the Carthaginians, gave the greatest shock of all others to the Roman grandeur, by a terrible devastation of Italy, Masinissa king of the Numidians, being received into the Roman alliance, by P. Scipio, afterwards firnamed Africanus, upon account of his putting a happy conclusion to that war, had distinguished himself b
postel

poſtea Africano cogno-
men ex virtute fuit, mul-
ta & præclara rei militaris
facinora fecerat. Obquæ,
victis Carthaginienſibus,
& capto Syphace, cujus
in Africa magnum atque
late imperium valuit, po-
pulus Romanus quaſ-
cumque urbis & agros
manu ceperat, regi dono
dedit. Igitur amicitia
Maſiniſſa bona atque ho-
neſta nobis permanſit Sed
imperii vitæque ejus finis
dem fuit. Dein Micipſa
ſilius regnum ſolus obti-
nuit, Maſtanabale &
Guluſſa fratribus morbo
ibſumptis. Is Atherba-
em & Hiempſalem ex
eſe genuit ; Jugurtham-
que filium Maſtanabalis
ſratris, quem Maſiniſſa,
quod ortus ex concubina
erat, privatum reliquerat,
eodem cultu, quo liberos
ſuos, domi habuit.

VI. Qui, ubi primum
adolevit, pollens viribus,
decora facie, ſed multo
maxume ingenio validus,
non ſe luxu neque inertiæ
corrumpendum dedit ;
ſed, uti mos gentis illius
eſt, equitare, jaculari,
curſu cum æqualibus cer-
tare ; &, cum omnis glo-
ria anteiret, omnibus ta-
men carus eſſe. Ad hoc,
pleraque tempora in ve-
nando agere ; leonem at-
que alias feras primus aut
in primis ferire ; pluri-

many brave and gallant actions :
in conſideration of which, after
the Carthaginians were conquered,
and Syphax taken, who was maſter of a great and powerful kingdom in Africa, the Roman people
made a preſent of all the cities
and territory they had taken to
king Maſiniſſa ; for which bounty
he was ever after a faſt and
faithful ally to us, continuing in
the enjoyment of his dominions 'till
his death. After which, they fell
into the hands of his ſon Micipſa,
his two brothers Maſtanabal and
Guluſſa, having died ſome time before. He had two ſons, Atherbal
and Hiempſal ; but neverthelſs
educated in his own court, and in
the ſame manner as his own ſons,
Jugurtha, the ſon of his brother
Maſtanabal, whom, as being be-
got of a concubine, Maſiniſſa had
left in the condition of a private
perſon.

VI. This youth, when he came
to man's eſtate, being conſpicuous
for ſtrength of body, handſomeneſs
of perſon, and great parts, did
not give himſelf up to luxury and
idleneſs : but, according to the
faſhion of his country, exerciſed
himſelf in riding, throwing the
lance, and racing ; in which exer-
ciſes though he was much ſuperior to
all his fellows, yet he was never-
theleſs exceedingly and univerſally
beloved by them. Beſides, he ſpent
moſt of his time in hunting. He
was ſure to be the firſt, or among
the foremoſt, in the encountering of

I 2   mium

mum· facere, & minu-
mum ipfe de fe loqui.
Quibus rebus Micipfa,
tametfi initio lætus fue-
rat, exiftumans virtutem
Jugurthæ regno fuo glo-
riæ fore, tamen, poft-
quam hominem adolef-
centem, exacta ætate fua,
& parvis liberis, magis
magifque crefcere intelligit, vehementer eo nego-
tio permotus, multa cum
animo fuo volvebat. I er-
rebat eum natura morta-
lium, avida imperii, &
præceps ad explendam
animi cupidinem ; ·præ-
terea, opportunitas fuæ
liberorumque ætatis, quæ
etiam mediocris viros fpe
prædæ tranfvorfos agit ;
ad hoc, ftudia Numida-
rum in Jugurtham accen-
fa ; ex quibus, fi talem
virum dolis interfeciffet,
ne qua feditio aut bellum
oriretur, anxius erat.

VII. His difficultatibus
circumventus, ·ubi videt,
neque per vim, neque
infidiis, opprimi poffe hominem tam acceptum po-
pularibus ; quod erat Ju-
gurtha manu promptus,
&· appetens gloriæ mili-
taris, ftatuit eum objec-
tare periculis, & eo mo-
do fortunam tentare.
Igitur bello Numantino
Micipfa, cum populo
Romano equitum atque
peditum auxilio mitteret,
fperans _vel oftentando

lions, and other wild beafts ; and
though he did the moft, yet he faid
the leaft of himfelf. With which
things though Micipfa was at firft
well pleafed, as looking upon the
gallant behaviour of Jugurtha as
redounding to the honour of his
kingdom ; yet, finding the young
man grow more and more in fame,
his days being now near an end,
and his children but fmall, he was
very much affected, and full of
perplexity about him. The nature
of man, greedy of power, and difpofed at any rate to gratify that
paffion, alarmed him ; but efpecially the opportunity which his own
age, and that of his children, gave
him ; a temptation that is apt to
lead men, otherwife not ambitious
aftray. But what terrified him
moft of all was the vaft fondnef
the Numidians had for Jugurtha
infomuch that he feared, if h
made him away privately, it migh
occofion a general mutiny, if no
a war.

VII. Perplexed with thefe dif
ficulties, and finding it impracti
cable to take him off, either b
open force, or fecret contrivance
confidering how popular he wa:
he refolved to try how favourab.
fortune might prove to him i
another way, that is, by expofin
him to dangers. For he was a
tive in fight, and vaftly fond c
military glory. Wherefore M
cipfa being to fend fome troops c
both horfe and foot to the a,
fiftance of· the Roman people in ti
war againft Numantia, hopin.
that his defire of diftinction, c

· virtu

virtutem, vel hoftium ævitia facile eum occaſurum, præfecit Numidis quos in Hifpaniam mittebat. Sed ea res longe aliter, ac ratus erat, evenit. Nam Jugurtha, ut erat impigro atque acri ingenio, ubi naturam P. Scipionis, qui tum Romanis imperator fuit, & morem hoftium cognovit, multo labore, multaque cura, præterea modeftiſſume parendo, & ſæpe obviam eundo periculis, in tantam claritudinem brevi pervenerat, uti noftris vehementer carus, Numantinis maxumo terrori effet. Ac fane, quod difficillumum in primis eft, & prælio ftrenuus erat, & bonus confilio. Quorum alterum ex providentia timorem, alterum ex audacia temeritatem adferre plerumque folet. Igitur imperator omnis fere res afperas per Jugurtham agere, in amicis habere, magis magiſque eum indies amplecti; quippe cujus neque confilium, neque inceptum ullum fruftra erat. animi & ingenii follertia manis familiari amicitia conjunxerat.

VIII. Ea tempeftate in exercitu noftro fuere complures novi atque nobilis, quibus divitiæ bono honeftoque potiores erant, factiofi, domi po-

the fury of the enemy might prove fatal to him, he made him commander of the forces he fent into Spain. But that matter ended quite otherwife than he expected. For Jugurtha, as he was of an active enterprifing genius, upon obferving the nature of P. Scipio, and the enemy's way of managing, did, by the utmoft pains and diligence in action, as alfo by a moft fubmiſſive obedience to all orders, and frequently expofing his perfon to all dangers, in a little time become fo very famous, that he was exceedingly beloved by our men, and was very terrible to the Numantines. And, what is very difficult indeed, he was brave in action, and wife in council. One of which qualities from a forefight of danger is apt to caufe fear, and the other rafhnefs. Accordingly the general executed all defperate projects by the means of Jugurtha, received him into the number of his friends, and grew every day more fond of him, as a man whofe advice and undertakings never failed of fuccefs; to which were added a great generofity of mind, and huge dexterity of parts; by which qualities he procured himfelf an intimate friendfhip with many of the Romans.

Huc accedebat munificentia Quibus rebus fibi multos ex Romanis

VIII. There was at that time in our army a great many, both of high and low rank, who preferred riches before virtue and honour, mighty party-men, and of great intereft in their feveral coun-

I 3   tentes,

tentes, apud focios clari magis quam honesti; qui Jugurthæ non mediocrem animum pollicitando accendebant, si Micipsa rex occidisset, fore uti solus imperio Numidiæ potiretur. In ipso maxumam virtutem, Remæ omnia venalia esse. Sed postquam, Numantia deleta, P. Scipio dimittere auxilia, & ipse revorti domum decrevit, donatum atque laudatum magnifice pro concione Jugurtham in prætorium adduxit; ibique secreto monuit, uti potius publice, quam privatim, amicitiam populi Romani coleret; neu quibus largiri insueret Periculose a paucis emi, quod multorum essent. Si permanere vellet in suis artibus, ultro illi & gloriam & regnum venturum. Sin properantius pergeret, ipsum pecunia præcipitem casurum.

IX. Sic locutus, cum litteris eum. quas Micipsæ redderet, dimisit; earum sententia hæc erat. Jugurthæ tui bello Numantino longe maxuma virtus fuit. Quam rem tibi certo scio gaudio esse. Nobis ob merita sua carus est. Ut idem S. P. Q. R. sit, summa ope nitemur. Tibi quidem pro

tries; better known than esteemed among st our allies; who inflamed the ambitious soul of Jugurtha by offers of their service, telling him, That when Micipsa dropped he might easily secure the kingdom of Numidia to himself alone. He was a person of great abilities, and all things were to be sold at Rome. But when, upon the reduction of Numantia, Scipio had determined to dismiss the auxiliary troops, and return home himself, he did, in the face of the army, present Jugurtha, and applaud him in terms of the highest approbation; but afterwards, taking him into his tent, he secretly advised him, to cultivate a friendship with the Roman people, by paying his court to the government rather than private persons, and to avoid bribery; since it would be hazardous to purchase that of a few which belonged to many. If he would but continue steady in the exercise of his own good qualities, glory and a kingdom too would drop into him of themselves; but, if he was too hasty, his money would be the ruin of him.

IX. After this advice, he dismissed him with a letter for Micipsa, to the following purpose: Your Jugurtha has behaved incomparably well in the war of Numantia; which, I am sure, must be matter of no small joy to you. We have, and very deservedly, the highest respect for him; and will endeavour to procure him the same from the senate and people of Rome. In re-
nostra

noſtra amicitia gratulor. En habes virum dignum te atque avo ſuo Maſiniſ- ſa. Igitur rex, ubi ea, quæ fama acceperat, ex litteris imperatoris ita eſſe cognovit, cum virtute, tum gratia viri permotus, flexit animum ſuum; & Jugurtham beneficiis vincere aggreſſus eſt. Statimque eum adoptavit, & teſtamento pariter cum filiis hæredem inſtituit. Sed ipſe, paucos poſt annos, morbo atque ætate confeſtus, cum ſibi finem vitæ adeſſe intelligeret, coram amicis & cognatis, itemque Atherbale & Hiempſale filiis, dicitur hujuſcemodi verba cum Jugurtha habuiſſe.

X. *Parvum ego te, Jugurtha, amiſſo patre, ſine ſpe, ſine opibus, in meum regnum accepi; exiſtumans non minus me tibi, quam ſi genuiſſem, ob beneficia carum fore. Neque ea res falſum me habuit. Nam, ut alia magna & egregia tua omittam, noviſſume rediens Numantia, meque regnumque meum gloria honoraviſti; tuaque virtute nobis Romanos ex amicis amiciſſumos feciſti. In Hiſpania nomen familiæ renovatum eſt. Poſtremo, quod difficillumum inter mortales eſt,*

gard to the friendſhip betwixt us, I congratulate you upon this occaſion. Herewith I return you a man, worthy of you, and his grandfather Maſiniſſa. *The king, finding what common fame had before informed him of confirmed by this letter of the general, moved as well by the fine accompliſhments of the man, as his intereſt with the Romans, reſolved to be eaſy with him, and endeavour to conquer him by kindneſs. Accordingly he immediately adopted him, and by a will made him joint-heir with his ſons. In a few years after, being worn out with infirmities and old age together, and finding himſelf a dying man, he is ſaid, in the preſence of his friends and relations, his two ſons Atherbal and Hiempſal too being by, to have addreſſed himſelf to Jugurtha in the Words following:*

X. I did, my dear Jugurtha, receive you into my court, left a little one by your father, without hopes or fortune, promiſing myſelf that you would be mindful of the favour, and love me no leſs than my own children, if I ſhould have any; nor was I deceived in that matter. For, to ſay nothing of other great and noble actions of yours, at your return from Numantia, you did me and my kingdom the utmoſt honour, by your excellent behaviour improved to the higheſt pitch the friendſhip that before ſubſiſted between the Romans and us; and revived afreſh the name of our family in Spain; and finally, what is the moſt difficult thing in the world,

I 4 *gloria*

128 C. CRISPI SALLUSTII

gloria invidia vicifti.
Nunc, quoniam mihi na-
tura finem vitæ facit, per
hanc dextram, per regni
fidem, moneo obteftorque,
uti hos, qui tibi genere
propinqui, beneficio meo
fratres funt, caros ha-
beas ; neu malis alienos
adjungere, quam fanguine
conjunctos retinere. Non
exercitus, neque thefauri,
præfidia regni funt, ve-
rum amici ; quos neque
armis cogere, neque auro
parare queas. Officio &
fide pariuntur. Quis au-
tem amicior, quam fra-
ter fratri ? Aut quem
alienum fidum invenies,
fi tuis hoftis fueris ? E-
quidem ego regnum vobis
trado firmum, fi boni eri-
tis ; fi mali, imbecillum.
Nam concordia res par-
væ crefcunt, difcordia
maxumæ dilabuntur. Cæ-
terum, ante hos, te, Ju-
gurtha, qui ætate & fa-
pientia prior es, ne ali-
ter quid eveniat, provi-
dere decet. Nam in omni
certamine, qui opulentior
eft, etiamfi accipit injuriam, tamen, quia plus
poteft, facere videtur.
Vos autem, Atherbal &
Hiempfal, colite, obfcr-
vate talem hunc virum ;
imitamini virtutem, &
enitimini, ne ego meliores
liberos fumpfiffe videar,
quam genuiffe.

you overcame envy itfelf by your
glory. Now, fince nature is juft
putting an end to my life, I befeech you by this right hand, by
the honour of a king too, I en-
treat and beg of you, to love my
children, your relations, and brothers by adoption ; and that you
would not transfer your affection
to ftrangers, rather than keep it
fixed upon thofe who are united
to you by blood. Armies and trea-
fures are not the fecurity of kingdoms, fo much as friends, whom
you can neither force to be fuch
by arms, nor purchafe with gold.
They are only procured by good
offices and fidelity. Who fhould
be more a fiiend than one brother
to another? Or what ftranger will
you find faithful to you, if you are
an enemy to your own relations?
I deliver up to you a kingdom,
ftrong indeed, if you are good to
one another, but weak, if you are
wicked. For fmall ftates grow
great by unanimity, whilft great
ones come to nothing by difcord.
But it behoves you, Jugurtha,
more than they, who are both
older and wifer than they, to take
care and guard againft any mifconduct in this affair. For in all
contefts, the more opulent party,
though he really receive wrong,
yet, becaufe he is the more powerful, is thought to do wrong. But
do you, Atherbal and Hiempfal,
refpect and reverence this worthy
man, imitate his noble behaviour,
and do your utmoft, that the
world may not think I have a-
dopted a fon preferable to thofe
nature beftowed upon me.

XI. Ad

XI. Ad ea Jugurtha, rametfi regem ficta locutum intelligebat, & ipfe longe aliter animo agitabat, tamen pro tempore benigne refpondit. Micipfa paucis poft diebus moritur. Poftquam illi more regio jufta magnifice fecerant, reguli in unum convenere, ut inter fe de negotiis cunctis difceptarent. Sed Hiempfal, qui minumus ex illis erat, natura ferox, etiam antea ignobilitatem Jugurthæ, quia materno genere impar erat, defpiciens, dextra Atherbalis adfedit ; ne medius ex tribus, quod apud Numidas honori ducitur, Jugurtha foret. Dein, tamen, ut ætati concederet, fatigatus a fratre, vix in alteram partem tranfductus eft. Ibi cum multa de adminiftrando imperio diflererent, Jugurtha inter alias res jacit, *Oportere quinquennii confulta & decreta omnia refcindi ; nam per ea tempora confectum annis Micipfam parum animo valuiffe.* Tum idem Hiempfal *placere fibi* refpondit; *nam ipfum illum tribus his proximis annis adoptatione in regnum perveniffe.* Quod verbum in pectus Jugurthæ altius, quam quifquam ratus erat, defcendit.

XI. *To this Jugurtha made a very complaifant reply, fuitable to the occafion, though he was fenfible the king was far from being fincere in what he faid, and he himfelf was as far from defigning what he declared for. Micipfa died a few days after. As foon as the funeral folemnity, which was very magnificent, was over, the three princes met together, in order to confer about the fettlement of their affairs. But Hiempfal, the youngeft of them, being naturally high-fpirited, who had before flighted Jugurtha for the meannefs of his birth by the mother's fide, placed himfelf on the right hand of Atherbal, to prevent Jugurtha's fitting himfelf in the middle betwixt him and his brother, which amongft the Numidians is reckoned the moft honourable pofition. And it was with much ado he was prevailed upon by the importunity of his brother to pay a deference to the age of Jugurtha by feating himfelf on the other fide. After a great deal of difcourfe upon a method of proceeding in the adminiftration of their kingdom, Jugurtha, among other things, propofed a repeal of all the refolutions and appointments of the five years foregoing, by reafon Micipfa was at that time but in a doating condition. Hiempfal faid he was of the fame mind ; for his adoption had happened within that time, to wit, about three years before. Which faying funk deeper into the mind of Jugurtha than any one imagined. Therefore from that day forward, being perplexed*

Itaque

Itaque, ex eo tempore ira & metu anxius, moliri, parare, atque ea modo in animo habere, quibus Hiempsal per dolum caperetur. Quæ ubi tardius procedunt, neque lenitur animus ferox, statuit quovis modo incœptum perficere.

betwixt anger and fear, he used his utmost endeavours, all the art and contrivance in his power, privately to make away with Hiempsal. But, finding he could not in that way of proceeding gain his purpose so soon as he desired, and his enraged soul being not to be pacified, he resolves at any rate to execute his design of murdering him.

XII. Primo conventu, quem ab regulis factum supra memoravi, propter dissensionem placuerat dividi thesauros, finisque imperii singulis constitui. Itaque tempus ad utramque rem decernitur, sed maturius ad pecuniam distribuendam. Reguli interea in loca propinqua thesauris, alius alio concessere. Sed Hiempsal in oppido Thirmida forte ejus domo utebatur, qui proxumus lictor Jugurthæ, carus acceptusque ei semper fuerat. Quem ille casu ministrum oblatum promissis onerat impellitque, uti tamquam suam domum visens erat, portarum claves adulterianas paret; nam veræ ad Hiempsalem referebantur. Cæterum, ubi res postularet, se ipsum cum magna venturum manu. Numida mandata brevi conficit; atque, uti doctus erat, noctu Jugurthæ milites introducit. Qui, postquam in ædes irrupe-

XII. In the first meeting which, we have above said, the princes had, they could not agree; and therefore resolved to divide the treasure and the kingdom too; and a time was accordingly fixed for both, but first for the partition of the money. In the mean time the princes had withdrawn separately into lodgings not far from the place where the money lay; particularly Hiempsal into the town of Thirmida, to the house of one that had been prime serjeant to Jugurtha, and ever highly in his favour and confidence. Now fortune presenting him with so fine an opportunity, he loads the fellow with promises, and prevails with him to go under pretence of visiting his house and provide false keys of the doors; for the true ones were always at night carried up to Hiempsal in his bed-chamber; and when all was ready, he told him, he would be sure to come with a considerable force. The Numidian quickly executed his orders; and, as instructed, let in Jugurtha's soldiers by night. After they were got in, they run some one way, and some another, in quest of the king. Some they killed asleep, and others standing re,

·fi regem quære-
iientis alios, alios
tis interficere ;
oca abdita; clau-
gere ; ſtrepitu &
omnia miſcere.
iterim Hiempſal
, occultans ſe
mulieris ancillæ,
o pavidus & ig-
oci profugerat.
caput ejus, uti
it, ad Jugurtham

upon their defence ; ſearched all
the private places about the houſe,
and broke open ſuch as were l.cked,
and filled every part with noiſe and
confuſion. Whilſt in the mean time
Hiempſal was found hiding himſelf
in the poor lodging of a maid-
ſervant ; whither, upon the firſt
alarm, he ran in a fright, being
not as yet well acquainted with
the houſe. The Numidians, according to their orders, carry his
head to Jugurtha.

Cæterum fama
:noris per omnem
brevi divulga-
therbalem, om-
qui ſub Micipſæ
fuerant, metus
In duas partis
t Numidæ ; plu-
erbalem ſequun-
l illum alterum
liores. Igitur Ju-
quam maxumas
opias armat. Ur-
m vi, alias vo-
imperio ſuo ad-
Omni Numidiæ
parat. Ather-
etſi Romam le-
iferat, qui ſena-
:erent de cæde
& fortunis ſuis,
·etus multitudine
, parabat armis
:re. Sed, ubi res
men venit, victus
o profugit in pro-
, ac dehinc Ro-
itendit. Cum Ju-
patratis conſiliis,
n omni Numidia

XIII. The fame of this villany
was ſoon ſpread all Africa over,
and ſtruck a mighty terror into A-
therbal, and all that had been ſubjects of Micipſa. The Numidians
were divided upon it into two parties ; the majority ſided with Atherbal, but the moſt warlike with
Jugurtha ; who, raiſing as great
an army as he could, reduces ſeveral cities, ſome by force, and
others by perſuaſion, under his ſub-
jection ; and, in ſhort, aims at nothing leſs than being maſter of all
Numidia. Atherbal, though he had
diſpatched embaſſadors to Rome, to
inform the ſenate of the murder
of his brother, and his own condition ; yet, depending upon the number of his troops, reſolved to give
his enemy battle. But being defeated therein, he made his eſcape
into the Roman province, and from
thence went to Rome. Jugurtha,
after he had thus finiſhed his work,
and was now become maſter of all
Numidia, conſidering the matter
coolly by himſelf, dreaded the Roman people, and could find no ſecurity againſt their reſentment,
potie-

potiebatur, in otio faci- / *ut in the avarice of the nobility,*
nus fuum cum animo re- *and his money. Wherefore in a*
putans, timeie populum *few days' time he difpatches away*
Romanum, neque ad- *embaſſadors to Rome with great*
vorfus iram ejus ulquam, *ſtore of ſilv r and gold, and orders*
nifi in avaritia nobilitatis, *them in the firſt place to glut all*
& pecunia fua, ſpem ha- *his old friends with prefents, and*
bere. Itaque, paucis di- *then to procure him new ones ; in*
ebus, cum auro argento- *ſhort, to ſtick at nothing, but bribe*
que multo legatos Ro- *all before them.˜ As ſoon as the*
mam mittit; queis præ- *gentlemen came to Rome, and, ac-*
cipit, uti primum veteres *coˑding to the king's inſtrucˑions,*
amicos muneribus exple- *diſtributed large prefents to the*
ant ; dein novos acqui- *perſons by whom they were enter-*
rant ; poſtremo, quem- *taiˑed, and others, leading men*
cunque poſſint largiundo *at that time in the ſenate, ſuch*
parare, ne cunctentur. *a wonderful change enſued upon*
Sed ubi Romam legati *it, that Jugurtha, inſtead of being*
venere, & ex præcepto *under a terrible odium, was migh-*
regis. hoſpitibus, aliiſque, *tily in the good graces of all the*
quorum ea tempeſtate in *nobility ; ſome of whom tempted*
fenatu auctoritas polle- *by hopes, and others by actual*
bat, magna munera mi- *bribes, made a-ſtrong intereſt in*
fere ; tanta commutatio *the houſe to prevent any ſevere*
inceſſit, ut ex maxuma *reſolution againſt him. Where-*
invidia in gratiam & fa- *fore, as ſoon as the embaſſadors*
vorem nobilitatis Jugur- *thought they had made all ſafe,*
tha veniret; quorum pars *they and Atherbal had an audience*
fpe, alii præmio inducti, *given them by the ſenate. Upon*
fingulos ex fenatu am- *which occaſion Atherbal, it is ſaid,*
biundo, nitebantur, ne *ſpoke to the following effect.*
gravius in eum confuleretur. Igitur, ubi legati fatis con-
fidunt, die conſtituto ſenatus utriſque datur. Atherbalem
hoc modo accepimus.

XIV. *P. C. Micipfa* XIV. Venerable fathers, Mi-
pater meus moriens mihi cipfa my father, at his death, gave
præcepit, uti regni Nu- me a charge to look upon the ad-
midiæ tantummodo pro- miniſtration of the kingdom of
curationem exiſtumarem me- Numidia only as mine, but the
am ; cæterum jus & im- right and ſovereignty to be in
perium penes vos eſſe ; ſi- you ; and at the ſame time to be
mul eniterer domi militi- as ſerviceable to the Roman people
æque quam maxumo uſui as poſſible, both in peace, and in
eſſe populo Romano ; vos war ; and regard you as my rela-
mih.

mihi cognatorum, vis in locum adfinium ducerem ; si ea f.cissem, in vestra amicitia exercitum, divitias, munimenta regni me habiturum. Quæ præcepta patris mei cum agitar.m, Jugurtha, homo omniu·i, quos terra susti·et, sceleratissumus, contempto imperio v.stro, Masinissæ me nepotem, etiam ab stirpe socium atque amicum populi Romani, regno fortunisque omnibus expulit. Atque ego, P. C. quoniam eo miseriarum venturus eram, vellem, potius ob mea, quam ob majorum meorum 'beneficia, posse me a vobis auxilium petere, ac maxume deberi mihi beneficia a populo Romano, quibus non egerem ; secundum ea, si desideranda erant, uti debitis uterer. Sed quoniam parum tuta per se ipsa probitas est ; neque mihi in manu fuit, Jugurtha qualis foret ; ad vos confugi, P. C. quibus, quod mihi miserrumum est, cogor prius oneri, quam usui, esse. Cæteri reges, aut bello victi, in amicitiam a vobis recepti sunt, aut in suis dubiis rebus societatem vestrum appetiverunt.

XV. Familia nostra cum populo Romano bello Carthaginiensi amicitiam instituit, quo tempore

tions and kinfmen; telling me, if I did fo, I fhould be fure to find forces, riches, and a fecurity to my kingdom, in your friendfhip. And whilft I was propofin r to put thefe orders of my father in execution, Jugurtha, the wickedeft wretch alive, in contempt of your high authority, ftripped me the grandfon of Mafiniffa, and born an ally and friend of the Roman people, of my kingdom, and every thing elfe in the world. And fince I was, moft illuftrious fathers, to be reduced to fo miferable a condition, I could wifh I might have had the advantage, however, to implore your affiftance for my own perfonal fervices rather than thofe of my forefathers; but above all, that I might have a debt of kindneffes due to me from the Roman people that I might never have occafion for; or, if I had, might only make ufe of fuch as were due to me. But becaufe integrity alone is no fufficient fecurity, nor was it in my power to direct the conduct of Jugurtha, I have fled to you, worthy fathers, for protection; to whom, to my unfpeakable forrow, I am obliged to be burthenfome before I could be of any fervice. Other kings have been either firft conquered in war, and then gracioufly received into your alliance, or elfe have in diftrefs follicited for the fame.

XV. Our family firft contracted an alliance with the Roman people, in a war of theirs againft the Carthaginians, at a time when

magis

magis fides ejus, quam
fortuna pendenda erat.
Quorum progeniem vos,
P. C. nolite pati me ne-
potem Masinissæ frustra
a vobis auxilium petere.
Si ad impetrandum nihil
cauffæ haberem, præter
miftrandam fortunam;
quod paullo ante rex ge-
nere, fama, atque copiis
potens, nunc deformatus
ærumnis, inopi, alienas
opes expecto; tamen erat
majeftatis populi Romani
prohibere injuriam, neque
pati cujufquam regnum
per fcelus crefcere. Ve-
rum ego iis finibus ejec-
tus fum, quos majoribus
meis populus Romanus de-
dit; unde pater & avus
meus una vcbifcum expu-
lare Syphacem & Car-
thaginienfes. Veftra be-
neficia mihi erepta funt,
P. C. vos in mea injuria
defpecti eftis. Eheu me
miferum! huccine, Mi-
cipfa pater, beneficia tua
evafere, uti quem tu
parem cum liberis tuis,
regnique participem fe-
cifti, is potiffumum ftir-
pis tuæ extinctor fit?
Numquamne ergo familia
noftra quieta erit? Sem-
perne in fanguine, ferro,
fuga verfabimur? Dum
Carthaginienfes incolu-
mes fuere, jure omnia
fæva patiebamur. Hoftis
ab latere; vos amici pro-
cul; fpes omnis in armis

their honour was more to be regarded, than their fortune. Suffer me not, mighty fathers, a de-
fcendant of that family, the grandfon of Mafiniffa, to implore your
affiftance in vain. If I had no
other pretenfions for procuring
the fame befides the mifery of my
circumftances, that I, who was
but lately a prince confiderable for
my extraction, fame, and forces,
am now reduced to the loweft
ftate of mifery, poverty, and dependance; yet would it highly
become the majefty of the Roman
people to vouchfafe me their protection, and not fuffer any prince
to grow great by the practice of
villainy. But I have been forced,
out of a country which the Roman people beftowed upon my anceftors; from whence my father
and grandfather, in conjunction
with you, drove Syphax and the
Carthaginians The favours you
conferred upon my family have
been taken from me, noble fathers;
you have been defpitefully treated
in the injuftice done to me. Alas,
wretch that I am! Is all your
kindnefs, my dear father Micipfa,
come to this, that the man you
had made equal to your own fons,
and joint-heir of your kingdom
with them, fhould, above all o-
thers, be the ruin of your iffue?
Muft our family then never be
at reft? Muft we be ever in blood,
war, or banifhment? Whilft the
Carthaginians flourifhed, we might
well fuffer every thing that was
difmal. Our enemies were our
next neighbours, and you our
friends far off. All our hopes were

erat,

erat. Poſtquam illa peſtis ex Africa ejecta eſt, læti pacem agitabamus ; quippe, queis hoſtis nullus erat, niſi forte quem vos juſſiſſetis. Ecce autem ex improviſo Jugurtha, intoleranda audacia, ſcelere atque ſuperbia ſeſe efferens, fratre meo atque eodem propinquo ſuo interfecto, primum regnum ejus ſceleris ſui prædam fecit ; poſt, ubi me iiſdem dolis nequit capere, nihil minus, quam vim aut bellum, expectantem, in imperio veſtro, ſicuti videtis, extorrem patria, domo ; inopem, coopertum miſeriis, effecit ut ubivis tutius, quam in meo regno, eſſem.

XVI. *Ego ſic exiſtumabam, patres conſcripti, uti prædicantem audiveram patrem meum ; qui veſtram amicitiam diligenter colerent, eos multum laborem ſuſcipere, cæterum ex omnibus maxume tutos eſſe. Quod in familia noſtra fuit, præſtitit ; uti in omnibus bellis adeſſet vobis ; nos uti per otium tuti ſimus, in manu veſtra eſt, patres conſcripti. Pater nos duos fratres reliquit ; tertium Jugurtham beneficiis ſuis ratus eſt nobis conjunctum fore. Alter eorum necatus ; alterius ipſe ego manus impias vix effugi. Quid a-*

in our arms. But when Africa was delivered from that peſtilent people, we enjoyed all the delights of peace, as having no enemy, unleſs ſuch as you had appointed us. When behold, unexpectedly, Jugurtha erecting his plumes with intolerable impudence, wickedneſs, and pride, and murdering my brother, his near relation, made his kingdom the firſt prize of his villainy ; and then, not finding it practicable to take me off by the like wicked contrivance, whilſt I expected nothing at all of violence or war, has, in the face of your mighty power, driven me, as you ſee, from my country, from my home, in want of every thing, and under the heavieſt load of miſery, and yet more ſecure any where than in my own kingdom.

XVI. I really thought, O venerable fathers, as I had heard my father often ſay, that ſuch as took care to cultivate a friendſhip with you, muſt do it at the expence of much labour and pains, but were of all mankind the moſt ſecure. All that was in the power of our family to do, it did, that is, it aſſiſted you in all your wars : it is in your power to make us a return of peace and ſecurity, mighty fathers. My father left behind him us two brothers, and thought he ſhould make Jugurtha a third brother to us by the favours he heaped upon him. One of the three is already murdered, and I had much ado to eſcape the wicked hands of the other. What ſhall I do ? Or whither ſhall I, unhappy man, apply myſelf ? All

gam? Aut quo potiſſu-
mum infelix accedam?
Generis præſidia omnia
extinĉta ſunt; pater, uti
neceſſe erat, naturæ con-
ceſſit; fratri, quem mi-
nume decuit, propinquus
per ſcelus vitam eripuit;
adfinis, amicos, propin-
quos cæteros meos, alium
alia clades oppreſſit;
capti ab Jugurtha, pars
in crucem aĉti, pars be-
ſtiis objeĉti ſunt; pauci,
quibus reliĉta eſt anima,
clauſi in tenebris cum
mœrore & luĉtu morte
graviorem vitam exi-
gunt. Si omnia, quæ aut
amiſi, aut ex neceſſariis
advorſa faĉta ſunt, in-
columia manerent; ta-
men, ſi quid ex improviſo
mali accidiſſet, vos im-
plorarem, patres con-
ſcripti; quibus pro mag-
nitudine imperii, jus &
injurias omnis curæ eſſe
decet. Nunc vero exſul
patria, domo, ſolus atque
omnium honeſtarum re-
rum egens, quos accedam,
aut-quos appellem? Na-
tioneſne an reges, qui
omnes familiæ noſtræ ob
veſtram amicitiam infeſti
ſunt? An quoquam mihi
adire licet, ubi non majorum meorum hoſtilia mo-
numenta plurima ſint?
An quiſquam noſtri miſe-
reri poteſt, qui aliquando
vobis hoſtis fuit?

the ſecurity to be had from my
own family is gone. My father
yielded, as neceſſity required, to
the order of nature. My brother
was villainouſly robbed of his life
by a relation, who of all men
ſhould have been the furtheſt from
ſuch a crime. My friends and relations, whether by blood or marriage, have been all ruined, ſome
one way, ſome another. Being
taken priſoners, part of them have
been crucified, whilſt others have
been thrown to wild beaſts. A
few whoſe lives were ſpared have
been clapped up in dungeons, and
lead a life in ſorrow and mourning, worſe than death. If I was
in full poſſeſſion of all I have loſt,
and my relations and friends were
none of them my enemies, or unfortunate; yet, in caſe of a ſudden
calamity ſurpriſing me, I ſhould
mighty fatheis, apply to you fo
deliverance, whom, by reaſon o
your vaſt dominion, it highly be
comes to ſee right and juſtice don
throughout the world. But now
whither ſhall I go, or to whom
ſhall I apply, baniſhed as I ar
from my country, my home, le
alone, and in want of every th
leaſt decent accommodation o
life? Shall I apply to foreign na
tions or princes, who are all mor
tal enemies to our family upo
account of our alliance with you
Or can I go any whither, whei
there are not very many monu
ments of the valour of my ai
ceſtors employed againſt the coui
try in your favour; Or can an
one have compaſſion on me wh
was ever an enemy to you?

XVI

XVII. *Poſtremo, Ma-*
ſiniſſa nos ita inſtituit, P.
C. ne quem coleremus,
niſi populum Romanum ;
ne· ſocietates, ne fœdera
nova acciperemus ; abun-
de magna · præſidia nobis
in· veſtra amicitia fore ;
ſi huic imperio fortuna
mutaretur, una occiden-
dum nobis eſſe. Virtute
ac diis volentibus, magni
eſtis & opulenti , omnia
ſecunda & obedientia
ſunt ; quo facilius ſocio-
rum injurias curare licet.
Tantum illud vereor, ne
quos privata amicitia Ju-
gurthæ, parum cognita,
transvorſos agat ; quos
ego audio maxuma ope
niti, ambire, fatigare vos
ſingulos, ne quid de abſen-
e, incognita cauſſa, ſta-
uatis; fingere me verba,
& fugam ſimulare, cui
licuerat in regno manere.
Quod utinam illum, cu-
jus impio facinore in has
miſerias projeſtus ſum,
adem hæc ſimulantem
videam ; & aliquando, aut
apud vos, aut apud deos
immortalis rerum huma-
narum cura oriatur ; ut
ille, qui nunc ſceleribus
ſuis ferox atque præcla-
rus eſt, omnibus malis ex-
cruciatus, impietatis in
parentem noſtrum, fra-
tris mei necis, mearum-
que miſeriarum gravis
bœnas reddat. Jam jam
frater animo meo cariſſu-

XVII. Finally, worthy fathers,
Maſiniſſa's inſtruction to our family ever was, to make no court
to any but the Roman people, to
engage in no alliances or treaties
with any other power whatever ;
alledging that we ſhould find a-
bundant ſecurity in your friendſhip
alone ; but that, if fortune ſhould
turn upon the Roman power to
its deſtruction, we muſt then of
neceſſity periſh with it. By your
own good conduct, and the favour
of the gods, you are great and
mighty ; ſuccefs and ſubmiſſion
attend you throughout the world,
whereby you are enabled to redrefs
with eaſe the injuries of your allies. All that I fear in the caſe is,
left the friendſhip of Jugurtha with
particular members of this ſtate,
to whom he is not ſufficiently
known, ſhould miſguide them in
their conduct upon this occaſion ;
who, I am informed, are uſing
their utmoſt endeavours, ſoliciting
and importuning you by a very
particular application, not to proceed to any reſolution againſt him,
as he is not here himſelf, without
a full hearing of his cauſe, 'Tis
ſaid, that what I alledge is pretence only ; as if I had not been
forced to fly my kingdom, but
might have continued in it if I
would. Heavens grant I could
but ſee the man, by whoſe impious
violence I have been plunged into
my preſent miſery, diſſembling as
I do ; and that at laſt either you,
or the immortal gods, would take
the affairs of mankind under your
care. Then would the wretch,
who now prides and triumphs in

K   *me,*

me, quamquam tibi im-
maturo, & unde minume
decuit, vita erepta eft,
tamen lætandum magis,
quam dolendum, puto ca-
fum tuum. Non enim
regnum, fed fugam, ex-
filium, egeftatem, & has
omnis, quæ me premunt,
ærumnas, cum anima fi-
mul amififti. At ego in-
felix, in tanta mala præ-
cipitatus, pulfus ex patrio
regno, rerum humanarum
fpectaculum præbeo; in-
certus quid agam, tuafne
injurias perfequar, ipfe
auxilii egens; an regno
confulam, cujus vitæ ne-
cifque poteftas ex opibus
alienis pendet. Utinam
emori, fortunis meis ho-
neftus exitus effet; ne vi-
vere contemptus viderer,
fi defeffus malis injuriæ
conceffiffem. Nunc, neque
vivere lubet, neque mori
licet fine dedecore. P. C.
per vos, per liberos atque
parentes veftros, per ma-
jeftatem populi Romani,
fubvenite mifero mihi; ite
obviam injuriæ; nolite
pati regnum Numidiæ,
quod veftrum eft, per fcelus
& fanguinem familiæ
noftræ tabefcere.

his villainy, by all imaginable mifery, fuffer the vengeance due to
him, for his wicked difregard to the
memory of our father, the murder of my brother, and reducing
me to the woful condition I am
now in. Now, now, O my dear,
dear brother, though you were cut
down in the prime of your days,
and by a hand of all others that
fhould leaft have been guilty of
fuch a fact; yet I cannot but think
I have reafon rather to rejoice at,
than lament, your fall. For you
did not fo much lofe your kingdom with your life, as you efcaped
the wretched neceffity of flight,
banifhment, want, and all that
weight of woe, which lies fo heavy upon me. But I, poor wretch
thrown headlong from the heigh
of my father's kingdom into the
loweft depths of mifery, am a no
torious inftance of the uncertaint
of human affairs, not knowing
what to do; whether to profecut
the revenge of the wrongs done to
you, helplefs as I am, or endeavou
only the recovery of my kingdom
whilft the difpofal of me, with re
fpect to life or death, is entirely i
the power of others. I could wift
death might put a decent end to
my life, to avoid the defpicable ap
pearance I muft make; if tire
out by my misfortunes I muft be o
bliged to be quiet under the injuf

tice I have fuffered. Now I have no inclination to life, and
yet I cannot die with honour. Now I beg of you, might
fathers, for the fake of yourfelves, your children and pa
rents, and the majefty of the Roman people, relieve a poo
wretch, curb the violence of Jugurtha, and fuffer not the
kingdom of Numidia, which is yours, to come to nothing
by villainy, and the murder of our family.

XVIII

XVIII. Poftquam rex finem loquendi fecit, legati Jugurthæ, largitione magis, quam cauffa, freti, paucis refpondent ; *Hiempfalem*, *ob fævitiam fuam*, *ab Numidis interfectum* : *Atherbalem ultro bellum inferentem*, *poftquam fuperatus fit*, *queri*, *quod injuriam facere nequiffet* ; *Jugurtham ab fenatu petere*, *ne fe alium putarent*, *ac Numantiæ cognitus effet* ; *neu verba inimici ante facta fua ponerent*. Deinde utrique curia egrediuntur. Senatus ftatim confulitur. Fautores legatorum, præterea magna pars gratia depravata, Atherbalis dicta contemnere ; Jugurthæ virtutem laudibus extollere; gratia, voce, denique omnibus modis pro alieno fcelere & flagitio, fua quafi pro gloria, nitebantur. At contra pauci, quibus bonum & æquum divitiis carius erat, fubveniundum Atherbali, & Hiemfalis mortem fevere vindicandam cenfebant. Sed ex omnibus maxume Æmilius Scaurus, homo nobilis, impiger, factiofus, avidus potentiæ, honoris, divitiarum, cæterum vitia fua calide occultans. Is, poftquam videt regis largitionem famofam impudentem-

XVIII. *After the king had made an end of his fpeech, the deputies of Jugurtha, depending more upon the bribes they had given than their caufe, made a fhort reply :* That Hiempfal had been murdered by the Numidians, becaufe of his cruelty ; that Atherbal had been the aggreffor in the late war, and becaufe he had been baffled therein, and could not do Jugurtha the mifchief he intended, he now complained ; that Jugurtha begged of the fenate, they would not take him to be any other man than what he had been known to be at Numantia, or fhew more regard to the words of his enemy than to his actions. *Upon this, both parties quit the houfe, and the fenate immediately went upon the affair. The favourers of the embaffadors, and a great party befide, made by the influence of their friends amongft the former, flighted what was faid by Atherbal, highly extolled the conduct of Jugurtha, and by their intereft, fpeeching, and, in fhort, all manner of means, ftruggled as hard to cover Jugurtha's wickednefs and infamous crimes, as if their own honour was at ftake. On the other hand, a fmall party, that regarded juftice and equity more than money, advifed to relieve Atherbal, and revenge feverely the death of Hiempfal. The moft eminent amongft thefe was Æmilius Scaurus, a perfon of noble defcent, active, factious, greedy of power, honour, and riches, but cunningly concealing his vices. He, finding that the bribery carried*

K 2   que,

que, veritus, quod in tali re folet, ne polluta licentia invidiam accenderet, animum a confueta lubidine continuit.

XIX. Vicit tamen in fenatu pars illa, quæ vero pretium aut gratiam anteferebat. Decretum fit, *uti decem legati regnum, quod Micipfa obtinuerat, inter Jugurtham & Atherbalem dividerent.* Cujus legationis princeps fuit L. Opimius, homo clarus, & tum in fenatu potens, quia conful, C. Graccho & M. Fulvio interfectis, acerrume vindictam nobilitatis in plebem exercuerat. Lum Jugurtha, tametfi Romæ in amicis habuerat, tamen accuratiffime recepit; dando & pollicendo multa perfecit, uti famæ, fidei, poftremo omnibus fuis rebus commodum regis anteferret. Reliquos legatos eadem via aggreffus, plerofque capit; paucis carior fides, quam pecunia fuit. In divifione, quæ pars Numidiæ Mauritaniam attingit, agro virifque opulentior, Jugurthæ traditur. Illam alteram, fpecie, quam ufu, potiorem, quæ portuofior, & ædificiis magis exornata erat, Atherbal poffedit. Res poftulare

on by the king was notorious and barefaced, fearing, as it ufually happens in fuch a cafe, left the vaft licence taken in that matter fhould inflame the general odium againft the parties guilty, had laid a reftraint upon his vicious inclination.

XIX. *However, the party that preferred money or favour before the truth prevailed in the fenate; and a vote paffed* for the appointment of ten commiffioners, to divide the kingdom which Micipfa had had betwixt Jugurtha and Atherbal. *The firft commiffioner was L. Opimius, a perfon of great figure, and of vaft weight at that time in the houfe; becaufe, when he was conful, he had taken off C. Gracchus and M. Fulvius, and after that fuccefs had furioufly executed the vengeance of the nobility upon the commons. And, tho' he had been one of Jugurtha's friends at Rome, yet, upon his arrival in Africa, he received him with huge ceremony; and by giving him money, and promifing more, he fo far wrought upon him, that he preferred the king's intereft before his own credit, honour, and, in fhort, every thing elfe. Jugurtha went to work in the fame manner with the reft of the commiffioners, and corrupted moft of them. A few of them valued their honour more than money. In the divifion of the kingdom, that part of Numidia which borders upon Mauritania, and is much the more confiderable for goodnefs of foil and number of people, was affigned to Jugurtha. Atherbal had the other, preferable in appearance, but not reality, as having more*
videtur

videtur Africæ fitum pau-
cis exponere ; & eas gen-
tis, quibufcum nobis bel-
lum aut amicitia fuit, attingere. Sed quæ loca &
nationes, ob calprem,
aut afperitatem, item fo-
litudines, minus frequen-
tata funt, de iis haud facile compertum narrave-
rim ; cætera quam pau-
ciffumis abfolvam.

XX. In divifione orbis
terræ, plerique in parte
tertia Africam pofuere ;
pauci tantummodo Afi-
am & Europam effe ; fed
Africam in Europa. Ea
finis habet ab occidente
fretum noftri maris &
oceani ; ab ortu folis de-
clivem latitudinem, quem
locum Catabathmon in-
colæ appellant. Mare
fævum, importuofum. A-
ger frugum fertilis, bonus
pecori, arbori infœcun-
dus ; cœlo terraque pe-
nuria aquarum ; genus
hominum falubri corpore,
velox, patiens laborum ;
plerofque feneƈtus diffol-
vit, nifi qui ferro aut a
beftiis interiere. Nam
morbus haud fæpe quem-
quam fuperat. Ad hoc,
malefici generis plurima
animalia. Sed qui mor-
tales initio Africam habuerint, quique poftea ac-
cefferint, aut quo modo
inter fe permixti fint ;
quamquam ab ea fama,
quæ plerofque obtinet,

*harbours and fine buildings in it.
And here, I judge, it may not be
improper to give a fhort account of
the fituation of Africa, and of
thofe nations we have had any war
or alliance with. But, as for thofe
parts and nations which, becaufe
of their exceffive heat, their being
rocky or defart, are lefs frequented,
I can fay little with any certainty ;
but the reft I fhall difpatch with
all poffible brevity.*

*XX. In the divifion of the
earth, moft authors reckon Africa
a third part. Some reckon indeed
but two, Afia and Europe ; but
then they count Africa in Europe.
That is bounded on the weft by the
ftreight, which makes the commu-
nication betwixt our fea and the
ocean, on the eaft by a wide decli-
vity, called by the natives Catabathmos. The fea bordering upon
it is boifterous, where there are
few or no harbours. The country
is fruitful in grain of all kinds,
and good for feeding of cattle, but
produces very few trees ; water is
fcarce, as well fpring water as
rain. The natives are healthy,
fwift of foot, and hardy. Moft
of them die of old age, except fuch
as perifh by the fword or wild
beafts : for a difeafe feldom difpatches them. But then it abounds
with noxious creatures. Now, as
to the firft inhabitants of this country, and thofe that in fucceeding
ages fettled there, and how they
incorporated, I fhall give a very
brief account, different indeed from
the common one, but fuch as was
interpreted to me out of the Carthaginian books, which were faid*

K 3   *diverfum*

diverfum eſt, tamen, ut ex libris Punicis, qui regis Hiempſalis dicebantur, interpretatum nobis eſt, utique rem feſe habere cultores ejus terræ putant, quam pauciſſimis dicam. Cæterum fides ejus rei penes auctores erit.

XXI. Africam initio habuere Gætuli & Libyes, aſperi incultique; queis cibus erat caro ferina, atque humi pabulum, uti pecoribus. Hi neque moribus, neque lege, aut imperio cujufquam regebantur ; vagi, palantes, quas nox coegerat, ſedes habebant. Sed poſtquam in Hiſpania Hercules, ficuti Afri putant, interiit; exercitus ejus, compoſitus ex gentibus variis, amiſſo duce, ac paſſim multis ſibi quifque imperium petentibus, brevi dilabitur. Ex eo numero Medi, Perſæ, & Armenii, navibus in Africam tranſvecti, proxumos noſtro mari locos occupavere. Sed Perſæ intra oceanum magis ; hique alveos navium inverſos pro tuguriis habuere ; quia neque materia in agris, neque ab Hiſpanis emundi aut mutandi copia erat. Mare magnum & ignara lingua commercia prohibebant. Hi paulatim per connubia Gætulos ſecum miſcuere ; & quia, ſæpe tentantes agros, alia deinde alia loca petiverant,

to be king Hiempſal's, and what the people of that country take to be fact. But let the authors anſwer for the credibility of it.

XXI. The original inhabitants of Africa were the Getulians and the Lybians, a rough unpoliſhed people, who lived upon fleſh taken in hunting, or upon herbs, like cattle. Theſe were under no manner of confinement from cuſtom, law, or government; but, ſtrolling about here and there, took up their lodging where the night happened to overtake them. But after Hercules died in Spain, as the Africans have it, his army, that was made up of divers nations, upon the loſs of their leader, and a buſtle made by a competition for the command, diſperſed in a ſhort time. Of that number the Medes, the Perſians, and Armenians, paſſing over by ſhipping into Africa, ſeized upon thoſe parts of it that lie upon our ſea. But the Perſians lay more upon the ocean. They made uſe of their ſhips turned bottom upwards for houſes; becauſe there was no wood in that country, nor had they any opportunity of buying any, or trucking for it with the Spaniards. A wide ſea, and a language to them unknown, rendered all commerce impracticable. By degrees, they by intermarriages mixed with the Getulians ; and, becauſe they were often ſhifting about from place to place to try the goodneſs of the ſoil, they called themſelves Numidians. To this

femet

BELLUM JUGURTHINUM. 143

femet ipfi Numidas ap-
pellavere. Cæterum ad-
huc ædificia Numidarum
agreſtium, quæ *Mapalia*
illi vocant, oblonga, in-
curvis lateribus tecta,
quafi navium carinæ funt.
Medis autem & Armeniis
acceffere Libyes. Nam
hi propius mare Africum
agitabant. Gætuli fub
fole magis, haud procul
ab ardoribus ; hique ma-
ture oppida habuere.
Nam freto divifi ab
Hifpania, mutare res in-
ter fe inſtituerant. No-
men eorum paullatim Li-
byes corrupere, barbara
linguâ Mauros pro Medis
appellantes. Sed res Per-
farum brevi adolevit ; ac
poſtea Nomo-Numidæ,
propter multitudinem, a
parentibus digreffi, pof-
fidere ea loca, quæ prox-
uma Carthaginem Nu-
midia appellatur. Deinde,
utrique alteris freti, finiti-
mos armis aut metu fub
imperium fuum coegere ;
nomen gloriamque · fibi
àddidere; magis hi, qui ad
noſtrum mare proceffe-
rant ; quia Libyes, quam
Gætuli, minus bellicofi.
Denique Africæ pars infe-
rior pleraque ab Numidis
poffeffa eſt. Victi omnes
in gentem nomenque im-
perantium conceffere.

XXII. Poſtea Phœni-
ces, alii multitudinis domi minuendæ gratia, pars

day the cottages of the Numidians,
which they call Mapalia, are of
an oblong form, with the fides
bending out, like the hulls of ſhips.
The Libyans joined the Medes and
Armenians, who lived nearer the
African fea. The Getulians lie more
to the fun, not far from the hot-
teſt part of the torrid zone. And
theſe quickly built towns. For,
being divided only by a narrow fea
from Spain, they carried on a traffick there. But the Libyans by
degrees altered their name, calling
them in their language Mauri,
inſtead of Medi. But the Per-
fians became in a ſhort time a
flouriſhing people. Afterwards too
the Nomo-Numidians, by reafon of
their vaſt numbers, feparating
from their parents, poffeffed themfelves of the country about Carthage, which is called Numidia.
After that, both parties depending
upon the mutual affiſtance of one
another did, by force of arms, or
the fear thereof, bring their neighbours under fubjection to them, and
acquired to themfelves a mighty
name and great glory ; but efpecially thofe who bordered upon our
fea, becaufe the Libyans are lefs
warlike than the Getulians. Finally, the lower part of Africa
was moſt of it over-run by the
Numidians. And the conquered
people mixed with, and went by
the name of, the conquerors.

XXII. Afterwards the Phœni-
cians, fome to leffen the over-great
crowds at home, and others out of

K 4 imperii

imperii cupidine, folicitata plebe, & aliis novarum rerum avidis, Hipponem, Hadrumetum, Leptim, aliafque urbis in ora maritima condidere. Hæque brevi multum auctæ, pars originibus suis præfidio, aliæ decori fuere. Nam de Carthagine filere melius puto, quam parum dicere; quoniam alio properare tempus monet. Igitur ad Catabathmon, qui locus Ægyptum ab Africa dividit, fecundo mari prima Cyrene est, colonia Thereon; ac deinceps duæ Syrtes, interque eas Leptis; deinde Philenon aræ; quem locum Ægyptum verfus finem imperii habuere Carthaginienfes; poft aliæ Punicæ urbes. Cætera loca ufque ad Mauritaniam Numidæ tenent. Proxume Hifpaniam Mauri funt. Super Numidiam Gætulos accepimus, partim in tuguriis, alios incultius vagos agitare; poft eos Æthiopas effe; dein loca exufta folis ardoribus. Igitur bello Jugurthino pleraque ex Punicis oppida, & finis Carthaginenfium, quos noviffume habuerant, populus Romanus per magiftratus adminiftrabat. Gætulorum magna pars, & Numidæ ufque ad flumen Mulucham fub Ju-

a defire of power, engaging many of the commonalty to put themfelves under their leading and direction, as well as others that were fond of novelty, built Hippo, Hadrumetum, Leptis, and other cities upon the fea-coaft. And thefe, growing confiderably in a little time, were partly a fecurity, and partly an ornament to their founders. For, as to Carthage, I think it better to fay nothing at all of it, than but a little, becaufe I am in hafte to return to my proper fubject. Wherefore by Catabathmos, which place divides Ægypt from Africa, down the fea, firft occurs Cyrene, a colony of the Thereans. Then follow the two Syrtes, and Leptis betwixt them; then the altars of the Philenians, which were the boundary of the Carthaginian empire to the fide of Ægypt; after them fucceed other Carthaginian cities. The reft of Africa, as far as Mauritania, the Numidians are poffeffed of. The Moors are next to Spain. The Getulians, we are told, lie about Numidia, who part of them live in huts, part wander about, without any fettled habitation. Beyond them lie the Æthiopians; beyond whom the country is burnt up with exceffive heat. In the time of the war againft Jugurtha, the Roman people governed moft of the Punick towns, as well as the country, that had been under the fubjection of the Carthaginians, by magiftrates of their own. A great part of the Getulians, and the Numidians as far as the river Mulucha, were under Jugurtha.

gurtha

rtha erant; Mauris om-
ɔus rex Bocchus im-
ritabat, præter nomen,
·tera ignarus populi Ro-
ini ; itemque nobis
que bello, neque pace
tea cognitus. De Africa
ejus incolis, ad necefſi-
linem rei fatis dictum.
XXIII. Poſtquam, di-
ɔ regno, legati Africa
ceſſere ; & Jugurtha,
ntra timorem animi,
æmia fceleris adeptum
è videt ; certum ratus,
od ex amicis apud Nu-
antiam acceperat, om-
i Romæ venalia eſſe ;
nul & illorum pollici-
:ionibus accenſus, quos
ullo ante muneribus
pleverat, in regnum
:herbalis animum in-
1dit. Ipſe acer, belli-
fus ; at is, quem pe-
ɔat, quietus, imbellis,
icido ingenio, opportu-
s injuriæ, metuens ma-
i, quam metuendus.
itur ex improviſo finis
is cum magna manu
vadit ; multos mortalis
m pecore atque alia
æda capit ; ædificia in-
ndit ; pleraque loca ho-
liter cum equitatu acce-
t. Dein cum omni
ultitudine in regnum
um convertit, exiſtu-
ans dolore permotum
therbalem injurias ſuas
anu vindicaturum, eam-
ie rem belli eauſſam
re. At ille, quod ne-

King Bocchus ruled over all the
Moors, a ſtranger to the Romans,
any farther than their name, and
not known to us before, either by
peace or war. But this may ſuf-
fice my purpoſe to ſay of Africa
and its inhabitants.

XXIII. After the Roman com-
miſſioners had divided the kingdom, and left Africa, and Jugurtha, contrary to his fears, ſaw
himſelf rewarded for his villainy,
taking it now for a certainty which
he had heard from his friends at
Numantia, that all things were
to be ſold at Rome, being likewiſe
puſhed on by the promiſes of thoſe
whom he had but a little before
loaded with preſents, he reſolved
to have Atherbal's kingdom from
him. He was himſelf an active,
warlike man ; but he whom he deſigned to attack, a quiet, weak,
meek-ſpirited creature, unable to
defend himſelf, and more fearful
of others, than to be feared by any.
Wherefore 'Jugurtha invades his
country with a great army, takes
abundance of men, cattle, and
other plunder ; fires towns, and
over-runs almoſt all the country
with his horſe. And when he had
done he returned with all his forces
into his own kingdom, ſuppoſing
Atherbal would reſent and revenge
the abuſe, and ſo a war would enſue upon it. But he, not looking upon
himſelf as a match for the other
in war, and depending more upon
the friendſhip of the Roman people
than his Numidian ſubjects, ſent
deputies to Jugurtha, to complain
que

que fe parem armis exi-
ftumabat, & amicitia po-
puli Romani magis, quam
Numidis, fretus erat, le-
gatos ad jugurtham de
injuriis queftum mifit;
qui, tametfi contumeliofa
dicta retulerant, prius tamen omnia pati decrevit,
quam bellum fumere;
quia tentatum antea fecus
cefferat. Neque eo magis
cupido Jugurthæ minue-
batur; quippe qui totum
ejus regnum animo jam
invaferat. Itaque non,
ut antea, cum prædato-
rio manu, fed magno ex-
ercitu comparato, bellum
gerere cœpit, & aperte
totius Numidiæ imperi-
um petere. Cæterum, qua pergebat, urbis, agros vaftare
prædas agere; fuis animum, hoftibus terrorem augere.

XXIV. Atherbal, ubi
intelligit eo proceffum,
uti regnum aut relinquen-
dum effet, aut armis retinendum, neceffario copi-
as parat, & Jugurthæ ob-
vius procedit. Interim,
haud longe a mari prope
Cirtam oppidum, utriuf-
que confedit exercitus;
&, quia diei extremum
erat, prælium non incep-
tum. Sed, ubi plerumque
noctis proceffit, obfcuro
etiam tum lumine, mili-
tes Jugurthini, figno da-
to, caftra hoftium inva-
dunt; femifomnos par-
tim, alios arma fumentis
fugant funduntque. A-
therbal cum paucis equi-

of the injuftice done him. And
though they brought but à rude an
fwer back again, yet he refolve
to fuffer any thing rather that
engage in a war, having had fuc
ill fuccefs in the former. However
Jugurtha's greedy humour was no
hereby leffened at all, as having
in his own thoughts already de
voured his whole kingdom. Where
fore he begun now to make wan
not, as before, with a band of plun
derers only, but with a numerou
and a regular army; and not
avowedly claimed for himfelf th
kingdom of all Numidia; and
wherever he came, laid waf
and plundered both town and cour
try, put life into his own mei
and encreafed more and more ti
fright the enemy was in.

XXIV. Atherbal, finding ma
ters were come to that pafs, th
he muft either quit his kingdom,
keep it by force of arms, was n
ceffitated to raife troops, and mar
againft Jugurtha. In the me
time, both armies encamped t
far from the fea, nigh the tot
of Cirta; and, becaufe the day w
almoft fpent, they did not enga
in battle. But when the night w
almoft over, about twilight, t
foldiers of Jugurtha had the fi
nal given them, and made an a
fault upon the enemy's camp, p
to flight and difperfed them, whi
fome were half afleep, and oth
were taking to their arms. Athe
bal, with a few horfe, made
efcape to Cirta; and, had there
been a good number of Romans
til

is Cirtam profugit ; ni multitudo togato- fuiffet, quæ Numi- infequentis mœnibus hibuit, uno die inter s reges cœptum atque ratum foret bellum. tur Jugurtha oppidum cumfedit ; vineis, tur- ufque & machinis nium generum expug- e aggreditur; maxume inans tempus legato- n antecapere, quos an- prælium factum Ro- m ab Atherbale miffos liverat. Sed, poftquam atus de bello eorum epit, tres adolefcentes Africam legantur, qui bos reges adeant ; S. Q. R. verbis nunciant, 'le & cenfere eos ab ar- s difcedere ; de contro- fiis fuis, jure potius am bello difceptare : ita ue illifque dignum effe.

XXV. Legati Africam aturantes veniunt ; eo agis, quod Romæ, dum oficifci parant, de prœ- facto, & oppugnatione irtæ audiebatur. Sed is mor clemens erat. uorum Jugurtha ac- pta oratione refpondit ; i neque majus quid- iam, neque carius aucto- tate fenati effe ; ab ado- fcentia fua ita fe enifum, ab optumo quoque pro- retur. Virtute, non alitia, P. Scipioni, fum- o viro placuiffe ; ob eaf-

town, who repulfed the Numi- dians in purfuit of him from the walls, the war betwixt the two kings had been begun and ended in one day. Upon this, Jugurtha laid clofe fiege to the town, and endeavours, by means of virea, towers, and engines of all forts, to take it ; making all the hafte he could to be before-hand with the deputies he heard had been fent to Rome by Atherbal before the battle. But, after the fenate were informed of this war, three young gentlemen were difpatched by them into Africa, with orders to apply to both kings, and acquaint them, That it was the pleafure of the fenate and people of Rome, they fhould both be quiet, and decide their difputes in the way of reafon, and not of war, as what would be more for the honour of the Romans and themfelves too.

XXV. The deputies make all poffible hafte into Africa, and the rather, becaufe whilft they were preparing for their journey, news arrived in Rome of the battle, and the fiege of Cirta ; but fuch too as leffened very much the odioufnefs of the facts. Jugurtha, upon hearing the deputies, replied, That he was ready to pay the utmoft deference to the authority of the fenate ; he had endeavoured from his youth to behave in fuch a manner as to gain the approbation of the beft of men, and had recommended himfelf to the favour of that great man P. Sci-

dem

dem artis a Micipfa, non
penuria liberorum, in regnum adoptatum effe. Cæ-
terum, quo plura bene
atque ftrenue feciffet, eo
animum fuum injuriam
minus tolerare. Ather-
balem dolis vitæ fuæ in-
fidiatum ; quod ubi com-
periffet, fceleri obvium
iffe. Populum Romanum
neque recte, neque pro
bono facturum, fi ab jure
gentium fefe prohibuerit.
Poftremo, de omnibus re-
bus legatos Romam brevi
miffurum. Ita utrique
digrediuntur. Atherbalis
appellandi copia non fuit.
Jugurtha, ubi eos Afiica
deceffiffe ratus eft, neque
propter loci naturam Cir-
tam armis expugnare po-
teft, vallo atque foffa
mœnia circumdat ; turris
extruit, eafque præfidiis
firmat ; præterea dies
noctifque, aut per vim,
aut dolis tentare ; defen-
foribus mœnium præmia
modo, modo formidinem
oftentare ; fuos hortando
ad virtutem erigere ;
prorfus intentus cuncta
parare. Atherbal ubi in-
telligit omnis fortunas
fuas in extremo fitas,
hoftem infeflum, auxilii
fpem nullam, penuria re-
rum neceffariarum bel-
lum trahi non poffe, ex
iis, qui una Cirtam pro-
fugerant, duos maxume
impigros delegit ; eos,

pio by his virtue, not wickednefs
He had likewife been adopted b:
Micipfa to fucceed in his king
dom for the fame good qualitie:
and not for want of fons. B
the better he had behaved, th
more he refented any abufe. 'I h:
Atherbal had formed a plot again
his life, upon the difcovery (
which he had endeavoured to pr
vent him. That the Roman pe
ple would not do well, or de
fairly by him, if they debarr(
him from the common right
nations. Finally, he told the
he fhould fhortly fend deputies
Rome about all matters. Aft
this anfwer they parted. T
Roman deputies could not get i
the town to fpeak to Atherb(
When Jugurtha thought they w(
departed from Africa, finding
impoffible to take Cirta by affau
becaufe of the natural ftrength
the place, he blocks it up clofely
all fides with a rampart and
ditch ; builds towers, and fills th
with armed men ; and, befid
makes frequent attempts upon
by day and by night, in the way
open force or ftratagem ; plyi
the befieged one while with p
mifes, and another while w
threats ; and at the fame ti
animating his men to do th
utmoft. In fhort, he pufhed
bufinefs with all poffible appli(
tion and eagernefs. Atherbal, fi
ing himfelf reduced to the laft (
tremity, his enemy bent upon
deftruction, no hopes of affiftan
and that the war could not be c(
tinued for want of neceffari
chufes from among thofe that h

mu

mise-
con-
ftium
ad
dein
Nu-
juffa
.ther-
tatæ,
: fuit.

' cul-
ratum
ſ Ju-
quem
extin-
neque
ırtalis
ıngui-
mnia,
intum
ami-
armis
e mihi
bene-
'ecreta
o an
, in-
·a de
dehor-
mea.
: fum,
effe.
·o il-
ſum,
ami-
reg-
; u-
lumet,
Nam
bſalem
deinde
xpulit.
noſtræ

eſcaped along with him to Cirta two. of the moſt active, and by large promiſes and lamenting his condition, prevails with them to get through the enemies' lines in the night-time down to the ſea, and from thence to go to Rome. The Numidians execute their orders in a few days. Atherbal's letter was read in the ſenate, which was to the following effect.

XXVI. 'Tis no fault of mine, illuſtrious fathers, that I trouble you with ſuch frequent meſſages ; but I am obliged to it by the violence of Jugurtha, who is ſo madly bent upon my deſtruction, that he has no regard to you or the immortal gods, but had rather have my blood than all things in the world beſides. And therefore I, an ally and friend of the Roman people, have been cloſely beſieged for five months together ; whilſt neither the ſervices of my father Micipſa, nor your decrees, avail at all to my relief. I am unable to tell you, whether I am more diſtreſſed by ſword or by famine. My circumſtances diſcourage me from enlarging in my complaints againſt Jugurtha. I have found by experience, the unfortunate have but little credit. But, however, I am ſenſible he has ſomething in view beyond my deſtruction, and never expects to enjoy your friendſhip and my kingdom together Which of the two he is moſt ambitiouſly fond of can be no ſecret to any body. For he firſt of all murdered my brother Hiempſal, and then forced me from my father's kingdom. Let thoſe be acts

injuriæ ;

injuriæ ; nihil ad vos.
Verum nunc regnum ve-
strum armis tenet ; me,
quem vos imperatorem
Numidis posuistis, clau-
sum obsidet ; legatorum
verba quanti fecerit,
pericula mea declarant.
Quid est reliquum, nisi
vis vestra, qua moveri
possit? Nam ego quidem
vellem, & hæc quæ scri-
bo, & illa quæ antea in
senatu questus sum, vana
forent potius, quam mise-
ria mea fidem verbis fa-
ceret. Sed quoniam eo
natus sum, ut Jugurthæ
scelerum ostentui essem ;
non jam mortem neque
ærumnas, tantummodo ini-
mici imperium, & cru-
ciatus corporis deprecor.
Regno Numidiæ, quod
vestrum est, uti lubet, con-
sulite, me ex manibus
impiis eripite, per maje-
statem imperii, per ami-
citiæ fidem, si ulla apud
vos memoria remanet avi
mei Masinissæ.

XXVII. His literis
recitatis, fuere qui exercitum in Africam mit-
tendum censerent, &
quam primum Atherbali
subveniundum ; de Ju-
gurtha interim uti confu-
leretur, quoniam legatis
non paruisset. Sed ab
iisdem illis regis fautori-
bus summa ope enisum,
ne tale decretum fieret.
Ita bonum publicum, ut

of injustice to us, which no wa[
affect you. Yet now he keeps,[
force of arms, a kingdom that
yours, and besieges me, whom y[
appointed king of the Numidian[
then too how much he mind[
the remonstrances of your dep[
ties, my danger sufficiently shew[
What remains therefore to me
him, but force on your par[
For I could wish, that what
now write, and what I befo[
complained of to you, had n[
thing of truth in it, rather th[
that my misery should gain cre[
to what I say. But, since I w[
born to manifest to the world
my person the villainies of J[
gurtha, I beg not a delivery fro[
death or misery, but the hands
Jugurtha, and the cruel torture[
must expect from him. Dispo[
of the kingdom of Numidi[
which is yours, as you please. B[
I beseech you, by the majesty[
your mighty power, and the h[
nour of our alliance, deliver m[
from those impious hands, if yo[
have any respect for the memo[
of my grandfather Masinissa.

XXVII. *After the reading*
this letter, some were for sendi[
an army over into Africa, and r[
lieving Atherbal forthwith, an[
considering in the mean while [
what way to proceed against Ju[
gurtha for slighting their messa[
to him. But this was strenuous[.
opposed by such as had before fa[
voured the cause of Jugurtha[
Thus was the publick good, as i[
commonly falls out, baffled by pri[
vate interest. However, some el[

in

n plerifque negotiis folet,
rivata gratia devictum.
Legantur tamen in Afri-
am majores natu nobi-
es, amplis honoribus ufi,
n queis fuit M. Scaurus,
e quo fupra memoravi-
nus, confularis, & tum
enati princeps. Hi, quod
n invidia res erat, fimul
t a Numidis obfecrati,
riduo navim adfcendere;
ein brevi Uticam adpul-
literas ad Jugurtham
nittunt, *quam ocyffume*
d provinciam accedat;
i ad cum ab fenatu mif-
is. Ille ubi accepit ho-
nines claros, quorum
uctoritatem Romæ pol-
re audiverat, contra in-
ceptum fuum veniffe;
rimo commotus metu
tque lubidine divorfus
gitabatur. Timebat iram
enati, ni paruiffet lega-
s; porro animus cupi-
ine cæcus ad incœptum
celus rapiebat. Vicit ta-
nen in avido ingenio
ravum confilium. Igi-
ur, exercitu circumdato,
umma vi Cirtam irrum-
ere nititur; maxume
perans, diducta manu
oftium, aut vi aut dolis
efe cafum victoriæ in-
enturum. Quod ubi
ecus procedit, neque,
quod intenderat, efficere
oteft, uti prius, quam
egatos conveniret, A-
herbalis potiretur; ne
mplius morando Scau-

*derly noblemen, that had run
through the great offices of state,
are difpatched over into Africa;
among whom was M. Scaurus
mentioned above, a confular gentleman, and then at the head of the
fenate. Thefe gentlemen, as there
was a general outcry againft Jugurtha's behaviour, and the Numidians vehemently preffed them
for difpatch, went aboard a fhip in
three days' time, and arriving foon
after at Utica, fend a letter to
Jugurtha, with orders to repair
forthwith to them in the province; for that they had a meffage
to him from the fenate. Upon
finding that perfons of high rank,
and of very great fway at Rome,
as he had been informed, were come
to oppofe his defigns, he was much
fhocked, and diftracted betwixt
fear and a paffionate defire to carry
his point againft Atherbal. He
feared the fenate's refentment, if
he did not obey the commiffioners;
and then again, his mind, blinded
with ambition, hurried him on to
the completion of his wicked enterprize. The worfe of the two things
propofed to his choice at laft
wrought upon his ambitious foul.
Wherefore, drawing his army quite
round the place, he ufes his utmoft
efforts to break into Cirta; being
in great hopes that, by thus dividing the force of the enemy, he
might hit upon fome lucky chance
for fuccefs, either by force or cunning. But, mifcarrying in his defign of getting Atherbal into his
hands before he attended the commiffioners, for fear of provoking
Scaurus, whom he much dreaded,
rum,*

rum, quem plurimum metuebat, incenderet, cum paucis equitibus in provinciam venit. Ac tametfi fenati verbis minæ graves nunciabantur, quod ab oppugnatione non defifteret ; multa tamen oratione confumpta, legati fruftra difceffere.

XXVIII. Ea poftquam Cirtæ audita funt, Italici, quorum virtute mœnia defenfabantur, confifi, deditione facta, propter magnitudinem populi Romani inviolatos fefe fore, Atherbali fuadent, uti feque & oppidum Jugurthæ tradat ; tantum ab eo vitam pacifcatur; de cæteris fenatui curæ fore. At ille, tametfi omnia potiora fide Jugurthæ rebatur, tamen, quia penes eofdem, fi advorfaretur, cogendi poteftas erat, ita, uti cenfuerant Italici, deditionem fecit. Igitur Jugurtha in primis Atherbalem excruciatum necat; dein omnis puberes Numidas atque negotiatores promifcue, uti quifque armatus obvius fuerat, interfecit.

XXIX. Quod poftquam Romæ cognitum eft, & res in fenatu agitari cœpta ; iidem illi miniftri regis, interpellando, ac fæpe gratia,

by his delay, he came, attended with a few horfe, into the province. And tho' they did, in the name of the fenate, threaten him very feverely, for not raifing the fiege, yet after a deal of wranglę upon the fubject, the commiffioners departed, without being able to move him in the leaft.

XXVIII. *When the news of this was brought to Cirta, the Italians, by whom the town had been defended, fuppofing, in cafe of a furrender, that they, upon account of the Roman grandeur, fhould come to no damage, advife Atherbal to deliver up himfelf and the town to Jugurtha, articling for life only ; fince other matters the fenate would take care of. But, though he abhorred above all things the thoughts of trufting Jugurtha, yet becaufe it was in their power, if he refufed, to force him to a compliance, he did furrender, as the Italians advifed him. Whereupon Jugurtha, in the firft place, puts Atherbal to death with torture ; and then put all the Numidians of age, and the merchants too, that appeared in arms, without diftinction, to the fword.*

XXIX. *As foon as this was known at Rome, and the matter begun to be debated in the fenate, the fame penfioners to the king, by obftructing proceedings, and fpinning out the bufinefs, by their* inter

interdum jurgiis trahendo tempus, atrocitatem facti leniebant. Ac ni C. Memmius, tribunus plebis defignatus, vir acer & infeftus potentiæ nobilitatis, populum Romanum edocuiffet, *id agi, uti per paucos faßiofos Jugurthæ fcelus condonaretur,* profeßo omnis invidia, prolatandis confultationibus, dilapfa foret. Tanta vis gratiæ atque pecuniæ regis erat. Sed ubi fenatus delißi confcientia populum timet; lege Sempronia provinciæ futuris confulibus Numidia atque Italia decretæ ; confules declarati P. Scipio Nafica, L. Beftia Calpurnius ; Calpurnio Numidia, Scipioni Italia obvenit. Dein exercitus, qui in Africam portaretur, fcribitur; ftipendium, aliaque, quæ bello ufui forent, decernuntur.

XXX. At Jugurtha, contra fpem nuncio accepto, quippe cui, Romæ omnia venire, in animo hæferat, filium & cum eo duos familiaris ad fenatum legatos mittit ; iifque, ut illis quos Hiempfale interfeßo miferat, præcipit, *omnis mortalis pecunia aggrediantur.* Qui poftquam Romam adventabant, fenatus a Beftia confultus eft, *placeretne legatos Ju-*

intereſt in the members, and wrangling together, endeavoured to leſſen the odiouſneſs of the faßt. And had not C. Memmius, tribune of the commons eleß, a briſk man, and an avowed enemy to the power of the nobility, informed the Roman people, that the defign was to fcreen Jugurtha from the punifhment due to his wickednefs,by the means of a few leading men, *all the odium of the thing, by the dilatory proceedings of the fenate, would have vaniſhed. Such weight had the king's intereſt and money together amongſt them. Eut when the fenate, from a fenfe of their own guilt, begun to be apprehenfive of the people's refentment, a bill was preferred to the people, and paffed, whereby the provinces appointed for the fucceeding confuls, were Numidia and Italy; P. Scipio Nafica, and L. Beftia Calpurnius,* were made confuls; *and Numidia fell to Calpurnius ; and Italy to Scipio. Then an army was levied for Africa; money, and other things neceffary for the war, voted.*

XXX. *But Jugurtha, furprifed at the news of this, as who had been full of a perfuafion, that all things were to be had for money at Rome, difpatches away his fon, and two ambaffadors with him, to the fenate, and orders them, as he had before done thofe he fent after the murder of Hiempfal,* to bribe all about them, wherever they came. *After their arrival at Rome, the fenate was confulted by Beſtia, to know their pleaſure,* Whether the ambaffadors of Jugurtha fhould be admitted into the

L.   *gurthæ*

gurthæ recipi mœnibus; iique decrevere, *ni regnum ipfumque deditum venifſent, ut in diebus proxumis decem Italia decederent.* Conful Numidis ex fenati decreto nunciari jubet. Ita infectis rebus illi domum difcedunt. Interim Calpurnius, parato exercitu, legat fibi homines nobilis, factiofos, quorum auctoritate, quæ deliquiffet, munito fore fperabat; in quein fuit Scaurus, cujus de natura & habitu fupra memoravimus. Nam in confule noftro multæ bonæque artes animi & corporis erant; quas omnis avaritia præpediebat. Patiens laborum, acri ingenio, fatis providens, belli haud ignarus, firmiſſumus contra pericula & infidias. Sed legiones per Italiam Rhegium, atque inde Siciliam, porro ex Sicilia in Africam tranfvectæ. Igitur Calpurnius, initio paratis commeatibus, acriter Numidiam ingreſſus eft; multofque mortalis & urbis aliquot pugnando cepit.

XXXI. Sed ubi Jugurtha per legatos pecunia tentare, bellique, quod adminiftrabat, afperitatem oftendere cœpit; animus æger avaritia facile converfus eft. Cæterum focius & adminifter

city, or no. *And the fenate voted thereupon,* That unlefs they were come to furrender both Jugurtha and his kingdom, they fhould be gone out of Italy in ten days time. *Which, by order of the fenate, the conful fignified to the Numidians; and accordingly they went home, without doing any thing. In the mean time, Calpurnius having raifed an army, chufes for his lieutenant-generals, noblemen of the greateft intereft; by the authority of whom, he hoped, the crimes he propofed to commit, might pafs unpunifhed. Amongft thefe was Scaurus, whofe character I have given above. For our conful had many excellent qualities, both of body and mind, the exercife whereof was much obftructed by his covetoufnefs. He was hardy, of fhrewd parts, a man of great forefight, and well verfed in the bufinefs of war, and much upon his guard againft all danger and furprize. The legions were led thro' Italy to Rhegium, from thence carried over to Sicily, and from Sicily to Africa. Where Calpurnius providing his army, in the firft place, with all neceffaries, very brifkly entered Numidia, took abundance of prifoners, and feveral cities fword in hand.*

XXXI. *But after Jugurtha begun by his meſſengers to lay the money-bait in his way, and to make him fenfible of the difficulty of the war, his mind, over-run with the diftemper of covetoufnefs, begun to faulter. Scaurus he made his partner and affiftant in all his mea-*
omni-

consiliorum af- *fures; who though at firft, when*
Scaurus; qui ta- *moft of his party had been corrupt-*
principio, plerif- *ed, he had violently oppofed the*
actione ejus cor- *king; yet was he at laft driven,*
icerrume regem *by the dint of hard bribery, from*
verat; tamen, *his integrity, to patronize the*
line pecuniæ, *wickednefs of Jugurtha; who at*
honeftoque in *firft purchafed only a fufpenfion of*
abftractus eft. *the war, in hopes to carry his point,*
gurtha primum *in the mean time, at Rome, by bri-*
iodo belli mo- *bery or intereft. But when he found*
imebat, exiftu- *Scaurus was engaged in his favour,*
e aliquid interim *in ftrong confidence of compaffing*
oretio aut gratia *a peace, he refolved to enter into a*
im. Poftea vero *perfonal treaty with them, in re-*
irticipem negotii *lation to all concerns whatever.*
accepit, in *But in the mean time, Sextius the*
m fpem adduc- *quæftor is difpatched, by way of*
uperandæ pacis, *fecurity, into a town of Jugurtha,*
im eis de omni- *called Vacca, under pretence of*
tionibus præfens *receiving corn, which Calpurnius*
Cæterum intérea *had ordered the deputies to provide*
iuffa mittitur a *for his army; becaufe there was*
Sextius quæftor *now a truce, in order to Jugur-*
idum Jugurthæ *tha's making a furrender of him-*
; cujus rei fpeci- *felf. Wherefore the king, accord-*
cceptio frumenti, *ing to his appointment, came into*
alpurnius palam *the camp. And after he had fpoke*
nperaverat; quo- *very briefly, with relation to the*
ditionis mora in- *odium his late conduct had brought*
jitabantur. Igitur *upon him, in the hearing of a coun-*
i conftituerat, in *cil of war, and defired he might*
enit; ac pauca *be admitted to an honourable fur-*
concilio locutus *render, he treated with Beftia and*
ia facti fui, atque *Scaurus in private about their o-*
editionem accipe- *ther affairs; and then the day af-*
eliqua cum Beftia *ter, the opinion of the council as*
o fecreta tranfigit; *to divers particulars, being taken*
tero die, quafi per *together, and in a hurry, he is*
fententiis exqui- *admitted to a furrender. But,*
deditionem acci- *agreeably to what had been enjoin-*
Sed, uti pro con- *ed him, in the prefence of the*
peratum erat, ele- *council, thirty elephants, fome cat-*
xxx, pecus atque *tle, and abundance of horfes, with*

equi

equi multi, cum parvo argenti pondere, quæftori traduntur. Calpurnius Romam ad magiſtratus rogandos proficifcitur. In Numidia & exercitu noſtro pax agitabatur.

XXXII. Poſtquam res in Africa geſtas, quoque modo actæ forent, fama divulgavit; Romæ per omnis locos & conventus de facto confulis agitari. Apud plebem gravis invidia; patres foliciti erant; probarentne tantum flagitium, an decretum confulis fubverterent, parum conſtabat. Ac maxume eos potentia Scauri, quod is auctor & focius Beſtiæ ferebatur, a vero bonoque impediebat. At C. Memmius, cujus de libertate ingenii, & odio potentiæ nobilitatis fupra diximus, inter dubitationem & moras fenati, concionibus populum ad vindicandum hortari, monere, ne rempublicam, ne libertatem fuam defererent; multa fuperba, & crudelia facinora nobilitatis oſtendere; prorfus intentus omni modo plebis animum accendebat. Sed, quoniam ea tempeſtate Romæ Memmii facundia clara pollenfque fuit, decere exiſtumavi unam ex tam multis orationem ejus prefcribere; ac potiſſumum ea dicam, quæ in

a *fmall quantity of filver, are delivered up to the quæſtor. Calpurnius goes to Rome, to prefide in the election of new magiſtrates; whilſt all was now quiet in Numidia, and our army.*

XXXII. *When common fam had now divulged the tranfaction in Africa, with the manner of them, the behaviour of the confu was the fubject of much converfa tion, in all places and companies a Rome. The commons were huget incenfed at the bufinefs; and th fenate in great perplexity. The knew not whether they fhould ra tify fo vile a piece of conduct, a make void all that had been refo ved on by the conful. What chief diverted them from the purfuit right and juſtice in the cafe, wi the power of Scaurus, who wi faid to have encouraged and fuj ported Beſtia in the defign. B C. Memmius, concerning who boldnefs and fpight to the nobilii we have fpoke above, during t. doubts and delays of the fenat did, by feveral harangues, exho the people to punifh the mifbehav our of the conful, and admonifh them not to defert the caufe the publick, and their own libert He gave many inſtances of t. infolent and cruel behaviour of t. nobility; and did, with the utmi application, endeavour to fpirit the commons againſt them. An. becaufe at that time he bore mighty character at Rome for el quence, I have thought it wou not be amifs, to prefent the read with one of the many fpeeches.*

concione, poft reditum Beftiæ, hujufcemodi verbis diſſeruit.

made on this occaſion; that I mean, which he made in an aſſembly of the people, after the return of Beſtia, in the following words.

XXXIII. *Multa me dehortantur a vobis, Quirites, ni ſtudium reipublicæ omnia ſuperet; opes faƈtionis, veſtra patientia, jus nullum; ac maxume, quod innocentiæ plus periculi, quam honoris, eſt. Nam illa quidem piget dicere, his annis xv. quam ludibrio fueritis ſuperbiæ paucorum; quam fæde, quamquam inulti, perierint veſtri defenſores; uti vobis animus ab ignavia atque ſecordia corruptus ſit; qui ne nunc quidem obnoxiis inimicis exſurgitis; atque etiam nunc timetis eos, quibus vos decet terrori eſſe. Sed quamquam hæc talia ſunt; tamen obviam ire faƈtionis potentiæ animus ſubigit. Certe ego libertatem, quæ mihi a parente meo tradita eſt, experiar; verum id fruſtra, an ob rem faciam, in veſtra manu ſitum eſt, Quirites.*

XXXIII. Many things would diſcourage me from applying to you, as I now do, gentlemen, did not a regard for the good of the publick prevail with me above all other conſiderations. The things I mean, are, the power of the faƈtion of the nobles, your tame ſubmiſſion, and want of authority; and above all, that innocency is now attended with more danger, than honour. For it is really irkſome to me to remind you, how inſolently you have been treated by ſome great men for theſe fifteen years laſt, and how baſely the patrons of your cauſe were taken off, without the leaſt puniſhment inflicted upon thoſe that were guilty of it, as alſo what a mean daſtardly ſpirit you ſhew, who ſtir not in your own defence, even now when your enemies are at your mercy; and are afraid of thoſe, to whom you ought to be a terror. But tho' matters be thus, yet I am determined to make a ſtand againſt the power of the faƈtion. I will try at leaſt, the liberty that has been left me by my father; but whether that my endeavour ſhall be attended with ſucceſs, or not, muſt depend entirely upon you, gentlemen.

XXXIV. *Neque ego vos hortor, quod ſæpe maores veſtri fecere, uti ontra injurias armati atis. Nihil vi, nihil iceſſione opus eſt. Neceſſe eſt, ſuomet ipſi more præ-*

XXXIV. Yet do I not adviſe you to what your forefathers often did, that is, to do yourſelves juſtice by force of arms. No, there is no occaſion for violence, or leaving the town. They muſt needs be ruined by their own way

L 3 . *cipites*

158   *C. CRISPI SALLUSTII*

*cipites eant. Occifo Ti.
Graccho, quem regnum
parare aiebant, in ple-
bem Romanam quæftiones
graves habitæ funt. Poft
C. Gracchi & M. Fulvii
cædem, item ordinis ve-
ftri multi mortales in carcere necati funt. Utriuf-
que cladis non lex, verum
lubido eorum finem fecit.
Sed fane fuerit regni pa-
ratio, plebi jura fua re-
ftituere. Quicquid fine
fanguine civium ulcifci
requitur, jure factum fit.
Superioribus annis taciti
indignabamini ærarium
expilari; reges & populos
liberos paucis nobilibus
vectigal pendere; penes
eofdem & fummam glori-
am, & maxumas divitias
effe. Tamen hæc talia fa-
cinora impune fufcepiffe,
parum habuere; itaque
poftremo leges, majeftas
veftra, divina & humana
omnia hoftibus tradita
funt. Neque eos, qui ea
fecere, pudet aut pœni-
tet; fed incedunt per ora
veftra magnifici, facerdotia, & confulatus, pars
triumphos fuos oftentan-
tes; perinde quafi ea ho-
nori, non prædæ, habe-
ant. Servi ære parati
injufta imperia dominо-
rum non perferunt; vos,
quirites, imperio nati,
æquo animo fervitutem
toleratis? At qui funt
hi, qui rempublicam oc-*

of proceeding. After Tiberius
Gracchus was flain, whom they
charged with a defign upon the fo-
vereignty, there was terrible execution done upon the commons of
Rome. After the murder of C.
Gracchus and M. Fulvius, a great
many perfons of your rank were
put to death in prifon. Nor was
an end put to thofe violent proceedings by law; but the humour
only of thofe that were guilty
thereof. But let the attempt to
reftore the commons to their right
pafs for a defign to feize the government. Let whatever cannot
be punifhed without fhedding the
blood of our fellow-citizens, be
warrantably fo done. For fome
years paft, tho' you faid nothing
yet you were full of indignation
to fee the treafury robbed, king
and free nations pay taxes to a few
of the nobility, who lived in the
greateft height of glory and plen
ty. Nor did it fuffice them to g
unpunifhed for fuch ftrange con
duct; and therefore at laft you
laws, majefty, and all things di
vine and human, were betraye
into the hands of your enemie
Nor are the perfons guilty of thi
treafon, afhamed of, or forry fo
it; but ftrut in the moft ftatel
manner before your eyes, pridin
themfelves in their facred dignitie
confulfhips, and triumphs, as
they valued them only for the ho
nour arifing from them, and n
for the convenience they thereb
had of robbing the publick. Slave
bought with money, refufe to fub
mit to the unreafonable infolenc
of their mafters, and do you, ger

cupavere

cupavere ? Homines fce-
leratiffumi, cruentis ma-
nibus, immani avaritia,
nocentiffumi, idemque fu-
perbiffumi ; quibus fides,
decus, pietas, poftremo,
honefta atque inhonefta
omnia quæftui funt. Pars
eorum occidiffe tribunos
plebis, alii quæftiones in-
juftas, plerique cædem in
vos feciffe, pro munimento
habent. Ita, quam quif-
que peffume fecit, tam max-
ume tutus eft. Metum a
fcelere fuo ad ignaviam
veftram tranftulere ; quos
omnis eadem cupere, eadem
odiffe, eadem metuere in
unum coegit. Sed hæc in-
ter bonos amicitia, inter
malos faƐio eft.

tlemen, who were born to dominion, endure to be enflaved with
patience ? But who are thefe that
have got the management of affairs into their hands ? The moft
wicked, bloody, avaricious, pernicious, infolent wretches, who
carry faith, honour, piety, and,
in fhort, every thing honourable,
or otherwife, to market. Some
have fecured themfelves by murdering your tribunes, others by
unjuft profecutions, and others
again by the murder of many
among yourfelves. And thus the
worfe any man behaves himfelf,
the fafer he is. And inftead of their
fearing you, left you fhould punifh
them for their wickednefs, you
are fo bafe fpirited as to be afraid
of them ; who are united among
themfelves by the conformity of
their difpofitions, as all coveting,
hating, and fearing the fame things. And this union among
good men is friendfhip, but among the wicked, faƐion.

XXXV. *Quod fi vos*
tam libertatis curam ha-
beretis, quam illi ad do-
minationem accenfi funt ;
profeƐo neque refpublica,
ficuti nunc, vaftaretur ;
& beneficia veftra penes
optumos, non audaciffu-
mos, forent. Majores
veftri, parandi juris, &
majeftatis conftituendæ
gratia bis per feceffionem
armati Aventinum occu-
pavere. Vos pro libertate,
quam ab illis accepiftis,
nonne fumma ope nitemi-
ni ? atque eo vehementi-
us, quo majus dedecus eft,
parta amittere, quam

XXXV. But if you had only
as great a concern for the preferva-
ation of your liberty, as they have
to acquire a defpotick power over
you, the publick would not be fo
wretchedly abufed, and your favours would fall upon the beft, and
not the moft audacious of men.
Your forefathers twice left the
town in arms, and poffeffed themfelves of the Aventine mount, in
order to affert their right, and
eftablifh their authority. And will
not you exert your utmoft endeavours in defence of the liberty you
have received from them ? and
the more fo, the more fhame it
is, to lofe what has been once got,
than never to have acquired it at

L 4   *omni-*

omnino non paravisse? Dicet aliquis, quid igitur censes? Vindicandum in eos qui hosti prodidere rempublicam, non manu, neque vi (quod magis vos fecisse, quam illis accidisse, indignum est) verum quæstionibus & indicio ipsius Jugurthæ. Qui si dedititius est, profecto jussis vestris obediens erit; sin ea contemnit; scilicet æstumabitis, qualis illa pax aut deditio sit, ex qua ad Jugurtham scelerum impunitas, ad paucos potentis maxumæ divitiæ, in rempublicam damna atque dedecora pervenerint. Nisi forte nondum etiam vos dominationis eorum satietas tenet; & illa, quam hæc tempora, magis placent; cum regna, provinciæ, leges, jura, judicia, bella atque paces, postremo divina & humana omnia penes paucos erant; vos autem, hoc est, populus Romanus, invicti ab hostibus, imperatores omnium gentium, satis habebatis animam retinere. Nam servitutem quidem quis vestrum audebat recusare? Atque ego, tametsi flagitiosissumum existumo impune injuriam accepisse; tamen vos hominibus sceleratissumus ignoscere, quoniam cives sunt, æquo animo paterer, ni misericordia in perniciem casura esset.

all. Some perhaps may afk, what I would have done then? To which I answer, that I would have those punished who have betrayed the republick to the enemy, yet not in the way of violence or force; which how much soever they may have deserved at your hands, yet would be a part unworthy of you to act. No, the way I would have you to proceed in, is that of a legal prosecution, and the evidence of Jugurtha himself. Who, if he has surrendered in good earnest, will be obedient to your orders; but if he slight them, you may thereby judge what kind of peace and submission that is, by virtue whereof Jugurtha is to reap impunity for all his crimes, a few great men immense riches, and the republick nothing but loss and disgrace. Unless you are not even yet weary of their tyranny, and those times please you best, when kingdoms, the provinces, laws, courts, war and peace, and in short, all things whatever, both divine and human, were at the disposal of a few great men: whilst you the Roman people, the invincible lords of the world, were content with life alone. For which of you durst refuse the yoke? and yet, tho' I think it highly dishonourable for a man to bear ill usage with a tame submission, I could be content you should pardon those wicked wretches, because they are your fellow-citizens, if your compassion to them would not end in your own destruction.

XXXVI.

XXXVI. *Nam & il-*
s, quantum importuni-
atis habent, parum eft
npune male feciffe, nifi
einde faciundi licentia
ripitur; & vobis æterna
licitudo remanebit, cum
ntelligetis, aut ferviun-
um effe aut per manus
bertatem retinendam.
Iam fidei quidem aut
ncordiæ quæ fpes eft?
Iominari illi volunt, vos
beri effe; facere illi in-
rias, vos prohibere.
oftremo fociis veftris,
luti hoftibus, hoftibus
o fociis utuntur. Po-
fine in tam divorfis
entibus pax aut amicitia
Ie? Quare moneo hor-
rque vos, ne tantum
:lus impunitum dimitta-
:. Non peculatus ærarii
Etus eft; neque per
m' fociis ereptæ pecu-
æ; quæ, quamquam
'avia funt, tamen con-
'etudine jam pro nihilo
ibentur. Hofti acerrumo
'odita fenati auctoritas,
'oditum imperium ve-
rum; domi militiæque
'fpublica venalis fuit
)uæ nifi quæfita erunt,
fi vindicatum in noxios,
iid erit reliquum, nifi
' illis, quia ea fecere, obe-
'entes vivamus? Nam
ipune quælibet facere,
! eft regem effe. Neque
'e vos, quirites, hortor,
'i jam malitis civis ve-
ros perperam, quam rec-

XXXVI. But fo violent is
their inclination to mifchief that
the letting them go unpunifhed for
paft crimes will avail you nothing,
unlefs the power of committing
the like be taken from them for
the future; and you muft live in
perpetual anxiety, when you find
yourfelves under a neceffity of being flaves, or maintaining your liberty by force of arms. For what
hope is there of preferving faith
or concord among us? They are
defirous to lord it over you at
pleafure, you to be free; they to
do mifchief, you to hinder it. Finally, they ufe your allies as enemies, your enemies as allies. Can
there be any peace or friendfhip
in minds fo differently difpofed?
Wherefore I advife and befeech
you, not to let fuch villainy go unpunifhed. The cafe now before
you is not that of robbing the
treafury, or oppreffing your allies,
which tho' very grievous things,
yet are grown fo fafhionable that
they pafs for trifles only. The
authority of the fenate, and your
mighty power have been betrayed
to your moft virulent enemy; and
the commonwealth fet to fale both
at home and abroad. And unlefs
ftrict enquiry be made into this
mifconduct, and the guilty be punifhed, what will be left for us,
but to live in a flavifh fubjection
to the villains? for to do with
impunity whatfoever a man pleafes is to be a king. I would not
hereby be thought to encourage
you to wifh your fellow-citizens
may be rather found guilty than
innocent; but only not to pardon

tc,

te, fecisse; sed ne ignoscendo malis, bonos perditum eatis. Ad hoc, in republica multo præstat, beneficii, quam maleficii, immemorem esse. Bonus tantummodo segnior fit, ubi neglegas; at malus improbior. Ad hoc, si injuriæ non sint, haud sæpe auxilii egeas.

such as shall really appear guilty, to the ruin of the innocent. Besides in the administration of the government, it is better to forget a kindness done the publick, than an offence committed against it. The good man only becomes less inclined to serve his country, if you overlook him; but the wicked becomes still worse. Besides, if no wickedness be acted against the state, you seldom want assistance

XXXVII. Hæc atque alia hujuscemodi sæpe dicundo, C. Memmius populo Romano persuadet uti L. Cassius, qui tum prætor erat, ad Jugurtham mitteretur; eumque, interposita fide publica, Romam duceret; quo facilius indicio regis, Scauri, & reliquorum, quos pecuniæ captæ arcessebant, delicta patefierent. Dum hæc Romæ geruntur, qui in Numidia relicti ab Bestia exercitui præerant, secuti morem imperatoris sui, plurima & flagitiosissuma facinora fecere. Fuere, qui auro corrupti elephantos Jugurthæ traderent; alii perfugas venderent; pars ex pacatis prædas agebant. Tanta avaricia in animos eorum, veluti tabes, invaserat. At Cassius prætor perlata rogatione a C. Memmio, ac perculsa omni nobilitate, ad Jugurtham proficiscitur;

XXXVII. *By frequently ha ranguing the people in this strain Memmius persuades them to sen L. Cassius, at that time Prætor to Jugurtha, to bring him to Rom upon the publick faith, in order i to use him as an evidence again Scaurus, and the rest, who wer charged with taking his money Whilst these things were doing Rome, they who were left by B. stia with the command of the ar my in Numidia, following the e: ample of their general, were guil of a great deal of very scandalo behaviour. Some were bribed return Jugurtha his elephant others to sell him deserters, othe again plundered the country th was at peace with us. To such degree had Covetousness, like t plague, infected their minds. B Cassius the Prætor, upon passe of the bill preferred by Memmiu to the great consternation of all t nobility, goes over to Jugurth and persuades him, being sore frighted, and from a sense of h guilt looking upon his case as desp rate, Since he had submitted t the Roman people, not to mak trial of their power, rather tha*

eiq

:ique timido, & ex con- *their clemency. Befides, he pri-*
cientia diffidenti rebus *vately engaged his own faith in*
uis,. perfuadet, *quoniam his behalf, which the other valued*
ſe populo Romano dedidiſ- as much as the publick faith itſelf.
ſet, ne vim, quam miſe- So excellent a character had Caſ-
ricordiam ejus, experiri ſius at that time.
nalit. Privatim præteria fidem fuam interponit, quam ille
non minoris, quam publicam, ducebat. Talis ea tempeſtate fama de Caſſio erat.

XXXVIII. Igitur Ju- *XXXVIII. Wherefore Jugur-*
gurtha, contra decus re-' *tha comes along with Caſſius to*
gium, cultu quam muxu- *Rome, with a very ſorry equipage,*
me miſerabili cum Caſſio *much below the dignity of a prince.*
Romam venit. At, tametſi *And tho' he had a good heart upon*
in ipſo magna vis animi *the matter, being encouraged by*
erat, confirmatus ab om- *all, by whoſe power and roguery*
nibus, quorum potentia *he had been ſupported in his wick-*
aut fcelere cuncta ea gef- *ed management above related ;*
ferat, quæ fupra memora- *yet he prevails with C. Bæbius,*
vimus, C. Bæbium tribu- *tribune of the commons, by an im-*
num plebis magna merce- *menſe bribe, to employ all his*
de parat, cujus impuden- *impudence, in order to protect him*
tia contra jus & injurias *againſt right, and the puniſhment*
omnis munitus foret. At *due to his crimes. But C. Mem-*
C. Memmius, advocata *mius ſummoning the people toge-*
concione, (quamquam *ther, although they were much en-*
regi infeſta plebes erat, & *raged againſt the king, and ſome*
pars *in vincula duci* jube- *were for* clapping him in jail, *and*
bat, pars, *ni ſocios ſcele- others for* puniſhing him capitally,
ris, aperiret, more majo- according to the antient Roman
rum de hoſte ſupplicium uſage, *unleſs he diſcovered thoſe*
ſumi) dignitati magis, *concerned with him in his wick-*
quam iræ, confulens, fe- *edneſs ; yet Memmius, I ſay, ha-*
dare motus, & animos *ving a regard to what honour re-*
eorum molire ; poſtremo *quired, rather than what paſſion*
confirmare, fidem pub- *directed, endeavoured to allay their*
licam per fefe inviola- *heat, and mollify them ; declaring*
tam fore. Poſt, ubi ſi- *finally, that he however would*
lentium cœpit, producto *have no hand in the violation of*
Jugurtha, verba facit ; *of the publick faith. And at laſt,*
Romæ Numidiæque fa- when ſilence was obtained, Jugur-
cinora ejus memorat, *tha being brought before the af-*
ſcelera in patrem fratreſ- ſembly, he ſpoke, and recounted all
que oſtendit ; *quibus ju-* his pranks at Rome, and in Nu-
vantibus

vantibus, quibufque mini-
ftris ea egerit, quamquam
intelligat populus Roma-
nus, tamen velle mani-
fefta magis ex illo habere;
fi verum aperiat, in fide
& clementia populi Ro-
mani magnam fpem illi
fitam; fin reticeat, non
fociis faluti fore, fed fe
fuafque fpes corrupturum.
Deia ubi Memmius di-
cendi finem fecit, & Ju-
gurtha refpondere juffus
eft, C. Bæbius tribunus
plebis, quem pecunia cor-
ruptum fupra diximus,
regem tacere jubet. Ac,
tametfi multitudo, quæ
in concione aderat, vehe-
menter accenfa, terrebat
eum clamore, vultu, fæpe
impetu, atque aliis om-
nibus, quæ ira fieri amat,
vicit tamen impudentia.
Ita populus, ludibrio ha-
bitus, ex concione difce-
dit. Jugurthæ, Beftiæ-
que, & ceteris, quos illa
quæftio exagitabat, ani-
mi augefcunt.

midia; *fet forth* his wicked beha.
viour towards his father, and his
brothers; *and gave him to under-*
ftand, that tho' the Roman people
knew by whofe affiftance and fupport he had done all thofe things
yet they had a mind to have a
more full difcovery of the fame
from himfelf, which if he woulc
truly and faithfully make, he migh
depend upon the honour and cle
mency of the Roman people; bu
if not, he would do his Friends no
fervice, and would moreover blaf
all his own hopes entirely. *Whei*
Memmius had done fpeaking, an
Jugurtha was ordered to reply, C
Bæbius, tribune of the commons
who had been fecured by a goo.
bribe, as I took notice above, com
mands the king to hold his tongue
And tho' the people there affemble
were mightily incenfed, and did b
fhouts, angry looks, and violenc
too very often, and all other mean
that paffion dictates, endeavour t
deter him from his purpofe, yet h
impudence prevailed. The peopl
being thus fooled, broke up and de
parted. Jugurtha, Beftia, an
the reft of them, againft whom thi
enquiry was pointed, took hear
upon it.

XXXIX. Erat ea
tempeftate Romæ Nu-
mina quidam, nomine
Maffiva, Guluffæ filius,
Mafiniffæ nepos; qui quia
in diffenfione regum, Ju-
gurthæ advorfus fuerat,
dedita Cirta, & Atherbale
interfecto, profugus ex
Africa abierat. Huic Sp.
Albinus, qui proxumo

XXXIX. *There was at tha*
time a certain Numidian at Rome
by name Maffiva, the fon of Gu
luffa, and grandfon of Maffiniffa
who, becaufe in the quarrel be
twixt the two kings, he had beei
againft Jugurtha, when Cirta wa
furrendered, and Atherbal put t
death, had fled out of Africa. Sp
Albinus, who the next year afiei
Beftia was conful with Q. Mi.
                              annc

anno poſt Beſtiam cum Q. Minucio Rufo confulatum gerebat, perſuadet, quoniam ex ſtirpe Maſiniſſæ ſit, Jugurtham ob ſcelera invidia cum metu urgeat, regnum Numidiæ ab ſenatu petat. Avidus conful belli gerundi, moveri, quam feneſcere, omnia malebat. Ipſi provincia Numidia, Minucio Macedonia evenerat. Quæ poſtquam Maſſiva agitare cœpit; neque Jugurthæ in amicis fatis præſidii eſt; quod eorum alium conſcientia, alium mala fama & timor animi impediebat; Bomilcari proxumo ac maxume fido ſibi imperat, *precio, ſiculi multa confecerat, inſidiatores Maſſiva paret; ac maxume occulte; ſin id parum procedat, quovis modo Numidam interficiat.* Bomilcar mature regis mandata exſequitur; &, per homines talis negotii artifices, itinera egreſſuſque ejus, poſtremo loca, atque tempora cuncta explorat; dein, ubi res poſtulabat inſidias tendit. Igitur unus, ex eo numero, qui ad cædem parati erant, paullo inconſultius Maſſivam aggreditur, illum obtruncat; ſed ipſe deprehenſus, multis hortantibus, & in primis Albino confule, indicium profitetur. Fit

nucius Rufus, perſuades him, ſince he was deſcended from Maſiniſſa, to aggravate the odiouſneſs of Jugurtha's crimes, and alarm him with fears, by making his ſuit to the ſenate for the kingdom of Numidia. The conſul being vaſtly deſirous of having the war continued under his command, was for kindling a new flame rather than have the old one die away. He had got by lot the province of Numidia, Minucius Macedonia. When Maſſiva begun to ſtir in the buſineſs, Jugurtha being not able to depend upon the protection of his friends, becauſe ſome where diſcouraged from meddling further in his behalf, by a ſenſe of their guilt; others by ſuſpicions conceived of them, and their fears together, orders Bomilcar, a very near relation, and heartily in his intereſt, to go to work in a way, wherein he had carried many of his points, and hire ſome perſons to take off Maſſiva, and privately, if poſſible; but if that ſhould not be found feaſible, by any way or means whatever. Bomilcar quickly puts the king's orders in execution; and by men well verſed in ſuch ſort of work watches all his motions and haunts; and when the matter ſeemed ripe for it, lays his plot. One of the rogues engaged in the deſign, falls upon Maſſiva, and kills him, but in ſo unguarded a manner that he was immediately apprehended; and being urged by many, and eſpecially Albinus the conful, to confeſs who ſet him on work, he did ſo. Bomilcar was proſecuted upon it, more

reus

reus magis ex æquo bonoque, quam ex jure gentium Bomilcar, comes ejus, qui Romam fide publica venerat. At Jugurtha, manifestus tanti sceleris, non prius omisit contra verum niti, quam animadvertit, super gratiam atque pecuniam suam invidiam facti esse. Igitur, quamquam in priore actione ex amicis quinquaginta vades dederat, regno magis quam vadibus confulens, clam in Numidiam Bomilcarem dimittit; veritus, ne reliquos popularis metus invaderet parendi sibi, si de illo supplicium sumptum foret. Et ipse paucis diebus eodem profectus est, jussus a senatu Italia decedere. Sed postquam Roma egressus est, fertur, sæpe tacitus eo-respiciens postremo dixisse, *Urbem venalem, & mature periituram, si emptorem invenerit.*

XL. Interim Albinus, renovato bello, commeatum, stipendium, aliaque, quæ militibus usui forent, maturat in Africam portare; ac statim ipse profectus, ut ante comitia, quod tempus haud longe aberat, armis, aut deditione, aut quovis modo bellum conficeret. At contra Jugurtha trahere omnia, & alias, de-

agreeably to the law of natural justice, than that of nations, as being one of the retinue of Jugurtha, who had come to Rome upon the publick faith. But Jugurtha, tho' manifestly guilty of so villainous a fact, did not give over facing down the truth, 'till he perceived the odium of the thing was quite too hard for all his interest and money together. And therefore, though in the first action he had given fifty of his friends as bail for Bomilcar's appearance, yet being more concerned for the preservation of · his kingdom than his bail, he sends him off privately into Numidia, fearing lest the rest of his subjects should be afraid of obeying him, if he should be punished. And in a few days after he went away himself, being ordered by the senate to depart out of Italy. It is reported of him, that after he was got out of Rome, he frequently looked back without saying any thing; but at last broke out into these words, that the city was to be sold, and would soon be ruined, if it did but meet with a chapman.

XL. The war being now revived, Albinus makes haste to transport into Africa provisions, money, and other necessaries for the army, and went forthwith himself, that he might by force of arms, the surrender of Jugurtha, or by any other means, dispatch the war before the election, which was not very far off. But, on the other hand, Jugurtha endeavoured to spin out the time, and contrived divers means for that purpose. He

as moræ cauffas
polliceri deditio-
c deinde metum
; inftanti cedere,
lo poft, ne fui
nt, inftare ; ita
)do, modo pacis
nfulem ludificare.
:, qui tum Albi-
ud ignarum con-
is exiftumarent ;
k tanta properan-
facile tractum bel-
)rdia magis, quam
'ederent.

Sed poftquam,
tempore, comi-
dies adventabat ;
, Aulo fratre in
roprætore relicto,
decefiit. Ea
ate Romæ fediti-
ribuniciis atrociter
ca agitabatur. P.
s & L. Annius
plebis, refiftenti-
legis, continuare
atum nitebantur ;
Tentio totius anni
impediebat. Ea
n fpem adductus
quem propræto-
caftris relictum fu-
mus, aut confici-
)elli, aut terrore
is ab rege pecuniæ
læ, milites menfe
o ex hibernis in
ionem evocat ;
]ue itineribus hie-
)era pervenit ad
n Suthul, ubi re-
auri erant. Quod

---

promifed to furrender, and then quickly excufed himfelf, under pretence of apprehending ill ufage. When the enemy pufhed him, he fled ; and prefently, for fear of difcouraging his men, came brifkly on again. and thus did he befool the conful, one while by pretenfions of war, and another while thofe of peace. There were fome at that time, who did believe that Albinus was no ftranger to the king's purpofe, and that after fo much hafte, the war was not protracted from carelefnefs, but defign.

XLI. But the time being now elapfed, and the day of election at hand, Albinus leaves his brother Aulus to fupply his place in the camp, and goes to Rome. At that time the commonwealth was put into great convulfions by fome broils among the tribunes. P. Lucullus, and L. Annius, tribunes of the commons, pretended to ftand candidates for the office the next year too, wherein they were oppofed by all their colleagues ; which difpute kept off all the other elections likewife. Upon occafion of this delay, Aulus, who, as we have juft faid, had been left proprætor in the camp, being put in hopes of either finifhing the war, or extorting money out of the king, by the terror of his army, draws his foldiers, in the month of January, out of their winter quarters upon an expedition, and came by great marches, in a fevere feafon, to the town of Suthul, where all the king's treafure lay. Which, tho' it could not be either taken, or be.
quam

quamquam, & fævitia temporis, & opportunitate loci, neque capi neque obfideri poterat, (nam circum murum fitum in prærupti montis extremo planicies limofa hiemalibus aquis paludem fecerat) tamen, aut fimulandi gratia, quo regi formidinem adderet, aut cupidine cæcus, ob thefauros oppidi potiundi, vineas agere, aggerem jacere, aliaque, quæ incœpto ufui forent, properare.

fieged, by reafon of the fharpnef of the weather, and the natura ftrength of the place ; for ther was a perfect marfh made by th winter's rains quite round th wall, built upon the extremity o a craggy mountain; yet either b way of feint, to fright the king or blinded with a greedy defire c taking the town, for the booty the was in it, he began to form vinea to caft up a mount, and make oth neceffary preparations for an a fault upon the place.

XLII. At Jugurtha, cognita vanitate atque imperitia legati, fubdolus ejus augere amentiam ; miffitare fupplicantis legatos ; ipfe, quafi vitabundus, per faltuofa loca & tramites exercitum ductare. Denique Aulum fpe pactionis perpulit, uti, relicto Suthule, in abditas regiones fefe, veluti cedentem infequeretur ; ita delicta occultiora fore. Interea per homines callidos diu noctuque exercitum tentabat. Centuriones ducifque turmarum partim, uti transfugerent, corrumpere ; alii, figno dato, locum uti deferent. Quæ poftquam ex fententia inftruxit ; intempefta nocte de improvifo multitudine Numidarum Auli caftra circumvenit. Milites Ro-

XLII. *But when Jugurth found out the weaknefs and u. fkilfulnefs of the lieutenant, craftily contrived how to impro his madnefs. He would frequen: fend deputies with very fubmiffi meffages, and he himfelf, as if purpofe to keep out of his wa would often lead his army throu woody parts of the country, a by-roads. Finally, he tempted A lus, by the hopes of a good bargai to quit Suthul, and follow him to a lonely part of the country, if he was flying before him, l in reality the better to conceal th vile pranks. In the mean time, was day and night tampering w: the army, by fome cunning agen Some centurions, and officers horfe, he bribed to defert to hi and others to quit their pofts, wh the fignal was givén. After had thus made fuch preparations he thought proper, very unexpei edly; in the dead of the night, enclofes Aulus's camp quite roun*
ma

nani perculfi tumultu nfolito, arma capere alii ; lii fe abdere ; pars terrios confirmare ; trepidarc innibus locis ; vis magna ioftium ; cœlum noctc tque nubibus obfcuraum ; periculum anceps ; ioftremo, fugerc, an maiere, tutius foret, in inerto erat. Sed ex eo nuaero, quos paullo ante orruptos diximus, sohors na Ligurum, cum duaus turmis Thracum, & aucis gregariis militibus, ranfire ad regem ; & enturio primi pili tertiæ :gionis per munitionem, uam, uti defenderet, cceperat, locum hoftibus itrocundi dedit ; eaque Jumidæ cuncti irrupere. Joftri fœda fuga, plerique bjectis armis, proxuium collcm occupavere. Jox atque præda caftroum hoftis, quo minus ictoria uterentur, remoata funt. Deinde Jugurha poftero die cum Aulo 1 colloquio verba facit ; ametfi ipfum cum exercitu ame ferroque claufum enet, tamen fe, memorem erum humanarum, fi feum fœdus faceret, incoymes omnis fub jugum iffurum ; præterea, uti 'iebus decem Numidia deederet. Quæ gravia uamquam & flagitii pleia erant ; tamen quia nortis metu mutabantur,

with a vaft number of his Numidians. The Roman foldiers being alarmed with an unufual hurry about the camp, fome of them took arms, others hid themfelves, fome endeavoured to encourage fuch as were frighted ; great conflernation there was in all places, the enemies very numerous, the night dark and cloudy, danger on all hands. Finally, it was impoffible to judge, whether it would be fafer to fly, or flay in the camp. But of the number of thofe, who, I have juft faid, had been bribed ; one battalion of Ligurians, with two troops of Thracian horfe, and a few common foldiers, went over to the king. And a centurion of the firft rank belonging to the third legion, gave the enemy entrance into the camp, by that part of the rampart where he was pofted for its defence, and there all the Numidians broke in. Our men by a fhameful flight, and moft of them throwing away their arms, got off to a neighbouring hill. Night, and the plunder of the camp hindered the enemy from making advantage of their victory. The next day Jugurtha, at a conference with Aulus, told him, That tho' he had him with his army in his power, diftreffed both by famine and fword, yet being fenfible of the uncertainty of human affairs, if he would conclude a treaty with him, he would give quarter to the army, but fhould oblige them to pafs under the yoke ; and furthermore infifted upon his quitting Numidia in ten days. And tho' the terms were hard and fcandalous, yet the fear of death made

M   ficuti

ficuti regi luberat, pax convenit.

XLIII. Sed, ubi ea Romæ comperta funt, metus atque mœror civitatem invafere. Pars dolere pro gloria imperii; pars infolita rerum bellicarum timere libertati; Aulo omnes infefti, ac maxume qui bello fæpe præclari fuerant, quod armatus dedecore potius, quam manu, falutem quæfiverit. Ob ea conful Albinus, ex delicto fratris invidiam, ac deinde periculum timens, fenatum de fœdere confulebat; & tamen interim exercitui fupplementum fcribere; ab fociis & nomine Latino auxilia accerfere; denique omnibus modis feftinare. Senatus ita, uti par fuerat, decernit, *fuo atque populi injuſſu nullum patuiſſe fœdus fieri.* Conful, impeditus a tribunis plebis, ne, quas paraverat copias, fecum portaret, paucis diebus in Africam proficifcitur. Nam omnis exercitus, uti convenerat, Numidia deductus in provincia hiemabat. Poftquam eo venit, (quamquam perfequi Jugurtham, & mederi fraternæ invidiæ animo ardebat) cognitis militibus, quos præter fugam, foluto imperio, licentia

them go down, and peace was accordingly concluded upon the conditions offered by the king.

XLIII. *As foon as the news of all this was carried to Rome, the city was full of fear and forrow both. Some were concerned for the honour of the empire; others, unacquainted with the bufinefs of war, thought their liberty in danger. All people were in a rage at Aulus, but principally thofe, who had often diftinguifhed themfelve by their gallant behaviour in the wars, that he, when he had arm in his hand, fhould fave himfelf by an infamous fubmiſſion, withou ſtriking a ſtroke. Upon this th conful Albinus being apprehenfive from the ill behaviour of his bro ther, of the publick odium, and danger thereby, confulted the fe nate upon the late treaty of his and yet at the fame time raifed re cruits for the army, and fent fo auxiliary forces from the allies and the people of Latium, an that with all poffible expedition The fenate, as it was fit the fhould, voted, That no valid treat could be conclued, without thei and the people's authority for i The conful being not fuffered by t tribunes of the commons, to car with him the troops he had raife in a few days time went over in Africa without them. For all t army, according to the late agre ment, had quitted Numidia, a wintered in the province. Aft his arrival, although he was po fionately defirous to go in queſt Jugurtha, and wipe off the odi occafioned by his brother's ill co*
atq

tque lafcivia corruperat, x copia rerum ftatuit, ibi nihil agitandum.

line, licence, and wantonnefs, whereby his brother had de-auched them, he refolved, confidering the bad fituation of affairs, to be quiet.

duct; yet finding the ill ftate the foldiery were in, not only from their late defeat, but the want of difci-

XLIV. Interea Romæ
C. Mamilius Limetanus
tribunus plebis rogatio-
nem ad populum pro-
mulgat, *uti quæreretur in eos, quorum confilio Jugurtha fenati decreta eglexiffet quique ab eo legationibus, aut impe-iis pecunias accepiffent; qui elephantos, quique rfugas tradidiffent; i-m, qui de pace aut bello cum hoftibus pactiones fe-ffent.* Huic rogationi partim confcii fibi, alii x partim invidia peri-ula metuentes, quoniam perte refiftere non pote-ant, quin illa, & alia alia placere fibi fateren-ur, occulte per amicos, c maxume per homines ominis Latini, & focios talicos, impedimenta pa-abant. Sed plebes, in-redibile memoratu eft, quantum intenta fuerit, uantaque vi rogationem afferit, decreverit, volu-rit; magis odio nobilita-is, cui mala illa paraban-ur, quam cura reipubli-æ: Tanta lubido in par-ibus erat. Igitur, cæteris metu perculfis, M. Scau-us, quem legatum Bef-iæ fuiffe fupra memora-

XLIV. *In the mean time at Rome, C. Mamilius Limetanus, tribune of the commons, preferred a bill to the people, for appointing a commiffion of enquiry, for the tryal of all thofe, by whofe encouragement Jugurtha had flighted the orders of the fenate; and fuch deputies or commanders, as had taken money of the king; fuch as had delivered up to him his elephants and deferters, as alfo thofe who had made any agreements with the enemy, relating to peace or war. Now fuch as were guilty, and others apprehenfive of danger from the odium of the party they had engaged in, durft not openly oppofe this bill; but pretended to be well pleafed with this, and other the like proceedings; yet underhand endeavoured to hinder its paffing, by means of their friends, and efpecially thofe of Latium, and the allies of Italy. But it is incredible to fay, how zealous the people were for the bill, and with what eagernefs they paffed it; more out of hatred to the nobility, againft whom it was levelled, than out of any concern for the public weal; fo violent was the fury of the parties at that time. Wherefore, whilft all the reft were heartily frighted, M. Scaurus, who was a lieutenant-general of Beftia's, as I have above faid, amidft the exultations of the common people, the*

M 2   vimus,

vimus, inter lætitiam plebis & fuorum fugam, trepida etiam tum civitate, cum ex Mamiliana rogatione tres quæfitores rogarentur, effeccrat, ut ipfe in co numero crearetur. Sed quæftione exercita afpere violenterque, ex rumore & lubidine plebis; uti fæpe nobilitatem, fic ea tempeftate plebem ex fecundis rebus infolentia ceperat.

XLV. Cæterum mos partium popularium, & fenati fanctionum, ac deinde omnium malarum artium, paucis ante annis Romæ ortus eft, otio atque abundantia eárum rerum, quæ prima mórtales ducunt. Nam, ante Carthaginem deletam, populus & fenatus Romanus placide modefteque inter fe rempublicam tractabant; nequæ gloriæ dominationis certamen inter civis erat; metus hoftilis in bonis artibus civitatem retinebat. Sed, ubi formido illa mentibus deceffit, fcilicet ea, quæ fecundæ res amant, lafcivia atque fuperbia inceffere. Ita quod in advorfis rebus optaverant, otium, poftquam adepti funt, afperius acerbiufque fuit. Namque cœpere nobilitas dignitatem, populus libertatem in lubidinem vertere; fibi quifque du-

flight of thofe of his party, and the diftraction of the town, procured himfelf to be chofen one of the three commiffioners appointed by Mamilius's bill. But as the commiffion was executed with great feverity and violence, in conformity to vulgar report, and the humour of the people: thefe grew at that time infolent upon their fuccefs, as the nobility had often been before.

XLV. Now the party of the commons, and the factions of the Senate, with all the mifchievous practices enfuing, took their rife at Rome but a few years before, from idlenefs, and plenty of fuch things as mankind are apt to fet the higheft value upon. For before the deftruction of Carthage, the people and Senate of Rome managed their affairs jointly, in perfect harmony and moderation, without the leaft bickering upon account of glory or power. The fear of their enemy kept the city in good order: but when that fear was now no more, then the conftant attendants upon a ftate of profperity, wantonnefs, and pride, came in fafhion. Thus they had no fooner attained what they had wifhed for in the time of their adverfity, peace, than they found the moft pernicious confequence from it, and their cafe to be really worfe than it was before. For the nobility begun to turn their power and the people their liberty, int licentioufnefs. Rapine and violenc now prevailed univerfally. An
cere

cere, trahere, rapere. Ita omnia in duas partis abstracta funt. Refpublica, quæ media fuerat, dilacerata. Cæterum nobilitas factione magis pollebat; plebis vis foluta atque difperfa, in multitudine minus poterat; paucorum arbitrio belli domique refpublica agitabatur; penes eofdum ærarium, provinciæ, inagiftratus, gloriæ, triumphique erant; populus militia, atque inopia urgebatur; prædas bellicas imperatores cum paucis diripiebant. Interea parentes, aut parvi liberi militum, uti quifque potentiori confinis erat, fedibus pellebantur. Ita cum potentia avaritia fine modo modeftiaque invadere, polluere & vaftare omnia; nihil penfi neque fancti habere, quoad femet ipfa præcipitavit. Nam, ubi primum ex nobilitate reperti funt, qui veram gloriam injultæ potentiæ anteponerent, moveri civitas, & diffenfio civilis, quafi permixtio terræ, oriri cœpit.

XLVI. Nam, poftquam Tiberius & C. Gracchus, quorum majores Punico, atque aliis bellis multum reipublicæ addiderant, vindicare plebem in libertatem, & paucorum fcelera patefa-

thus was the commonwealth rent into two parties, by which it was miferably torn to pieces. The faction of the nobility proved the moft prevalent; that of the commons being more loofe and divided, by reafon of their numbers, was obliged to give ground; whereupon the management of all affairs, both in peace and war, fell into the hands of a few. They had the difpofal of the treafury, provinces, places, glory, and triumphs. The populace were oppreffed by fervice in wars and want. The generals, with a few friends, made prize of all the fpoils of victory. In the mean time the parents, or the young children of the foldiers, according as they happened to be neighbours to any of the grandees, were forced from the poffeffion of their eftates. Thus did avarice, in conjunction with power, feize, ravage, and lay wafte all before it, without the leaft regard to moderation or modefty at all, without thought or diftinction, 'till it plunged itfelf into inextricable difficulties. For as foon as fome of the nobility ftarted up, who preferred true glory before unjuft power, the city began to be in an uproar, and civil diftraction and confufion, not unlike a disjointing of the very earth itfelf, to arife upon it.

XLVI. For after Tiberius and C. Gracchus, whofe anceftors had, in the Carthaginian and other wars, been highly ferviceable to the ftate, begun to affert the liberty of the commons, and to expofe the wickednefs of the other party; the nobility being guilty, and therefore

M 3 cere

cere cœpere; nobilitas noxia, atque eo perculfa, modo per. focios ac nomen Latinum, interdum per equites Romanos, quos fpes focietatis a plebe dimoverat, Gracchorum actionibus obviam ierat; & primo Tiberium, dein paucos poft annos eadem ingredientem Cajum, Tribunum plebis alterum, alterum triumphirum coloniis deducendis, cum M. Fulvio Flacco, ferro necaverat. Et fane Gracchis, cupidine victoriæ, haud fatis animus moderatus fuit. Sed bono vinci fatius eft, quam malo more injuriam vincere. Igitur ea victoria nobilitas ex lubidine fua ufa, mortalis multos ferro aut fuga exftinxit; plufque in reliquum fibi timoris, quam potentiæ, addidit; quæ res plerumque magnas civitates peffum dedit; dum alteri alteros vincere quovis modo, & victos acerbius ulcifci volunt. Sed, de ftudiis partium, & omnibus civitatis moribus, fi fingillatim aut pro magnitudine parem differere, tempus, quam res, maturius deferet, quamobrem ad incœptum redeo.

XLVII. Poft Auli fœdus, exercitufque noftri fœdam fugam, Metellus

---

under terrible apprehenfions, did one while by our Italian allies, and thofe of Latinum, another while by the Roman knighs, whom the hopes of fharing in the fpoils with them, had feparated from the intereft of the commons, endeavour to oppofe the pretenfions of the Gracchi, and killed by the fword Tiberius; and a few years after C. pufuing the fame meafures, the one a Tribune of the commons, and the other one of the three commiffioners appointed for the planting of colonies; as alfo M. Fulvius Flaccus. And indeed the Gracchi, from too keen a defire of carrying their point, pufhed matters too far. But a good man would rather chufe to be baffled in any caufe, than carry it by ill meafures. Wherefore the nobility making a moft infolent ufe of their fuccefs in that ftruggle, put to death, or banifhed, great number. of the commons, and rendered themfelves for the future more terrible, rather than more powerful; a thing that has often proved ruinou. to mighty ftates, whilft parties are for fubduing one another at any rate, and ufing their victory with a vengeance upon their enemies, when they have once got them under. But fhould I propofe to defcant upon the fury of parties, and all the other corruptions of the city at large, and according to the extent of the fubject, time would fooner fail me than matter. I fhall therefore again take up the thread of my hiftory.

XLVII. After the treaty of Aulus, and the fcandalous return of our army into the province, the

R

s, confules defig-
)vincias inter fe
nt; Metelloque
evenerat, acri
quamquam ad-
)uli partibus, fa-
m æquabili & in-
Is, ubi primum
tum ingreffus eft,
i fibi cum colle-
nunia ratus, ad
quod gefturus
iimum intendit.
ffidens veteri ex-
milites fcribere,
undique accerfe-
)a, tela, equos,
:ra inftrumenta
)arare; ad hoc,
:um affatim; de-
nia, quæ in bello
rerum multarum
ufui effe folent.
i ad ea patranda
uctoritate, focii,
c Latinum, &
:ro auxilia mit-
)oftremo omnis
immo ftudio ad-
. Itaque, ex
omnibus rebus
)mpofitifque, in
m proficifcitur,
)e civium, cum
irtis bonas, tum
quod advorfum
invictum ani-
ebat; & avaritia
uum ante id
Numidia noftræ
ufæ, hoftiumque
int.

II. Sed, ubi in
venit, exercitus
M 4

Confuls elect, Metellus and Silanus, divided the provinces betwixt
them by lot, and Numidia fell to
Metellus, a brifk man, and though
an enemy to the popular party, yet
of a general good character; and
without blemifh. As foon as he
entered upon his office, thinking all
other things concerned his colleague
as much as him, he applied himfelf
to make preparations for the war
he was to command in, as what
was his proper and peculiar bufinefs.
Wherefore, as he put no great confidence in the old army, he made
new levies, and fent for troops
from all parts, and provided arms
of all forts, horfes, and other in-
ftruments of war, befides plenty of
provifions; and finally, all things
neceffary for a war that would require no fmall variety. And to
help forward the bufinefs, the
Senate contributed their authority;
our allies, and the Latins, and foreign princes too, fent in troops of
their own accord; and finally, the
whole city exerted itfelf ftrenuoufly
upon the occafion. Wherefore, when
now all things were prepared and
regulated to his mind, he paffes
over into Numidia, whilft the Romans were now all in full expectations of fuccefs, as well becaufe of
the other excellent qualities of the
general, as efpecially, becaufe he
had a foul invincibly fortified a-
gainft the temptation of money;
whereas our affairs in Africa had
been ruined, and the ftrength of the
enemy increafed by the avarice of
our own commanders.

XLVIII. But after his arrival
in Africa, the army of the Procon-
&

ei traditur Sp. Albini proconfulis, iners, imbellis neque periculi, neque laboris patiens, lingua, quam manu, promptior, prædator ex fociis, & ipfe præda hoftium, fine imperio & modeftia habitus. Ita imperatori novo plus ex malis moribus folicitudinis, quam ex copia militum auxilii, aut bonæ fpei, accedebat. Statuit tamen Metellus, (quamquam & æftivorum tempus comitiorum mora imminuerat, & exfpectatione eventi civium animos intentos putabat) non prius bellum attingere, quam majorum difciplina milites laborare coegiffet. Nam Albinus, Auli· fratris exercitufque clade perculfus, poftquam decreverat non egredi provincia, quantum temporis æftivorum in imperio fuit, plerumque milites in ftativis caftris habebat ; nifi cum odos, aut pabuli egeftas, locum mutare fubegerat. Sed neque more militari vigiliæ deducebantur. Uti cuique lubebat, ab fignis aberat. Lixæ permifti cum militibus diu noctuque vagabantur ; & palantes agros vaftare, villas expugnare, pecoris & mancipiorum prædas certantes agere ; eaque mutare cum mercatoribus vino advectitio,

ful Sp. Albinus was delivered up to him, not at all difpofed for action, but heartlefs, and neither capable of enduring danger or fatigue, much more ready with their tongues than their hands, accuftomed to plunder the allies, whilft they themfelves were a prey to the enemy, as being under no proper command, in no order at all. Thus the new general had more trouble with the vicious manners of the foldiers, than he had either help or hope from their numbers. However, Metellus was refolved, notwithftanding the latenefs of the election had left but a fhort time for that year's campaign, and he did fuppofe that the minds of the people at Rome would wait the iffue of the war with impatience, not to enter upon action, 'till he had, by due difcipline, brought the foldiers to bear fatigue. For Albinus being quite difmayed with the late defeat of the army under the command of his brother, and refolving thereupon not to ftir out of the province, kept the foldiers, during the time of his command that fummer, in ftanding camps, which he changed not, 'till the ftench of them, or the want of forage, obliged him to be gone. But neither was the watch kept, as is ufual in war ; and every man ftrolled from the camp at pleafure ; and the fervants, together with the foldiers, ran about night and day, wafting the country, and forcing gentlemen's houfes, carried off vaft numbers of cattle and flaves continually, and exchanged them with merchants for wine they brought them, and
&

& aliis talibus. Præterea, rumentum publice da-um vendere, panem in hes mercari. Poftremo, juæ cunque dici aut fingi jueunt ignaviæ luxuriæ-jue proba, in illo exer-itu cuncta fuere, & alia mplius.

XLIX. Sed in ea dif-icultate Metellum non ninus, quam in rebus oftilibus, magnum & ipientem virum fuiffe omperior; tanta tem-erantia inter ambitio-em fævitiamque mode-itum. Namque edicto rimo adjumenta ignaviæ iftuliffe, *ne quifquam in iftris panem, aut quèm lium cibum coctum ven-ret ; ne lixæ exercitum querentur, ; ne miles regarius in caftris, neve i agmine fervum, aut imentum haberet.* Cæ-ris arte modum ftatuif-:. Præterea, tranfvorfis ineribus quotidie caftra novere ; juxta ac fi ho-es adeffent, vallo at-ue foffa munire ; vigi-as crebras ponere, & eas fe cum legatis circuire ; em in agmine in primis nodo, modo in poftre-nis, fæpe in medio adeffe, e quifquam ordine egre-eretur ; uti cum fignis equentes incederent, mi-s cibum & arma porta-et. Ita prohibendo a elictis magis, quam vit.-

other fuch things. Befides, they would fell the corn allowed them by the government, and buy bread every day. In fhort, all the moft fcandalous effects of idlenefs and luxury, that can be mentioned or imagined, were every one of them in that army, and more too.

XLIX. But I find Metellus fhewed himfelf as great and able a man under this difficulty, as in his conduct againft the enemy ; he obferved fo due a mean betwixt fneaking to gain the favour of his troops, and cruelty. For in the firft place, he ordered out of the camp by proclamation, all the fupports of idlenefs ; as that no body fhould fell bread, or any other drefs'd victuals, in the camp ; that no fetchers of wood fhould follow the camp, nor any common foldier have in the camp, or upon the march, a fervant, or any beaft of burden. And in refpect of other things, was very fparing of his allowance of them. Befides, he would daily march his army, not directly forward, but to the right and left alternately, and fecure his camp by a rampart and ditch, juft as if an enemy was at hand, kept due watch in the fame, and went the rounds himfelf, attended by his lieutenant generals ; and upon a march, he would fometimes be in the van, fometimes in the rear, and oftentimes in the main body, to fee that no man quitted his rank, but all duly attended their own ftandards, and carried their own provifion, and arms. Thus, in a fhort time, he infufed vigour and fpirit into his

dicando,

dicando, exercitum brevi confirmavit.

L. Interea Jugurtha, ubi, quæ Metellus agebat, ex nunciis accepit, fimul de innocentia ejus certior Romæ factus, diffidere fuis rebus, ac tum demum veram deditionem facere conatus eft. Igitur legatos ad confulem cum fuppliciis mittit, qui tantummodo ipfi liberifque vitam paterent, alia omnia dederent populo Romano. Sed Metello jam antea experimentis cognitum erat, genus Numidarum infidum, ingenio mobili, novarum rerum avidum effe. Itaque legatos alium ab alio diverfos aggreditur; ac paullatim tentando, poftquam opportunos fibi cognovit, multa pollicendo perfuadet *uti Jugurtham maxume vivum, fin id parum procedat, necatum fibi traderent*; cæterum palam, quæ ex voluntate forent, regi nunciari jubet. Dein ipfe paucis diebus intento atque infeflo exercitu in Numidiam procedit; ubi, contra belli faciem, tuguria plena hominum, pecora, cultorefque in agris erant; ex oppidis & mapalibus præfecti regis obviam procedebant, parati frumentum dare,

army, *rather by keeping them from the breach of orders, than punishing them.*

L. *In the mean time, Jugurtha being adviſed of what Metellus was doing, and having been informed at Rome of his integrity begun now to deſpair of ſucceſs in the war, and to think of making a ſurrender of himſelf in good earneſt. Wherefore he diſpatches meſſengers to the Conſul, to capitulate only for the lives of himſelf and children, ſubmitting every thing beſides to the pleaſure of the Roman people. But Metellus had before found ſufficiently by experience the nation of the Numidians to be faithleſs, fickle, and fond of change. Wherefore he tampered with the meſſengers apart, and when, by ſifting of them, he found them for his purpoſe, he, by large promiſes, perſuades them, to deliver up to him Jugurtha alive, if poſſible, but if not, dead. But openly orders them to carry an anſwer to the King, agreeable to his deſire: and a few days after marches into Numidia with his army ready for action, where there was not the leaſt appearance of war, the country houſes being full of men, and the lands of cattle and people at work upon their ground; the King's governors too came from the towns and cottages to meet Metullus, ready to furniſh him with corn, and other proviſions; and, in ſhort, to execute all his commands whatever. But Metellus notwithſtanding marched with his army in a poſture of defence, as if the enemy were* comme

commeatum portare; postremo omnia, quæ imperarentur, facere. Neque Metellus idcirco minus, sed, pariter ac si hostes adessent, munito agmine incedere, late explorare omnia, illa deditionis signa ostentui credere, & insidiis locum tentare. Itaque ipse cum expeditis cohortibus, item funditorum & sagittariorum delecta manu apud primos erat. In postremo C. Marius legatus cum equitibus curabat. In utrumque latus equites auxiliarios tribunis legionum & præfectis cohortium dispertiverat; uti cum his permixti velites, quocumque accederent, equitatus hostium propulsarent. Nam in Jugurtha tantus dolus, tantaque peritia locorum & militiæ erat, ut, absens an præsens, pacem an bellum gerens, perniciosior esset, in incerto haberetur

at hand; sent his scouts into all quarters round, as looking upon those tokens of submission designed for shew only, and in order to trepan him. Wherefore he marched in the van, attended by some battalions clear of baggage, and a body of slingers and archers. In the rear commanded his lieutenant-general C. Marius with the horse; and the auxiliary horse he disposed of in the flanks, under the command of the Tribunes of the legions, and the commanders of the battalions, with which were mixed some light-armed foot; and all this he did in order to repulse the enemy's horse, in what quarter soever they should make their attack. For Jugurtha was a man of so much subtilty, and so well acquainted with the Country, and the business of war, that it was hard to say, whether he was more mischievous, when absent or present, in peace or war.

LI. Erat haud longe ab eo itinere, quo Metellus pergebat, oppidum Numidarum, nomine Vacca, forum rerum venalium totius regni maxume celebratum; ubi & incolere & mercari consueverant Italici generis multi mortales. Huc consul, simul tentandi gratia, &, si paterentur opportunitates loci, præsidium imposuit; præterea imperavit frumentum, & alia, quæ bello usui fo-

LI. There was not far from the rout Metellus was in, a town of the Numidians, called Vacca, a place of the greatest trade of any in the kingdom, where a great many Italian merchants were settled, upon account of traffick. Metellus, as well to try the submission of the people, as upon account of the advantages of the place, put a garrison into it; and further made a demand of corn, and other necessaries for his army, supposing, as it was natural to do, that the great number of merchants there would be very convenient,

rent, comportare ; ratus id, quod res monebat, frequentiam negotiatorum & commeatum juvaturum exercitum, & jam paratis rebus munimento fore. Inter hæc negotia Jugurtha impensius modo legatos supplices mittere, pacem orare, præter suam liberorumque vitam omnia Metello dedere. Quos item, uti priores, consul illectos ad proditionem domum dimittebat ; regi pacem, quam postulabat, neque abnuere, neque polliceri, & inter eas moras promissa legatorum expectare. x

LII. Jugurtha, ubi Metelli dicta cum factis composuit, ac suis, se artibus tentari animadvertit, (quippe cui verbis pax nunciabatur, cæterum re bellum asperrimum erat, urbs maxima alienata, ager hostibus cognitus, animi popularium tentati) coactus rerum necessitudine, statuit armis certare. . Igitur, explorato hostium itinere, in spem victoriæ adductus, ex opportunitate loci, quam maxumas potest copias omnium generum parat, ac per tramites occultos exercitum Metelli antevenit. Erat in ea parte Numidiæ, quam Atherbal in divisione possederat, flumen

nient for the supplying his troops with provisions, and a means to secure his conquests. In the mean time, Jugurtha was continually sending messengers, and begging peace in the most submissive manner, leaving all things to the disposal of Metellus, but his own and his children's lives; whom the Consul wheedled into a design of betraying their master, as he had done by those that were sent before, neither absolutely refusing, nor promising the King the peace he desired, but in the mean while waiting the execution of the promises made him by the messengers.

LII. *Jugurtha comparing Metellus's words with his deeds, and finding himself attacked by the arts he himself had before practised, as having, notwithstanding the hopes given him of a peace, a very smart war upon his hands, the principal city in his kingdom being taken from him, the country well known to the enemy, and his subjects tampered with to seduce them from their allegiance, being forced by the necessity of his affairs, he resolved to give battle to Metellus. Wherefore having got sufficient intelligence of the march of the enemy, and being in hopes of a victory from the advantage their situation presented, he raises as great a force as possible, of both horse and foot; and by some private cross routs gets before Metellus's army. There was in that part of Numidia, which Atherbal had, upon orien*

-iens a meridie, nomine
luthul; quo aberat
ions ferme millia paffuu-
m viginti, tractu pari,
aftus ab natura & hu-
ano cultu; fed ex eo
edio quafi collis orieba-
ir, in immenfum perti-
ens, veftitus oleaftro ac
yrtetis, aliifque gene-
ibus arborum, quæ hu-
i arido atque arenofo
ignuntur. Media autem
lanicies deferta, penuria
quæ, præter fluminis
ropinqua loca: Ea con-
ta arbuftis, pecore atque
ultoribus frequentaban-
ur.

LIII. Igitur in eo col-
e, (quem tranfvorfo itine-
e porrectum docuimus)
fugurtha extenuata fuo-
um acie confedit; ele-
hantis & parti copiarum
edeftrium Bomilcarem
ræfecit; eumque edocet
quæ ageret. Ipfe propior
nontem cum omni equi-
atu & peditibus delectis
uos collocat; dein fingu-
as turmas & manipulos
ircumiens monet atque
bteftatur, uti, *memores*
riftinæ virtutis & victo-
iæ, fefe regnumque fuum
ab Romanorum avaritia
lefendant. Cum his certa-
nen fore, quos antea victos
ub jugum miferint; ducem
llis, non animum, muta-
um. Quæ ab imperatore
lecuerint, omnia fuis pro-
nifa; locum fuperiorem

the *division thereof, a river run-*
ning from the fouth, by name Mu-
thul, at above twenty miles diftance
from which there was a mountain
parallel to the river, wafte and
uncultivated, from the middle of
which rofe a hill of a vaft height,
covered with wild olives, myrtles,
and other trees, which are apt to
grow in a dry fandy foil. The
plain betwixt the river and moun-
tain was all defart for want of
water, except the parts bordering
upon the river. Thofe were full
of brufhwood, cattle, and inha-
bitants.

LIII. *In this hill,* (which, we
have already taken notice, lay a-
crofs the rout Metellus was taking,)
Jugurtha fat down with his army,
ftretched out to a great length.
He gave the command of the elephants, with a part of the infantry, to Bomilcar, and inftructs
him what to do. He pofts himfelf
nigher the mountain, with all the
horfe, and the choiceft of the foot;
and then riding round the feveral
troops and companies, he begs and
befeeches them, to be mindful of
their former bravery and fuccefs,
and to defend themfelves and his
dominions from the avarice of the
Romans. They were now to engage with thofe, whom they had
before conquered, and obliged to
pafs under the yoke; that they
had only changed their general, not their temper. That he
had made all the preparations for
the battle that could be expected

uti

uti prudentes cum imperi- from a commander; so that they
tis, ne pauciores cum plu- had the advantage of the ground,
ribus, 'aut rudes cum bello surprize, numbers, and skill in
melioribus manum confere- war, on their side; and therefore
rent. Proinde parati in- ought to be upon their guard, and
tentique essent, signo dato ready, when the signal should be
Romanos invadere; illum given, to fall upon the Romans.
diem aut omnis labores & That that day would either secure
victorias . confirmaturum, to them the fruit of their former
aut maxumarum ærumna- labours and victories, or prove the
rum initium fore. Ad beginning of the most extreme
hoc viritim, uti quemque *misery. Besides, he addressed*
ob militare facinus pecu- *himself singly to such as he had for*
nia aut honore extulerat, *their gallant behaviour raised to*
commonefacere beneficii *riches or honour, put them in mind*
sui, & eum ipsum aliis . *of his kindness, and shewed them*
ostentare. Postremo, pro *to the rest. In short, he endea-*
cujusque ingenio pollicen- *voured to rouse the courage of one*
do, minitando, obtestan- *in one way, and another another,*
do, alium alio modo ex- *by promising, threatening, or en-*
citare;   cum   interim *treating them, according to their*
Metellus, ignarus hosti- *several tempers. Whilst in the*
um, monte degrediens *mean time Metellus, being not a-*
cum exercitu conspicaba- *ware of the enemy, was spied coming*
tur. Primo dubius, quid- *down the mountain with his army.*
nam insolita facies osten- *And being at first in some doubt,*
deret (nam inter virgul- *what that unusual appearance*
ta equi Numidæque con- *should mean (for the Numidians*
federant, neque plane oc- *with their horses were among the*
cultati humilitate arbo- *brush-wood, but not sufficiently co-*
rum, & tamen incerti *vered, by reason of the lowness of*
quidnam esset, cum natu- *the trees, nor yet appearing so as*
ra loci tum dolo ipsi atque *to discover what they were, as be-*
signa militaria obscurati) *ing themselves and their standards*
dein, brevi cognitis insi- *concealed by the nature of the place,*
diis, paullisper agmen *and other ways designedly) but*
constituit. Ibi commu- *in a short time perceiving the stra-*
tatis ordinibus, in dextro *tagem of the enemy, he ordered*
latere, quod proxumum *his army to halt a little; and*
hostis erat, triplicibus sub- *then altering the disposition there-*
sidiis aciem instruxit; in- *of, he reinforced it in the right*
ter manipulos funditores *wing, which was next the enemy,*
& sagittarios dispertit, e- *with three several bodies of re-*
quitatem omnem in cor- *serves, for their support, if occa-*

                                    nibus

ibus locat; ac pauca pro empore milites hortatus, ciem, ficut inftruxerat, ranfvorfis principiis in lanum deducit.

LIV. Sed, ubi Numilas quietos, neque colle legredi animadvertit, veritus ex anni tempore & nopia aquæ, ne fiti conficeretur exercitus, Rutilium legatum cum expeditis cohortibus, & parte equitum, præmifit ad flumen, uti locum caftris antecaperet; exiftumans hoftis crebro impetu, & tranfvorfis prœliis, iter fuum remoraturos; &, quoniam armis diffiderent, laffitudihem & fitim militum tentaturos. Dein ipfe pro re atque loco, ficuti monte defcenderat, paullatim procedere; Marium poft principia habere; ipfe cum finiftræ alæ equitibus effe, qui in agmine principes facti erant. At Jugurtha, ubi extremum agmen Metelli primos fuos prætergreffum videt, præfidio quafi duum millium peditum montem occupat, qua Metellus defcenderat; ne forte cedentibus adverfariis receptui, ac poft munimento foret; dein, repente figno dato, hoftis invadit. Numidæ alii

fion required; diftributes the flingers and archers among ft the feveral companies, and places all the horfe in the wings, and making a fhort fpeech fuitable to the occafion, for the encouragement of his men, he drew down his army into the plain.

LIV. But finding the Numidians keep their ground, without offering to quit the hill, and fearing from the feafon of the year, and the want of water in thofe parts, left his army fhould be diftreffed by thirft, he fent his lieutenant-general Rutilius with a light detachment of infantry, and a part of the cavalry, down to the river, to fecure a proper place for his camp, as fuppofing the enemy would, by frequent attacks upon their flank, endeavour to retard their march; and as they had little hopes of fucceeding by force of arms, would endeavour to diftrefs our foldiers by continual fatigue and thirft. Upon this, he advanced leifurely, in the fame order as he came down the mountain, fo far as the nature of the place would admit. He kept Marius behind the principes; he marched with the horfe on the left wing, who were now become the foremoft in the march. But when Jugurtha faw that the rear of Metellus was now got by his van, he feizes upon the mountain Metellus had quitted, with a body of two thoufand men, that the enemy, if routed, might not betake themfelves thither for fecurity; and then fuddenly giving the fignal, he falls upon the enemy. The Numidians fome of

poftre-

poftremos cædere ; pars a finiftra ac dextra tentare ; infenfi adeffe atque inftare, omnibus locis Romanorum ordines conturbare. Quorum etiam qui firmioribus animis obvii hoftibus fuerant, ludificati incerto prælio, ipfi modo eminus fauciabantur, neque contra feriundi aut conferendi manum copia erat. Ante jam docti ab Jugurtha equites, ubicumque Romanorm turma infequi cœperat, non confertim, neque in unum fefe recipiebant, fed alius alio quam maxume divorfi. Ita numero priores, fi a perfequendo hoftis deterrere nequiverant, disjectos ab tergo aut lateribus circumveniebant. Sin opportunior fugæ collis, quam campi fuerant, ea vero confueti Numidarum equi facile inter virgulta evadere ; noftros afperitas & infolentia loci retinebat.

LV. Cæterum facies totius negotii varia, incerta, fœda atque miferabilis. Difperfi a fuis, pars cedere, alii infequi. Neque figna, neque ordines obfervare. Ubi quemque periculum ceperat, ibi refiftere ac propulfare. Arma, tela, equi, viri, hoftes, cives permixti. Nihil

of them attacked the rear, whilft others did the fame upon the flanks, being very preffing and furious, infomuch that they every where put the Romans into fome diforder. Of which thofe that made the moft gallant oppofition were yet befooled by the enemy's unfteady way of fighting ; and being themfelves wounded by the difcharge of the enemy's weapons, made upon them at a diftance, could not come to ftrokes or clofe fight with them at all. For the horfe, as they had before been inftructed by Jugurtha, whenfoever any troop of the Roman cavalry began to purfue them, did not fly off together, or to any one certain place, but difperfed, one one way, and another another, as much as poffible. And fo being fuperior in numbers, if they could not by that means difcourage the enemy's purfuit, they attacked them upon their dividing, in rear, or flank. But if a hill lay more convenient for their flight, than the plain, the horfes of the Numidian, being ufed to the work, would eafily make their way through the bufhes which ours, for want of being exercifed in fuch rough work, could not do.

LV. But the appearance of things during the whole tranfaction, was various, uncertain, difmal, and miferable. Some, feparated from their main body, fled, whilft others were engaged in the purfuit of the enemy. They neither kept by their ftandards nor companies. Where danger overtook any one, there he made a ftand, and repulfed his adverfary. Arms of all

con-

onfilio, neque imperio gi ; fors omnia regere. taque multum diei pro-efferat, cum etiam tum ventus in incerto erat. Denique, omnibus labore & æftu languidis, Metel-us, ubi videt Numidas ninus inftare, paullatim nilites in unum conducit; rdines reftituit, & co-ortis legionarias quatuor dvorfum pedites hoftium ollocat ; eorum magna ars fuperioribus locis fef-a confederat. Simul ora-e, hortari milites, *ne de-icerent, neu paterentur oftes fugientis vincere : æque illis caftra effe, ne-ue munimentum ulium, uo cedentes tenderent : n armis omnia fita.* Sed ec Jugurtha quidem in-erea quietus erat; circu-re, hortari, renovare rælium, & ipfe cum lelectis tentare omnia ; ubvenire fuis, hoftibus lubiis inftare ; quos fir-mos cognoverat, eminus ugnando retinere.

forts, horfes, men, both enemies and Romans were all jumbled toge-ther ; nothing was done under any certain conduct or command ; chance ruled all. *Wherefore the day was now far fpent, whilft the event was ftill uncertain. Finally, when all were now quite faint with the fatigue of action, and heat of the day, Metellus percei-ving the Numidians to abate of their vigour, draws by degrees his foldiers into one place, puts them in due order, and pofts four legiona-ry battalions againft the enemy's foot ; a great part of which being heartily tired, were fat down up-on fome rifing grounds. At the fame time Metellus entreated and encouraged his men* not to faint, or fuffer the flying enemy to get the victory. They had no camp or any fortification to fly to ; all their hopes were in their arms. *Nor was Jugurtha idle in the mean time, but rid round his troops to encou-rage them, and renew the fight, and did, with a body of choice troops, make all imaginable ef-forts for the purpofe, relieving his own men, and pufhing home upon the enemy, where they were in dif-trefs ; and fuch as ftood firm, he kept in play, by annoying them at a diftance.*

LVI. Eo modo duo imperatores, fummi viri, nter fe certabant ; ipfi pares, cæterum opibus difparibus. Nam Metello virtus militum erat, locus advorfus.: Jugurthæ alia omnia, præter milites, opportuna. Denique Ro-

LVI. *And thus did thefe two great commanders ftruggle toge-ther for victory, equally matched indeed in their own perfons, but in very different circumftances as to other refpects. Metellus had the advantage with regard to the cou-rage of his men, but the difadvan-tage as to ground. Jugurtha had*

N mani,

mani, ubi intelligunt, neque fibi profugium effe, neque ab hofte copiam pugnandi fieri (& jam die vefper erat) advorfo colle, ficuti præceptum fuerat, evadunt. Amiffo loco Numidæ fufi fugatique, pauci interiere. Plerofque velocitas & regio hoftibus ignara tutata funt. Interea Bomilcar, quem elephantis & parti copiarum pedeftrium præfectum ab Jugurtha fupra diximus, úbi eum Rutilius prætergreffus · eft, paullatim fuos in æquum locum deducit; ac, dum legatus ad flumen, quo præmiffus erat, feftinans pergit, quietus, uti res poftulabat, aciem exornat; neque remittit, quid ubique hoftes agerent, explorare. Poftquam Rutilium confediffe jam, & animo vacuum accepit, fimulque ex Jugurthæ prælio clamorem augeri, veritus ne legatus, cognita re, laborantibus fuis auxilio foret, aciem, quam diffidens virtuti militum arte ftatuerat, quo hoftium itineri officeret, latius porrigit ; eoque modo ad Rutilii caftra procedit.

the better of it in all other re-fpects, excepting his men. Finally, the Romans finding no other means of fecurity left them, fince the enemy, by keeping at a diftance, would give them no opportunity of engaging them, and night was now coming on apace, advance, as they were ordered, up the hill ; whereupon the Numidians quitting their ground were routed, and put to flight, and fome few of them flain. But the moft of them were faved by the goodnefs of their heels, and the enemy's want of fufficient acquaintance with the country, together. In the mean time Bomilcar, to whom Jugurtha, as we have above faid, had given the command of the elephants, and a part of the infantry, as foon as Rutilius was paft him, draws down his men very leifurely into the plain ; and whilft the lieutenant-general, according to his orders, purfues his march with all expedition to the river, he, unmolefted, puts his troops into fuch a difpofition, as the nature of the cafe required, and does not neglect to get intelligence what the enemy was every where doing. And after he was advifed, that Rutilius was encamped, and under no apprehenfions of an enemy, and perceived too, that the fhouting, where Jugurtha was engaged, grew louder and louder, fearing left the lieutenant-general, upon underftanding

the matter, fhould return to the relief of his friends in diftrefs. he extends his forces, which, in diftruft of their courage, he had drawn up in clofe array, to a confiderable length, in order to obftruct his paffage, and in that difpofition advances toward the camp of Rutilius.

LVII

LVII. Romani ex improvifo pulveris vim magnam animadvertunt; nam profpectum ager arbuſtis conſitus prohibebat. Et primo rati humum aridam vento agitari; poſt, ubi æquabilem manere, &, ſicuti acies movebatur, magis magiſque appropinquare vident; cognita re, properantes arma capiunt, ac pro caſtris, ſicuti imperabatur, conſiſtunt. Deinde, ubi propius ventum eſt, utrimque magno clamore concurritur. Numidæ, tantummoʼo remorati, dum in elephantis auxilium putant, poſtquam eos impeditos ramis arborum, atque ita disjectos circumveniri vident, fugam faciunt; ac plerique, abjectis armis, collis, aut noctis, quæ jam aderat, auxilio integri abeunt. Elephanti quatuor capti, reliqui omnes numero quadraginta interfecti. At Romani, quamquam itinere, atque opere caſtrorum & prælio feſſi, lætique erant, tamen, quod Metellus amplius opinione morabatur, inſtructi intentique obviam procedunt. Nam dolus Numidarum nihil languidi neque remiſſi patiebatur. Ac primo obſcura nocte, poſtquam haud procul inter ſe erant, ſtrepitu,

LVII. *The Romans were ſurprized with the ſudden appearance of a mighty duſt raiſed; for the country being thick ſet with ſhrubs, hindered the view at any diſtance: and at firſt ſuppoſed it was only occaſioned by the wind's ſweeping the dry plain; but perceiving it to be conſtant, and approach nearer and nearer, as the army advanced, and thereupon diſcovering the matter, they fly to their arms, and by order of their commander drew up before the camp. And after the enemy was come within proper diſtance, both ſides engage with a great ſhout. The Numidians only made a ſtand, whilſt they thought the elephants might be of ſervice to them; but when they ſaw them entangled amongſt the bruſh-wood, and ſeparately encloſed by the enemy, they take to their heels, and moſt of them throwing away their arms, got off ſafe by the advantage of a hill and the night together, which was now come on. Four elephants were taken; all the reſt, forty in number, were ſlain. But the Romans, although fatigued with their march, the work of encamping, and battle too, and all in the height of joy for their ſucceſs; yet as Metellus ſtaid beyond their expectation, put themſelves in due order, and advance to meet him: for the wiles of the Numidians admitted no ſlackneſs or remiſneſs at all. And when now they were not far aſunder, the night being dark, the noiſe alarmed both ſides with the apprehenſions of an enemy advancing, the conſequence whereof had like to velut*

velut hoftes adventarent, alteri apud alteros formidinem fimul & tumultum facere ; & pene imprudentia admiffum facinus miferabile, ni utrimque præmiffi equites rem exploraviffent. Igitur pro metu repente gaudium exortum. Milites alius alium læti appellant, acta edocent, atque audiunt; fua quifque fortia facta ad cœlum fert. Quippe res humanæ ita fefe habent ; in victoria vel ignavis gloriari licet; advorfæ res etiam bonos detrectant.

have been fatal, but that fome horfe, difpatched by both parties, difcovered the truth. Whereupon their fear was followed with joy, and the foldiers fell to congratulating one another, and mutually imparting their accounts of the two actions, whilft each man extolls his own behaviour to the heavens. For fuch is the condition of mankind; upon a victory cowards may boaft; but ill fuccefs finks the fpirits of the brave themfelves.

LVIII. Metellus, in iifdem caftris quatriduo moratus, faucios cum cura reficit ; meritos in præliis more militiæ donat ; univerfos in concione laudat, atque agit gratias ; hortatur, *ad cætera, quæ levia funt, parem animum gerant ; pro victoria fatis jam pugnatum, reliquos labores pro præda fore.* Tamen interim transfugas & alios opportunos, Jugurtha ubi gentium, aut quid agitaret, cum paucis ne effet, an exercitum haberet, uti fefe victus gereret, exploratum mifit. At ille fefe in loca faltuofa & natura munita receperat ; ibique cogebat exercitum, numero hominum ampliorem, fed hebetem infirmumque, agri ac pecoris magis, quam belli, cultorem. Id ea gratia eve-

LVIII. *Metellus continued four days in the fame camp, took due care for the recovery of his wounded men, confers prefents, as is ufual in war, upon fuch as had diftinguifhed themfelves in the late fight, commends them all in a fpeech he made them, and gives them thanks, advifing them* to fhew the like courage for the difpatch of the work remaining upon their hands, which was but inconfiderable. They had fought fufficiently for victory; all they had now to labour for, was plunder. *Yet in the mean time he fent out fome deferters, and other proper perfons, to enquire where Jugurtha was, or what he defigned to do ; whether he was only attended by few, or an army ; and how he behaved himfelf after his defeat. But he was already retired to a woody part of the country, that was naturally very ftrong ; and was there raifing an army, already greater than the former, but unfit for action, and of no account ; as be-*

niebat

niebat, quod, præter e- quites regios, nemo om- nium Numidarum ex fu- ga regem fequitur. Quo cujufque animus fert, eo difcedunt. Neque id fla- gitium militiæ ducitur; ita fe mores habent. Igitur Metellus, ubi videt etiam tum regis animum fero- cem efle; bellum renova- ri, quod nifi ex illius lu- bidine geri non poffet; præterea iniquum certa- men fibi cum hoftibus, minore detrimento illos vinci, quam fuos vincere; ftatuit non præliis, neque acie, fed alio more bellum gerendum. Itaque in loca Numidiæ opulentiffuma pergit; agrcs vaftat; multa caftella & oppida, temere munita, aut fine præfidio, capit incendit- que; puberes interfici ju- bet, alia omnia militum prædam effe. Ea formi- dine multi mortales Ro- manis dediti obfides; fru- mentum, & alia, quæ ufui forent, affatim præ- bita; ubicumque res po- ftulabat, præfidiam im- pofitum. Quæ negotia multo magis, quam proe- lium male pugnatum ab fuis, regcm terrebant. Quippe cujus fpes omnis in fuga fita erat; fequi cogebatur; &, qui fua loca defendere nequive- rat, in alienis bellum ge- rere. Tamen ex inopia,

ing more acquainted with hufban- dry and grazing, than the bufi- nefs of war. The reafon whereof was, that not a man of the Numi- dians attends their prince upon a defeat, excepting his own horfe- guards, but go where they pleafe. Nor is this any blemifh upon their honour at all, as being the fafhion. Wherefore Metellus perceiving the King's fpirit to be ftill undaunted, and that the war was like to grow upon him again, which could not be carried on but as Jugurtha pleafed; and that he was not upon an equal footing with the enemy in the conteft; that they fuftained lefs damage by a defeat, than his men did by a victory, he refolved not to carry on the war in the way of pitch'd field-battles, but after a different manner. Wherefore a- way he marches into the richeft parts of Numidia, where he rava- ges the country, and takes abun- dance of caftles, and towns, that were but flightly fortified, or with- out any garrifon in them, and burns them, orders all the males of age to be put to the fword, granting all befides to his foldiers as plunder. Upon the confterna- tion occafioned by this manner of proceeding, a great many people fubmitted themfelves to the Ro- mans, gave hoftoges, and fupplied the army with corn, and other ne- ceffaries, in great plenty. Garri- fons were likewife placed where occafion required. Which things ftruck a much greater terror into the King, than the late unfortu- nate battle had done. For he, whofe hopes lay entirely in avoiding

quod

quod optumum videbatur, confilium capit; exercitum plerumque in iifdem locis opperiri jubet; ipfe cum delectis equitibus Metellum fequitur; nocturnis & aviis itineribus ignoratus, Romanos palantis repente aggreditur. Eorum plerique inermes cadunt, multi capiuntur; nemo omnium intactus profugit. Et Numidæ, priufquam ex caftris fubveniretur, ficuti juffi erant, in proxumos collis difcedunt.

his enemy, was now obliged to purfue him; and he that could not defend thofe parts of his dominions, where in fight he would have confiderable advantages, was forced to carry on the war in thofe where he would labour under difadvantages. Yet in this ftraight he takes fuch a courfe as feemed moft advifeable. He orders the army to keep generally in the fame parts, and attends the motions of Metellus himfelf with a choice body of horfe, and by marching in the night, and through by-roads, comes unexpectedly upon the Romans that had ftrolled from the camp, who, being moft of them unarmed, were all either killed or taken prifoners, except fome few that got off, yet not without being much wounded. And the Numidians, before any relief could come from the camp, according to orders, draw off to the next hills.

LIX. Interim Romæ gaudium ingens ortum, cognitis Metelli rebus; ut feque & exercitum more majorum gereret; in adverfo loco victor tamen virtute fuiffet; hoftium agro potiretur; Jugurtham, magnificum ex Auli focordia, fpem falutis in folitudine aut fuga coegiffet habere. Itaque fenatus, ob ea feliciter acta, diis immortalibus fupplicia decernere. Civitas, trepida antea, & folicita de belli eventu, læta agere; de Metello fama præclara effe. Igitur eo intentior ad victoriam niti; omnibus modis feftinare; cavere tamen nec

LIX. *In the mean time there was huge joy at Rome upon the news of Metellus's fuccefs; how he conducted himfelf and his army, in a manner conformable to that of the brave old Romans; had by his galiant behaviour gained a victory, though with the difadvantage of the ground, and had made himfelf mafter of the enemy's country, having obliged Jugurtha, who was hugely elated with his fuccefs againft Aulus, to put all his hopes in flying about with fmall parties. Wherefore the fenate orders publick thanfgivings to the gods upon account of the fame. The city, that was before in no fmall fear, and much concerned for the iffue of the war, was now full of joy, and cried up Metellus moft mightily; which infpired him with frefh zeal*

ubi

inus fic-
ioft glo-
ui. Ita,
magis
jue poft
: effufo
Ubi
ilo opus
m omni
n.agita-
partem
rius du-
magis,
r vafta-
cis haud
a facie-
is erat,
cæte-
atque
efceret,
to tem-
r collis
: locum
; qua
audie-
quarum
penuria
Mo-
terdum
poftre-
:entare,
egredi;
liis mi-
rælium
m pati,
em ab

to bring the war to a happy conclufion, for which purpofe he ufed all poffible application; but yet, notwithftanding his hafte, took care to be upon his guard againft the ftratagems of the enemy, remembring at the fame time that envy ufually attends upon glory, and therefore the more famous he was, the more anxious he was too; and after that ambufcade of Jugurtha's, never fuffered his army to difperfe for the plunder of the country. But, when he had occafion for corn and forage, fome battalions of foot, with all the horfe, went as a guard to thofe employed in that fervice. He conducted one part of the army, and Marius the other. But the country was wafted more by the firing of towns, and other buildings, than plundering them. They ufed to pitch their camps at a fmall diftance from one another, and, when there was occafion for any confiderable action, they joined in it, but, to fpread terror and defolation more effectually, they generally acted feparately. At that time Jugurtha kept within view of them upon the hills, watching all the advantages of time and place for the attacking of them. And wherefoever he could learn the eneny defigned to march, he deftroyed the forage and the fprings, of which there was great fcarcity in that

bile he fhewed himfelf to Metellus, another to fall upon their rear, then prefently make off :, and by and by alarm them again, firft in ' then in ancther, neither engaging them in · fuffering them to be quiet, but only hirder- c execution of their defign.

N 4   LX.

LX. Romanus impc-
rator, ubi se dolis fatigari
videt, neque ab hoste co-
piam pugnandi fieri, ur-
bem magnam, & in ea
parte, qua sita erat, ar-
cem regni, nomine Za-
mam, statuit oppugnare;
ratus id, quod negotium
poscebat, Jugurtham la-
borantibus suis auxilio
venturum, ibique præli-
um fore.   At ille, quæ
parabantur,   a perfugis
edoctus, magnis itineri-
bus Metellum antevenit;
oppidanos hortatur, mœ-
nia defendant, additis auxilio perfugis; quod genus
ex copiis regis, quia fal-
lere nequibat, firmissi-
mum erat. Præterea pol-
licetur, in tempore semet
cum exercitu adfore. Ita,
compositis rebus, in loca
quam maxume occulta
discedit ;   ac paulo post
cognoscit,   Marium ex
itinere frumentatum cum
paucis cohortibus Siccam
missum,   quod oppidum
primum omnium post
malam pugnam ab rege
defecerat. Eo cum delec-
tis equitibus noctu pergit,
& jam egredientibus Ro-
manis in porta pugnam
facit; simul magna voce
Siccenses hortatur,   uti
cohortes ab tergo circum-
veniant ; fortunam illis
præclari facinoris casum
dare. Si id fecerint, postea sese in regno, illos in

LX. *When the Roman general
found himself so harrassed by the
wily conduct of the enemy, with
out any possibility of coming to an
engagement with him, he resolved
to attack Zama, the most considerable town in that part of the kingdom wherein it lies; supposing, as
the case indeed required, that Jugurtha would come to the relief of
his subjects in that distress, and
that a battle would ensue thereupon. But he, being apprized of this
intention by some deserters, by great
marches got thither before Metellus, and encouraged the townsmen
to stand out, putting some deserters
into the place for their assistance,
which of all the king's troops were
the most to be relied on, as who
could not deceive him.   Moreover,
he assures them he would be there
again in due time with an army.
And, after he had thus ordered his
affairs, he withdrew, and got off
into some very private parts of
the country, where soon after he
was informed that Marius had
been dispatched from the army, then
upon a march, to Sicca, with a
few battalions, to fetch in corn;
which was the first town that revolted from the king after the late
unfortunate battle. Thither he goes
with a few choice horse in the night,
and as the Romans were coming
out of town, falls upon them at the
very gate. At the same time, with
a loud voice, he begged of the Sic-
cen*sians to attack the battalions in
rear ; that fortune had put into
their hands an opportunity of performing a noble feat, which if
they did but lay hold of, that he*
liber-

libertate fine metu ætatem aĉturos. Ac ni Marius figna inferre, atque evadere oppido properaviffet ; profeĉto cunĉti, aut magna pars Siccenfium, fidem mutaviffent ; tanta nobilitate fefe Numidæ agunt. Sed milites Jugurthini, paulifper ab rege fuftentati, poftquam majore vi hoftes urgent, paucis amiffis, profugi difcedunt.

LXI. Marius ad Zamam pervenit. Id oppidum in campo fitum ; magis opere, quam natura, munitum erat ; nullius idoneæ rei egens, armis virifque opulentum. Igitur Metellus, pro tempore atque loco paratis rebus, cunĉta mœnia exercitu circumvenit ; legatis imperat. ubi quifque curaret ; deinde, figno dato, undique fimul clamor ingens oritur. Neque ea res Numidas terret ; infenfi intentique fine tumultu manent ; prælium incipitur. Romani, pro ingenio quifque, pars eminus glande aut lapidibus pugnare ; evadere alii ; alii fuccedere ; ac murum modo fuffodere, modo fcalis aggredi ; cupere prælium in manibus facere. Contra ea oppidani in proxumos faxa volvere ; fudes, pila, præterea pice & fulphure tædam

fhould for the future enjoy his kingdom, and they their liberty, in great fecurity. *And had not Marius, by pushing forward, got hastily out of the.town, all, or the greatest part of the Siccensians, would certainly have changed fides ; fo fickle are the Numidians. But the foldiers of Jugurtha, being for fome time kept in courage by the king, upon the enemy's making a vigorous refiftance, fcour off at laft, with the lofs of fome few of their men.*

LXI. *Marius came to Zama. That town was fituated in a plain, better fortified by art than nature, abounding in all the conveniences of life, and well fraught with arms and men. Metellus, having provided all things that the time and occafion required, draws his army quite round the town, and affigns his lieutenant-generals the feveral quarters they were to take care of ; and then immediately, upon a fignal given, a great fhout is fet up on all fides. Which did not terrify the Numidians at all, who ftood undaunted, ready for the reception of the enemy ; and accordingly a battle enfues. The Romans, according as each man was difpofed, fome fought with bullets or ftones ; fome withdrew ; others came in their room ; and one while undermined, another fcaled, the wall, eager to come to clofe fight with the enemy. On the other fide, the townfmen tuumbled great ftones upon thofe that were under the wall, and difcharged fharp ftakes and lances, with pitch and fulphur on fire, upon them. Now were thofe,*

miftam,

miftam, ardentia mittere. Sed ne illos quidem, qui procul manferant, timor ánimi fatis muniverat. Nam plerofque jacula, tormentis, aut manu emif-fa vulnerabant ; parique periculo, fed tama impari, boni atque ignavi erant.

LXII. Dum apud Za-mam fic certatur, Ju-gurtha ex improvifo ca-ftra hoftium cum magna manu invadit ; remiffis, qui in præfidio erant, & omnia magis, quam præ-lium, exfpectantibus, por-tam irrumpit. At noftri, repentino metu perculfi, fibi quifque pro moribus confulunt ; alii fugere, alii arma capere , magna pais vulnerati aut occifi. Cæte-rum ex omni multitudine non amplius quadraginta, memores nominis Roma-ni, grege facto locum cepere paullo, quam alii, editiorem ; neque inde maxuma vi depelli qui-verunt ; fed tela eminus miffa remittere, pauci in pluribus minus fruftrati ; fin Numidæ propius ac-ceffiffent, ibi vero virtu-tem oftendere, & eos maxuma vi cædere, fun-dere, atque fugare. In-terim Metellus, cum a-cerrume rem gereret, cla-morem & tumultum ho-ftilem a tergo accepit ; deinde, converfo equo, animadvertit fugam ad

whofe fears kept them further off, fecure ; moft of them being wound-ed with weapons difcharged from engines, or the hand ; and fo the brave, and the cowardly, were in equal danger, though not in equal credit.

LXII. *During this fight at Zama, Jugurtha falls unexpect-edly upon the enemy's camp, with a confiderable force ; and thofe left for the defence of it being off their guard, as expecting not in the leaft to be attacked, he breaks in at one of the gates. But our men, being counfounded with the furprife, provide for themfelves, each ac-cording to his natural difpofition. Some ran away, others took up arms ; a great part of them were wounded or flain. And of all the number not above forty, being mind-ful of the Roman name, form-ed themfelves into a body, and feized upon a rifing ground ; nor could be diflodged from thence by all the fury of the enemy, but threw back upon them their own weapons, and with the more fuc-cefs becaufe they were fo many of them ; and, if the Numidians came near them, they then laid about them with the utmoft bra-very, flaughtering, routing, and putting them to flight. In the mean time, whilft Metellus was furioufly engaged in the affault up-on the town, he heard from his rear the fhouting and noife of an enemy ; upon which turning his horfe, he perceived a rout of per-fons flying towards him ; a plain*
fe

vorfum fieri; quæ res licàbat popularis. effe. tur equitatum omnem caftra propere mifit, ftatim C. Marium, m cohortibus focio- n; eumque lacrumans · *amicitiam, perque rem- blicam, obfecrat, ne quam tumeliam remanere in rcitu victore, neve hof- inultos abire finat.* e brevi mandata efficit. Jugurtha, munimen- caftrorum impeditus, m alii fuper vallum ecipitarentur, alii in zuftiis ipfi fibi prope- ites officerent, multis iiffis, in loca munita fe- recipit. Metellus, infec- negotio, poftquam nox erat, in caftra cum ex- :itu revortitur.

LXIII. Igitur poftero :, prius quam ad op- gnandum egrederetur, uitatum omnem in ea rte, qua regis adventus it, pro caftris agitare :et; portas, & proxu- loca tribunis difpertit; inde ipfe pergit ad op- lum, atque, uti fupe- re die, murum aggre- :ur. Interim Jugurtha occulto repente nof- s invadit. Qui in oxumo locati fuerant, ullifper territi pertur- ntur; reliqui cito fub- niunt. Neque diutius umidæ refiftere quivif- nt, ni pedites cum equi-

fign of their being friends. Where- fore he fent away all the horfe im- mediately to the camp, and pre- fently ufter them C. Marius, with fome auxiliary battalions; and with tears begs of him by their friend- fhip, and the commonwealth, that he would not fuffer any ftain to fix upon the honour of their vic- torious army, or the enemy to get off unrevenged. *He prefently exe- cutes his orders. But Jugurtha, hindered by the rampart of the camp, whilft fome threw them- felves headlong down the fame, and others by crowding and fqueez- ing through the ftraight paffage of the gates, ftopped one another, af- ter the lofs of a great many men, gets away again into his faftneffes. Metellus, upon the approach of night, draws off his army into the camp, without being able to com- pafs his defign.*

LXIII. *Wherefore the next day, before he drew out to renew the attack, he orders all the caval- ry to patrole before the camp, on the fide the king was to come; the gates, and the parts adjoining, he affigns to fome tribunes; and then he himfelf advances up to the town, and makes an affault upon the wall, as he had done the day before. In the mean time, Jugurtha from his cover comes fuddenly upon our men. Thofe upon whom the brunt fell were put for a while into fome dif- order, but were foon relieved by the reft. Nor would the Numidi- ans have been able to have ftood it any long time, had not their foot, mixing with the horfe, done great execution in the battle. Upon*

tibus

tibus permifti magnam cladem in congreflu facerent. Quibus illi freti, non uti equæftri prælio folet, fequi, dein cedere, fed advorfis equis concurrere, implicare, ac perturbare aciem ; ita, expeditis peditibus fuis, hoftis pœne victos dare.

LXIV. Eodem tempore apud Zamam magna vi certabatur ; ubi quifque legatus, aut tribunus curabat, eo acerrume niti ; neque alius in alio magis, quam in fefe, fpem habere ; pariterque oppidani agere, oppugnare, aut parare omnibus locis ; avidius alteri alteros fauciare, quam femet tegere. Clamor permiftus hortatione, lætitia, gemitu ; item ftrepitus armorum ad cœlum ferri ; tela utrimque volare. Sed illi, qui mœnia defenfabant, ubi hoftes paullulum modo pugnam remiferant, intenti prælium equeftre profpectabant. Eos, uti quæque Jugurthæ res erant, lætos modo, modo pavidos, animadverteres ; ac, ficuti audiri a fuis, aut cerni poffent, monere alii, alii hortari, aut manu fignificare, aut niti corporibus ; huc & illuc, quafi vitabundi, aut jacientes tela, agitare. Quod ubi Mario cognitum eft, nam

whom the horfe depending, th did not, according to their ordina cuftom, purfue one while, and another, but charged breaft to brea, confounding our troops, and putti them into fuch diforder, that th did in a manner deliver them u nigh conquered, to their own lig foot to difpatch.

LXIV. In the mean time, th was very warm work at Zam each lieutenant general and t bune, in their feveral pofts, exe ing all the might they were m ters of ; placing their hopes of f cefs not in others, but themfeh Nor were the townfmen lefs vi rous in their refiftance. B fides, in fhort, were more ea to wound the enemy, than fee themfelves. Shouts were mi with encouragements, exultatic and groans. The din of a reached the very heavens, weapons flew thick on both fi The befieged upon the wall, as as the fury of the befiegers abai did with great attention view engagement of the horfe. And might have feen them, accora as matters went with Jugurt one while glad, and another w. frighted. And where they co be heard or feen by their friei fome admonifhed them of what t thought proper for them to do ; oth encouraged them, or made fign them with their hands, putt their bodies upon the ftretch, moving them this way or that, if they themfelves were avoidi or difcharging of weapons amor them. Which being obferved

n ea parte curabat, fulto lenius agere, ac dentiam rei fimulare; Numidas fine tumul- regis prælium vifere. illis ftudio fuorum rictis, repente magna nurum aggreditur; & fcalis adgreffi milites pe fumma ceperant, 1 oppidani concur- t, lapides, ignem, alia terea tela ingerunt. ftri primo refiftere; 1de, ubi unæ atque ræ fcalæ comminutæ, fuperfteterant afflicti t; cæteri, quo quifque do potuere, pauci in- ri, magna pars con- i vulneribus, abeunt. inde utrimque præ- n nox diremit.

LXV. Metellus poft- m videt fruftra in- ptum; neque oppi- n capi, neque Jugur- m, nifi ex infidiis, aut loco, pugnam facere; jam æftatem exactam :; ab Zama difcedit, in iis urbibus, quæ ab defecerant, fatifque initæ loco, aut mæni- erant, præfidia impo- . Cæterum exercitum provinciam, quæ prox- ia eft Numidiæ, hic- indi gratia collocat. eque id tempus ex alio- m more quieti, aut xuriæ, concedit; fed, oniam armis bellum

Marius, for he commanded in that quarter, he defignedly flackened his fpeed, under pretence of being difheartened, fuffering the Numidians to look on and fee the engagement of the king. But then, whilft they were very intent upon the fight, he fuddenly renews the affault upon the wall with the utmoft violence. And now fome of the foldiers were advanced upon ladders nigh the top of it, when the townfmen, flocking to the place, pour upon them ftones, fire, and all manner of weapons befide. Our men at firft ftood ftifly to it; but fome of them tumbling headlong to the Ground, upon the breaking of a ladder or two they were upon, the reft fhifted for themfelves, as well as they could, a great many of them being fadly mauled, and few without wounds. At laft night put an end to the fray.

LXV. Metellus finding his attempt upon the town to no purpofe, and that it was impoffible to take it, and that Jugurtha would not fight him, but in the way of furprize, or upon great advantage of ground, and that the fummer was now almoft over, marches away from Zama, and places garrifons in thofe cities which had revolted from him, and were fufficiently ftrong by nature or art. But his army he puts into winter-quarters in the province where it borders upon Numidia. Yet he did not, according to the cuftom of others, fpend the time in idlenefs and luxury; but, fince he had but fmall fuccefs in the ufe of arms, he refolves to lay a trap for Jugurtha,
parun

parum procedebat, infidias regi per amicos tendere, & eorum perfidia pro armis uti parat. Igitur Bomilcarem, qui Romæ cum Jugurtha fuerat, & inde, vadibus datis clam Maſſivæ de nece, judicium fugerat ; quod ei per maxumam amicitiam maxuma copia fallendi erat, multis pollicitationibus aggreditur ; ac primo efficit, uti ad ſe colloquendi gratia occultus veniat ; dein, fide data, *ſi Jugurtham vivum, aut necatum, ſibi tradidiſſet, fore, ut illi Senatus impunitatem, & ſua ommia concederet* ; facile Numidæ perſuadet, cum ingenio infido, tum metuenti ne, ſi pax cum Romanis fieret, ipſe per conditiones ad ſupplicium traderetur.

LXVI. Is, ubi primum opportunum fuit, Jugurtham anxium, ac miſerantem fortunas ſuas accedit ; monet, atque lacrumans obteſtatur, *uti aliquando ſibi liberiſque, & genti Numidarum optume merenti, provideat ; omnibus prœliis ſeſe victos, agrum vaſtatum, multos mortales captos, occiſos ; regni opes comminutas eſſe ; ſatis ſœpe jam & virtutem militum, & fortunam tentatam ; caveat, ne illo cunctante, Numi-*

by means of his friends, and mak, uſe of their treachery, inſtead of arms. Accordingly he attacks with mighty promiſes Bomilcar, who had been at Rome with Jugurtha, and by deſerting his bail, and flying from thence, had evaded his tryal for the murder of Maſſiva ; becauſe he had, by reaſon of his great intimacy with him, the beſt opportunity of deceiving him. He firſt prevails upon him to come privately, and confer with him ; and then giving him his word and honour upon it, that if he delivere Jugurtha alive, or dead, the Senate ſhould grant him a pardon, an all his eſtate ; he eaſily perſuade the Numidian, who was naturally perfidious, and withal afraid left, upon the concluſion of a peace with the Romans, he ſhould, l the articles of it, be delivered u to puniſhment.

LXVI. He, as ſoon as opportunity preſented, accoſts Jugurtha full of perplexity, and lamenting his caſe ; adviſing and beſeeching him with tears, to take at laſt proper meaſures for his own ſafety with that of his children, and th whole nation of the Numidians which had deſerved very well a his hand. That they had, *b* ſaid, been defeated in every battle the country laid waſte, and a work of people made priſoners, and ſlain whereby the ſtrength of his king dom had been reduced to nothing That he had ſufficiently tried both the valour of his troops, and hi

d

'æ fibi confulant. His, tque talibus aliis ad de- itionem regis animum mpellit. Mittuntur ad mperatorem legati, qui ugurtham imperata fac- urum dicerent, ac fine illa pactione fefe, reg- iumque fuum, in illius idem tradere. Metellus ropere cunctos Senato- ii ordinis ex hibernis ac- :erfiri jubet; eorum, at- que aliorum, quos idone- is ducebat, confilium habet. Ita more majo- um, ex confilii decreto, er legatos *Jugurthæ* im- erat, argenti pondo du- enta millia, elephantos mnis, equorum & armo- um aliquantum. Quæ poftquam fine mora facta unt, jubet omnis perfu- gas vinctos adduci. Eo- rum magna pars, uti juf- fum erat, adducti; pau- ci, cum primum deditio cœpit, ad regem Bocchum in Mauritaniam abierant. Igitur Jugurtha, ubi ar- mis, virifque, & pecunia fpoliatus eft, cum ipfe ad imperandum Tifidium vocaretur, rurfus cœpit flectere animum fuum, & ex mala confcientia digna timere. Denique, multis diebus per dubitati- onem confumptis, cum modo tædio rerum ad- vorfarum omnia bello potiora duceret; inter= dum fecum ipfe reputa-

fortune too; and therefore ought to have a care, left, if he demurred any longer upon the matter, the Numidians fhould provide for their own fecurity without him. *With thefe, and the like arguments, he at laft prevails upon the King to think of making a furrender. Ac- cordingly deputies are difpatched to the Roman General, to let him know, that Jugurtha would fubmit to his pleafure, and, without infift- ing upon any terms, would caft himfelf, and his kingdom, upon his honour. Metellus immediately or- ders all the gentlemen of Senato- rian rank to be fummoned from their winter-quarters, to hold a council with them, and others, fuch as he judged proper to advife with upon the occafion. And fo, accord- ing to ancient Roman ufage, upon a determination of the council to that effect,* he, by the deputies, or- ders Jugurtha to deliver up two hundred thoufand pound of filver, all his elephants, and fome horfes and arms. *Which being immedi- ately done accordingly, he commands all the deferters from him to be brought to him in chains; and a great part of them were brought, as ordered. Some few of them, as foon as the affair of the furrender begun, fled off to King Bocchus in Mauritania. Wherefore Jugur- tha being thus ftript of arms, men, and money, upon his being fummoned to Tifidium, to receive further com- mands, begun again to change his mind, and, from a fenfe of his guilt, to fear meeting with his de- ferts. Finally, after he had fpent many days in doubt with himfelf* ret,

ret, quam gravis cafus in fervitium ex regno foret; multis, magnifque præfidiis nequicquam perditis, de integro bellum fumit. Et Romæ fenatus, de provinciis confultus, Numidiam Metello decreverat.

what to do, as one while, from an uneafinefs under his misfortunes, thinking any terms whatever preferable to war; and then again confidering how heavy a fall he fhould have from the height of royal majefty into a ftate of flavery; after he had now thrown away a confiderable part of his ftrength to no

purpofe, refolves a-frefh upon war. Now the fenate at Rome, being confulted about the difpofal of the provinces, had voted Numidia for Metellus.

LXVII. Per idem tempus Uticæ forte C. Mario, per hoftias diis fupplicanti, *magna, atque mirabilia portendi,* harufpex dixerat; *proinde, quæ animo agitabat, fretus diis ageret; fortunam quam fæpiffume experiretur; cuncta profpere eventura.* At illum jam antea confulatus ingens cupido exagitabat; ad quem capiundum, præter vetuftatem familiæ, alia omnia abunde erant; induftria, probitas, militiæ magna fcientia, animus belli ingens, domi modicus, lubidinis, & divitiarum victor, tantummodo gloriæ avidus Sed is natus, & omnem pueritiam Arpini altus, ubi primum ætas militiæ patiens fuit, ftipendiis faciundis, non Græca facundia, neq; urbanis munditiis, fefe exercuit; ita inter artis bonas integrum ingenium brevi adolevit. Ergo ubi primum tribu-

LXVII. *About the fame time as Caius Marius was at Utica, paying his devotion to the gods by facrifice, the harufpex told him, that there appeared therein prognofticks of great and wonderful favours defigned him by heaven; and therefore he might depend upon the protection and bleffing of the gods in the execution of his defigns, and might pufh his fortune as much as he pleafed, with affurance of fuccefs. Now he had, fome time before this, been feized with a paffionate defire of the confulfhip, and indeed was abundantly furnifhed with all the qualifications requifite for obtaining it, befides that of a noble defcent, fuch as induftry, integrity, fkill in the military art, a fpirit great in war, but moderate in peace, far above covetoufnefs and riches, and ambitious of glory alone. He was born and brought up at Arpinum, and as foon as he came of age to bear arms he applied himfelf to the fervice of his country in the wars, not to the ftudy of the Græcian eloquence, or the fopperies of the town; and thus was his noble genius advanced to the higheft pitch of improve-*
natum

natum militarem a populo petit, plerifque faciem ejus ignorantibus, facile notus per omnis tribus declaratur. Deinde ab eo magiſtratu, alium poſt aliuni ſibi ¡peperit; femperque in poteſtatibus eo modo agitabat, ut ampliore, quam gerebat, dignus haberetur. Tamen is ad id locorum talis vir, (nam poſtea ambitione præceps datus eſt) conſulatum appetere non audebat. Etiam tum alios magiſtratus plebes, conſulatum nobilitas inter ſe per manus tradebat. Novus nemo tam clarus, neque tam egregius factis erat, quin is indignus illo honore, & quaſi pollutus haberetur.

ment, in the practice of laudable qualities. And therefore, when he made his firſt ſuit to the people for a tribune's commiſſion, though moſt of them were ſtrangers to his face, yet being ſoon known by his character, he was choſen by all the tribes, without exception. After that he roſe from one degree of honour to another, and behaved himſelf in them all ſo, that he was always thought worthy of a greater poſt than that he was in. Yet, as valuable a man as he was 'till that time (for afterwards he was hurried away into ſtrange exceſſes by his ambition) he durſt not venture to offer himſelf a candidate for the conſulſhip. For at that time the commons were admitted to other offices; but the conſulſhip the nobility engroſſed to themſelves, tranſmitting it from one to another. No perſon of low birth, how famous or valuable ſoever he was upon the ſcore of his own merit, was thought worthy of it, but rather a ſcandal to it.

LXVIII. Igitur, ubi Marius haruſpicis dicta eodem intendere videt, quo cupido animi hortabatur, ab Metello petundi gratia miſſionem rogat ; cui quamquam virtus, gloria, atque alia optanda bonis ſuperabant, tamen inerat contemptor animus, & ſuperbia, commune nobilitatis malum. Itaque primum commotus inſolita re, mirari ejus conſilium, & quaſi per amicitiam monere, ne tam prava inciperet, neu ſuper

LXVIII. Wherefore Marius finding the predictions of the ſoothſayer concur with his own ambitious inclinations, he requeſts of Metellus his diſcharge, in order to ſue for the conſulſhip. And tho' Metellus had virtue, glory, and other deſirable qualifications in abundance, yet had he a haughty ſpirit, and pride withal, the common bane of the nobility. Wherefore, being at firſt much ſtartled with the novelty of the thing, he wondered what he meant, and pretended in friendſhip to adviſe him, not to engage in ſo wild a project, or ſuffer his thoughts to tower above his fortune. All things were not to be

fortu-

202 C. CRISPI SALLUSTII

fortunam animum gere-
ret ; non omnia omnibus
cupienda effe ;· debere illi
res fuas fatis placere ; po-
firemo caveret id petere a
populo Rom. quod illi jure
negaretur. Poftquam hæc,
atque alia talia dixit, neque
animus Marii. flectitur ;
refpondit, *ubi primum*
potuiffet per negotia publi-
ca, facturum fefe, quæ
peteret. Ac poftea, fæ-
pius eadem poftulanti,
fertur dixiffe, *ne feftina-*
ret abire ; fatis mature,
illum cum filio fuo con-
fulatum petiturum. Is eo
tempore contubernio pa-
tris ibidem militabat, annos natus circiter xx.
Quæ res Marium cum pro
honore, quem affectabat,
tum contra Metellum
vehementer accenderat.
Ita cupidine, atque ira,
peffumis confultoribus,
graffari ; neque facto
ullo, neque dicto abfti-
nere, quod modo am-
bitiofum foret ; milites,
quibus in hibernis præ-
erat, laxiore imperio,
quam antea, habere ; a-
pud negotiatores, quo-
rum magna multitudo
Uticæ erat, criminofe
fimul & magnifice de bel-
lo loqui ; *dimidia pars*
exercitus, fi fibi permitte-
retur, paucis diebus Ju-
gurtham in catenis habi-
turum ; ab imperatore
confulto trahi, quod, ho-

coveted by all men ; he ought to be abundantly fatisfied with his prefent condition. Finally, *he bid him* have a care of afking that of the Roman people which they might very reafonably deny him. *After he had faid this, and other things to the like purpofe, but without being able to divert Marius from his defign, he told him,* that as foon as the publick occafions would permit, he fhould comply with his requeft. *And upon Marius's repeated inftances to him for his difcharge, he at laft, they fay, told him,* he need not be in fo much hafte to be gone ; he might fue time enough for the conful-fhip with his fon. *He at that time ferved under his father, being a youth of about twenty years of age. This only made Marius more eager of carrying his point, and very much incenfed him againft Metellus. Wherefore he now proceeded according to the inftigation of two of the worft of counfellors, ambition and anger ; by all his words and actions he endeavoured to render himfelf popular ; keeping the foldiers he commanded in their winter-quarters under a very loofe difcipline ; and reflecting amongft the merchants, whereof there was a great number at Utica, upon the conduct of Metellus in the war, and boaft-ing mightily what he would do ;* that with half the army he would in a few days have Jugurtha in chains ; the war was defignedly prolonged by the general, who, being a vain man, and having al the haughtinefs of a king in him, was too fond of his command

m

mo inanis, & regiæ fuper-
biæ, imperio nimis gau-
deret. Quæ omnia illis
eo firmiora videbantur,
quod diuturnitate belli res
familiaris corruperant ; &
animo cupienti nihil fatis
feftinatur.

LXIX. Erat præterea
in exercitu noftro Numi-
da quidam, nomine Gau-
da, Maftanabalis filius,
Mafiniffæ nepos, quem
Micipfa teftamento fe-
cundum hæredem fcrip-
ferat, morbis confe&tus,
& ob eam cauffam mente
paullum imminuta. Cui
Metellus petenti, more
regum, uti fellam juxta
poneret, item poftea
cuftodiæ cauffa turmam
equitum Romanorum,
utrumque negaverat ;
honorem, quod eorum
modo foret, quos popu-
lus Romanus reges appel-
laviffet ; præfidium, quod
contumeliofum in eos
foret, fi equites Romani,
fatellites Numidæ trade-
rentur. Hunc Marius
anxium aggreditur, atque
hortatur, ut contumeli-
arum in imperatorem,
cum fuo auxilio pœnas
petat ; hominem ob mor-
bos animo parum valido
fecunda oratione extollit ;
illum regem, ingentem vi-
rum, Mafiniffæ nepotem
effe ; fi Jugurtha captus,
aut occifus foret, imperi-
um Numidiæ fine mora

All which things appeared to them
the more plaufible, becaufe the long
continuance of the war affected
their trade ; and no expedition
feems fufficient to the man that is
in hafte to be rich.

LXIX. *There was befides in*
our army a certain Numidian, by
name Gauda, the fon of Mafta-
nabal, and grandfon of Mafinif-
fa, whom Micipfa in his will had
made his fecond heir ; a man di-
ftempered to fuch a degree that it
affected his mind. He had requefted of Metellus the honour of a
chair next him, as kings had, and
afterwards a troop of Roman
horfe for his guard : but he refufed him both ; the firft, becaufe it
was an honour only paid to fuch as
the Roman people complimented
with the title of kings ; and the
latter, becaufe it would be an af-
front upon Roman knights to be
made to attend upon a Numidian
as his guard. In his concern for
this refufal, Marius addreffes him,
and encourages him, by the promife of his affiftance, to apply for
fatisfaction for the affronts put upon him by the general. He mag-
nifies the poor mortal, who from
the influence of his diftempers upon his mind was little better than
crazed, telling him, he was a
prince, a great man, the grandfon of Mafiniffa. If Jugurtha was
but taken prifoner, or flain, he
would, without more ado, forthwith get the kingdom of Numidia,
which might luckily be brought
about, if he was made conful for

hati-

habiturum; *id adeo ma-*
ture poffe evenire, fi ipfe
conful ad id bellum miffus
foret. Itaque & illum,
& equites Romanos, mi-
lites, & negotiatores, alios
ipfe, plerofque fpes pacis
impellit, uti Romam ad
fuos neceffarios afpere in
Metellum de bello fcri-
bant, Marium imperato-
rem pofcant. Sic illi a
multis mortalibus ho-
neftiffuma fuffragatione
confulatus petebatur. Si-
mul ea tempeftate plebes
nobilitate fufa per legem
Mamiliam, novos extol-
lebat. Ita Mario cuncta
procedere.

LXX. Interim Jugur-
tha, poftquam, omiffa
deditione, bellum incipit,
cum magna cura parare
omnia, feftinare, cogere
exercitum; civitates, quæ
ab fe defecerant, formidine, aut oftentando præ-
mia adfectare; com-
munire fuos locos; arma,
tela, aliaque, quæ fpe
pacis amiferat, reficere,
aut commercari; fervitia
Romanorum allicere, &
eos ipfos, qui in præfidiis
erant, pecunia tentare;
prorfus nihil intactum,
neque quietum pati;
cuncta agitare. Igitur
Vaccenfes, quo Metellus
initio, Jugurtha pacifi-
cante, præfidium impo-
fuerat, fatigati regis fuppliciis, neque antea vo-

the management of the war.
Wherefore he, the Roman knights,
foldiers, and merchants, were all
encouraged, part by Marius, but
moft of them by the hopes of peace,
to write to their friends at Rome,
in a very reflecting manner, upon
the conduct of Metellus in the
war, at the fame time wifhing
Marius might be made general
therein. Thus was he fupported
in his pretenfions to the confulfhip,
by a very honourable intereft made
for him. At the fame time tho the
commons, having baffled the nobility
by the Mamilian law, were for
raifing your upftart gentlemen.
And thus all things went on Ma-
rius's fide.

LXX. *In the mean time Jugur-*
tha, having dropped his intention
of furrendering, and renewed the
war, was making preparations for
it with all poffible application and
expedition, and raifing an army. He
endeavoured too, partly by threats,
and partly by promifes, to engage
the cities which had revolted from
him, to return to their allegiance;
was bufy in fortifying places; in
making or buying up arms of all
forts, and other things, which he
had parted with in hopes of peace.
He likewife attempted to wheedle
over to him the Roman flaves, and
tampered, by the influence of his
money, to engage fuch as were in
garrifons to betray the towns to
him. In fhort, he left no means
untried for his defence, but pufhed
at all. Wherefore fome of the
principal inhabitants of Vacca,
wherein Metellus had put a garri-
luntate

luntate alienati, principes civitatis, inter fe conjurant ; nam vulgus, uti plerumque folet, & maxume Numidarum, ingenio mobili, feditiofum, atque difcordiofum erat, cupidum novarum rerum, quieti & otio advorfum ; dein, compofitis inter fe rebus, in diem tertium cónftituunt, quod is feftus celebratufqué per omnem Africam, ludum & lafciviam magis, quam formidinem, oftentabat. Sed, ubi tempus fuit, centuriones, tribunofque militaris, & ipfum præfectum oppidi T. Turpilium Silanum, alius alium domos fuos invitant ; eos omnis, præter Turpilium, inter epulas obtruncant ; poftea milites palantis, inermis, quippe in tali die, ac fine imperio, aggrediuntur. Idem plebes facit, pars edocti ab nobilitate, alii ftudio talium rerum incitati, quis acta, confiliumque ignorantibus tumultus ipfe, & res novæ fatis placebant.

fon, when Jugurtha made an offer of fubmitting, being wearied out by the follicitations of the king, and indeed not diffaffected to him before, the heads of them enter into a confpiracy for betraying the town. For the common people, according to their ufual temper, efpecially among the Numidians, were fickle, feditious, and contentious, fond of change, and enemies to peace and quietnefs. Thefe gentlemen, having formed their plot, pitched upon the third day after for the execution of it, becaufe that, being a feftival much obferved throughout all Africa, naturally gave occafion to expect mirth and jollity, and nothing of terror at fuch a time. When the day was come, they invite the centurions and tribunes, with the governor of the town, T. Turpilius Silanus, to their houfes, one one, and another another of them, and murdered them all during the feaft, excepting Turpilius ; after which they fall upon the foldiers, difperfed about town, and unarmed, being holyday, and confequently under no command. The commonalty too do the like, part of them at the inftigation of the nobility, and others out of a fondnefs for the work ; who, though they knew not well what was doing, or the defign, yet liked the commotion, and the novelty of the thing.

LXXI. Romani milites, improvifo metu, incerti ignarique, quod potiffumum facerent, trepidare ad arcem oppidi, ubi figna & fcuta erant ; præfidium hoftium, por-

LXXI. The Roman foldiers, upon this unexpected alarm, being in great doubt and uncertainty what courfe to take, ran in great hurry to the citadel of the town, where their ftandards and fhields were ; but found the gates fhut,

O 3

ta

tæ ante clausæ fugam prohibebant ; ad hoc mulieres puerique pro tectis ædificiorum saxa, & alia, quæ locus præbebat, certatim mittere. Ita neque cavere anceps malum, neque a fortissumis infirmissumo generi resisti posse ; juxta boni, malique, strenui, & imbelles inulti obtruncati. In ea tanta asperitate, sævissumis Numidis, & oppido undique clauso, Turpilius præfectus unus ex omnibus Italicis profugit intactus ; id misericordiane hospitis, an pactione, an casu ita evenerit, parum comperimus ; nisi, quia illi in tanto malo, turpis vita integra fama potior fuit, improbus intestabilisque videtur. Metellus, postquam de rebus Vaccæ actis comperit, paullisper mœstus e conspectu abit ; dein, ubi ira & ægritudo permista sunt, cum maxuma cura ultum ire injurias festinat. Legionem, cum qua hiemabat, & quam plurimos potest Numidas equites pariter cum occasu solis expeditos educit ; & postera die, circiter horam tertiam, pervenit in quamdam planitiem, locis paullo superioribus circumventam. Ibi milites fessos itineris magnitudine, & jam ab-

and a guard posted to prevent their getting in. Besides, the women and children upon the tops of the houses plied them off with stones, and aught else that came to hand. In this double distress, it was impossible for them to take any proper measures for their own security, nor could the bravest resist the weakest. The courageous and the cowardly, the vigorous and unactive, perished all alike unrevenged. In this dismal case, the Numidians breathing nothing but destruction, and the gates being all close, Turpilius the governor was the only man of all the Italians that got safe off ; whether through the compassion of the person that entertained him, by compact, or chance, does not appear. But however, as in the common calamity he preferred a scandalous life before his honour, he must, I think, pass for a detestable scoundrel. When Metellus heard of the transactions at Vacca, he was so much affected that for some time he declined all company ; but at last, resentment mixing with his sorrow, his mind was wholly taken up with the thoughts of revenge. Accordingly he draws out the legion he wintered with, and as many light Numidian horse, as he could get together, about sun-set ; and the next day, by three of the clock, he came into a plain enclosed on all sides with rising ground. There the soldiers being much fatigued with their march, and now refusing to obey orders, he tells them that the town of Vacca was not above a mile off, and that they

nuentis

nuentis omnia, docet op-
pidum Vaccam non am-
plius mille paffuum abef-
fc ; decere illos reliquum
laborem æquo animo pa-
ti, dum pro civibus fuis,
viris fortiffumis, atque
miferrumis, pœnas cape-
rent. Præterea prædam
benigne oftentat. Sic animis eorum arrectis, equi-
tes in primo latere, pe-
dites quam arctiffume ire,
& figna occultare jubet.

LXXII. Vaccenfes ubi
animadvertere ad fe vor-
fum exercitum pergere ;
primo, uti res erat, Me-
tellum effe rati, portas
claufere; dein, ubi ne-
que agros vaftari, & eos,
qui primi aderant, Nu-
midas equites vident ; rur-
fum Jugurtham arbitrati,
cum magno gaudio obvii
procedunt. Equites pedi-
tefque, repente figno da-
to, alii vulgum effufum
oppido cædere ; alii ad
portas feftinare ; pars tur-
res capere ; ira, atque
fpes prædæ amplius, quam
laffitudo, poffe. Ita Vaccenfes biduum modo ex
perfidia lætati ; civitas
magna, & opulens, pœ-
næ cuncta aut prædæ fuit.
Turpilius, quem præfec-
tum oppidi unum ex om-
nibus profugiffe, fupra
oftendimus, juffus a Me-
tello cauffam dicere ;
poftquam fefe parum ex-
purgat, condemnatus,

ought to bear with patience the
little remaining fatigue, to take
vengeance for the murder of their
brave, but unhappy, countrymen.
At the fame time he civilly made
them an offer of the plunder of the
place. The hearing of this putting new life into them, he orders
the horfe to advance firft, and the
foot to follow after in clofe array,
concealing their ftandards.

LXXII. The Vaccenfians, upon the firft difcovery of an army
coming againft them, fuppofing it
to be Metellus, as it was, fhut
their gates ; but, perceiving no
ravage made, and that thofe in
the van were Numidian horfe,
concluding that Jugurtha was
there, they fally out to meet him
with great joy. Whereupon both
horfe and foot, upon a fudden fignal given, fome made havock of
the mob that came from the town,
whilft others haftened to the gates,
and others got into the towers upon
the wall ; and now their paffion,
and the hopes of plunder, made
them forget all their fatigue. Thus
the Vaccenfians, a great and wealthy people, after a joy of two days
continuance for the fuccefs of their
late treachery, were all either put
to the fword or plundered. Turpilius, the governor of the town,
who, we have already faid, was
the only one that made his efcape,
was called before a court martial
by Metellus ; where, making but a
poor defence, he was fentenced to
die, and, being firft lafhed, was

O 4   verbe-

verbaratufque, capite pœnas folvit; nam is civis ex Latio erat.

LXXIII. Per idem tempus Bomilcar, cujus impulfu Jugurtha deditionem, quam metu deferuit, inceperat, fufpectus regi, & ipfe eum fufpiciens, novas res cupere; ad perniciem ejus dolum quærere; diu noctuque fatigare animum; denique, omnia tentando, focium fibi adjungit Nabdalfam, hominem nobilem, magnis opibus clarum, acceptumque popularibus fuis; qui plerumque feorfum ab rege exercitum ductare, & omnis res exfequi folitus erat, quæ Jugurthæ feffo, aut majoribus adftricto, fuperaverant; ex quo illi gloria, opefque inventæ. Igitur utriufque confilio dies infidiis ftatuitur; cætera, ut res pofceret, ex tempore parari placuit. Nabdalfa ad exercitum profectus; quem inter hiberna Romanorum juffus habebat, ne ager inultis hoftibus vaftaretur. Is poftquam, magnitudine facinoris perculfus, ad tempus non venit; metufque rem impediebat: Bomilcar, fimul cupidinibus incœpta patrandi, & timore focii anxius, ne, omiffo vetere confilio, novum quæreret; litteras ad eum per

afterwards beheaded. For he was a Roman only with the privilege of Latium.

LXXIII. About the fame time Bomilcar, at whofe inftigation Jugurtha had begun to make a furrender of his kingdom, which defign he afterwards relinquifhed through fear, being fufpected by the King, and himfelf fufpicious of him, out of a defire to get rid of him, was wracking his invention day and night in the contrivance of a plot for his deftruction; and, after a variety of projects for the purpofe, at laft engages Nabdalfa in the defign, a nobleman of great eftate and intereft in the country, who ufed generally to command an army apart from the king, and take charge of fuch affairs relative to the war as the king was at any time too much fatigued to attend upon in perfon, or prevented from fo doing by bufinefs of higher concern; by which means he had acquired to himfelf great glory, and a vaft eftate. Wherefore by joint confent a day was fixed for the execution of their plot, the manner whereof was to be regulated according to the exigency of the time. Upon this, Nabdalfa went to the army, which by order of the king he had within the enemy's winter-quarters, in order to oppofe or revenge any ravage of theirs in the country. But he, ftaggering at the greatnefs of the undertaking, and fearful of the iffue, came not at the time appointed, which prevented the execution of the defign. Whereupon Bomilcar, as well from an eager defire

ho-

homines fidelis mittit ; in queis mollitiem, focor-diamque viri accufare ; teftari .deos, per quos juraviffet ; monere, ne præmia Metelli in peftem converteret ; Jugurthæ exitium adeffe ; cæterum, fua ne, an virtute Metelli periret, id modo agitari ; proinde reputaret cum a-nimo fuo, præmia an cru-ciatum mallet.

LXXIV. Sed cum hæ litteræ adlatæ, forte Nab-dalfa, exercito corpore feffus, in lecto quiefcebat. Ubi, cognitis Bomilcaris verbis, primo cura, dein-de, uti ægrum animum folet, fomnus cepit. Erat ei Numida quidam nego-tiorum curator, fidus, ac-ceptufque, & omnium confiliorum, nifi noviffu-mi, particeps. Qui poft-quam-allatas litteras au-divit, ex confuetudine ratus opera, aut ingenio fe opus effe, in taberna-culum introiit ; dormi-ente illo, epiftolam, fu-per caput in pulvino te-mere pofitam, fumit, ac perlegit ; dein propere, cognitis infidiis, ad regem pergit. Nabdalfa, poft paullo experrectus, ubi neque epiftolam reperit,

of accomplifhing his purpofe, as alfo from a concern at the timorouf-nefs of his friend, left he, drop-ping their former defign, fhould en-gage in a new one to his deftruction, difpatches a letter to him by fome confidents ; in which he upbraided him with cowardice and want of fpirit ; called the gods, by whom they had fworn, to witnefs againft him ; and advifed him to have a care of turning the rewards they had to expect from Metellus, to their common deftruction ; that Jugurtha was on the brink of ruin ; but whether that was to be effected by their r fo-lution, or that of Metellus, was the only thing they wer to confider. Wherefore he would do well to think with him elf, which he would make choice of, rewards, or a cruel death.

LXXIV. When this letter came to the hands of Nabdalfa, he hap-pened to be refting himfelf upon the bed after a fatigue of exercife. Upon reading of it he was full of perplexity ; and, after he had wea-ried himfelf with mufing upon the matter, as it often happens in fuch cafes, he fell afleep. He had a faithful fervant, a Numidian, much entrufted by him in the ma-nagement of his affairs, highly in his favour, and acquainted with all his defigns, excepting the laft. Who, upon hearing a letter was brought for his mafter, fuppofing he might, as ufual, have occafion for his fervice or advice upon it, entered his tent, and finding him afleep takes the letter, that was carelefly laid above his head upon his pillow, and reads it. Having by this means difcovered the plot, he goes in all hafte to the king. Nabdalfa, awaking foon after, miffed his letter, and, being informed

&

& rem omnem, uti acta erat, ex perfugis cognovit; primo indicem persequi conatus; postquam id fruſtra fuit, Jugurtham placandi gratia, accedit; dicit quæ ipſe paraviſſet facere, perfidia clientis ſui præventum; lacrumans *obteſtatur per amicitiam, perque ſua antea fideliter aſta, ne ſuper tali ſcelere ſuſpeſtum ſeſe haberet.*

by *ſome deſerters of what had paſſed, he firſt of all endeavoured to overtake the informer; but, finding he could not do that, he goes himſelf to the king, in order to mollify him, telling him* that he had been prevented in what he deſigned to do himſelf. by the perfidiouſneſs of his ſervant; and *with tears* beſeeches him by his favour for him, and the merit of his former ſervices, not to ſuſpect him.

LXXV. Ad ea rex aliter, atque animo gerebat, placide reſpondit. Bomilcare, aliiſque multis, quos ſocios inſidiarum cognoverat, interfectis, iram oppreſſerat, ne qua ex eo negotio feditio oriretur. Neque poſt id locorum Jugurthæ dies, aut nox ulla quieta fuit; neque loco, neque mortali cuiquam aut tempori ſatis credere; civis, hoſtis juxa metuere; circumſpectare omnia, & omni ſtrepitu paveſcere; alio, atque alio loco ſæpe contra decus regium, noctu requieſcere; interdum ſomno excitus, arreptis armis tumultum facere; ita formidine, quaſi vecordia exagitari.

LXXV. *The king, diſſembling the real ſentiments of his mind, gave him a kind anſwer. And then putting Bomilcar, and many others he found concerned with him in the plot, to death, ſuppreſſed his reſentment againſt Nabdalſa, for fear of an inſurrection in his favour. From this day forward Jugurtha had no quiet day or night, as not knowing how to truſt himſelf in any place or company, and fearing his ſubjects and enemies all alike. He was ever looking round him, affrighted with the leaſt noiſe, and reſted at nights ſometimes in one place, ſometimes another, unbecoming a prince. Sometimes he would ſtart ſuddenly, in great diſorder, out of ſleep, and take to his arms, and was haunted with his fears to diſtraction.*

LXXVI. Igitur Metellus, ubi de caſu Bomilcaris, & indicio patefacto ex perfugis cognovit; rurſus tanquam ad integrum belluni cuncta parat,

LXXVI. *When Meiellus heard by ſome deſerters of the fate of Bomilcar, and the diſcovery of the plot, he makes, in all haſte, freſh preparations for the renewal of the war. And, as Marius was per-* rat,

at, feſtinatque. Marium, atigantem de profecti- ne, ſimul & invitum, z offenſum ſibi parum Joneum ratus, domum imittit. Et Romæ ple- ies, litteris, quæ de Me- ello ac Mario miſſæ rant, cognitis, volenti nimo dc ambobus ac- eperant. Imperatori no- ilitas, quæ antea decori uerat, invidiæ eſſe ; at lli alteri generis humilitas avorcm addiderat ; cæ- erum in utroque magis tudia partium, quam bo- ia, aut mala ſua, mode- ata. Præterea ſeditioſi nagiſtratui vulgum exa- ;itare, Metellum omni- ius concionibus capitis rceſſere, Marii virtutem n majus celebrare. De- iique plebes ſic accenſa, iti opifices, agreſtiſque ɔmnis, quorum res, fideſ- jue in manibus ſitæ erant, elictis operibus frequen- iarent Marium, & ſua iieceſſaria poſt illius hono- iem ducerent. Ita per- :ulſa nobilitate, poſt nultas tempeſtates, novo iomini conſulatus man- latur ; & poſtea populus i tribuno plebis Manlio Mantino rogatus, quem vellet cum Jugurtha bel- lum gerere, frequens Ma- rium juſſit. Sed ſenatus paullo ante Metello Nu- midiam decreverat, ea res fruſtra fuit.

petually ſolliciting him for his dif- charge, and he thought he would be of ſmall ſervice to him, if de- tained againſt his will, and out of humour, he ſends him home. At Rome too, when the commons came to know the contents of the letters relating to Metellus and Marius, they were well pleaſed with the treatment of both. The general's noble deſcent, which before had been an ornament to him, now ex- poſed him to the hatred of the peo- ple, whilſt the low birth of the other procured him their favour. But party-rage prevailed more in the caſe of both than their own good or bad qualities. Beſides, ſome factious magiſtrates inflamed the popular heat, by charging Me- tellus in all their harangues with capital crimes, and magnifying pro- digiouſly the great conduct of Ma- rius. In ſhort, the people were ſo fired, that the mechanicks in town, with the boors from the country, whoſe ſubſtance and credit lay all in their daily labour, quitting their ſeveral employments, gave conſtant attendance upon Marius, and poſt- poned their own neceſſary concerns to his honour. The nobility being by this means quite diſpirited, af- ter much buſtle, the conſulſhip is put into the hands of this upſtart gentleman Marius. And by a bill, which the tribune of the commons, Manlius Mantinus, preferred to the people, in a full aſſembly, he was ordered to manage the war with Jugurtha. The ſenate indeed had a little before voted the province of Numidia for Metellus, but all in vain.

LXXVII.

LXXVII. Eodem tempore Jugurtha, amiſſis amicis, quorum plerofque ipfe necavcrat, cæteri formidine, pars ad Romanos, alii ad regem Bocchum profugerant; cum neque bellum geri fine adminiſtris poſſet, novorumque fidem in tanta perfidia veterum experiri periculofum duceret, varius incertufque agitabatur. Neq; illi res, neque confilium, aut quifquam hominum fatis placebat; itinera, præfectofque in dies mutare; modo advorfum hoſtes, interdum in folitudines pergere; fæpe in fuga, at poſt paullo fpem in armis habere; dubitare, virtuti an fidei popularium minus crederet. Ita, quocumque intenderat, res advorſæ erant. Sed inter eas moras repente ſefe Metellus cum exercitu oſtendit. Numidæ ab Jugurtha pro tempore parati, inſtruĉtique; dein prælium incipitur. Qua in parte rex pugnæ adfuit, ibi aliquamdiu certatum; ceteri omnes ejus milites primo congreſſu pulfi, fugatique; Romani fignorum, & armorum, & aliquanto numero hoſtium potiti. Nam ferme Numidas in omnibus præliis magis pedes, quam arma, tuta funt.

LXXVI. *In the mean time Jugurtha having loſt all his friends, the greateſt part of them being put to death by himſelf, and the reſt, for fear of the like fate flying over to the Romans, or King Bocchus, being not in a condition to carry on the war without miniſter, or proper aſſiſtants; and thinking it dangerous, after the perfidious uſage he had met with from his old friends, to try the faith of new ones, he was in vaſt perplexity and uncertainty what to do. Nothing no advice, no body could pleaſe him. He changed his marches, and the governors of towns, every day. Sometimes he advanced againſt the enemy, ſometimes he made off in the deſarts. He oftentimes placed his hopes in flight, and preſen after in his arms; being in doubt whether the courage, or the fidelity of his ſubjeĉts, was leſs to be confided in. Thus, turn his thoughts which way he would, all things ſeemed to be againſt him. Whilſt was in this wavering condition, a ſudden Metellus appears with army. The Numidians were put order of battle, and drawn up, well as the ſhortneſs of the time would allow; after which the fight begun; which continued ſome time where the king was perſonally preſent; but the reſt of the army was routed and put to flight, at the very firſt ſhock. The Romans took their ſtandards and arms, with ſmall number of priſoners. For almoſt all the battles that we fought, their heels ſecured the Numidians more than their arms.*

LXXVII

ι fuga
s mo-
fidens,
parte
dines,
nit, id
ι, &
erique
ιe ejus
cultus
tquam
funt,
'halam
mum,
quin-
a, at-
ςnave-
trandi
i poti-
ρerita-
natu-
ιggre-
ia ju-
ιri ju-
lierum
utres
ε ido-
εterea
quam
domiti
nponit
ι, ple-
&a ex
ι. Ad
ιt, qui
ι Me-
quam-
aquæ
ocum-
orent,
ιmine,
ρppido
ςimus,
ιo mo-

LXXVIII. *After this defeat,
Jugurtha despairing more than
ever of success, got off with some
deserters, and a part of the horse,
into the deserts, from whence he
came to Thala, a great and wealthy town ; where most of his treasure lay, and his sons were generally educated. Upon advice of
which, Metellus, tho' all the country betwixt Thala and the next
river, of fifty miles extent, was
dry and waste ; yet in hopes of
finishing the war, if he could but
make himself master of that town,
he resolves to encounter all manner
of hardships, and conquer even nature itself. Wherefore he orders
all the beasts of burden to be eased
of all their luggage, in order to
carry corn sufficient for ten days,
with leathern bottles, and other
vessels proper to put up water in.
Moreover, he picks up out of the
country as many horses, and the like
animals that had been broke, as he
could ; and loads them with vessels
of all kinds, but mostly of wood,
taken out of the cottages of the
Numidians. Besides, he orders the
neighbouring people, who, after the
defeat of the King, had submitted to
Metellus, to carry every one of them
as much water as they could ; and
appoints time and place for their
rendezvous. He loads the beasts of
carriage out of the river, which,
we have above said, was the nigh-
est water to the town. Being thus
provided, away he marches for
Thala ; and when he was arrived
at the place where he had appointed
the Numidians to meet him, and the
camp was pitched and fortified,*

do

do inftructus ad Thalam proficifcitur. Deinde ubi ad id loci ventum, quod Numidis præceperat; & caftra pofita, munitaque funt; tanta repente cœlo miffa vis aquæ dicitur ut ea modo exercitui fatis fuperque fore. Præterea commeatus fpe amplior; quia Numidiæ, ficuti plerique in nova deditione, officia intenderant. Cæterum milites, religione, pluvia magis ufi; eaque res multum animis eorum addidit; nam rati fefe Diis immortalibus curæ effe. Deinde poftero die, contra opinionem Jugurthæ, ad Thalam perveniunt. Oppidani, qui fe locorum afperitate munitos crediderant, magna atque infolita re perculfi, nihilo fegnius bellum parare; idem noftri facere.

LXXIX. Sed rex nihil jam Metello infectum credens, quippe qui omnia arma, tela, locos, tempora, denique naturam ipfam, cæteris imperitantem, induftria vicerat, cum liberis, & magna parte pecuniæ ex oppido noctu profugit; neque poftea in ullo loco amplius una die, aut una nocte moratus, fimulabat, fefe negotii gratia properare; cæterum proditionem timebat, quam vitare poffe celeritate putabat. Nam

there fell fuch a vaft quantity of rain, they tell you, that that alone would have been fufficient for the army, and more than fufficient. And provifions too were brought in greater plenty than was expected; becaufe the Numidians, like moft other people after a fubmiffion, had executed the orders given them, with extraordinary care. But the foldiers, from a fuperftitious whim, chofe rather to ufe the rain than river water; and the thing animated them exceedingly; becaufe they fuppofed by that, the immortal gods took care of them. The day following, contrary to Jugurtha's expectations, they arrived at Thalia. The towns-people, who imagined themfelves fufficiently fecured by the adjoining wildernefs, being furprized at fo great and uncommon an event, did, notwithftanding, prepare for a vigorous defence; as our men did, on the other hand, for the attack.

LXXIX. But the King thinking now nothing impoffible for Metellus, as who had by his induftry conquered arms, places, times, and finally, nature itfelf, that rules over all things elfe, fled out of the town in the night-time, with his children, and a great part of his money; and never after ftay'd above one day, or one night, in the fame place, pretending himfelf to be upon bufinefs that required hafte. But indeed he was afraid of being betrayed, which he hoped to prevent by his expedition; becaufe fuch defigns are ufually hatched by virtue of thofe advantages, which a

talia

talia confilia per otium & ex opportunitate capi. At Metellus, ubi oppidanos prælio intentos, fimul oppidum & operibus et loco munitum videt, vallo foffaque mœnia circumvenit. Deinde jubet locis ex copia maxume idoneis vineas agere, fuperque eas aggerem jacere, & fuper aggerem impofitis turribus opus & adminiftros tutari. Contra hæc oppidani feftinare, parare; prorfus ab utrifque nihil reliquum fieri. Denique Romani, multo ante labore, præliifque fatigati, poft dies quadraginta, quam eo ventum erat, oppido modo potiti; præda omnis a perfugis corrupta. Ii poftquam murum arietibus feriri, refque fuas afflictas vident, aurum, atq; argentum, & alia, quæ prima ducuntur, domum regiam comportant; ibi vino, & epulis onerati, illaque, & domum, & femet igni corrumpunt; & quas victi ab hoftibus pœnas metuerant, eas ipfi volentes pependere. Sed pariter cum capta Thala legati ex oppido Lepti ad Metellum venerant, orantes uti præfidium præfectumque eo mitteret; *Hamilcarem quendam, hominem nobilem, factiofum, novis rebus ftudere; advorfum*

time of eafe and reft affords. Metellus, finding the townf-people refolved upon the defence of the place, and that it was well fecured both by nature and art, draws a line of circumvallation quite round; and then orders his men to pufh up their vineæ in fuch places as would moft conveniently admit of them, to caft up a mount, and from towers erected thereupon to defend the works and thofe concerned therein. On the other hand, the townf-men were not idle, but provided all things for their defence. In fhort, nothing was left unattempted on either fide. At length the Romans, within forty days after they came before the place, with a world of fatigue and hard fighting, made themfelves mafters of it. But the plunder was all deftroyed by the Roman deferters in town. For they, as foon as they found the rams begun to play upon the wall, and what a defperate cafe they were in, carry the gold and filver, and every thing elfe that was valuable, to the royal palace; and there, after they had glutted themfelves with wine and good cheer, they deftroyed all the treafure, and themfelves too, by fetting fire to the houfe, and voluntarily inflicted upon themfelves the punifhment they apprehended from the enemy, if they fell into their hands. Juft at the juncture when Thala was taken, fome deputies came from the town of Leptis to Metellus, begging of him to fend a garrifon and a governor thither; that one Hamilcar there, a perfon of great birth and intereft, was in a plot againft the

quem

quem neque imperia magistratuum, neque leges valerent ; ni id festinaret, in summo periculo suam salutem, illorum socios, fore. Nam Leptitani jam inde a principio belli Jugurthini ad Bestiam consulem, & postea Romam miserant, amicitiam, societatemq; rogatum. Deinde, ubi ea impetrata, semper boni, fidelesque mansere, & cuncta a Bestia, Albino, Metelloque imperata nave fecerant. Itaque ab imperatore facile, quæ petebant, adepti. Emissæ eo cohortes Ligurum quatuor, & Caius Annius præfectus.

government, and was like to be to strong for the magistrates and laws ; unless ·he dispatched away the assistance forthwith, they, the allies of the Romans, would be in the utmost danger. *For the Leptitani, at the very beginning of the war with Jugurtha,-had sent first to the consul Bestia, and afterwards to Rome, to desire our friendship and alliance ; and, their request being granted,they remained: true and trusty ever after, and punctually executed all orders received from Bestia, Albinus, and Metellus. Wherefore they found from the general a ready compliance with their desires. Four battalions of Ligurians were sent thither, under the command of C. Annius.*

LXXX. Id oppidum ab Sidoniis conditum est, quos, accepimus, profugos ob discordias civilis navibus in eos locos venire ; cæterum situm inter duas Syrtis, quibus nomen ex re inditum. Nam duo sunt sinus prope in extrema Africa, impares magnitudine, pari natura; quorum proxuma terræ præalta sunt ; cætera, uti fors tulit, alta ; alia in tempestate vadosa. Nam ubi mare magnum esse, & sævire cœpit ventis, limum arenamque, & saxa ingentia fluctus trahunt ; ita facies locorum cum ventis simul mutatur. *Syrtes ab tractu nominatæ.* Ejus civitatis lingua

LXXX. *That town was built by the Sidonians, who, as tradition says, being obliged by civil broils at home to leave their native country, came by shipping into those parts. It is situated betwixt the two Syrtes, which are so called from the nature of them.· For they are two bays, almost in the extremity of Africa, unequal in bigness, but of like nature, whereof the parts nigh the shore are very deep ; the rest are some deep, some shallow, especially much so in a storm. For when the sea begins to swell, and grow boisterous by the winds, the waves drag the mud,)and, and huge stones about, whereby the appearance of the places is perpetually changing with the wind ; and from this dragging they are called Syrtes. The language of that town has undergone an alteration from*

modo

modo converfa connubio Numidarum; legum, cultufque pleraque Sidonica; quæ eo facilius retinebant, quod procul ab imperio regis ætatem agebant. Inter illos, & frequentem Numidiam multi vaftique loci erant.

LXXXI. Sed, quoniam in has regiones per Leptitanorum negotia venimus, non indignum videtur, egregium, atque mirabile facinus duorum Carthaginienfium memorare ; eam rem nos locus admonuit. Qua tempeftate Carthaginienfes pleræque Africæ imperitabant, Cyrenenfes quoque magni, atque opulenti fuere. Ager in medio arenofus, una fpecie; neque flumen, neque mons erat, qui finis eorum difcerneret; quæ res eos in magno diuturnoque bello inter fe habuit. Poftquam utrimque legiones, item claffes fæpe fufæ, fugatæque, & alteri alteros aliquantum attriverant; veriti, ne mox victos, victorefque defeffos alius aggrederetur, per inducias fponfionem faciunt, *uti certo die legati domo proficifcerentur ; quo in loco inter fe obvii fuiffent, is communis utriufque populi finis haberetur.* Igitur Carthagine

their inter-marriages with the Numidians ; but moft things in their laws and way of living are derived from the Sidonians, which they retained the more eafily becaufe of their being at fo great a diftance from the power and influence of the king of Perfia. Betwixt them and the well inhabited parts of Numidia lies a vaft defart.

LXXXI. *But fince we are got into thefe parts, upon occafion of mentioning the Leptitani, I think it may not be amifs to give an account of an extraordinary wonderful action performed by two Carthaginians, which the mention of Leptis puts me in mind of. At the time the Carthaginians ruled over the greateft part of Africa, the Cyrenians were a great and wealthy people. The country lying betwixt them and the Carthaginians was all fandy, without variety or diftinction, of one uniform appearance, having neither river nor mountain to fix the limits of each dominion ; which thing proved the occafion of a terrible and tedious war. After great loffes had been fuftained on each fide by land and by fea, to the weakening of both, fearing left fome third people fhould fall upon the conquered or conquerors together, when weary, they came to a ceffation of arms, and thereupon an agreement that deputies fhould, upon a day appointed, depart from each place, and where they met fhould be the common boundary of their dominions. Accordingly two brothers, called Philænis, were fent from Carthage, who made their journey*

P   duo

duo' fratres miffi, quibus nomen Philænis erat, maturavere iter pergere ; Cyrenenfes tardius iere. Id focordiane, an cafu acciderit, parum cognovi. Cæterum folet in illis locis tempeftas haud fecus, atque in mari retinere. Nam, ubi per loca æqualia, & nuda gignentium, ventus coortus arenam humo excitavit, ea magna vi agitata, ora, oculofque implere folet; ita profpectu impedito, morari iter. Poftquam Cyrenenfes aliquanto pofteriores fe effe vident, & ob rem corruptam domi pœnas metuunt; criminari Carthaginienfes ante tempus domo digreffos; conturbare rem; denique omnia malle, quam victi abire. Sed cum Pœni aliam conditionem, tantummodo æquam, peterent, Græci optionem Carthaginienfium faciunt, *ut vel illi, quos finis populo fuo peterent, ibi vivi obruerentur; vel eadem conditione fefc, quem in locum vellent, proceffuros.* Philæni, conditione probata, feque, vitamque fuam reipublicæ condonavere; ita vivi obruti. Carthaginienfes in eo loco Philænis fratribus aras confecravere ; aliique illis dom honores inftituti. Nunc ad rem redeo.

LXXXII. Jugurtha poftquam, amiffa Thala, nihil fatis firmum contra

with all due difpatch. But the Cyrenians were not fo quick, whether through lafinefs, or fome ill chance, I do not find. For in thofe parts a ftorm will detain travellers as effectually as by fea. A wind arifing upon that level and naked foil heaves up the fand, and with great violence drives it in their faces and eyes, and fo preventing their feeing the way before them ftops them. When the Cyrenians found themfelves behind the other, fearing to be punifhed at home for their mifconduct, they charged the Carthaginians with fetting out before the time appointed for it, making a mighty buftle upon it, as being willing to do any thing rather than go off baffled. The Carthaginians defiring any other way of deciding the matter that was fair and equal, the Greeks made them this propofal, either to be buried alive there where they were for fixing the boundary of their dominion, or that they would advance as far as they thought proper upon the like condition. The Philæni, accepting the offer, made a facrifice of themfelves and their lives to their country, and wert buried alive. The Carthaginian. dedicated altars in that place t the memory of the two brothers the Philæni, and inftituted feve ral other honours to be paid t them at home. But now to m purpofe again.

LXXXII. *Jugurtha. after th lofs of Thala, thinking nothing fu ficiently fecure againft Metellus, fi*

M(

Metellum putat ; per magnas folitudines cum paucis profeſtus, pervenit ad Gætulos, genus hominum ferum, incultumque, & eo tempore ignarum nominis Romani. Eorum multitudinem in unum cogit ; ac paullatim confuefacit ordines habere, figna fequi, imperium obfervare, item alia militaria facere. Præterea regis Bocchi proxumos magnis muneribus, & majoribus promiſſis ad ſtudium fui perducit ; queis adjutoribus regem aggreſſus, impellit, uti advorfum Romanos bellum fufcipiat. Id ea gratia facilius, proniufque fuit, quod Bocchus initio hujufce belli legatos Romam miferat, foedus, & amicitiam petitum. Quam rem opportuniſſumam incœpto belli, pauci impediverant, cæci avaritia, queis omnia honefta, atque inhonefta vendere mos erat. Etiam antea Jugurthæ filia Bocchi nupferat. Verum ea neceſſitudo apud Numidas, Maurofque levis ducitur ; quia finguli pro opibus, quifque quam plurimas uxores, denas alii, alii plures habent , fed reges eo amplius. Ita animus multitudine diſtrahitur ; nullam pro focia obtinet; pariter omnes viles funt.

with a ſmall retinue, through vaſt defarts, into the land of the Getulians, a wild unpoliſhed people, unacquainted with the Roman name, He muſters up a great number of them, and teaches them to form companies, follow their ſtandards, obſerve command, and to behave in all refpeEts like foldiers. He likewiſe, by great preſents, and greater promiſes, engages in his intereſt ſome of the greateſt favourites of King Bocchus, by whoſe aſſiſtance he at laſt prevails with the king to undertake a war againſt the Romans. Which was the more eaſily brought about, becauſe Bocchus, in the beginning of this war, had ſent embaſſadors to Rome, to treat upon an alliance with the Roman people. Which thing, tho' likely to prove of fingular ſervice in the war, yet ſome gentlemen, blinded with avarice, who were ready for any kind of work, honourable or otherwiſe, if they were but well paid for it, had obſtruEted. Bocchus's daughter had likewiſe before this been married to Jugurtha. But the tie of affinity is little regarded among the Numidians and Moors, becauſe with them every man may have as many wives as he can maintain, and accordingly ſome have ten, others more, but the kings more than any body. Thus the mind being divided by the number, they look upon none as a friend or companion, but treat them all with contempt alike.

LXXXIII. Igitur in locum ambobus placitum exercitus conveniunt ; ibi, fide data, & accepta, Jugurtha Bocchi animum oratione accendit ; *Romanos injuſtos, profunda avaritia, communes omnium hoſtis eſſe ; eandem illos cauſſam belli cum Boccho habere, quam ſecum, & cum aliis gentibus, lubidinem imperitanti, queis omnia regna advorſa ſint ; tum ſeſe, paullo ante Carthaginienſes, item regem Perſen, poſt, uti quiſque opulentiſſimus videatur, ita Romanis hoſtem fore.* His, atque aliis talibus dictis, ad Cirtam oppidum iter conſtituunt ; quod ibi Q. Metellus prædam, captivoſque, & impedimenta locaverat. Ita Jugurtha ratus, aut capta urbe, operæ pretium fore ; aut, ſi Romanus auxilio ſuis veniſſet, prælio ſeſe certaturos. Nam callidus id modo feſtinabat, Bocchi pacem imminuere ; ne, moras agitando, aliud, quam bellum, mallet.

LXXXIII. *Wherefore the two armies meet in a place appointed by the kings ; where, after they had pledged their faith to one another, Jugurtha fired the ſoul of Bocchus, by talking to the following effect;* That the Romans were an unjuſt people, of inſatiable avarice, and the common enemies of mankind. They had juſt as much cauſe of war with Bocchus, as with himſelf and other nations, the luſt of dominion, for the ſake of which they looked upon all kings as enemies. At that time he was ; not long before the Carthaginians, and king Perſes, bad been their enemies, and ſo would every prince hereafter be, eſpecially of conſiderable power and ſtrength. *After he had ſaid this, and other things to the like purpoſe, they reſolve to march together to the town of Cirta, becauſe Q. Metellus had there lodged the booty and priſoners he had taken in the war, together with the baggage of the army. Jugurtha ſuppoſed the enterprize would either be well worth their while if they took the city, or, if the Romans came to the aſſiſtance of their friends, a battle muſt enſue. For he ſtily endeavoured, with all the haſte he could, to break the peace betwixt Bocchus and the Romans, leſt upon demurring he ſhould change his mind.*

LXXXIV. Imperator poſtquam de regum ſocietate cognovit, non temere, neque uti ſæpe, jam victo Jugurtha conſueverat, omnibus locis pugnandi copiam facit ; cæ-

LXXXIV. *When the Roman general heard of this alliance betwixt the two kings, he does not upon all occaſions, and in all places, as before, after Jugurtha had been ſeveral times defeated, offer the enemy battle ; but, pitching his*
terum,

terum, haud procul ab Cirta caſtris munitis, reges opperitur; melius eſſe ratus, cognitis Mauris, quoniam is novus hoſtis acceſſerat, ex commodo pugnam facere. Interim Roma per litteras certior fit, provinciam Numidiam Mario datum. Nam Conſulem factum ante acceperat. Quibus rebus ſupra bonum, aut honeſtum perculſus, neque lacrumas tenere, neque moderari linguam; vir egregius in aliis artibus, nimis molliter ægritudinem pati. Quam rem alii in ſuperbiam vortebant; alii bonum ingenium contumelia accenſum eſſe; multi, quod jam parta victoria ex manibus eriperetur; nobis ſatis cognitum eſt, illum magis honore Marii, quam injuria ſua excruciatum, neque tam anxie laturum fuiſſe, ſi adempta provincia alii, quam Mario, traderetur.

LXXXV. Igitur eo dolore impeditus, & quia ſtultitiæ videbatur, alienam rem periculo ſuo curare, legatos ad Bocchum mittit, poſtulatum, *ne ſine cauſſa hoſtis populo Romano fieret; habere eum magnam copiam ſocietatis, amicitiæque conjungendæ, quæ potior bello eſſet;* quam-

camp not far from Cirta, he waits for the kings, thinking it not proper to engage with the Moors, an enemy he was not yet acquainted with, but upon ſome advantage. In the mean time, he had notice by letters from Rome that the province of Numidia was aſſigned to Marius. For he had heard before that he was made conſul. With which things he was prodigiouſly affected, to a degree inconſiſtent with all equity and decency, inſomuch that he could neither refrain from tears, or govern his tongue; and, tho' he was an extraordinary perſon in other reſpects, yet under trouble of mind he was too impatient, which ſome imputed to his pride, others to a juſt reſentment of the contumelious uſage he had, many to a concern that the victory he had got ſhould be ſnatched out of his hands. But it appears pretty plain to me that he was more diſturbed at the advancement of Marius than the injury done to himſelf, and would not have borne it ſo heavily if the province that was taken from him had been given to any body elſe but Marius.

LXXXV. Wherefore, as well upon account of this reſentment, as becauſe it ſeemed a folly to take care of another man's buſineſs, at his own hazard, he diſpatches meſſengers to Bocchus, to deſire he would not become an enemy to the Roman people without any occaſion given for it. That he had now a fine opportunity of entering into the Roman alliance, which would be much better for him than a war.

P 3

quam

quam opibus suis confideret, tamen non debere incerta pro certis mutare; omne bellum sumi facile, cæterum ægerrume desinere; non in ejusdem potestate initium ejus, & finem esse; incipere cuivis etiam ignavo licere; deponi, cum victores velint; proinde sibi, regnoque suo consuleret; neu florentis res suas cum Jugurthæ perditis misceret. Ad ea rex placide verba facit; sese pacem cupere, sed Jugurthæ fortunarum misereri; si eadem illi copia fieret, omnia conventura. Rursus imperator, contra postulata Bocchi, nuncios mittit. Ille probare partim, alia abnuere. Eo modo, sæpe ab utroque missis remissisque nunciis, tempus procedere, & ex Metelli voluntate bellum intactum trahi.

LXXXVI. At Marius, ut supra diximus, cupientissuma plebe, consul factus, postquam ei provinciam Numidiam populus jussit, antea jam infestus nobilitati, tum vero multus, atque ferox instare; singulos modo, modo universos lædere; dictitare, sese consulatum ex victis illis spolia cepisse; alia præterea magnifica pro se, & illis dolentia; interim, quæ bello

What confidence soever he might repose in his own strength, yet he ought not to change certainties for uncertainties. That it was an easy matter to begin a war, but not so easy to end it; since the beginning and ending thereof were not in the same hands. Any coward might begin; but the end must depend upon the pleasure of the conqueror. Wherefore he advised him to have a care of doing any thing that might affect the security of his person and kingdom, and not engage his happy circumstances in the desperate cause of Jugurtha. *To this the king made a very smooth reply*; That he was desirous of peace, but pitied the case of Jugurtha; if he might but have the same terms, they should soon agree. *Again the Roman general sends messengers with an answer to Bocchus's demand, wherein something was granted, other things denied. And, by sending messengers backward and forward in this manner, the time was spun out, and the war, as Metellus wished, kept at a stand.*

LXXXVI. *But Marius, as was said above, having been made consul by the people with a very extraordinary zeal, and got by their grant too the province of Numidia, was now more violent and furious against the nobility than ever, tho' he was keen enough in that way before. Sometimes he would reflect upon them singly, sometimes upon the whole body; and would often say, that he had vanquished them, and had taken from them the consulship as spoil from a conquered enemy. And other things too he* opus

opus erant, prima habere; poftulare legionibus fupplementum ; auxilia a populis, & regibus, fociifque arceffere ; præterea ex Latio fortiffumum quemque, plerofque militia, paucos fama cognitos accire, & ambiendo cogere homines emeritis ftipendiis proficifci. Neque illi fenatus, quamquam adverfus erat, de ullo negotio abnuere audebat ; cæterum fupplementum etiam lætus decreverat ; quia, neque plebi militiam volenti, putabatur, & Marius, aut belli ufum, aut ftudium vulgi amiffurus. Sed ea res fruftra fperata. Tanta lubido cum Mario eundi plerofque invaferat ; fefe quifque præda locupletem fore, victorem domum rediturum, alia hujufcemodi animis trahebant ; & eos non paullum oratione fua Marius arrexerat. Nam poftquam, omnibus, quæ poftulaverat, decretis, milites fcribere vult, hortandi cauffa, fimul & nobilitatem, uti confueverat, exagitandi, concionem populi advocavit. Deinde hoc modo differuit.

faid boaftingly of himfelf, and that heartily vexed them. But the making of due preparations for the war was his principal care. He demanded recruits for the army ; fent for auxiliary forces from kings and ftates in alliance with us ; particularly from Latium he fummoned the choiceft men, moft of them known well enough in the army, but few elfewhere. He did likewife by his perfuafions prevail with old foldiers, that had ferved up their time in the wars, to engage in the fervice again. And tho' the fenate hated him; yet they durft refufe him nothing ; nay, they were forward enough to vote him recruits, becaufe it was fuppofed the commonalty would not much care for the fervice, and fo Marius would either not be able to make his levies, or incur their difpleafure by fo doing. But herein they were baulked, fo fond were moft of them of going along with Marius, each man flattering himfelf with the hopes of returning home victorious, and enriched with the fpoils of war, or of other fuch-like advantages. And Marius had, by a fpeech of his to them, contributed not a little to the raifing of fuch expectations in them. For refolving, after what he defired had been voted for him, to raife recruits, he fummoned the people to an affembly, as well to encourage them to favour his defign, as to take occafion, according to his cuftom, of inveighing againft the nobility. Both which he did in the following manner.

LXXXVII. *Scio ego, Quirites, plerofque non*

LXXXVII. I am fenfible, gentlemen, that the generality of

P 4 *iifdem*

iisdem artibus imperium a
vobis petere, &, postquam
adepti sunt, gerere; pri-
mo industrios, supplices,
modicos esse; dehinc per
ignaviam, & superbiam,
ætatem agere; sed mibi
contra videtur. Nam, quo
universa respublica pluris
est, quam consulatus, aut
prætura, eo majore cura
illam administrari, quam
hæc peti debere. Neque
me fallit, quantum cum
maxumo beneficio vestro
negotii sustineam. Bellum
parare, simul & ærario
parcere; cogere ad militiam eos, quos nolis offende-
re; domi, forisque omnia
curare; & ea agere inter
invidos, occursantis, fac-
tiosos; opinione, Quiri-
tes asperius est. Ad hoc,
alii si deliquere, vetus nobilitas, majorum facta fortia, cognatorum & affini-
um opes, multæ clientelæ,
omnia hæc præsidio ad-
sunt; mihi spes omnes in
memet sitæ; quas necesse
est & virtute, & inno-
centia tutari; nam alia
infirma sunt. Et illud
intelligo, Quirites, om-
nium ora in me conversa
esse; æquos, bonosque fa-
vere; quippe benefacta
mea reipublicæ procedunt;
nobilitatem locum inva-
dendi quærere. Quo mihi
acrius adnitendum est;
uti neque vos capiamini,
& illi frustra sint. Ita

such as apply to you for preferment in the state behave not in
the same manner after they have
compassed their designs as before.
At first they are industrious, submissive, and modest; after their
advancement, lazy and proud.
But I have quite different sentiments in the case: for, as the good
of the community is of much
higher importance than the con-
sulate or prætorship, with just so
much the more care ought that to
be pursued than these. Nor am
I insensible what a weight of business your late kindness has laid upon me. To make preparations for
the war, and at the same time to
be sparing of the public money;
to oblige those to the service a-
broad that one is loth to offend; to
take care for the due management
of all affairs, both at home and a-
broad; and this amidst numbers of
envious, thwarting, factious people, all this, I say, gentlemen, is
difficult beyond imagination. Besides, others, if they fail in the
performance of their duty, are
protected by their quality, the gallant behaviour of their ancestors,
the power of their relations and
friends, and their own numerous
dependants. But all my hopes are
in myself. My good behaviour
and integrity must be my only
protection, for I have nothing else
to trust to. I am well aware too,
gentlemen, that the eyes of all
people are upon me; that the just
and the good are my friends, as
being sensible of the services I have
done my country; but that the
nobility are watching all advanta-
ad

ad hoc ætatis a pueritia fui, ut omnis labores, pericula confueta habeam. Quæ ante veſtra beneficia gratuito faciebam, ea uti, accepta mercede, deferam, non eſt confilium, Quirites. Illis difficile eſt in poteſtatibus temperare, qui per ambitionem fefe probos fimulavere ; mihi, qui omnem ætatem in optumis arſibus egi, bene facere jam ex confuetudine in naturam vertit. Bellum me gerere cum Jugurtha juſſiis ; quam rem nobilitas ægerrume tulit. Quæfo, reputate cum animis veſtris, num id mutari melius fit, fi quem ex illo globo nobilitaris ad hoc, aut aliud tale negotium mittatis, hominem veteris profapiæ, & multarum imaginum, & ullius ſtipendii ; filicet ut in tanta re ignarus omnium trepidet, feſtinet, fumat aliquem ex populo monitorem officii fui. Ita plerumque evenit, ut, quem vos imperare juſſiſtis, is fibi imperatorem alium quærat.

ges to be upon me. And therefore I am the more obliged to ufe my utmoſt endeavours that you may not be baulked, but they may. I have from my youth up been inured to hardfhip and danger of all kinds. Which, before your favours conferred upon me, I did folely out of a principle of generofity, I fhall not, to be fure, gentlemen, neglect to do, now that I have received my reward. It is a hard matter to thofe to keep within any bounds, when poffeffed of power, who, to obtain it, only put on a counterfeit fhew of goodnefs. But with me, who have fpent all my days in the practice of the moſt laudable qualities, ufe is become fecond nature. You have commanded me to make war with Jugartha, to the great vexation of the nobility. I befeech you, confider with yourfelves, whether it would not be better to fend upon this, or any other the like occafion, one of the tribe of the nobility, a man of an ancient and noble family, and that has never been in the fervice of his country abroad. Ay, why not ? He would, though frighted and confounded in the midft of bufinefs, for want of experience, get fome of the commons to direct him in his duty.

And fo it commonly happens, that the perfon you have appointed to command, is obliged to get fome body to command him.

LXXXVIII. At ego fcio, Quirites, qui, poſtquam confules facti funt, acta majorum, &. Græcorum militaria præcepta legere cœperint ; homines

LXXXVIII. I have, indeed, gentlemen, known fome, who after they were made confuls read the noble actions of our anceftors, with the military inftructions laid down by the Greeks. Prepofterous

præ-

præposteri. Nam gerere, quam fieri, tempore posterius, re, atq; usu prius est. Comparate nunc, Quirites, cum illorum superbia me hominem novum. Quæ illi audire, & legere solent, eorum partem vidi, alia egomet gessi; quæ illi litteris, ea ego militando didici. Nunc vos existumate, facta, an dicta pluris sint. Contemnunt novitatem meam; ego illorum ignaviam. Mihi fortuna, illis probra objectantur. Quamquam ego naturam unam, & communem omnium existumo, sed fortissumum quemque generosissumum. Ac si jam ex patribus Albini, aut Bestiæ quæri posset, mene, an illos ex se gigni maluerint; quid responsuros creditis, nisi, sese liberos quam optumos voluisse? Quod si jure me despiciunt; faciant idem majoribus suis; quibus, uti mihi, ex virtute nobilitas cœpit. Invident honori meo; ergo invideant labori, innocentiæ, periculis etiam meis; quoniam per hæc illum cepi. Verum homines corrupti superbia, ita ætatem agunt, quasi vestros honores contemnant; ita hos petunt, quasi honeste vixerint. Næ illi falsi sunt, qui diversissumas res pariter ex-

creatures! For the management of an office is indeed posterior, in point of time, to the choice of the person to officiate; but with respect to the qualifications necessary for the same, it is prior to it. Compare me, gentlemen, the first of my family that has attained to any considerable station in the government, with your haughty nobles. What they are accustomed only to hear and read, I have in part seen, and in part managed myself in person. What they have learnt from books, the same I have learnt by serving in the wars. Now do you yourselves judge, whether actions or words are of more account. They despise the meanness of my descent; I despise their incapacity for business. I am upbraided with my fortune, they with their scandalous vices. Tho' I think the nature of man to be one and common to all, but that the bravest is the most noble. And if now the fathers of Albinus, or Bestia, could be consulted, whether they would rather have chosen me for their descendant, or them, what answer do you think they would make, but that they should have desired the most deserving men might have been their sons? But if they have reason to despise me, let them do the same by their ancestors, whose nobility, like mine, took its rise from their noble behaviour. They envy my advancement; let them then envy my activity, my integrity, and dangers too; because it was by these I attained to the former. But men corrupted with pride,

*ſpectant, ignaviæ volup-
tatem, & præmia virtu-
tis. Atque etiam cum
apud vos, aut in ſenatu
verba faciunt, pleraque
oratione majores ſuos ex-
tollunt ; eorum fortia facta memorando clariores
ſeſe putant ; quod contra
eſt. Nam, quanto vita
illorum præclarior, tanto
horum ſocordia flagitio-
ſior. Et projecto ita ſe
res habet ; majorum glo-
ria poſteris quaſi lumen
eſt, neque bona eorum,
neque mala in occulto pa-
titur. Hujuſce rei ego
inopiam patior, Quirites.
Verum id, quod multo
præclarius eſt, meamet
facta mihi dicere licet.
Nunc videte, quam iniqui
ſint. Quod ex aliena vir-
tute ſibi arrogant, id mihi
ex mea non concedunt ;
ſcilicet quia imagines non
habeo, & quia mihi nova
nobilitas eſt ; quam certe
peperiſſe, quam acceptam
corrupiſſe melius eſt.*

*LXXXIX. Equidem
ego non ignoro, ſi jam
mihi reſpondere velint,
abunde illis facundam, &
compoſitam orationem fore.
Sed in Maxumo veſtro
beneficio, cum omnibus
locis me, voſque maledictis
lacerent, non placuit reti-*

live as if they deſpiſed the honours
you have to beſtow, and yet ſue
for them, as if they had lived ho-
nourably. Truly, they are much
miſtaken, who expect at once two
things of very different nature, the
pleaſure of idleneſs, and the rewards of virtue. And when they
harangue too before you, or in the
ſenate, they are ever running out
into the praiſes of their anceſtors,
and think they receive a luſtre from
the relation of their noble actions;
whereas it is quite the reverſe. For
the more illuſtrious their lives were,
the more ſcandalous is the baſe behaviour of theſe their deſcendants.
And indeed the caſe is thus. The
glory of the antients is a light
held out before their poſterity, that
ſuffers neither their good or ill qualities to be concealed. This is what
I want, gentlemen. But I can tell
you of ſomething elſe, which is
much greater, my own actions.
Now mind how unreaſonable they
are. What they arrogate to themſelves from the noble behaviour
of others, that they will not allow
me to reap from my own; for no
other reaſon truly, but that I have
no images of my anceſtors to ſhew, and becauſe my nobility is of very late date ; which it is certainly better for a
man to be the founder of in his own family than to be a
diſgrace to that received from his anceſtors.

LXXXIX. I know indeed, if
they have a mind to reply upon
me, they will find plenty of elegant polite language for the purpoſe. But however, ſince upon
your late advancement of me to
the high dignity I poſſeſs, they e-
very where let looſe their tongues
againſt both you and me in the
cere;

cere ; ne quis modefliam in confcientiam duceret. Nam me quidem, ex animi mei fententia, lædere nulla oratio potefl. Quippe vera, neceffe efl bene prædicet ; falfam, vita morefque mei fuperant. Sed quoniam veflra confilia accufantur, qui mihi fummum honorem, & maxumum negotium impofuiflis ; etiam atque etiam reputate, num eorum pœnitendum fit. Non poffum, fidei cauffa, imagines, neque triumphos, aut confulatus majorum meorum oflentare ; at, fi res poflulet, haflas, vexillum, phaleras, alia militaria dona, præterea cicatrices advorfo corpore. Hæ funt meæ imagines hæc nobilitas, non hereditate relicta, ut illa illis, fed quæ ego meis plurimis laboribus , & periculis quæfivi. Non funt compofita verba mea; parvi id facio ; ipfa fe virtus fatis oflendit ; illis artificio opus efl, ut turpia facta oratione tegant. Neque litteras Græcas didici. Parum placebat eas difcere, quippe quæ ad virtutem doctoribus nihil profuerunt. At illa multo optuma reipublicæ doctus fum ; hoflem ferire, præfidia agitare, nihil· metuere, nifi turpem famam; hiemem, & æfla-

vileft reproaches, I was refolved not to be filent; left any one fhould take my modefty for an argument of guilt. For indeed, their language, in my opinion, cannot affect me ; fince, if what they fay be true, it muft be to my honour ; but if falfe, my life and behaviour confute it. But becaufe your conduct is blamed, who have laid upon me the greateft honour, and bufinefs of the higheft importance, confider again and again, whether you have any occafion to repent what you have done. I cannot indeed, to raife your confidence in me, boaft of the images, triumphs, and confulfhips of my anceftors ; but, if occafion requires, I can fhew you fpears, a banner, horfetrappings, and other military prefents made me, with fcars all over my body before. Thefe are my images, this my nobility, not, like theirs, left me by inheritance; but procured by infinite hardfhips and dangers. My language is unpolifhed ; that I little regard. My virtue, without words, fhews itfelf fufficiently. They ftand in need of all the art of eloquence, to varnifh over their infamous pranks. I never applied myfelf to the Græcian literature ; nor did I care to learn that, which rendered not the teachers a whit the more virtuous or able men. But I have been inftructed in other things, highly conducive to the publick good ; fuch as bravery and vigilance in war ; to dread nothing but an infamous character ; to bear cold and heat ; to lodge upon the ground ; and endure, at the fame

tem juxta pati, humi re-
quiefcere; eodem tempore
inopiam, & laborem tole-
rare. His ego præceptis
milites hortabor; neque
illos arcte colam, me opu-
lenter; neque gloriam
meam laborem illorum fa-
ciam. Hoc eft utile, hoc
civile imperium. Namque,
cum tute per mollitiem
agas, exercitum fupplicio
cogere, id eft, dominum
effe, non imperatorem.
Hæc, atque alia majores
veftri faciundo, feque, &
rempublicam celebravere.
Quis nobilitas freta, ipfa
diffimilis moribus, nos illorum æmulos contemnit;
& omnes honores non ex
merito, fed quafi debitos,
a vobis repetit. Cæterum
homines fuperbiffumi pro-
cul errant. Majores eo-
rum omnia, quæ licebat,
illis reliquere, divitias,
imagines, memoriam fui
præclaram; virtutem non
reliquere; neque poterant;
ea fola neque datur dono,
neque accipitur.

XC. Sordidum me, &
incultis moribus ajunt;
quia parum fcite convivium
exorno; neque hiftrionem
ullum, neque pluris pretii
coquum, quam villicum,
habeo. Quæ mihi lubet
confiteri, Quirites. Nam
& ex parente meo, & ex
aliis fanctis viris ita accepi, munditias mulieri-
bus, viris laborem conve-

time, hunger and fatigue. With
thefe leffons fhall I animate my
foldiers. Nor fhall I treat them
hardly, but myfelf with indulgence, or make their toil the matter of my glory. This manner of
command is ufeful and modeft.
For to keep the foldiery, by feverity, to ftrict difcipline, whilft you
take your eafe yourfelf, is to act
the part of a tyrant, not a general.
By this and the like conduct did
your anceftors render themfelves,
and the Roman ftate, famous in
the world; which our nobility
depending upon, tho' nothing like
them in their behaviour, defpife
us that follow their glorious ex-
ample; and demand from you all
places of power and truft, not upon the foot of merit, as having deferved them, but as other ways
their due. But thofe haughty gen-
try are very widely miftaken.
Their anceftors left them all they
could; riches, images, and their
own glorious memory. But did
not leave them their noble qualities; nor could they. Thofe are
neither given, nor received.

XC. They upbraid me as a
rough unpolifhed mortal; becaufe
I am not nice in my entertainments, or have a player, or cook,
of higher price than my fteward;
all which I very frankly own, gentlemen. For I have learnt from my
father, and other excellent perfons, that nicenefs belongs to women, rugged induftry to men;
and that the brave ought to excel
more in glory than riches; that
nire,

nire, omnibufque bonis oportere plus gloriæ, quam divitiarum effe; arma, non fupellectilem, decori effe. Quin 'ergo, quod juvat, quod carum æftumant, id femper faciant; ament, potent; ubi adolefcentiam habuere, ibi fenectutem agant, in conviviis, dediti ventri, & turpiffumæ parti corporis; fudorem, pulverem, & alia talia relinquant nobis quibus illa epulis jucundiora funt. Verum non eft ita. Nam, ubi fe omnibus flagitiis dedecoravere turpiffumi viri, bonorum præmia ereptum eunt. Ita injuftiffume luxuria, & ignavia, peffumæ artes, illis, qui coluere eas, nihil officiunt, reipublicæ innoxiæ cladi funt. Nunc, quoniam illis, quantum mei mores, non illorum flagitia pofcebant, refpondi; pauca de republica loquar. Primum omnium de Numidia bonum habetote animum, Quirites; nam, quæ ad hoc tempus Jugurthum tutata funt, omnia removiftis, avaritiam, imperitium, fuperbiam. Deinde exercitus ibi eft locorum fciens, fed mehercule, magis ftrenuus, quam felix; nam magna pars ejus avaritia, aut temeritate ducum attrita eft. Quamobrem vos, quibus militaris eft ætas,

arms, and not fine furniture, was an honour to fuch. Let them then ever mind what pleafes them, what they hold fo dear. Let them whore and drink, and let them fpend their old days, as they did their young, in revelling, and pampering their bellies, and the vileft part about them. Let them leave fweat and duft, with other things of like kind, to us, who prefer them before all their fine entertainments. But this they will not do. For after thofe vileft of men have covered themfelves with infamy, by the practice of the moft fcandalous vices, they will needs deprive the brave of the rewards that are their due. Thus, contrary to all juftice, luxury and idlenefs, the worft of qualities, are no ways detrimental to thofe who practife them; at the fame time that they prove of pernicious confequence to the innocent commonwealth. And now, having anfwered them fo far as my character, not their infamous behaviour, required, I fhall add a word or two in relation to the prefent ftate of affairs. In the firft place, as to Numidia, have a good heart, gentlemen; for you have removed all that hitherto fecured Jugurtha, avarice, ignorance, and pride. There is an army there indeed acquainted with the country, but, upon my word, active rather than fortunate. For the greateft part of it has been deftroyed by the avarice or rafhnefs of their commanders. Wherefore you that are of an age fit for war, join your endeavours with mine, and ftand by the publick; nor let any one conceive any

adni-

adnitimini mecum, & ca-
peſſite rempublicam, neque
quemquam ex calamitate
aliorum, aut imperatorum
ſuperbia metus ceperit.
Egomet in agmine, in
prælio conſultor idem, &
ſocius periculi vobiſcum
adero ; meque voſque in
omnibus rebus juxta ge-
ram. Et profecto, diis
juvantibus, omnia matura
ſunt, victoria, præda,
laus ; que ſi dubia, aut
procul eſſent, tamen omnis
bonos reipublicæ ſubvenire
decet. Etenim ignavia
nemo immortalis factus ;
neque quiſquam parens li-
beris, uti æterni forent,
optavit ; magis, uti boni,
honeſtique vitam exige-
rent. Plura dicerem,
Quirites, ſi timidis vir-
tutem verba adderent ;
nam ſtrenuis abunde dic-
tum puto.

XCI.. Hujuſcemodi
oratione habitâ, Marius
poſtquam plebis animos
arrectos videt, propere
commeatu, ſtipendio,
armis, aliiſque utilibus
navis onerat ; cum his A.
Manlium legatum profi-
ciſci jubet. Ipſe interea
milites ſcribere, non mo-
re majorum, neque ex
claſſibus, ſed uti cujuſque
libido erat, capite cenſos
pleroſque. Id factum
alii inopia bonorum, alii
per ambitionem conſulis
memorabant ; quod ab

apprehenſions from the miſcarriage
of others, or the haughtineſs of
the commanders. I in march, in
battle, will be your adviſer, ſhare
every danger with you, and treat
you upon all occaſions no otherwiſe than I do myſelf. And indeed,
with the help of the gods, all
things are now ready for you, victory, ſpoil, and glory ; and tho'
they were uncertain, and at a diſtance, yet it would become, ne-
vertheleſs, all gallant men to ſupport the cauſe of their country.
For no man was ever rendered
immortal by a lazy inactivity ;
nor did ever any father wiſh his
ſons might never die, but rather
that they might live like brave
and worthy men. I ſhould ſay
more, gentlemen, if words would
put courage into cowards ; for
to the valiant, I think, I have ſaid
enough.

XCI. *Marius, perceiving the*
ſpirits of the people to be much ele-
vated by this ſpeech of his, ſhips
with all haſte, proviſions, money,
and other things requiſite for the
war ; and orders his lieutenant-
general, A. Manlius, to go along
with them. In the mean time he
levies troops, not according to for-
mer uſage, nor out of the ſeveral
claſſes of the people, but volunteers
only, and moſt of them of the very
loweſt rank. Which, ſome ſay, he
did for want of better ; but others,
that he did it to render himſelf ſtill
more popular ; becauſed he had been
much cried up and advanced by that

eo genere celebratus, auctufque. erat ; & homini potentiam quærenti egentiſſumus quiſque opportuniſſumus ; cui neque ſua curæ, quippe quæ nulla ſunt, & omnia cum pretio honeſta videntur. Igitur Marius cum aliquanto majore numero, quam decretum erat, in Africam profectus, paucis diebus Uticam advehitur. Exercitus ei traditur a P. Rutilio legato. Nam Metellus conſpectum Marii fugerat ; ne videret ea, quæ audita animus tolerare nequiverat.

XCII. Sed Conſul, expletis legionibus, cohortibuſque auxiliariis, in agrum fertilem, & præda onuſtum proficiſcitur. Omnia ibi capta militibus donat ; dein caſtella, & oppida natura, & viris parum munita adgreditur ; prœlia multa, cæterum alia levia aliis locis facere. Interim novi milites ſine metu pugnæ adeſſe ; videre fugientis capi, aut occidi ; fortiſſimum quemque tutiſſimum ; armis libertatem, patriam, parenteſque, & alia omnia tegi ; gloriam, atque divitias quæri. Sic brevi ſpatio novi, veterefque coaluere, &. virtus omnium æqualis facta. At reges ubi de adventu

ſort of people ; and to a man ambitious of power, the moſt needy are the moſt for his purpoſe ; as who regard nothing of their own, having nothing to regard, and thinking every thing honourable, that is but gainful. Wherefore Marius ſetting ſail for Africa, with a number of troops, ſomewhat larger than what had been voted for him, in a few days arrives at Utica. Where the army was delivered up to him by the lieutenant-general P. Rutilius. For Metellus declined coming near Marius, for fear of ſeeing thoſe things, which he could not ſo much as hear with patience.

XCII. But the conſul having completed his legions, and the auxiliary battalions, out of his new levies, directs his march into a fruitful country, full of plunder ; where he made a preſent of all he took to the ſoldiers. Then he fell upon ſuch forts and towns as were neither very ſtrong, nor well garriſoned. He fought likewiſe ſeveral battles in different places, but not conſiderable. In the mean time, the new-raiſed men, from the eaſineſs of the ſervice, were under no apprehenſions. They ſaw ſuch as fled taken priſoners, or ſlain ; whilſt the braveſt were ſtill the ſafeſt. That liberty, their country, parents, and every thing elſe were ſecured, and glory and riches got, by arms. Thus, in a ſhort time, the new and the old ſoldiers embodied, and were upon a par in point of courage. But the two kings, as

Ma-

Marii cognoverunt, diverſi in locos difficilis abeunt. Ita Jugurthæ placuerat, ſperanti, mox effuſos hoſtis invadi poſſe; Romanos ſicuti plerofque, remoto metu laxius, licentiuſque futuros.

ſoon as they heard of Marius's arrival, retired different ways into places of difficult acceſs. This was Jugurtha's contrivance, in hopes that the enemy in a little time, by not keeping cloſe together, might afford an opportunity of falling on them to good advantage; as ſuppoſing the Romans, like moſt other men, when their apprehenſions of an enemy were removed, would be more looſe and licentious.

XCIII. Metellus interea Romam profeĉtus, contra ſpem ſuam lætiſſumis animis accipitur; plebi, patribuſque, poſtquam invidia deceſſerat, juxta carus. Sed Marius impigre, prudenterque ſuorum, & hoſtium res pariter attendere; cognoſcere quid boni utriſque, aut contra eſſet; explorare itinera regum; conſilia, & inſidias eorum antevenire; nihil apud ſe remiſſum, neque apud illos tutum pati. Itaque & Gætulos, & Jugurtham, ex ſociis noſtris prædas agentis, ſæpe adgreſſus itinere fuderat, ipſumque regem haud procul ab oppido Cirta armis exuerat. Quæ poſtquam glorioſa modo, neque belli patrandi cognovit, ſtatuit urbis, quæ viris, aut loco pro hoſtibus, & advorſum ſe opportuniſſumæ erant ſingulas circumvenire; ita Jugurtham aut præſidiis nuda-

XCIII. *In the mean time Metellus, upon his arrival in Rome, was, contrary to his expeĉtations, very joyfully received; being equally acceptable to the Commons, and the Senate, now that the ſpirit of envy had left them. But Marius, with all poſſible application and prudence, weighing well the circumſtances of the enemy, and his own, diſcovered thereby what was advantageous for each, or otherwiſe. He watched all the movements of the two Kings, prevented all their plots and deſigns; ſuffered no remiſſneſs in his own men, or ſecurity with the enemy. Accordingly he had oftentimes, when upon a march, attacked and routed, both the Getulians and Jugurtha, as they were making off with the ſpoils they had got from our allies; and diſarmed the King himſelf, not far from the town of Cirta. But finding all this, how ſpecious an appearance ſoever it made, availed nothing towards bringing the war to a concluſion, he reſolved to inveſt all the cities that, by their number of people and ſituation, gave the enemy an advantage againſt us; ſince Jugur-*

Q   tum

tum, si ea pateretur, aut prœlio certaturum. Nam Bocchus nuncios ad eum sæpe miserat, velle populi Romani amicitiam, ne quid ab se hostile timeret. Id simulaveritne, quo improvisus gravior accederet, an mobilitate ingenii pacem, atque bellum mutare solitus, parum exploratum est.

tha by that means, would either b¸ stript of those strong holds, if h¸ suffered it, or else engage in battle For Bocchus had frequently sen¸ messengers to him, to let him know that he was desirous of the friend ship of the Roman people, and tha Marius need not fear any hostili ties from him. Whether he onl pretended so, that he might fall th heavier on him by surprize, ¸ through the fickleness of his temper he was accustomed never to persi¸ long ei her in peace or war, I ha¸ not been able to discover.

XCIV. Sed Consul, uti statuerat, oppida, castellaque munita adire, partim vi, alia metu, aut præmia ostentando, avortere ab hostibus. Ac primo mediocria gerebat, existumans Jugurtham ob suos tutandos in manus venturum. Sed ubi illum procul abesse, & aliis negotiis intentum accepit; majora, & magis aspera aggredi tempus visum est. Erat inter ingentis solitudines oppidum magnum, atque valens, nomine Capsa; cujus conditor Hercules Libys memorabatur. Ejus cives apud Jugurtham immunes, levi imperio, & ob ea fidelissumi habebantur; muniti advorsum hostis non mœnibus modo & armis, atque viris, verum etiam multo magis locorum asperitate. Nam, præter oppido

XCIV. But the Consul, accor¸ ing to his resolution, now went ¸ work with the towns and castl of any strength; some of which ¸ took by assault; others he broug¸ over to him by threats or promis¸ At first indeed he only attempt small places, supposing Jugurtha, protest his subjects, would come ¸ a battle with him. But when found that he was at a consider¸ ble distance from him, taken ¸ with other affairs, he thought time to attack the larger tow¸ and such as were more difficult take. There was in the midst a vast wildernefs, a great a strong town, by name Capsa; ¸ builder whereof was said to be H¸ cules the Lybian. The people the¸ of were excused from the paym¸ of taxes; and being under a v¸ gentle government in other respe¸ too, were therefore thought v¸ faithful to Jugurtha; and t¸ were secured against an enemy, ¸ only by their walls, arms, ¸ men, but much more by the situat¸ of the place. For, excepting ¸

P¸

propinqua, alia omnia vasta, inculta, egentia aquæ, infesta serpenti-bus; quarum vis, sicuti omnium ferarum, inopia cibi acrior; ad hoc, natura serpentum ipsa perniciosa, siti magis, quam alia re accenditur. Ejus potiundi Marium maxuma cupido invaserat, cum propter usum belli, tum quia res aspera videbatur; & Metellus oppidum Thalam magna gloria ceperat, haud dissimiliter situm, munitumque; nisi quod apud Thalam non longe a mœnibus aliquot fontes erant; Capfenfes una modo, atque ea intra oppidum jugi aqua, cætera pluvia utebantur. Id ibique, & in omni Africa, quæ procul a mari incultius agebat, eo facilius tolerabatur, quia Numidæ plerumque lacte, & ferina carne vescebantur, neque salem, neque alia irritamenta gulæ quærebant. Cibus illis advorsum famem, atque sitim, non libidini, neque luxuriæ erat.

XCV. Igitur Conful, omnibus exploratis, credo diis fretus, nam contra tantas difficultates consilio satis providere non poterat; quippe etiam frumenti inopia tentabatur, quod Numidæ pa-

parts nigh the town, all the rest of the country about it was waste and uncultivated, without water, and infested with serpents, who, like all other wild beasts, are made keener by want of food; besides, the nature of serpents, mischievous enough in itself, is inflamed by thirst above all things. Marius was very desirous of mastering this place, as well for the better convenience of carrying on the war, as because it seemed a matter of vast difficulty; and because Metellus had acquired much reputation by the taking of Thala, a town for situation and strength much like Capfa; but that at Thala there were some springs not far from the town. The Capfenfians had but one spring, and that within the town, which flowed the year round; all the water they had besides, was from the heavens. This scarcity of water both there, and in other parts of Africa, which lying at a distance from the fea, were but indifferently cultivated, was the more easily born, because the Numidians live mostly upon milk, and the flesh of wild beasts, without the use of salt, or any other seasoning or sauce, to whet the appetite. Their food was designed against hunger and thirst, and not made subservient to whimsy and luxury.

XCV. Wherefore the Conful having strictly examined into all circumstances, proceeds in his designs, depending, I suppose, upon the Gods; for he could hardly, by any contrivance of his own, provide effectually against so many difficulties; for he was but poorly

Q 2　　　　　　　　bulo

bulo pecoris magis, quam arvo, ftudent, &, quodcumque natum fuerat, juffu regis in loca munita contulerant ; ager autem aridus, & frugum vacuus ea tempeftate; nam æftatis extremum erat; tamen pro rei copia fatis providentur exornat; pecus omne, quod fuperioribus diebus prædæ fuerat, equitibus auxiliariis agendum attribuit; A. Manlium legatum cum cohortibus expeditis ad oppidum Laris, ubi ftipendium, & commeatum locaverat, ire jubet; dicitque fe prædabundum poft paucos dies eodem venturum. Sic incœpto fuo occultato, pergit ad flumen Tanam.

XCVI. Cæterum in itinere quotidie pecus exercitui per centurias, item turmas æqualiter diftribuerat ; & ex coriis utres uti fierent, curabat; fimul &, inopiam frumenti lenire, &, ignaris omnibus, parare, quæ mox ufui forent; denique fexto die, cum ad flumen ventum eft, maxuma vis utrium effecta. Ibi caftris levi munimento pofitis, milites cibum capere, atque, uti fimul cum occafu folis egrederentur, paratos effe jubet; omnibus farcinis abjectis, aqua modo feque & jumenta onerare. Dein,

fupplied with corn, becaufe the Numidians apply themfelves more to grazing than tillage; and what corn there was, had, by the King's order, been carried off into fortified towns. The land too was parched, and afforded nothing at that time, being the end of fummer. Yet, confidering all circumftances, he provided pretty well for the fupply of his army. He gave the cattle they had picked up fome days before to the auxiliary horfe to drive; orders Aulus Manlius, his lieutenant general, to march with a light detachment of foot to a town called Laris, where he had laid up the money for the pay of the army, an provifions; and tells him, that he would in a few days come to the fame place a plundering. Thus concealing his defign, he goes to th river Tana.

XCVI. But in his march daily diftributed cattle to the fevral foot companies, and troops horfe in the army; and took ca for the making of leathern bott out of their hides; at once to ma amends to them for the want corn, and to provide, whilft people were ignorant of his inte tions, fuch things as would by a by be of ufe to him; fo that up his arrival fix days after at river, a great quantity of leathe bottles were made. Then pitchi a camp, with a flight fortificatio he orders the foldiers to refre themfelves, and to be ready for march at fun-fet; as alfo to afide all other baggage, and lo themfelves, and their beafts of bu

P

poſtquam tempus viſum, caſtris egreditur; noctemque totam itinere facto, confedit; idem proxuma facit. Dein tertia multo ante lucis adventum pervenit in locum tumuloſum, ab Capſa non amplius duum millium intervallo; ibique, quam occultiſſume poteſt, cum omnibus copiis opperitur. Sed, ubi dies cœpit; & Numidæ nihil hoſtile metuentes, multi oppido egreſſi; repente omnem equitatum, & cum his velociſſimos pedites curſu tendere ad Capſam, & portas obſidere jubet; deinde ipſe intentus propere ſequi, neque milites prædari. ſinere. Quæ poſtquam oppidani cognovere; res trepidæ, metus ingens, malum improviſum, ad hoc pars civium extra mœnia in hoſtium poteſtate, coegere, uti deditionem facerent. Cæterum oppidum incenſum; Numidæ puberes interfecti; alii omnes venumdati; præda militibus diviſa. Id facimus contra jus belli non avaritia, neque ſcelere Conſulis admiſſum; ſed quia locus Jugurthæ opportunus, nobis aditu difficilis; genus hominum mobile, jnfidum, ante neque beneficio, neque metu coercitum.

den, with water only. Then, at the time appointed, he draws out of the camp, and marching all night, encamped again. The ſame he did the next night too; and in the third, he arrived a little before day at a hill, not above two miles from Capſa; and there he ſtays, as privately as poſſible, with all his army. But as ſoon as day appeared, and the Numidians, as being under no apprehenſions at all of an enemy, many of them came out of the town: on a ſudden he orders all his horſe, and with them the nimbleſt of the foot, to make directly for Capſa with all ſpeed, and ſecure the gates. At the ſame time he follows them with all diligence and expedition, and ſuffers not the ſoldiers to plunder. When the towns-people found this, they were in the utmoſt confuſion and fright, with ſo unexpected a calamity; and as part of their people were without the wall, in the hands of the enemy, they found it neceſſary to ſurrender. Yet notwithſtanding, the town was burnt, the Numidians of age put to the ſword, all the reſt ſold, and the plunder of the place given to the ſoldiers. This piece of execution, contrary to the rules of war, was not occaſioned by the avarice or cruelty of the Conſul, but from a conſideration that the place was very advantageous for Jugurtha, and difficult for us to come at; the people too being fickle and faithleſs, and by no means, fair or foul, to be wrought upon.

Q 3 XCVII.

XCVII. Poftquam
tantam rem Marius fine
ullo fuorum incommodo
patravit; magnus, &
clarus antea, major, at-
que clarior haberi cœpit;
omnia non bene confulta
in virtutem trahebantur.
Milites modefto imperio
habiti, fimul & locuple-
tes, ad cœlum ferre;
Numidæ magis, quam
mortalem, timere; pof-
tremo omnes focii, atque
hoftes credere, illi aut
mentem divinam effe, aut
Deorum nutu cuncta
portendi. Sed Conful,
ubi ea res bene evenit, ad
alia oppida pergit; pauca,
repugnantibus Numidis,
capit; plura deferta
propter Capfenfium mi-
ferias, igni corrumpit;
luctu, atque cæde omnia
complentur. Denique
multis locis potitis, ac
plerifque exercitu incru-
ento, aliam rem aggredi-
tur, non eadem afperitate,
qua Capfenfium, cæte-
rum haud fecus difficilem,
Namque haud longe a
flumine Muluchæ, quod
Jugurthæ, Bocchique
regnum disjungebat, erat
inter cæteram planitiem
mons faxeus, mediocri
caftello, fatis patens, in
immenfum editus, uno
perangufto aditu relicto;
nam omnia natura, velut
opere, atque confulto,
præceps. Quem locum

XCVII. *After Marius had exe-*
cuted this fo important a project,
without any detriment to his own
troops, though he was great and
famous before, he now begun to be
look'd upon as greater and more fa-
mous; and all his performances,
though but ill advifed, were placed
to the account of his good conduct.
The foldiers too, being under a very
gentle command, and at the fame
time enriched with plunder, cried
him up to the heavens; and the
Numidians dreaded him as fome-
thing more than man. In fhort,
all, both allies and enemies, did
really believe he had either a di-
vine mind in him, or that all things
were fignified to him by the inti-
mation of the Gods. But the Con-
ful, after this fuccefs, marches
againft fome other towns. Some,
where he met with oppofition from
the Numidians, he takes by force;
but moft of them, being deferted
becaufe of the terrible ufage of the
Capfenfians, he burnt to the ground.
And fo all parts are filled with
mourning and flaughter. Finally,
having made himfelf mafter of ma-
ny places, and moft of them with-
out lofs of blood, he goes upon an-
other defign, of full as much diffi-
culty, but not of the fame nature
as that againft the Capfenfians.
For, not far from the river Mu-
lucha, which divided the kingdoms
of Jugurtha and Bocchus, there
was, in the midft of a plain, a
rocky mountain, with a fmall caftle
upon it. The mountain was large,
and vaftly high, with one only ve-
ry ftrait way up to the top. For it
was by nature fteep on all fides, as

Ma-

Marius, quod ibi regis thefauri erant, fumma vi apere intendit ; fed ea es forte, quam confilio, nelius gefta. Nam caftello virorum, atque armorum fatis magna vis, & frumenti, & fons aquæ ; aggeribus, turriufque, & aliis machinaionibus locus importunus.; iter caftellanorum inguftum admodum, urimque præcifum ; vineæ cum ingenti periculo ruftra agebantur. Nam cum eæ paullo proceffeant, igni, aut lapidibus corrumpebantur ; milites neque pro opere confiftere, propter iniquitatem oci ; neque inter vineas fine periculo adminiftrare ; optumus quifque cadere, aut fauciari ; cæteris metus augeri.

if it had been defignedly made fo by the hands of men. Which place Marius attempts with all his might and main to take, becaufe the king's treafure was lodged there ; and fucceeded in his attempt, more by chance, than good management. For there was in the caftle ftore of men, arms, and corn, with a fpring of water. And the place was rendered ftill more troublefome to take by ramparts, caftles, and other works. The way up to the caftle was very narrow, with a precipice on both fides; the pufhing of vineæ along which was attended with vaft hazard, and fignified nothing. For after they had advanced a little they were deftroyed by fire or great ftones. The foldiers were neither able to ftand before their works, becaufe of the great difadvantage or inconvenience of the ground ; nor could they manage their bufinefs within the vineæ without danger. The braveft of them were either flain or wounded, and the reft fadly difcouraged.

XCVIII. At Marius, multis diebus, & laboribus confumptis, anxius trahere cum animo fuo, omitteretne incœptum, quoniam fruftra erat; an fortunam opperiretur ; qua fæpe profpere ufus fuerat. Quæ cum multos dies, noctefque æftuans agitaret, forte quidam Ligus, ex cohortibus auxiliariis miles gregarius, caftris aquatum egreffus, haud procul ab latere caftelli, quod advorfum

XCVIII. *But Marius, after he had fpent many days and much pains to no purpofe, was in great doubt with himfelf, whether he fhould drop his undertaking, which had hitherto proved in vain, or wait fome lucky turn of fortune, which he had often found favourable to him. Whilft he was taken up with thefe thoughts, for feveral days and nights together, by chance a certain Ligurian, a common foldier of the auxiliary battalions, going out of the camp to get water, obferved fome fnails creeping among the ftones, not far from that fide of*

Q 4 *præ-*

prœliantibus erat, animadvertit inter faxa repentes cochleas; quarum cum unam, atque alteram, dein plures peteret, ſtudio legundi, paullatim prope ad ſummum montis egreſſus eſt. Ubi poſtquam ſolitudinem intellexit, more humanæ cupidinis ignara viſundi animum vortit. Et forte in eo loco grandis ilex coaluerat inter ſaxa, paullulum modo prona, deinde inflexa, atque aucta in a'titudinem, quo cuncta gignentium natura fert; cujus ramis modo, modo eminentibus ſaxis niſus Ligus, caſtelli planitiem perſcribit; quod cuncti Numidæ intenti prœliantibus aderant. Exploratis omnibus, quæ mox uſui fore ducebat, eadem regreditur, non temere, uti aſcenderat, ſed tentans omnia & circumſpiciens. Itaque Marium propere adit; acta edocet; hortatur, *ab ea parte, qua ipſe aſcenderat, caſtellum tentet; pollicetur ſeſe itineris periculique ducem.* Marius cum Ligure, promiſſa ejus cognitum ex præſentibus miſit; quorum, uti cujuſque ingenium erat, ita rem difficilem, aut facilem nunciavere. Conſulis animus tamen paullum arrectus. Itaque ex copia tubici-

the caſtle, which was oppoſite to the beſiegers. After he had picked up a few of them, from a deſire of having more, he was by little and little got almoſt up to the top of the mountain. And finding all quiet in that quarter, from a curioſity, natural to man, of prying into things unknown, he looks about him. By chance, in the place where he was, there grew a great oak-tree out of the ſide of the rock, with the bole tending downwards a little, but preſently taking a turn, and mounting up to a vaſt height, as all things that grow out of the earth naturally tend upwards. The Ligurian climbing up one while by the boughs of the tree, another while by pieces of the rock ſtanding out from the reſt, takes a pretty good ſurvey of the plain of the caſtle; becauſe all the Numidians were buſily engaged in fight with the beſiegers. After he had made ſuch obſervations as he thought might be of ſervice, he returns the ſame way as he came, not careleſsly as he went up, but trying and viewing all things well as he went along. Upon this, he applies himſelf to Marius in all haſte, tells him what he had done, and adviſes him to make an attempt upon the caſtle on that ſide where he went up, and promiſes him that he would lead the way, and be the foremoſt in the danger. *Marius ſends ſome of thoſe that attended him along with the Ligurian, to ſee whether what he promiſed was feaſible or no, who brought word according to their different tempers, ſome that the matter was difficult, others that

num,

num, & cornicinum, numero quinque quam velociſſumos delegit, & cum his, præſidio qui forent, quatuor centuriones ; omniſque Liguri parere jubet ; & ei negotio proxumum diem conſtituit.

XCIX. Sed ubi ex præcepto tempus viſum, paratis, compoſitiſque omnibus, ad locum pergit. Cæterum illi, qui centuriis præerant, prædocti ab duce, arma, ornatumque mutaverant, capite, atque pedibus nudis, uti proſpectus, niſuſque per ſaxa facilius foret ; ſuper terga gladii, & ſcuta ; verum ea Numidica ex coriis, ponderis gratia ; ſimul & offenſa, quo levius ſtreperent. Igitur prægrediens Ligus, ſaxa, & ſi quæ vetuſtate radices eminebant, laqueis vinciebat, quibus allevati milites facilius aſcenderent, interdum timidos inſolentia itineris levare manu ; ubi paullo aſperior adſcenſus erat, ſingulos præ ſe inermes mittere ; deinde ipſe cum illorum armis ſequi ; quæ dubia niſui videbantur, potiſſumum tentare ; ac ſæpius eadem adſcendens, deſcendenſque, dein ſtatim digrediens, cæteris

it was eaſy. However, the mind of the conſul was rouſed upon the occaſion. Wherefore he chuſes out of all the trumpeters, belonging to both horſe and foot, five of the ſwifteſt, and four centurions to go along with them as a guard, ordering them to follow the direction of the Ligurian, and appoints the next day for the execution of the deſign.

XCIX. When the time fixt was come, the Ligurian, having provided and got all things ready for the buſineſs, goes to the place. But the centurions, as they had been inſtructed by him, had changed their arms and dreſs, being bareheaded and bare-foot too, that they might look about them, and climb the rock with more eaſe. Their ſwords and ſhields were upon their backs. The latter were of the Numidian kind, made of hides for lightneſs, and that they might not make a noiſe, if they chanced to daſh againſt the rock. The Ligurian mounted firſt, and tied cords about the ſtones, or old tree-roots which ſtuck out here and there, for the ſoldiers to climb up by. Sometimes, when they were diſcouraged by the extraordinary ruggedneſs of their paſſage, he would lend them a hand to give them a lift. Where the aſcent was a little more difficult than ordinary, he ſent them up unarmed before him, and then followed himſelf with their arms. And places, where it ſeemed doubtful whether they could paſs or no, he tried ; and by going up and down the ſame ſeveral times, and then advancing again, encouraged the reſt to fol-

auda-

audaciam addere. Igitur
diu, multumque fatigati,
tandem in castellum per-
veniunt, desertum ab ea
parte; quod omnes, si-
cuti aliis diebus, advor-
sum hostes aderant. Ma-
rius, ubi ex nunciis, quæ
Ligus egerat, cognovit;
quamquam tota die in-
tertos prælio Numidas
habuerat, tum vero co-
hortatus milites, & ipse
extra vineas egressus, tes-
tudine acta succedere,
& simul hostem tormen-
tis, sagittariisque, & funditoribus eminus terrere.
At Numidæ, sæpe antea
vineis Romanorum sub-
versis, item incensis, non
castelli mœnibus sese tu-
tabantur; sed pro muro
dies, noctesque agitare;
*maledicere Romanis, ac
Mario vecordiam objecta-
re; militibus nostris Ju-
gurthæ servitium minari;
secundis rebus feroces esse.*
Interim, Romanis om-
nibus, hostibusque prælio
intentis, magna utrimque
vi, pro gloria atque im-
perio his, illis pro salute
certantibus, repente a
tergo signa canere; ac
primo mulieres, & pueri,
qui visum processerant,
fugere; deinde, uti quis-
que muro proxumus erat,
postremo cuncti armati,
inermesque. Quod ubi
accidit, eo acrius Roma-
ni instare, fundere, ac

*low. After a tedious deal of fa-
tigue, they came to the castle, which
was naked on that side, because the
whole garrison, as on other days,
were attending the motions of the
besiegers. When Marius was informed by messengers what the Ligurian had done, tho' he had kept
the Numidians under a constant
alarm all day long, yet then encouraging his men, he sallied out of
the vineæ, and forming a testudo
advanced towards the wall of the
castle, and at the same time terrified the enemy with his engines,
archers, and slingers, at a distance.
But the Numidians, having often
before ruined the vineæ of the Romans, and burnt them, did not
use to defend themselves with their
walls, but posted themselves before
them day and night,* railing at the
Romans, and upbraiding Marius
with madness. They threatened
our soldiers too, that they should
be all slaves to Jugurtha, and
were greatly elevated with their
advantage. *In the mean time, while
the Romans and the enemies were
intent upon the fight, which was
warmly carrried on on both sides,
one party contending eagerly for
glory and dominion, and the other
for their lives, on a sudden the
trumpets sounded in the rear of the
enemy. And first the women and
children, who ran to see what the
matter was, fled; after them those
nearest the wall; and after them
all the rest, both armed and unarmed. Upon which the Romans
pushed forward with more violence
in pursuit of them. The most of
them they only wounded, making*
ple-

plerofque tantummodo fauciare, dein fuper occiforum corpora vadere, avidi gloriæ certantes murum petere ; neque quemquam omnium prædamorari. Sic forte correcta Marii temeritas, gloriam ex culpa invenit.

C. Cæterum, dum ea res geritur, L. Sulla quæftor cum magno equitatu in caftra venit; qui, uti ex Latio, & a fociis exercitum cogeret, Romæ relictus erat. Sed quoniam nos tanti viri res admonuit ; idoneum vifum eft, de natura, cultuque ejus paucis dicere. Neque enim alio loco de Sullæ rebus dicturi fumus; & L. Sifenna optume, & diligentiffume omnium, qui eas res dixere, perfecutus, parum mihi libero ore locutus videtur. Igitur Sulla gentis patriciæ nobilis fuit, familia prope jam extincta majorum ignavia, litteris Græcis, atque Latinis juxta, atque doctiffume eruditus, animo ingenti, cupidus voluptatum, fed gloriæ cupidior ; otio luxuriofo effe ; tamen ab negotiis numquam voluptas remorata, nifi quod de uxore potuit honeftius confuli ; facundus, callidus, & amicitia facilis ; ad fimulanda negotia altitudo ingenii incredibilis ; mul-

their way in all hafte over the bodies of the flain to the wall ; all greedy of glory, and not to be diverted by a regard to plunder. Thus the rafh conduct of Marius being happily corrected, made even a fault in him turn to his glory.

C. During this tranfaction, his quæftor L. Sulla came with a great body of horfe to the camp, who had been left at Rome to draw together the troops furnifhed by the Latins, and our allies. But as the thread of the ftory has led us to the mention of this man, I judge it may not be amifs to give his character in a few words ; for I fhall have no further occafion to take notice of him ; and L. Sefenna, who has given us his hiftory with the greateft accuracy and exactnefs, of all that have pretended to write it, does not however appear to me to lay down his character with all the freedom that was requifite. Sulla was of a Patrician family, but almoft extinct by the want of fpirit and activity in his anceftors. He was well educated in all the learning both of Greece and Rome ; of a great foul ; a lover of pleafure, but yet fonder of glory. He would, in a time of leifure be guilty of a luxurious indulgence ; but was never hindered by his pleafures from the profecution of bufinefs, excepting only the cafe of his marriage, in which he might have acted more for his honour. He was eloquent, artful, and open to any that fought his friendfhip ; had a prodigious talent for diffimulation, and would

tarum

tarum rerum, ac maxume pecuniæ largitor, atque illi, feliciſſumo omnium ante civilem victoriam, numquam ſuper induſtriam fortuna fuit; multique dubitavere, fortior, an felicior eſſet. Nam, poſtea quæ fecerit, incertum habeo, pudeat an pigeat diſſerere.

CI. Igitur Sulla, uti ſupra dictum eſt, poſtquam in Africam, atque in caſtra Marii cum equitatu venit, rudis antea, & ignarus belli, ſollertiſſumus omnium in paucis tempeſtatibus factus eſt, Ad hoc milites benigne appellare; multis rogantibus, aliis per ſe ipſe dare beneficia, invitus accipere; ſed ea properantius, quam æs mutuum, reddere; ipſe ab nullo repetere; magis id laborare, ut illi quam plurimi deberent; joca, atque ſeria cum humillumis agere; in operibus, in agmine, atque ad vigilias multus adeſſe; neque interim, quod prava ambitio ſolet, conſulis, aut cujuſquam boni famam lædere; tantummodo neque conſilio, neque manu priorem alium pati; plerofque antevenire. Quibus rebus, & artibus brevi Mario, militibuſque cariſſumus factus.

readily part with any thing to ſhew his generoſity, eſpecially money. And tho' he was, before the civil war, the moſt fortunate of all men; yet his fortune was never ſuperior to his induſtry; inſomuch that many have made a queſtion of it, whether he was more brave, or more fortunate. For as to his behaviour in the civil war, I am uncertain, whether the relation of it would give me more of ſhame or ſorrow.

CI. When Sulla, as has been before ſaid, was come into Africa, and arrived at Marius's camp with the horſe, tho' he had been before unſkilled and ignorant in the art of war, yet in a ſhort time he became the ableſt man that way in the army. Beſides, he was very complaiſant in his addreſs to the ſoldiers. He granted favours to many upon their requeſt; to others without it, of his own accord, whilſt he cared not to receive any himſelf; but when he did, would be in more haſte to repay them than a debt; tho' he never demanded any return from others, but rather made it his buſineſs to have others as much indebted to him as poſſible. He would engage either in ſerious or merry converſation with perſons of the loweſt rank. He was ſure to be every where with the ſoldiers in their encampments, marches, and upon the watch. Nor did he in the mean time, what wicked ambition is apt to prompt men to, go about to leſſen the character of the conſul, or any other worthy man whatever. He only would not ſuffer any one to outſtrip him in counſel, or action;

tion ; and excelled moſt. By all which behaviour, in a ſhort time he rendered himſelf highly acceptable to Marius, and the whole army.

CII. At Jugurtha poſtquam oppidum Capſam, aliofque locos munitos, & ſibi utilis, ſimul & magnam pecuniam amiſerat ; ad Bocchum nuncios mittit, quam primum in Numidam copias adduceret ; prœlii faciundi tempus adeſſe. Quem ubi cunctari accepit, dubium belli, atque pacis rationes trahcre ; rurſus, uti antea, proxumos ejus donis corrumpit ipſique Mauro pollicetur Numidiæ partem tertiam, ſi aut Romani Africa expulſi, aut, integris ſuis finibus, bellum compoſitum foret. Eo præmio illectus Bocchus, cum magna multitudine Jugurtham accedit. Ita, amborum exercitu conjuncto, Marium jam in hiberna proficiſcentem, vix decima parte die reliqua invadunt, rati noctem, quæ jam aderat, victis ſibi munimento fore ; &, ſi viciſſent, nullo impedimento, quia locorum ſcientes erant ; contra Romanis utrumque caſum in tenebris difficiliorem fore. Igitur ſimul conful ex multis de hoſtium adventu cognovit ; & ipſi hoſtes aderant ; & prius quam cxercitus aut

CII. *But Jugurtha, after he had loſt Capſa, with other ſtrong holds of great uſe to him, and a vaſt treaſure beſides ; ſends away meſſengers to Bocchus, to haſten his march into Numidia ; becauſe it was now time, he ſaid, to give the enemy battle. But finding him demur upon the matter, and doubtful with himſelf what courſe to take, whether that of war or peace ; he again, as he had done before, bribes thoſe about him to his intereſt, and promiſes the Moor himſelf a third part of Numidia, if the Romans ſhould be driven out of Africa, or he left in the poſſeſſion of his dominions entire, upon the concluſion of the war. Bocchus, tempted by this bait, comes to Jugurtha with a vaſt army. After they were joined, they fall upon Marius, as he was now marching into his winter-quarters, ſo far on the day, that there was ſcarce a tenth part of it left ; ſuppoſing the night, which was near at hand, would protect them, if worſted ; and if they prevailed, would be no impediment to the proſecution of the victory, by reaſon they were ſo well acquainted with the country ; whereas the Romans, which way ſoever the matter went, would have but a bad chance for it in the dark. Wherefore the conful no ſooner had notice, as he had from ſeveral, of the enemy's approach, than they were upon him. And before the army could be put in order of battle, or draw their baggage together ; in ſhort,*

inſtrui,

inftrui, aut farcinas colligere, denique, antequam fignum, aut imperium ullum accipere quivit, equites Mauri, atque Gætuli, non acie, neque ullo more prœlii, fed catervatim, uti quofque fors conglobaverat, in noftros incurrunt. Qui omnes trepidi, improvifo metu ac tamen virtutis memores, aut arma capiebant, aut capientis alios ab hoftibus defenfabant ; pars equos afcendere, obviam ire hoftibus ; pugna latrocinio magis, quam prœlio fimilis fieri ; fine fignis, fine ordinibus, equites pedites permixti ; cædere alios, alios obtruncare ; multos, contra adverfos acerrume pugnantes ab tergo circumvenire ; neque virtus, neque arma fatis tegere ; quia hoftes numero plures, & undique circumfufi erant. Denique Romani veteres, novique, & ob ea fcientes belli, fi quos locus, aut cafus conjunxerat, orbes facere ; atque ita ab omnibus partibus fimul tecti, & inftructi, hoftium vim fuftentabant.

CIII. Neque in eo tam afpero negotio Marius territus, aut magis, quam antea, demiffo animo fuit ; fed cum turma fua, quam ex fortiffumis magis, quam familiariffumis

before they could receive any fignal, or word of command, the Moorish and Getulian horfe, not in due order, or any regular method of fighting, but in fcattered companies, as chance had brought them together, came pell-pell upon the Romans, who were alarmed indeed with fo unexpected an onfet ; yet mindful of their former bravery, they either took to their arms, or defended fuch as were doing fo, from the enemy. Part of them mounting their horfes, advanced againft them. The fight was more like an engagement with a gang of banditti than foldiers. The Romans were without their ftandards, in confufion, horfe and foot jumbled together ; whilft the enemy's hacked and hewed among them, and attacked here and there fuch of them as were engaged in the rear, whom neither their courage, nor arms, could fufficiently fecure; becaufe the enemy were more numerous, and on all fides of them. Finally, the Romans, both old and new foldiers, as chance happened to join them, formed themfelves into round bodies ; and fo being fecured on all fides, and pofted in proper order, they bravely withftood the enemy.

CIII. In this defperate cafe, Marius was not daunted, or a whit more difmayed than at other times ; but with his own troop, which he had formed not fo much of friends, as the braveft fellows in the army, flew about every where ; one while

para-

paraverat, vagari paffim; ac modo laborantibus fuis, fuccurrere, modo hoftis, ubi confertiffumi obftiterant, invadere manu; eonfulere militibus, quoniam imperare conturbatis omnibus non poterat. Jamque dies confumptus erat, cum tamen barbari nihil remittere; atque, uti reges præceperant, noctem pro fe rati, acrius inftare. Tum Marius ex copia rerum confilium trahit; atque, uti fuis receptui locus effet, collis duos propinquos inter fe occupat. Quorum in uno, caftris parum amplo, fons aquæ magnus erat; alter ufui opportunus, quia magna parte editus, & præceps; pauca munimento egebat. Cæterum apud aquam Sullam cum equitibus noctem agitare jubet. Ipfe paullatim difperfos milites, neque minus hoftibus conturbatis, in unum contrahit; dein cunctos pleno gradu in collem fubducit. Ita reges, loci difficultate coacti, prœlio deterrentur; neque tamen fuos longius abire finunt, fed, utroque colle multitudine circumdato effufi confedere. Dein, crebris ignibus factis, plerumque noctis barbari more fuo lætari, exfultare, ftrepere vocibus;

relieving his own men in diftrefs; another while falling in among ft the thickeft of the enemy; and by fighting himfelf in perfon, endeavoured to ferve his foldiers all he could; fince in this univerfal confufion, it was impoffible for him to act the proper part of a general. And tho' the day was now quite fpent, yet did not the fury of the enemy abate at all; but as the kings had inftructed them beforehand, fuppofing night would give them the advantage, they charged more defperately than before. Marius, upon this, takes the moft proper meafures his prefent circumftances would admit of; and, to provide for the retreat of his troops, feizes upon two hills that were near together; in one of which, not large enough to encamp on, there was a plentiful fpring of water; the other was convenient for the purpofe, becaufe the main of it was high and fteep, and would require but little fortifying. However, he orders Sulla with his horfe to fpend the night by the water. He draws by degrees his fcattered troops together, the enemy being now in as much confufion as they; and then carries them all, upon a full march, up the hill. Thus the kings were obliged, by the difficulty of attacking them in that fituation, to give over the fight; but yet fuffered not their men to withdraw to any diftance; but enclofing both the hills within their two armies, lay fcattered here and there. And then the barbarians, making many fires, fpent the greateft part of the night in mirth and jollity, and yelling

&

& ipfi duces feroces ; quia non fugere, ut pro victoribus agere. Sed ea cuncta Romanis, ex tenebris, & editioribus locis facilia vifu, magnoque hortamento erant.

CIV. Plurimum vero Marius imperitia hoftium confirmatus, quam maxumum filentium haberi jubet ; ne figna quidem, uti per vigilias folebant, canere ; deinde, ubi lux adventabat, defeffis jam hoftibus, ac paullo ante fomno captis, de improvifo vectigalis, item cohortium, turmarum, legionum tubicines fimul omnis figna canere, milites clamorem tollere, atque portis erumpere. Mauri, atque Gætuli, ignoto & horribili fonitu repente exciti, neque fugere, neque arma capere, neque omnino facere, aut providere quidquam poterant ; ita cunctos ftrepitu, clamore nullo fubveniente, noftris inftantibus tumultu, terrore, formidine, quafi vecordia, ceperat. Denique omnes fufi, fugatique ; arma, & figna militaria pleraque capta ; plurefque eo prœlio, quam omibus fuperioribus, interempti. Nam fomno, & metu infolito impedita fuga.

CV. Dein Marius, uti cœperat, in hiberna proficifcitur, quæ propter commeatum in oppidis maritimis agere decreve-

after their fafhion. And their leaders, proud to think they had not run away, behaved as conquerors. All thefe things were very vifible to the Romans, who were in the dark upon the hills ; and gave them no little encouragement.

CIV. Marius being much animated by the folly of the enemy, orders a profound filence to be kept, and that no trumpets fhould found, as ufual, at the end of every watch. Towards break of day, when the enemy were now weary and afleep, he orders the trumpeters throughout the army to found at once, and the foldiers to make a fally upon the enemy with a great fhout. The Moors and Getulians being fuddenly awakened with fo unexpected and difmal a noife, could neither fly, nor take arms ; neither act, nor think of any thing for their own fecurity ; being all perfectly ftupified with the clamour and din about their ears ; whilft our men poured in upon them in this helplefs condition, with confufion, terrour, and diftraction attending them. In fhort, they were all routed and difperfed, moft of their arms and military ftandards were taken, and more men killed in that battle than all the former. For their flight was in a great meafure prevented by fleep and furprize together.

CV. Now Marius purfued his former defign of marching, in order to quarter his foldiers, for the winter, in the towns upon the fea-coaft, becaufe of the plenty of pro-

rat ;

rat; neque tamen victoria focors, aut infolens factus; fed pariter, atque in confpectu hoftium, quadrato agmine incedere. Sulla cum equitatu apud dextimos, in finiftra parte. A. Manlius cum funditoribus, & fagittariis, præterea cohortes Ligurum curabat; primos, & extremos cum expeditis manipulis tribunos locaverat. Perfugæ, minime cari, & regionem fcientiffimi, hoftium, iter explorabant. Simul Conful, quafi nullo impofito, omnia providere; apud omnis adeffe, laudare, increpare merentis. Ipfe armatus, intentufque item milites cogebat; neque fecus, atque iter facere, caftra munire, excubitum in porta cohortis ex legionibus, pro caftris equites auxiliarios mittere; præterea alios fuper vallum in munimentis locare, vigilias ipfe circuire, non diffidentia futuri, quæ imperaviffet, quam uti militibus exæquatus cum imperatore labos volentibus effet. Et fane Marius illo & aliis temporibus Jugurthini belli, pudore magis, quam malo, exercitum coercebat; quod multi per ambitionem fieri agebant; pars; quod a pueritia confuetam duritiam, & alia, quæ cæteri mifærias

vifions in thofe parts. However, he was not rendered either carelejs, or infolent, by his fuccefs; but marched with his army in a fquare figure, as if he had been in view of an enemy. Sulla was with the horfe upon the right; A. Manlius with the flingers and archers, as alfo fome battalions of the Ligurians, on the left. In the van and rear he had pofted the Tribunes of the army, with feveral companies of foot, clear of baggage. Deferters, who were but little fet by, and befides beft acquainted with the country, were fent out to reconnoitre the enemy. At the fame time, the conful overlooked every thing, as if no one had been entrufted in any fhare of the command with him. He was every where, commending or reprimanding fuch as deferved it. He was armed, and upon his guard himfelf; and obliged the foldiers to be fo too. Nor did he ufe this great caution only in his march, but in encamping, pofting the ufual guard of legionary foldiers at the gates within the camp, and auxiliary horfe without, as alfo upon the ramparts; and going the rounds to vifit the watch himfelf, not fo much from a diftruft of thofe employed to execute his orders, as to make the foldiers more eafy under their fatigue, by taking an equal fhare with them in it. And indeed Marius both then, and all the time he was employed in the war againft Jugurtha, kept up good order in the army, more by the dint of fhame, than punifhment; which, many faid, was done purely to court the foldiery; but others were of opi-

R   vocant,

vocant, voluptati habuiſſet. Niſi tamen Reſpub. pariter, ac ſæviſſumo imperio, bene atque decore geſta.

xion, he took a real pleaſure in that way of behaviour, as having from his youth been inured to hardſhip, and ſuch things as others count very diſmal. However, affairs were as well, and as glorioufly managed, as they could have been under the moſt ſevere commander.

CVI. Igitur quarto deniq; die, haud longe ab oppido Cirta undique ſimul ſpeculatores citi ſeſe oſtendunt; qua re hoſtis adeſſe intelligitur. Sed quia diverſi redeuntes, alius ab alia parte, atque omnes idem ſignificabant; Conſul incertus, quonam modio aciem in ſtrueret, nullo ordine commutato, advorſum omnia paratus, ibidem opperitur. Ita Jugurtham ſpes fruſtrata, qui copias in quatuor partis diſtribuerat, ratus ex omnibus æque aliquos ab tergo hoſtibus venturos. Interim Sulla, quem primum hoſtes attigerant, cohortatus ſuos, turmatim, & quam maxume confertis equis, ipſe aliique Mauros invadunt; cæteri in loco manentes, ab jaculis eminus emiſſis corpora tegere, & ſi qui in manus venerant, obtruncare.

CVI. *At laſt, four days after the battle, ſeveral ſcouts ſuddenly appeared on all ſides, not far from the town of Cirta; a certain ſign that the enemy was not far off. But becauſe the parties that brought intelligence from all quarters round, were in the ſame ſtory, the conſul not knowing how to draw up his army, without altering the diſpoſition of his troops at all, waits, in the place where he then was, the coming of the enemy; prepared to receive them, let them attack him in what quarter they would; which was a baulk upon Jugurtha. For he had divided his troops into four parts, ſuppoſing ſome of them would certainly ſurprize the enemy in their rear. In the mean time Sulla, whom the enemy firſt came up with, encouraging his men, with ſeveral troops of horſe, in cloſe order, fall upon the Moors. The reſt keeping their ground, only endeavoured to guard againſt the weapons, which the enemy poured in upon them at a diſtance; and if any of them came up to them, cut them down.*

CVII. Dum eo modo equites præliantur, Bocchus cum peditibus, quos Volux ſilius ejus adduxerat, neque in priore pug-

CVII. *During this engagement of the horſe, Bocchus with the foot, which his ſon Volux had brought him, but who loitering upon their march, had not been at*

na;

na, in itenere morati, ad-
fuerant, poftremam Ro-
manorum aciem inva-
dunt. Tum Marius apud
primos erat, quod ibi
Jugurtha cum plurimis
inftabat. Dein Numida,
eognito Bocchi adventu,
clam cum paucis ad pedi-
tes convertit; ibi Latine,
nam apud Numantiam
loqui didicerat, exclamat
noftros fruftra pugnare;
paullo ante Marium fua
manu interfectum; fimul
gladium fanguine oblitum
oftendere, quem in pug-
na, fatis impigre occifo
pedite noftro, cruenta-
verat. Quod uti milites
accepere, magis atrocitate
rei, quam fide nuncii,
terrentur; fimulque bar-
bari animos tollere, & in
perculfos Romanos acrius
incedere. Jamque paul-
lum a fuga aberant, cum
Sulla, profligatis iis, quos
advorfum ierat, rediens
ab latere Mauris incurrit.
Bocchus ftatim avertitur.
At Jugurtha, dum fuf-
tentare fuos, & prope jam
adeptam victoriam reti-
nere cupit, circumventus
ab equitibus dextra, fi-
niftra, omnibus occifis,
folus inter tela hoftium
vitabundus erumpit. At-
que interim Marius, fu-
gatis equitibus, accurrit
auxilio fuis, quos pelli
jam acceperat. Denique
hoftes jam undique fufi.

the former battle; falls upon the
hinder part of the Roman army.
Marius was then in the van, becaufe Jugurtha was there with a
numerous body of troops; who receiving intelligence of Bocchus's coming, wheels off privately with a
few attendants to the Roman foot,
and there cries out in Latin, which
he had learnt to fpeak at Numantia, that our men fought to no
purpofe, fince he had flain Marius but a little before with his
own hand; and at the fame time
fhewed them his fuord all bloody,
which he had made fo by killing a
foot-man belonging to our army.
Which, when the foldiers heard,
they were fhocked with the horrid-
nefs of the thing, more than any
credit they gave to it; and at the
fame time the barbarians took frefh
courage, and made a very fmart attack upon the difheartened Romans,
who were now ready to fly; when
Sulla having routed thofe he was
engaged with, in his return from
the purfuit of them, falls upon the
Moors in their flank; whereupon
Bocchus immediately flies. But Jugurtha, defirous to fupport his
friends, and make fure of the victory, which he had now almoft got,
was hemmed in upon the right and
left by our horfe; and all his attendants being flain, made good his retreat, as he was by himfelf, by cauti-
oufly keeping upon his defence againft
the weapons poured in upon him. And
in the mean time, Marius routing
the horfe, comes to the relief of his
men, who, he was advertifed, gave
ground before the enemy. Finally, they
were now routed in all quarters.

CVIII.

CVIII. Tum fpecta-
culum horribile in campis
patentibus; fequi, fuge-
re; occidi, capi; equi
atque viri adflicti; ac
multi, vulneribus accep-
tis, neque fugere poffe,
neque quietem pati; niti
modo, ac ftatim concide-
re; poftremo omnia, qua
vifus erat, conftrata telis,
armis, cadaveribus; & in-
ter ea humus infecta fan-
guine. Poftea loci Con-
ful, haud dubie jam victor,
pervenit in oppidum Cir-
tam, quo initio profectus
intenderat. Eo poft diem
quintum, quam iterum
barbari male pugnave-
rant, legati a Boccho
veniunt; qui regis verbis
ab Mario petivere, *duos
quam fidiffumos ad eum
mittere; velle de fuo, &
de populi Romani commo-
do cum iis differere.* Ille
ftatim L. Sullam, & A.
Manlium ire jubet. Qui
quamquam acciti ibant;
tamen placuit verba apud
regem facere; uti ingeni-
um aut averfum flecte-
rent; aut cupidum pacis
vehementius accenderent.
Itaque Sulla, cujus fa-
cundiæ, non ætati, a
Manlio conceffum, pauca
verba hujufcemodi locu-
tus.

CIX. *Rex Bocche,
magna nobis lætitia eft,
cum te talem virum dii
monuere, uti aliquando*

CVIII. *And now there was a
dreadful fight to be feen all over
the fields, to a vaft extent; fome
purfuing, others flying; fome were
killed, fome taken; horfes and men
tumbled together on the ground;
and many that were wounded, could
neither fly, nor be quiet; but endeavouring to rife, immediately fell
down again. Finally, all parts, as
far as fight could reach, were covered with arms of all forts, and
dead bodies; and the ground ftain-
ed with blood. The conful having
now got an unqueftionable victory,
continued his march to Cirta, the
place he before defigned for. Thither, five days after the barbarians had been beaten, came deputies
from Bocchus, who, in the King's
name, requefted of Marius to fend
to him two perfons to be confided
in, that he might treat with them
concerning the joint intereft of
himfelf, and the Roman people.
He immediately difpatches away L.
Sulla and A. Manlius; who, notwithftanding they went upon the
King's requeft, yet they refolved to
fpeak firft, in order to work upon
him, if he was ftill obftinate; or
if he was defirous of peace, to
encourage that difpofition in him.
Wherefore Sulla, to whom Manlius gave place, in confideration of
his eloquence, and not his age, fpoke
briefly to the following effect.*

CIX. King Bocchus, it is no
fmall joy to us, to find the Gods
have put it into the heart of fo fine
a prince as you are, to chufe at laft
pacem

pacem, quam bellum, mal-
les; neu te optumum cum
peſſumo omnium Jugur-
tha miſcendo commacula-
res; ſimul nobis demeres
acerbam · neceſſitudinem,
pariter te errantem, &
illum ſceleratiſſumum per-
ſequi. Ad hoc, populo Ro-
mano, jam a principio
inopi, melius viſum, ami-
cos, quam ſervos, quære-
re; tutiuſque rati, vo-
lentibus, quam coaɛlis,
imperitare. Tibi vero
nulla opportunior amicitia
noſtra; primum quod
procul abſumus; in quo
effenſæ minumum, gracia
par, ac ſi prope adeſſe-
mus; dein, quod parentes
abunde habemus; amico-
rum, neque nobis, neque
cuiquam omnium ſatis fu-
it. Atque hoc utinam a
principio tibi placuiſſet.
profeɛlo ex P. R. ad hoc
tempus multo plura bona
accepiſſes, quam mala
pepeſſus eſſes. Sed quo-
niam humanarum rerum
fortuna pleraque regit;
cui ſcilicet placuiſſe & vim,
& gratiam noſtram expe-
riri; nunc, quando per il-
lam licet, feſtina; atque,
uti cœpiſti, perge. Mul-
ta, atque opportuna ha-
bes, quo facilius errata
officiis ſuperes. Poſtremo
hoc in peɛlus tuum dimit-
te, numquam P. R. · be-
neficiis viɛlum eſſe. Nam,
bello quid valeat, tute
ſcis.

rather to be at peace, than war
with us; and no longer diſparage
yourſelf, a moſt excellent perſon,
by uniting with the worſt man a-
live, Jugurtha; and at the ſame
time deliver us from the odious neceſſity of purſuing you, guilty only
of a miſtake, and that moſt vile
wretch, with the like vengeance. It
has ever been a maxim with the
Roman people, ſince their firſt riſe
in the world, which was but low,
to procure themſelves friends, rather than ſlaves; and they have always thought it ſaſer to rule over
willing ſubjects, than by compulſi-
on. No alliance can be more com-
modious for you than ours. In the
firſt place, becauſe we are a great
way off; in which caſe, there can
be very ſmall occaſion of difference, and yet there may be the
ſame good underſtanding as if we
were near neighbours; and in the
next place, becauſe we have ſubjects enough; but neither we, nor
any one elſe, had ever friends e-
nough. And I could have wiſhed,
you had taken this courſe at firſt!
You would certainly, by this time,
have received more good at the
hands of the Roman people, than
you have now ſuffered evil. But as
the concerns of mankind are, in
the main, ſubjected to the power
of fortune, who had a mind, it
ſeems, that you ſhould as well feel
the effects of our force, as of our
favour; now that ſhe puts the
latter in your power, be quick,
and go on, as you have begun.
Now you have great advantages
for correcting your former miſtakes, by future ſervices. Finally,

R 3   let

let this thought sink deep into your mind, that the Roman people were never yet out-done in acts of kindnefs by any one. For as to their ability in war, you know that well enough yourfelf.

CX. Ad ea Bocchus placide, & benigne; fimul pauca pro delicto fuo verba facit; fe non hoftili animo, fed eb regnum tutandum arma cepiffe; nam Numidiæ partem, unde vi Jugurtham expulerit, jure belli fuam factam, eam vaftari a Mario, pati nequiviffe; præterea, miffis antea Romam legatis, repulfum ab amicitia; cæterum vetera omittere, ac tum, fi per Mariam liceret, legatos ad Senatum miffurum. Dein, copia facta, animus barbari ab amicis flexus, quos Jugurtha, cognita legatione Sullæ, & Manlii, metuens id quod parabatur, donis corruperat. Marius interea, exercitu in hibernaculis compofito, cum expeditis cohortibus, & parte equitatus proficifcitur in loca fola, obfeffum turrim regiam, quo Jugurtha perfugas omnis præfidium impofuerat. Tum rurfus Bocchus felicitur, feu reputando, quæ fibi duobus præliis venerant, feu admonitus ab aliis amicis, quos incorruptos Jugurtha reliquerat, ex omni copia neceffariorum quinque delegit, quorum & fides cognita, & inge-

CX. To all this Bocchus made a very foft and civil reply; at the fame time making a brief apology for his mifconduct; alledging, that he had not taken up arms out of any hoftile intention againft the Romans, but for the defence of his kingdom; for that part of Numidia, out of which he had driven Jugurtha, was by the right of war, become his own; which he could not fuffer to be laid wafte by Marius. Befides, upon his applying formerly, by his ambaffadors at Rome, for an alliance with us, he had been rejected, but; however, he fhould decline all further mention of what was paft; and now, if Marius pleafed to give him leave, he fhould fend ambaffadors again to the Senate. Yet tho' this liberty was afterwards granted him, the mind of the barbarian received a different turn, from the influence of fuch friends, as Jugurtha, upon hearing of the difpatch of Sulla and Manlius to him, had bribed. In the mean time Marius, having put his army into winter-quarters, marches into the defart, with a detachment of foot and horfe, to befiege a tower of the king's, wherein Jugurtha had put a garrifon of Roman deferters. Then again Bocchus, either from a confideration of what he had fuffered in the two battles, or upon the advice of other friends, whom Jugurtha had left uncorrupted, chofe out of the number of his friends five, the moft emi-
nia

nia validiſſuma erant. Eos ad Marium, ac dein, ſi placeat, Romam legatos ire jubet; agendarum rerum, & quocumque modo belli componendi licentiam ipſis permittit.

CXI. Illi mature ad hiberna Romanorum proficiſcuntur; deinde a Gætulis latronibus in itinere circumventi, ſpoliatique, pavidi, ſine decore ad Sullam pergunt; quem conſul, in expeditionem proficiſcens, pro prætore reliquerat. Eos ille non pro vanis hoſtibus, uti meriti erant, ſed accurate & liberaliter habuit. Qua re barbari & famam Romanorum avarⁿiæ falſam, & Sullam ob munificentiam in ſeſe amicum rati. Nam etiam tum largitio multis ignota erat; munificus nemo putabatur, niſi pariter volens; dona omnia in benignitate habebantur. Igitur Quæſtori mandata Bocchi patefaciunt; ſimul ab eo petunt, uti fautor, conſultorque ſibi adſit; *copias, fidem, magnitudinem regis ſui & alia, quæ aut utilia, aut benevolentia eſſe credebant,* oratione extollunt; dein, Sulla omnia pollicito, docti quo modo apud Marium, item apud Senatum verba facerent, circiter dies XL. ibidem opperiuntur.

nent for their good affection and parts. Theſe he orders to go to Marius, and if he gave conſent, to Rome; and furniſhes them with full powers for the concluding of a peace at diſcretion.

CXI. *They quickly depart for the winter-quarters of the Romans; but being trepanned in the way, and ſtript of all they had, by ſome Getulian robbers, in great fright, and a ſorry equipage, they purſue their way to Sulla; whom the conſul, when he went upon his expedition, had left proprætor. He did not treat them like fickle enemies, as they had deſerved; but with great kindneſs and generoſity. Whereupon the barbarians believed the report of the Roman avarice to be falſe; and concluded Sulla, from his generous reception of them, to be their friend. For the practice of giving, in order to corruption, was even at that time unknown to many; and no body was thought generous, but out of good will; and all preſents were reckoned arguments of kindneſs. Wherefore they acquainted the quæſtor with the inſtructions they had received from Bocchus; and at the ſame time requeſt of him to favour and aſſiſt them in their buſineſs; magnifying extremely the forces, honeſty, and greatneſs of their prince, with other things they thought might be ſubſervient to their deſign, or a means to procure favour. Sulla promiſed all they deſired; and being by him inſtructed how they ſhould addreſs Marius, and likewiſe the Senate, they waited there about forty days.*

CXII.

CXII. Marius poftquam infecto negotio, quo intenderat, Cirtam redit; de adventu legatorum certior factus, illofque, & Sullam venire jubet, itemque L. Bellienum prætorem, Utica, præterea omnis undique fenatorii ordinis; quibufcum mandata. Bocchi cognofcit; in quibus, legatis poteftas eundi Romam fit; & ab confule interea induciæ poftulabantur. Ea Sullæ & plerifque placuere; pauci ferocius décernunt, fcilicet ignari humanarum rerum, quæ fluxæ, & mobiles femper in advorfa mutantur.   Cæterum Mauri impetratis omnibus, tres Romam profecti cum C. Octavio Rufone, qui quæftor ftipendium adportaverat; duo ad regem redeunt. Ex his Bocchus cum cætera, tum maxume benignitatem, & ftudium Sullæ lubens accepit. Romæque legatis ejus poftquam, *erraffe regem, & Jugurthæ fcelere lapfum,* deprecati funt, amicitiam & fœdus petentibus hoc modo refpondetur.

S. & P. R. beneficii, & injuriæ memor effe folet. Cæterum Boccho, quoniam pœnitet, delicti gratiam facit; fœdus & amicitia dabuntur, cum meruerit.

CXII. *Marius not fucceeding in his attempt upon the tower, return to Cirta; where being informed of the arrival of the ambaffadors, he orders them and Sulla to come to him; and likewife fummons L. Bellienus the prætor, from Utica, and befides him, all others of fenatorian rank, in order to advife with them about the propofals of Bocchus; the fum whereof was liberty for his ambaffadors to proceed to Rome, and a ceffation of arms in the mean time. Which Sulla, with a majority of the council, approved of; but others ftifly oppofed, being not fufficiently fenfible of the uncertainty and inconftancy of human affairs, fubject to very unlucky revolutions. The Moors, having obtained all they defired, three of them went for Rome, with C. Octavius Rufo, who had come as Quæftor into Africa, with pay for the army; two return to the king, and, befides other things, acquaint him more particularly with Sulla's kindnefs and concern for him; which was very agreeable. At Rome, the ambaffadors confeffing their king had been in an error, which he was led into by the wickednefs of Jugurtha; and defiring the favour to be admitted into the Roman alliance, they received an anfwer in the following words.*

The fenate and people of Rome are ever mindful of any kindnefs or injury done them; however, they pardoned Bocchus's offence, in confideration of his repentance; and fhould admit him into their alliance, when he deferved it.

CXIII. Quibus rebus cognitis, Bocchus per litteras a Mario petivit, ut Sullam ad fe mitteret; cujus arbitratu de communibus negotiis confuleretur. Is miffus cum præfidio equitum, atque peditum, funditorum Baleariorum; præterea iere fagittarii, & cohors Peligna cum velitaribus armis, itineris properandi cauffa; neque his fecus, atque aliis armis, advorfum tela hoftium, quod ea levia funt, muniti. Sed in itinere, quincto denique die, Volux, filius Bocchi, repente in campis patentibus cum mille non amplius equitibus fefe oftendit; qui temere & effufe euntes, Sullæ, aliifque omnibus & numerum ampliorem vero, & hoftilem metum efficiebant. Igitur fe quifque expedire; arma atque tela tentare, intendere; timor, aliquantus, fed fpes amplior, quippe victoribus, & advorfum eos, quos fæpe vicerant. Interim equites, exploratum præmiffi, rem, uti erat, quietam nunciant.

CXIII. Bocchus, upon advice of this, requefted of Marius, by a letter, to fend Sulla to him, that he might advife with him about their common concerns; who was fent accordingly, with a guard of horfe and foot, Balearian flingers, bowmen, and a battalion of Pelignians, with arms ufed by the Velites, for the better expedition in their march, and becaufe they would be as well fecured by that fort of arms, as any other, againft the enemies, who ufed the like themfelves. Upon the fifth day of their march, Volux, the fon of Bocchus, all on a fudden appeared upon a wide plain, with no more than a thoufand horfe, but who, by the loofe order of their march, gave occafion to Sulla, and all that were with him, to imagine them to be more numerous, and enemies too. Whereupon, every man now ftands to his arms, ready to receive them. Their hopes, however, were above their fears, as being to engage with an enemy which they had often conquered. In the mean time, fome horfe being fent to reconnoitre them, bring word again how the matter was, and that there was no danger.

CXIV. Volux adveniens Quæftorem appellat, fe a patre Boccho obviam illis fimul, & præfidio miffum. Deinde eum, & proximum diem fine metu conjuncti eunt. Poft, ubi caftra locata, & diei vefper erat; repen—

CXIV. Volux, coming up, addreffes himfelf to the quæftor, and tells him, that he had been fent by his father to meet him, and to wait upon him with that guard to his court. Accordingly they continue their march together, for that and the next day, very quietly. But in the evening, when they had now te

te Maurus, incerto vultu pavens, ad Sullam adcurrit; dicitque, *fibi ex fpeculatoribus cognitum, Jugurtham, haud procul abeffe; fimul, uti noctu clam fecum profugeret, rogat, atque hortatur.* Ille animo feroci; negat fe *toties fufum Numidam pertimefcere; virtuti fuorum fatis credere; etiam fi certa peftis adeffet, manfurum potius, quam proditis quos ducebat, turpi fuga incertæ, ac forfitan paullo poft morbo inte-rituræ vitæ parceret.* Cæterum ab eodem monitus, *uti noctu proficifcerentur,* confilium adprobat; ac ftatim milites cœnatos effe in caftris; ignefque creberrimos fieri, dein prima vigilia filentio egredi jubet. Jamque nocturno itinere feffis omnibus, Sulla pariter cum ortu folis caftra metabatur; cum equites Mauri nunciant, *Jugurtham, circiter duum milium intervallo, ante confedilfe.* Quod poftquam auditum eft, tum vero ingens metus noftros invadit; credere fe proditos a Voluce, & infidiis circumventos. Ac fuere.qui dicerent, *manu vindicandum, neque apud illum tantum fcelus inultum relinquendum.*

pitched their camp, all on a fudden the Moor comes in a great fright, to Sulla, and tells him, that he was informed by his fcouts that Jugurtha was not far off, and at the fame time begs and entreats him to fly away privately with him in the night. To which he very boldly replied, that he feared not the Numidian, who had been fo often beat by him; nor did he diftruft the courage of his men: but however, tho' he was fure to perifh, yet would he ftand his ground, rather than fave his life, which might otherwife, perhaps in a fhort time, have an end put to it by a diftemper, by a fcandalous flight, and betraying thofe he conducted. But however, being advifed by the fame Volux to continue his march in the night, he approved of that advice, and immediately gives order for the foldiers to go to fupper in the camp; and, when they had done, to make a good many fires up and down the fame, and march filently off in the firft watch. All being heartily tired with that night's march, Sulla pitched his camp again about fun-rife, when the Moorifh horfe bring word, that Jugurtha had fat down about two miles on the road before them. Upon hearing of which, our men were in a mighty confternation, as believing themfelves betrayed, and led into a fnare by Volux. And fome cried out for vengeance upon him, and that fuch a piece of villainy might not go unpunifhed.

CXV.

CXV. At Sulla, quam-
quam eadem exiſtumabat,
tamen ab injuria Mau-
rum prohibet ; ſuos hor-
tatur, *uti fortem animum
gererent ; ſæpe ante pau-
cis ſtrenuis advorſus multitudinem bene pugnatum ;
quanto ſibi in prælio mi-
nus pepercissent, tanto
tutiores fore ; nec quem-
quam decere, qui manus
armaverit, ab inermis
pedibus auxilium petere,
in maxumo metu nudum
& cæcum corpus ad hoſtis
vertere. Deinde Volu-
cem, quoniam hoſtilia
faceret, Jovem maxu-
mum obteſtatus, ut ſceleris,
atque perfidiæ Bocchi teſtis
adeſſet, caſtris abire jubet.
Ille lacrumans orare, ne
ea crederet ; nihil dolo
factum, ac magis callidi-
tate Jugurthæ ; cui vi-
delicet ſpeculanti iter ſuum cognitum eſſet. Cæ-
terum, quoniam neque in-
gentem multitudinem ha-
beret ; & ſpes, opeſque
ejus ex patre ſuo pende-
rent ; credere illum nihil
auſurum palam, cum ipſe
filius teſtis adeſſet ; quare
optumum factum videri,
per media ejus caſtra pa-
lam tranſire ; ſeſe, vel
præmiſſis, vel ibidem re-
lictis Mauris, ſolum cum
Sulla iturum. Ea res, uti
in tali negotio, probata ;
ac ſtatim profecti, quia de
improviſo acceſſerint, du-*

CXV. *But Sulla, tho' he was
of the ſame opinion, yet would not
ſuffer the Moor to be hurt ; but encourages his men to have a good
heart ; that a few brave fellows had
oftentimes prevailed againſt multitudes ; the leſs they ſpared themſelves in battle, the more ſecure
they would be ; nor ought any
one, that had armed his hands, to
ſeek aſſiſtance from his unarmed
feet, or in the midſt of danger turn
his naked back, that had no eyes in
it, upon his enemy. Then, invok-
ing Jupiter as a witneſs of the villainy and treachery of Bocchus,
he orders Volux, as acting like a
baſe enemy, to be gone out of the
camp. He, with tears in his eyes,
begs of him, not to harbour any
ſuch ſuſpicion of him ; that nothing of all this was owing to any
baſeneſs of his, but to the ſubtlety
of Jugurtha only, who had by his
ſpies diſcovered their march. However, ſince he had no great numbers with him, and all his hopes and
ſtrength depended upon his father,
he did not believe he would dare
to make any open attempt upon
them whilſt the ſon was by to be
a witneſs of his behaviour. For
which reaſon, he thought their beſt
way would be to take their rout
fairly through the middle of his
camp ; that he would either ſend
his Moors before, or leave them
there, and go ſingle along with
Sulla. This propoſal was, as the
caſe ſtood, approved of, and immediately they went ; and Jugurtha, being ſurprized with their
coming, and unreſolved what to
do, they paſſed ſafe, and arrived
bio,*

bio, atque hæfitante Jugurtha, incolumes tranfeunt. Deinde paucis diebus, quo ire intenderant, perventum eft.

CXVI. Ibi cum Boccho Numida quidam Afpar nomine ; multum, & familiariter agebat, præmiffus ab Jugurtha, poftquam Sullam accitum audierat, orator, & fubdole fpeculatum Bocchi confilia ; præterea Dabar, Maffugradæ filius, ex gente Maffiniffæ, cæterum materno genere impar ; nam pater ejus ex concubina ortus erat ; Mauro ob ingenii multa bona carus, acceptufque, quem Bocchus fidum effe Romanis, multis ante tempeftatibus expertus, illico ad Sullam nunciatum mittit, *paratum fefe facere, quæ populus Rom. vellet ; colloquio diem, locum, tempus ipfe deligeret ; confulta fefe omnia cum illo integra habere ; neu Jugurthæ legatum pertimefceret ;* accitum effe, quo res communis licentius gereretur ; nam ab infidiis ejus aliter caveri nequiviffe. Sed ego comperior, Bocchum magis Punica fide, quam ob ea, quæ prædicabat, fimul Romanos, & Numida fpe pacis attinuiffe ; multumque cum animo fuo volvere folitum,

---

in a few days at the place they defigned for.

'CXVI. *There was at that time in Bocchus's court a Numidian named Afpar, who pretended to great freedom and familiarity with him, having been difpatched thither by Jugurtha, as foon as he heard that Sulla had been fent for, as his envoy, and flily to difcover Bocchus's intentions ; and, befides him, one Dabar, the fon of Maffagrada, of the family of Mafiniffa, but of mean defcent by the mother, for her father was the fon of a concubine, but in great favour with the Moor for his excellent parts, whom Bocchus having found upon feveral occafions before to be entirely in the Roman intereft, he immediately difpatches him to Sulla, to tell him, that he was ready to comply with the pleafure of the Roman people in every thing ; that he might fix time and place for the interview betwixt them ; that he was at full liberty to conclude matters as they two, upon confideration, fhould find reafonable, without being under any obligations to the contrary from Jugurtha, whofe agent he need not fear. He had been fent for only that their common affair might be tranfacted with more freedom ; for otherwife it would have been impoffible to have guarded effectually againft the fly arts of Jugurtha. But I find that Bocchus herein acted double, rather than with the defign he pretended, in order to keep both*

Ju-

Jugurtham Romanis, an illi Sullam traderet; libidinem advorfum nos, metum pro nobis fuafiffe.

CXVII. Igitur Sulla refpondit, *pauca fe coram Afpare locuturum, cætera occulte aut nullo, aut quam pauciffumis præfentibus*; fimul edocet, quæ refponderentur. Poftquam, ficuti voluerant, congreffi; dicit *fe miffum a confule veniffe, quæfitum ab eo, pacem an bellum agitaturus foret.* Tunc rex, uti præceptum fuerat, poft diem decimum redire jubet; ac nihil etiam nunc decreviffe, fed illo die refponfurum. Deinde ambo in fua caftra digreffi. Sed ubi plerumque noctis proceffit; Sulla a Boccho occulte accerfitur; ab utroque tantummodo fidi interpretes adhibentur. Præterea Dabar internuncius, fanctus vir, ex fententia jurat ambobus; ac ftatim fic rex incipit.

CXVIII. *Numquam ego ratus fum fore, uti rex maxumus in hac terra, & omnium, quos novi, opulentiffimus, privato homini gratiam deberem. Et hercule Sulla, ante te cognitum, multis orantibus aliis ultro ego-*

the Romans and Jugurtha at a bay with the hopes of peace; and that he was a long time in debate with himfelf, whether fhe fhould deliver up Jugurtha to the Romans, or Sulla to him, his inclination pleading againft, and his fear for, us.

CXVII. *Sulla therefore replied,* that he fhould fay but little in the prefence of Afpar; the reft in private, with no one, or but very few by. At the fame time he inftructs him what anfwer he fhould return him. After they met according to appointment, Sulla tells him, that he had been fent by the conful to know of him whether he was for peace or war. Then the King, according to his inftruction, bids him come to him again after ten days time, feeing he was as yet undetermined in that matter, but would then give him an anfwer. Whereupon they both departed into their feveral camps. But when the night was now far fpent, Sulla is privately fent for by Bocchus, and trufty interpreters alone allowed to be prefent, except the meffenger Dabar, a man of honour, who was fworn to fecrecy. Whereupon the king opened the conference as follows.

CXVIII. I never imagined that I, the greateft prince in this part of the world, and the moft opulent that I know, fhould ever be indebted for a favour to a private perfon, or any one under the rank of a king. And indeed, Sulla, before I was acquainted with you, I have granted favours to

met

A

met opem tuli, nullius in-
digui. Id imminutum,
quod cæteri dolere solent,
ego lætor. Fuerit mihi
pretium, eguisse aliquan-
do tuæ amicitiæ; qua a-
pud animum meum [nihil
carius habeo. Id adeo
experiri licet; arma, vi-
ros, pecuniam, postremo
quicquid animo libet, su-
me, utere; & quoad vi-
ves, numquam tibi reddi-
tam gratiam putaveris;
semper apud me integra
erit; denique nihil me
sciente frustra voles.
Nam, ut ego existumo,
regem armis, quam muni-
ficentia, vinci, flagitiosum
minus. Cæterum de re-
publ. vestra, cujus cura-
tor huc missus es, paucis
accipe. Bellum ego po-
pulo Rom. neque feci, ne-
que factum umquam vo-
lui; finis meos advorsum
armatos armis tutus sum.
Id omitto; quando vobis
ita placet, gerite, uti
vultis, cum Jugurtha
bellum. Ego flumen Mu-
lucham, quod inter me &
Micipsam fuit, non egre-
diar, neque Jugurtham
id intrare sinam. Præ-
terea, si quid meque vobis
bisque dignum petiveris,
haud repulsus abibis.

many, upon their application for
them, and to others without; but
never stood in need of any myself.
I am glad the case is altered with
me in that respect; a thing which
others are apt to be sorry for. It
was worth my while to stand in
need of your friendship, to which
I prefer nothing in the world besides, which you may try. Take
use my arms, men, money, in
short, whatsoever you have a mind
to; and, after all, whilst you live,
never think I have made you a
sufficient requital for your favours.
My obligation to you will ever be
the same. Finally, you shall never
desire any thing in my power to
do for you, if I am but sensible of
it, but you shall have it. For I
thing it less dishonourable for a
prince to be outdone in arms than
generosity. But, as to your repub-
lic, whose affairs you have been
sent hither to take care of, I shall
let you know my mind in a few
words. I never made war upon
the Roman people, or ever so
much as desired it. I only defended my dominions with arms
against an armed force. But I say
no more of that. Since you are so
minded, carry on a war with Jugurtha, as you please. I shall never stir beyond the river Mulucha,
which was the boundary betwixt
me and Micipsa; nor will I ever
suffer Jugurtha to come within it.
And, if you have any thing further
to demand, worthy of me and
yourselves, you shall not be denied.

CXIX. Ad id Sulla
pro se breviter, & modi-
ce; de pace, & de com-

CXIX. To this Sulla replied
briefly and modestly so far as it
related to himself; but spoke large-
muni-

múnibus rebus multis dif-feruit. Denique regi pa-tefecit; *quod polliceatur, fenatum & populum Romanum, quoniam amplius armis valuiffent, non in gratia habituros; faciundum aliquid, quod illorum magis, quam fua, retuliffe videretur; id adeo in promptu effe; quoniam Jugurthæ copiam haberet; quem fi Romanis tradidiffet, fore, ut illi plurimum deberetur; amicitiam, fœdus, Numidiæ partem, quam nunc peteret, tunc ultro adventuram. Rex primum negitare; affinitatem, cognationem, præterea fœdus interveniffe; ad hec metuere, ne fluxa fide ufus popularium animos averteret; queis & Jugurtha carus, & Romani invifi effent.* Denique fæpius fatigatus, lenitur; & ex voluntate Sullæ omnia fe facturum promittit. Cæterum ad fimulandam pacem, cujus Numida, defeffus bello, avidiffumus, quæ utilia vifa, conftituunt. Ita, compófito dolo, digrediuntur.

CXX. At rex poftero die Afparem, Jugurthæ legatum, appellat; dicitque fibi per Dabarem ex Sulla cognitum, *poffe con-*

ly as to the public concerns. Finally, *he gave the king to underftand,* That, as the fenate and people of Rome had been fuccefsful in the war, they would never thank him for what he promifed. He muft do fomething that might appear to be more for their intereft than his own; which was an eafy matter for him to do, fince he had Jugurtha in his power, whom, if he would deliver up to the Romans, they would then be under a very great obligation to him; that then the Roman friendfhip and alliance, with the third part of Numidia, which he demanded, would come into him without more a-do. *The king at firft, refufed over and over to comply with this propofal, alledging* their relation both by blood and marriage, with the treaty of alliance that had been betwixt them. He was moreover afraid, he faid, left by acting fo treacherous a part he fhould lofe the affections of his fubjects, who all loved Jugurtha, and hated the Romans. *But repeated inftances to the fame purpofe foftened him at laft; and he accordingly promifed to do all that Sulla defired of him. But to carry on the pretence of concluding a peace that fhould include Jugurtha, which he, being weary of the war, was very defirous of,* they fettle matters as they judged proper for that purpose. And having thus laid their plot, they part.

CXX. *The following day, the king fpeaks to Afpar, and tells him that he was informed from Sulla by Dabar, that the war might be ended upon terms;* he
ditioni-

ditionibus bellum comp̃oni ;
quamobrem regis fui fen-
tentiam exquireret. Ille
lætus in caftra Jugurthæ
venit. Deinde ab illo
cuncta edoctus: propera-
to itinere, poft diem
octavum redit ad Boc-
chum ; & ei nunciat,
Jugurtham cupere om-
nia, quæ imperarentur,
facere ; fed Mario parum
fidere ; fæpe antea cum
imperatoribus Romanis
pacem conventam, fruftra
fuiffe. Cæterum Bocchus,
fi ambobus confultam, &
ratam pacem vellet, daret
operam, ut una ab omni-
bus, quafi de pace, in col-
loquium veniretur ; ibi-
que fibi Sullam traderet ;
cum talem virum in pote-
ftate haberet, tum fore,
uti juffu S. P. Q. R. *fœdus fieret ; neque hominem nobilem*
non fua ignavia, fed ob rempubl. in hoftium poteftate relictum iri.

CXXI. Hæc Maurus
fecum ipfe diu volvens,
tandem promifit. Cæ-
terum dolo, an vere cunc-
tatus, parum comperi-
mus. Sed plerumque
regiæ voluntates, ut ve-
hementes, fic mobiles,
fæpe ipfæ fibi advorfæ.
Poftea tempore & loco
conftituto, in colloquium
uti de pace veniretur,
Bocchus Sullam modo,
modo Jugurthæ legatum
appellare ; benigne habe-
re ; idem ambobus polli-
ceri. Illi pariter læti, ac
fpei bonæ pleni effe. Sed

might learn his mafter's fentiments
about it. *He went, full of joy, to*
Jugurtha's camp, and taking his in-
ftructions returns with all expedi-
tion eight days after to Bocchus, and
tells him, that Jugurtha was ready
to comply with any thing, but
durft not truft Marius ; that the
peace he had concluded with feveral Roman commanders before
him they had never ftood to. Bocchus, if he would provide effectually for them both, and make a
peace to laft, fhould procure a joint
conference under that pretence,
and deliver up Sulla to him. If he
had but fuch a man as him in his
hands, a treaty of peace would then
be concluded by order of the fenate
and people of Rome. For a man
of his quality would never be left
in the enemy's hands, into which
he came, not by his own want of
courage, but in ferving his country.

CXXI. *The Moor mufing up-*
on this propofal a good while, at
laft promifed he would ; but whe-
ther with a fraudulent defign, or
fincerely, I do not find. But
princes humours, as they are moftly
very violent, fo are they fickle, and
often inconfiftent. After this, time
and place being appointed for the
conference, Bocchus one while talked
with Sulla, another while with
Jugurtha's agent ; treated them
kindly, and promifed both the fame
thing. They were both alike well
pleafed, and full of hopes. But in
the night before the day appointed
for the conference, the Moor
gathering his friends about him,

no fte

nocte ea, quæ proxuma fuit ante diem colloquio decretum, Maurus adhibitis amicis, ac ftatim immutata voluntate, remotis cæteris dicitur fecum ipfe multa agitaviffe, vultu, colore, motu corporis pariter atq; animo varius; quæ fcilicet, tacente ipfo, occulta oris patefeciffe. Tamen poftremo Sullam arceffi jubet; & ex ejus fententia Numidæ infidias tendit. Deinde, ubi dies advenit, & ei nunciatum eft, Jugurtham haud procul abeffe; cum paucis amicis, & Quæftore noftro, quafi obvius honoris cauffa, procedit in tumulum facillumum vifu infidiantibus. Eodem Numida cum plerifque neceffariis fuis inermis, ut dictum erat, accedit; ac ftatim figno dato, undique fimul ex infidiis invaditur. Cæteri obtruncati; Jugurtha Sullæ vinctus traditur, & ab eo ad Marium deductus eft.

CXXII. Per idem tempus advorfum Gallos ab ducibus noftris Q. Cæpione, & M. Manlio male pugnatum. Quo metu Italia omnis contremuerat. Illique, & inde ufque ad noftram memoriam Romani fic habuere; alia omnia virtuti fuæ prona effe; cum Gallis pro falute, non pro glo-

and immediately changing his mind, after he had ordered all but his friends to withdraw, he did, they tell you, ruminate upon the matter a long time, with ftrange alterations in his countenance, and a variety of fentiments; which, tho', he was filent, was difcoverable in his looks. However, at laft, he orders Sulla to be fent for, and, by his advice, lays a plot for the Numidian. Then, as foon as it was day, and he was informed that Jugurtha was not far off, he, with a few friends, and our Quæftor, goes, under pretence of doing him honour, to meet him, as far as a hill that was in view of thofe who were ordered to trepan him. Thither, as had been appointed, the Numidian came unarmed with many friends. And immediately, upon a fignal given, he was furrounded on all hands, and feized. The reft were killed; but Jugurtha was delivered in chains to Sulla, and by him conducted to Marius.

CXXII. About the fame time, our generals, Q. Cæpio and M. Manluis, were very unfortunate againft the Gauls; which occafioned a general confternation throughout Italy. And the Romans then were, and from that time to this, have been always of opinion, that other wars had no difficulty in them; but that they fought with the Gauls for their very being, not glory. But after the

S ria

ria certare. Sed poft-quam bellum in Numidia confectum; & Jugur-tham victum adduci Romam nunciatum eft; Marius conful abfens factus eft; & ei decreta provincia Gallia; ifque Kalendis Januariis magna gloria conful triumpha-vit. Ex ea tempeftate fpes, atque opes civitatis in illo fitæ.

war in Numidia was at an end, and news was carried to Rome that Jugurtha was coming in chains, Marius, tho' abfent, was made conful again; and the province of Gaul affigned him; and he triumph-ed, when conful, upon the firft of January with great glory. From that time forward, the hopes and fecurity of the Roman ftate refted upon him.

ORA-

ORATIONES DUÆ
A . D
C. CÆSAREM,
SALLUSTIO Adfcriptæ.

ORATIO I.
A D
C. CÆSAREM,
D E
REPUBLICA ORDINANDA.

I. **P**OPULUS R. antea obtinebat, regna atque imperia, fortunam dono dare, item alia, quæ per mortalis avide cupiuntur ; quia & apud indignos fæpe erant, quafi Pe lubidinem data; neque cuiquam incorrupta perman-ferant. Sed res docuit in verum effe, quod in carminibus Appius ait, *Fabrum effe fuæ quemque fortunæ* ; atque in te maxume, qui tantum alios prætergreffus es, uti prius defeffi fint homines laudando facta tua, quam tu laude digna faciundo. Cæterum uti fabricata, fic virtute parta, quam magna induftria haberi decet ; ne incuria deformentur, aut corruant infir-mata. Nemo enim alteri imperium volens concedit; & quamvis bonus atque clemens fit, qui plus poteft; tamen, quia malo effe licet, formidatur. Id evenit, quia plerique rerum potentes perverfe confulunt; & eo fe munitiores putant, quo illi, quibus imperitant, nequiores fuere.

II. At

II. At contra id eniti decet; cum ipfe bonus, atque ftrenuus fis, uti quam optumis imperites. Nam peffumus quifque
afperrime rectorem patitur. Sed tibi hoc gravius eft, quam
ante te omnibus, armis parta componere. Bellum aliorum
pace mollius geffifti; ad hoc victores prædam petunt, victi
cives funt. Inter has difficultates evadendum eft tibi; atque
in pofterum firmanda refpub. non armis modo, neque adverfum hoftes, fed, quod multo majus, multoque afperius eft,
bonis pacis artibns. Ergo omnes magna mediocrique fapientia
res huc vocat; quæ quifque optuma poteft, ut dicat. Ac mihi
fic videtur; qualicumque modo tu victoriam compofueris, ita
alia omnia futura. Sed jam, quo melius, faciliufque conftituas, paucis, quæ me animus monet, accipe.

III. Bellum tibi fuit, imperator, cum homine claro, magnis
opibus, avido potentiæ, majore fortuna, quam fapientia;
quem fecuti funt pauci, per fuam injuriam tibi inimici, item
quos affinitas, aut alia neceffitudo traxit. Nam particeps dominationis neque fuit quifquam; neque, fi pati potuiffet, orbis terrarum bello concuffus foret. Cætera multitudo vulgi,
more magis quam judicio, poft alius alium, quafi prudentio-
rem, fecuti. Per idem tempus maledictis iniquiorum occu-
pandæ reipubl. in fpem adducti homines, quibus omnia probro ac luxuria polluta erant, concurrere in caftra tua; & aperte
quietis mortem, rapinas, poftremo omnia, quæ corruptus
animus jubebat, miniteri.

IV. Ex quis magna pars, ubi neque creditum condonare,
neque te civibus, ficuti hoftibus, uti vident, defluxere; pauci
reftitere, quibus majus otium in caftris, quam Romæ, futurum
erat; tanta vis creditorum impendebat. Sed ob eafdem cauffas, immane dictu eft, quanti, & quam multi mortales poftea
ad Pompejum difcefferint; eoque per omne tempus belli quafi
facro, atque infpoliato fano debitores ufi. Igitur, quoniam
tibi victori de bello, atque pace, agitandum eft; hoc uti civi-
liter deponas, illa ut quam juftiffima, & diuturna fit; de te
ipfo primum, quia compofiturus es, quod optumum factu eft,
exiftima. Equidem ego cuncta imperia crudelia, magis acerba, quam diuturna, arbitror, neque quemquam a multis me-
tuendum effe, quin ad eum ex multis formido recidat; eam
vitam bellum æternum & anceps gerere; quoniam neque adverfus, neque ab tergo, aut lateribus tutus fis, femper in periculo, aut metu agites.

V. Contra qui benignitate, & clementia, imperium tem-
peravere, his læta & candida omnia vifa, etiam hoftes, æquiores,
quam aliis cives. An qui me his dictis corruptorem victoriæ
tuæ

tuæ, nimifque in victos bona voluntate prædicent ? Scilicet quod ea, quæ exteris nationibus, natura hoftibus, nofque ma-jorefque noftri fæpe tribuere, ea civibus danda arbitror ; neq; barbaro ritu cæde cædem, & fanguine fanguinem expiandum. An illa, quæ paullo ante hoc bellum in Cn. Pompejum vic-toriamque Sullanam increpabantur, oblivio abftulit; interfecit Domitium, Carbonem, Brutum, alios item non armatos, neque in prælio belli jure, fed poft ea fupplices per fummum fcelus interfectos; plebem Romanam in villa publica pecoris modo confciffam.

VI. Heu quam illa occulta civium funera, & repentinæ cædes in parentum, aut liberorum finum, fuga mulierum, & puerorum, vaftatio domorum ! ante partam a te victoriam omnia fæva atque crudelia erant. Ad quæ te illi iidem hor-tantur; & fcilicet id certatum effe utrius veftrum arbitrio, in-juriæ uti fierent; neque receptam, fed captam a te remp. & ea cauffa exercitus ftipendiis confectis, optimos, & veterrimos omnium adverfum fratres, parentefque, alii liberos armis con-tendere ; ut ex alienis malis deterrimi mortaies ventri atque profundæ libidini fumtus quærerent ; atque effent opprobria victoriæ ; quorum flagitiis commacularetur bonorum laus.

VII. Neque enim te præterire puto, quali quifque eorum more aut modeftia, etium tum dubia victoria, fefe gefferit; quoque modo in belli adminiftratione fcorta, aut convivia, exercuerint nonnulli; quorum ætas ne per otium quidem tales voluptates fine dedecore attigerit. De bello fatis dictum. De pace firmanda quoniam tuque, & omnis tui agitatis; primum id, quæfo, confidera, quale id fit, de quo confultas; ita, bonis, malifque dimotis, patenti via ad verum perges. Ego fic exiftumo quoniam orta omnia intereunt, qua tempeftate ur-bi Romanæ fatum excidii adventarit ; cives cum civibus ma-nus conferturos ; ita defeffos, & exfangues regi, aut nationi prædæ futuros. Aliter non orbis terrarum, neque cunctæ gentes conglobatæ, movere, aut contundere queunt hoc im-perium. Firmanda igitur funt concordiæ bona & difcordiæ mala expellenda.

VIII. Id ita eveniet, fi fumtuum, & rapinarum licentiam demferis ; non ad vetera inftituta revocans, quæ jam pridem corruptis moribus, ludibrio funt ; fed fi fuam cuique rem fa-miliarem finem fumtuum ftatueris ; quoniam his inceffit mos, ut homines adolefcentuli, fua atque aliena confumere, nihil lubidini, atque aliis rogantibus denegare, pulcherrumum pu-tent ; eam virtutem, & magnitudinem animi, pudorem, at-que modeftiam pro focordia æftiment. Ergo animus ferox,

prava

prava via ingreſſus, ubi conſueta non ſuppetunt, fertur accenſus in ſocios modo, modo in cives; movet compoſita, & res
novas veteribus acquirit. Quare tollendus fenerator in poſte-
rum, uti ſuas quiſque res curemus; ea vera, atque ſimplex
via eſt magiſtratum populo, non creditori, gerere; & magnitudinem animi in addendo, non demendo reipubl. oſtendere.

IX. Atque ego ſcio, quam aſpera hæc res in principio futura ſit, præſertim iis, qui ſe in victoria licentius liberiuſque,
quam artius, futuros credebant; quorum ſi ſaluti potius,
quam lubidini, conſules; illoſque noſque & ſocios in pace firma conſtitues. Si eadem ſtudia, arteſque juventuti erunt;
næ iſta egregia tua fama ſimul cum urbe Roma brevi concidet.
Poſtremo ſapientes pacis cauſſa bellum gerunt, laborem ſpe
otii ſuſtentant. Niſi illam firmam efficis, vinci, an viciſſe,
quid retulit? Quare capeſſe per deos rempubl. & omnia aſpera,
uti ſoles, pervade. Namque aut tu mederi potes; aut omit-
tenda eſt cura omnibus. Neque quiſquam te ad crudeles pœnas, aut acerba judicia invocat, quibus civitas vaſtatur magis
quam corrigitur, ſed uti pravas artes, malaſque lubidines, ab
juventute prohibeas.

X. Ea vera clementia erit conſuluiſſe, ne immerito cives
patria expellerentur; retinuiſſe ab ſtultitia, & falſis voluptatibus; pacem concordiamque ſtabiliviſſe; non ſi flagitiis obſe-
cutus, delicta perpeſſus, præſens gaudium cum mox futuro
malo conceſſeris. Ac mihi animus, quibus rebus alii timent,
maxume fretus eſt, negotii magnitudine; & quia tibi terræ,
& maria ſimul omnia componenda ſunt, (quippe res parvas
tantum ingenium attingere nequit) magnæ curæ magna merces eſt. Igitur provideas oportet, uti plebes, largitionibus,
& publico frumento, corrupta, habeat negotia ſua, quibus ab
malo publico detineatur; juventus probitati, & induſtriæ, non
ſumtibus, neque divitiis, ſtudeat. Id ita eveniet, ſi pecuniæ,
quæ maxuma omnium pernicies eſt, uſum, atque decus
demſeris.

XI. Nam ſæpe ego cum animo meo reputans, quibus
quiſque rebus clariſſumi viri magnitudinem inveniſſent; quæ
res populos nationeſve magnis auctoribus auxiſſent; ac deinde quibus cauſſis ampliſſuma regna & imperia corruiſſent; eadem ſemper bona atque mala reperiebam, omniſque victores
divitias contempſiſſe, & victos cupiviſſe. Neque aliter quiſquam extollere ſeſe, & divina mortalis attingere poteſt, niſi
omiſſis pecuniæ & corporis gaudiis, animo indulgens, non aſ-
ſentando, neque concupita præbendo, perverſam gratiam
gratificans; ſed in labore, patientia, boniſque præceptis, &

factis

factis fortibus exercitando. Nam domum aut villam exftrue-
re, eamque fignis, aulæis, aliifque operibus exornare, & omnia potius, quam femet, vifendum efficere; id eft, non divitias decori habere, fed ipfum illis flagitio effe.

XII. Porro ii, quibus bis die ventrem onerare, nullam
noctem fine fcorto quiefcere mos eft; ubi animum, quem
dominari decebat, fervitio oppreffere; nequicquam eo poftea
hebeti, atque claudo pro exercito uti volunt. Nam imprudentia pleraque, & fe præcipitant. Verum hæc & omnia mala pariter cum honore pecuniæ definent, fi neque magiftratus, neque alia vulgo cupienda, venalia erunt. Ad hoc providendum eft, quonam modo Italia atque provinciæ tutiores
fint; id quod factu haud obfcurum eft. Nam iidem omnia
vaftant, fuas deferendo domos, & per injuriam alienas occu-
pando. Item ne, ut adhuc, militia injufta aut inæqualis fit;
cum alii triginta, pars nullum ftipendium faciet; & frumentum id, quod antea præmium ignaviæ fuit, per municipia, &
colonis illis dare conveniet, cum ftipendiis emeritis domos
reverterint. Quæ reipublicæ neceffaria, tibique gloriofa ratus fum, quam pauciffumis abfolvi.

XIII. Non pejus videtur, pauca nunc de facto meo differere. Plerique mortales ad judicandum fatis ingenii habent, aut
fimulant; veruntamem ad reprehendenda aliena facta, aut
dicta ardet omnibus animus; vix fatis apertum os, aut lingua
promta videtur, quæ meditata pectore evolvat; quibus me
fubjectum haud pœnitet, magis reticuiffe pigeret. Nam five
hac, feu meliore alia via perges; a me quidem pro virile
parte dictum, & adjutum fuerit. Reliquum eft, optare, uti,
quæ tibi placuerint, ea dii immortales approbent, beneque
evenire finant.

ORA-

ORATIO II.

AD

C. CÆSAREM,

DE

REPUBLICA ORDINANDA.

I. SCIO ego, quam difficile, atque afperum factu fit, confilium dare regi, aut imperatori; poftremo cuiquam mortali, cujus opes in excelfo funt; quippe cum & illis confultorum copiæ adfint; neque de futuro quifquam fatis callidus, fatifque prudens fit. Quinetiam fæpe prava magis, quam bona confilia profpere eveniunt; quia plerafque res fortuna ex lubidine fua agitat. Sed mihi ftudium fuit adolefcentulo rempublicam capefere; atque in ea cognofcenda multam, magnamque curam habui non ita, uti magiftratum modo caperem, quem multi malis artibus adepti erant; fed etiam uti rempubl. domi, militiæ, quantumque armis, viris, opulentia poffet, cognitum haberem. Itaque mihi multa cum animo agitanti confilium fuit, famam, modeftiamque meam poft tuam dignitatem habere, & cujus rei lubet periculum facere, dum quid tibi ex eo gloriæ accederet. Idque non temere, neque ex fortuna tua, decrevi; fed quia in te, præter cæteras, artem unam egregie mirabilem comperi, femper tibi majorem in adverfis, quam in fecundis rebus animum effe. Sed per cæteros mortales illa res clarior eft, quod prius defeffi fint homines laudando atque admirando munificentiam tuam, quam tu faciendo, quæ gloria digna effent.

II. Equidem mihi decretum eft, nihil tam ex alto reperiri poffe, quod non cogitanti tibi in promtu fit. Neque ego, quæ vifa funt, de rep. tibi fcripfi, quia mihi confilium, atque ingenium meum amplius æquo probaretur; fed inter labores militiæ, interque prælia, victorias, imperium, ftatui admonendum te de negotiis urbanis. Namque tibi fi id modo in

pectore

pectore confilii eft, uti te ab inimicorum impetu vindices, quoque modo contra adverfum Confulem beneficia populi retineas; indigna virtute tua·cogites. Sin in te ille animus eft, qui jam a principio nobilitatis factionem difturbavit; plebem Rom ex gravi fervitute in libertatem reftituit; in prætura inimicorum arma inermis disjecit; domi militiæque tanta, & tam præclara facinora fecit, uti ne inimici quidem queri quidquam audeant, nifi de magnitudine tua; quin accipe tu ea quæ dicam de fumma republ. quæ profecto aut vera invenies, aut certe haud procul a vero.

III. ˈed quoniam Cn. Pompejus aut animi pravitate, aut quia nihil maluit, quam quod tibi obeffet, ita lapfus eft, ut hoftibus tela in manus jaceret; quibus ille rebus rempubl. conturbavit, eifdem tibi reftituenda eft. Primum omnium, fummam poteftatem moderandi, de vectigalibus, fumtibus, judiciis, fenatoribus paucis tradidit; plebem Romanam, cujus ante fumma poteftas erat, ne æquis quidem legibus in fervitute reliquit, Judicia tametfi, ficut antea, tribus ordinibus tradita funt; tamen iidem illi factiofi regunt, dant, adimunt quæ lubet, innocentes circumveniunt; fuos ad honorem extollunt.

IV. Non facinus, non probrum, aut flagitium obftat, quo minus magiftratus capiant; quod commodum eft, trahunt, rapiunt; poftremo, tanquam urbe capta, lubidine, ac licentia fua, pro legibus utuntur. Ac me quidem mediocris dolor angeret, fi virtute partam victoriam more fuo per fervitium exercerent. Sed homines inertiffumi, quorum omnis vis, virtufque in lingua fita eft, forte, atque alterius focordia dominationem oblatam infolentes agitant. Nam quæ feditio, ac diffenfio civilis tot tamque illuftres familias ab ftirpe evertit? aut quorum unquam victoria animus tam præceps, tamque immoderatus fuit? L. Sulla, cui omnia in victoria lege belli licuerunt, tametfi fupplicio hoftium partes fuas muniri intelligebat; tamen paucis interfectis cæteros beneficio, quam metu, retinere maluit. At hercule nunc cum Catone, L. Domitio, cæterifque ejufdem factionis, quadraginta fenatores, multi præterea cum fpe bona adolefcentes, ficuti hoftiæ, mactati funt; cum interea importuniffuma genera hominum tot miferorum civium fanguine fatiari nequiere; non orbi liberi, non parentes exacta ætate, non gemitus virorum, luctus mulierum immanem eorum animum inflexit; quin, acerbius in dies male faciendo, ac dicundo, dignitate alios, alios civitate everfum ierent.

V. Nam,

V Nam, quid ego de te dicam, cujus contumelium homines ignaviffiumi vita fua commutare volunt, fi liceat? neque illis tanta voluptati eft (tametfi infperantibus accidit) dominatio, quanto mœrori tua dignitas; quin optatius habent, ex tua calamitate periculum liberatis facere, quam per te populi R. imperium maximum ex magno fieri. Quo magis tibi etiam atque etiam animo profpiciendum eft, quonam modo rem ftabilias communiafque. Mihi quidem quæ mens fuppetit, eloqui non dubitabo. Cæterum tui erit ingenii probare, quæ vera, atque utilia factu putes. In duas partes ego civitatem divifam arbitror, ficut a majoribus accepi, in patres, & plebem. Antea in patribus fumma auctoritas erat, vis multo maxuma in plebe.

VI. Itaque fæpius in civitate fecefiio fuit; femperque nobilitatis opes diminutæ funt, & jus populi amplificatum. Sed plebes eo libere agitabat; quia nullius potentia fuper leges erat; neque divitiis, aut fuperbia fed bona fama, factifque fortibus nobilis ignobilem anteibat; humillimus quifque in armis, aut militia, nullius honeftæ rei agens, fatis fibi, fatifque patriæ erat. Sed, ubi eos paullatim expulfos agris, inertia, atque inopia incertas domos habere fubegit; cœpere alienas opes petere, libertatem fuam cum republica venalem habere. Ita paullatim populus, qui dominus cunctis gentibus imperitabat, dilapfus eft; & pro communi imperio, privatim fibi quifque fervitutem peperit. Hæc igitur multitudo primum malis moribus imbuta, deinde in artes, vitafque varias difpalata, nullo modo inter fe congruens, parum mihi quidem idonea videtur ad capeffendam rempubl.

VII. Cæterum, additis novis civibus, magna me fpes tenet, fore, ut omnes expergifcantur ad libertatem; quippe cum illis libertatis retinendæ, tum his fervitutis amittendæ cura orietur. Hos ego cenfeo, permixtos cum veteribus novos in coloniis conftituas; ita & res militaris opulentior erit, & plebes bonis negotiis impedita malum publicum facere definet. Sed non infcius, neque imprudens fum, cum ea res agetur; quæ fævitia, quæque tempeftates hominum nobilium futuræ fint, cum indignabuntur omnia funditus mifceri, antiquis civibus hanc fervitutem imponi, regnum denique ex libera civitate futurum, ubi unius munere multitudo ingens in civitatem pervenerit. Equidem ego fic apud animum meum ftatuo, malum facinus in fe admittere, qui incommodo reipubl. gratiam fibi conciliet. Ubi bonum publicum etiam privatim ufui eft; id vero dubitare aggredi, focordiæ, atque ignaviæ duco. M. Livio Drufo femper confilium fuit, in tribunatu

bunatu fumma ope niti pro nobilitate; neque ullam rem in principio agere intendit, nifi illi auctores fierent. Sed homines factiofi, quibus dolus, atque militia, fide cariora erant, ubi intellexerunt, per unum hominum maxumum beneficium multis mortalibus dari; videlicet & fibi quifque confcius, malo atque infido animo effe, de M. Livio Drufo juxta, ac fe, exiftimaverunt. Itaque metu, ne per tantam gratiam folus rerum potiretur, contra eum nixi, fua ipfius confilia difturbaverunt.

VIII. Quo tibi, imperator, majore cura fideque amici, & multa praefidia paranda funt. Hoftem adverfum opprimere, ftrenuo homini haud difficile eft; occulta pericula neque facere, neque vitare, bonis in promptu eft. Igitur, ubi eos in civitatem adduxeris; quoniam quidem revocata plebes erit, in ea re maxume animum exercitato, uti colantur boni mores; concordia inter veteres, & novos coalefcat. Sed multo maxumum bonum patriae, civibus, tibi, liberis, poftremo humanae genti, pepereris, fi ftudium pecuniae aut fuftuleris, aut, quoad res feret, minueris. Aliter neque privata res, neque publica, neque domi, neque militiae, regi poteft. Nam ubi cupido divitiarum invafit; neque difciplina, neque artes bonae, neque ingenium ullum fatis pollet; quin animus magis, aut minus mature, poftremo tamen fuccumbit. Saepe jam audivi, qui reges, quae civitates, & nationes, per opulentiam magna imperia amiferint, quae per virtutem inopes ceperant, id adeo haud mirandum eft. Nam ubi bonus deteriorem divitiis magis clarum, magifque acceptum videt; primo aeftuat multaque in pectore volvit; fed ubi gloria honorem magis in dies, virtutem opulentia vincit; animus ad voluptatem a vero deficit.

IX. Quippe gloria induftria aliter; ubi eam demferis, ipfa per fe virtus amara, atque afpera eft. Poftremo, ubi divitiae clarae habentur, ibi omnia bona vilia funt, fides, probitas, pudor, pudicitia. Nam ad virtutem una, & ardua via eft; ad pecuniam, qua cuique lubet, nititur; & malis, & bonis rebus ea creatur. Ergo in primis auctoritatem pecuniae demito; neque de capite, neque de honore ex copiis quifquam magis, aut minus judicaverit; fi neque praetor, neque conful, ex opulentia, verum ex dignitate creetur. Sed de magiftratu facile populi judicium fit. Judices a paucis probari, regnum eft; ex pecunia legi, inhoneftum. Quare omnes primae claffis juditare placet, fed numero plures, quam judicant. Neque Rhodios, neque alias civitates umquam fuorum judiciorum paenituit; ubi promifcue dives, & pauper,

ut

ut cuique fors tulit, de maxumis rebus juxta, ac de minumis
difceptat. Sed de magiftratibus creandis haud mihi quidem
abfurde placet lex, quam C. Gracchus in tribunatu promul-
gaverat; ut ex confufis quinque claffibus forte centuriæ voca-
rentur. Ita coæquati dignitate, pecunia, virtute anteire
alius alium properabit. Hæc ego magna remedia contra divitias ftatuo. Nam perinde omnes res laudantur, atque appe-
tuntur, ut earum rerum ufus eft; malitia præmiis exercetur.

X. Ubi ea demferis, nemo omnium gratuito malus eft.
Cæterum avaritia bellua fera, immanis, intoleranda eft; quo
intendit, oppida, agros, fana, atque domos, vaftat; divina
cum humanis permifcet; neque exercitus, neque mœnia obftant, quo minus vi fua penetret; fama, pudicitia, liberis,
patria, atque parentibus cunctos mortales fpoliat. Verum,
fi pecuniæ decus ademeris; magna illa vis avaritiæ facile bonis
moribus vincetur. Atque hæc ita fefe habere, tametfi omnes
æqui, atque iniqui memorent; tamen tibi cum factione nobilitatis haud mediocriter certandum eft; cujus fi folum ca-
veris, alia omnia in proclivi erunt. Nam hi, fi virtute fatis
valerent, magis æmuli bonorum, quam invidi, effent. Quia
defidia, & inertia, & ftupor eos, atque torpedo, invafit;
ftrepunt, obtrectant, alienam famam bonam fuum dedecus
exiftumant. Sed, quid ego plura, quafi de ignotis, memorem? M. Bibuli fortitudo, atque animi vis, in confulatum
erupit; hebes lingua, magis malus, quam callidus ingenio.
Quid ille audeat, cui confulatus maxumum imperium maxumo dedecori fuit? An L. Domitii magna vis eft, cujus nullum membrum a flagitio aut facinore vacat? lingua vana,
manus cruentæ, pedes fugaces; quæ honefte nominari ne-
queant, inhoneftiffuma.

XI. Unius tamen M. Catonis ingenium verfutum, lo-
quax, callidum haud contemno. Parantur hæc difciplina
Græcorum. Sed virtus, vigilantia, labos, apud Græcos
nulla funt. Quippe, qui domi libertatem fuam per inertiam
amiferunt; cenfefne eorum præceptis, imperium haberi poffe? Reliqui de factione funt inertiffimi nobiles; in quibus,
ficut in ftatua, præter nomen, nihil eft additamenti. L.
Pofthumus, & M. Favonius, mihi videntur quafi magnæ
navis fupervacua onera effe, ubi falvi pervenere, ufui funt; fi
quid adverfi coortum eft, de illis potiffumum jactura fit, quia
pretii minumi funt. Nunc quoniam, ficut mihi videor, de
plebe renovanda, corrigendaque differui; de fenatu, quæ tibi
agenda videntur, dicam. Poftquam mihi ætas ingeniumque
adolevit, haud ferme armis, atque equis corpus exercui, fed

ani-

animum in litteris agitavi; qued natura firmius erat, id in laboribus habui. Atque ego in ea vita multa legendo, atque audiendo ita comperi, omnia regna, civitates, nationes ufque eo profperum imperium habuiffe, dum apud eos vera confilia valuerunt; ubicumque gratia, timor, voluptas, ea corrupere; poft paullo imminutæ opes, deinde adeintum imperium, poftremo fervitus impofita eit.

XII. Equidem ego fic apud animum meum ftatuo; cuicumque in fua civitate amplior, illuftriorque locus, quam aliis eft, ei magnam curam effe reipubl. Nam cæteris, falva urbe, tantummodo libertas tuta eft; qui per virtutem fibi divitias, decus honorem pepererunt; ubi paullum inclinata refpubl. agitari cœpit, multipliciter animus curis, atque laboribus fatigatur; aut gloriam aut libertatem, aut rem familiarem defenfat; omnibus locis adeft, feftinat; quanto in fecundis rebus florentior fuit, tanto in adverfis afperius magifque anxie agitat. Igitur ubi plebes fenatui, ficuti corpus animo, obedit, ejufque confulta exfequitur, patres confilio valere decet, populo fupervacanea eft calliditas. Itaque majores noftri cum bellis afperrimis premerentur, equis, viris, pecunia amiffa, nunquam defeffi funt armati de imperio certare. Non inopia, ærarii, non vis hoftium, non adverfa res ingentem eorum animum fubegit; quin, quæ virtute ceperant, fimul cum anima retinerent. Atque ea magis fortibus confiliis, quam bonis præliis, patrata funt. Quippe apud illos una refpubl. erat, ei omnes confulebant; factio contra hoftes parabatur; corpus atque ingenium, patriæ, non fuæ quifque potentiæ, exercitabat.

XII. At hoc tempore contra homines nobilis, quorum animos focordia, atque ignavia, invafit, ignari laboris, hoftium, militiæ, domi factione inftructi, per fuperbiam cunctis gentibus moderantur. Itaque patres, quorum confilio antea dubia refpubl. ftabiliebatur, oppreffi, ex aliena libidine huc atque illuc fluctuantes agitantur; interdum alia, deinde alia decernunt; ut eorum, qui dominantur, fimultas ac arrogantia fert, ita bonum malumque publicum exiftumant. Quod fi aut libertas æqua omnium, aut fententia obfcurior effet; majoribus opibus refpubl. & minus potens nobilitas effet. Sed quoniam coæquari gratiam omnium difficile eft; quippe cum illis majorum virtus partam reliquerit gloriam, dignitatem, clientelas; cætera multitudo pleraque infcia; fit fententia eorum a metu libera. Ita occulto fibi quifque alterius potentia carior erit. Libertas juxta bonis, & malis, ftrenuis, atque ignavis optabilis eft. Verum eam plerique metu deferunt, ftultiffimi mortales; quod in certamine dubium eft, quorfum accidat,

id

id per inertiam in fe, quafi victi, recipiunt. Igitur duabus rebus confirmari poffe fenatum puto; fi numero auctus per tabellam fententia feret.

XIV. Tabella obtentui erit, quo magis animo libero facere audeat; in multitudine, & præfidii plus, & ufus amplior eft. Nam fere, his tempeftatibus, alii judiciis publicis, alii privatis fuis atque amicorum negotiis implicati, haud fane reipubl. con-. filiis adfuerunt; neque eos magis occupatio, quam fuperba imperia diftinuere. Homines nobiles cum paucis fenatoriis, quos additamenta factionis habent, quæcumque libuit probare, reprehendere, decernere, ea, uti libido tulit, fecere. Verum ubi, numero fenatorum aucto, per tabellam fententiæ dicentur; næ illi fuperbiam fuam dimittent, ubi iis obediendum erit, quibus antea crudeliffume imperitabant. Forfitan, imperator, perlectis litteris defideres, quem numerum fenatorum fieri placeat; quoque modo is in multa, & varia officia diftribuatur; & quoniam judicia primæ claffis mittenda putem, quæ defcriptio, qui numerus in quoque genere futurus fit. Ea mihi omnia generatim defcribere haud difficile factu fuit; fed prius laborandum vifum eft de fumma confilii, idque tibi probandum verum effe. Si hoc itinere uti decreveris, cætera in promptu erunt. Volo ego confilium meum prudens, maximeque ufui effe. Nam ubicunque tibi res profpere cedet, ibi mihi bona fama eveniet. Sed me illa magis cupido exercet, uti quocumque modo, & quamprimum refpubl. a juvetur. Libertatem gloria cariorem habeo, atque ego te oro, hortorque, ne clariffumus imperator, Gallica genta fubacta, populi R. fummum atque invictum imperium tabefcere vetuftate, ac per fummam difcordiam dilabi, patiaris. Profecto, fi id accidat, neque tibi nox, neque dies curam animi fedaverit, quin infomniis exercitus, furibundus, atque amens alienata mente feraris. Namque mihi pro vero conftat, omnium mortalium vitam divino numine invifi; neque bonum, neque malum facinus cujufquam pro nihilo haberi; fed ex natura diverfa præmia bonos, malofque fequi. Interea forte ea tardius procedunt; fuus cuique animus ex confcientia fpem præbet.

XV. Quod fi tecum patria, atque parentes poffent loqui, fcilicet hæc tibi dicerent; O Cæfar, nos te genuimus fortiffumi viri, in optuma urbe, decus, præfidiumque nobis, hoftibus terrorem. Quæ multis laboribus, & periculis ceperamus, ea tibi nafcenti cum anima fimul tradidimus, patriam maximam in terris; domum, familiamque in patria clariffumam, præterea bonas artes, honeftas divitias; poftremo omnia honeftamenta nestamenta pacis, & præmia belli. Pro his amplissumis beneficiis non flagitium a te, neque malum facinus, petimus; sed uti libertatem everfam restituas. Qua re patrata, profecto per gentes omnes fama virtutis tuæ volitabit. Namque hac tempestate, tametsi domi, militiæque præclara facinora egisti; tamen gloria tua cum multis viris fortibus æqualis est; si vero urbem amplissumo nomine, & maxumo imperio, prope iam ab occafu restitueris; quis te clarior, quis major in terris fuerit? Quippe si morbo jam, aut fato huic imperio fecus accidat; cui dubium est, quin per orbem terrarum vastitas, bella, cædes oriantur? Quod fi tibi vana lubido fuerit, patriæ, parentibus gratificandi; postero tempore republ. restituta, super omnis mortalis gloria agnita, tuaque unius mors vita clarior erit. Nam vivos interdum fortuna, fæpe invidia, fatigat; ubi anima naturæ cessit, demtis obtrectationibus ipfa fc virtus magis magifque extollit. Quæ mihi utilia factu vifa funt, quæque tibi ufui fore credidi quam, pauciffumis potui, perfcripfi. Cæterum deos immortales obteftor, uti, quocumque modo ages, ea res tibi, reique publicæ profpere eveniat.

F I N I S.